The Persimmon Tree Narrative

Michael Brookshire

1ˢᵗ Printing by BookBaby

The Persimmon Tree Narrative
© 2022 Mike Brookshire, Author
Rob Cleland, Cover Design
David Clendenning, Line Editor

ISBN: 978-1-66786-156-2

Acknowledgements

Let me begin by acknowledging the help and support of Tree, who of course made this narrative possible. Thank you to all the family, friends, teachers, students, colleagues, and strangers who brought my thinking and laughing together.

Especially important to me were my early readers: Nanya, Lynn, Mary Margaret, Nancy, Howard, Carol, Chloe, Frank and David. Thank you to Rob Cleland for the cover art, David Clendenning for detailed editing, Aniah Hall for social media support, and Gail Fisher for her early help and support.

Most important is my wife Lynn, my valued partner in bringing this project to fruition, for her help, love, and patience. This book is dedicated to you.

TABLE OF CONTENTS

CHAPTER ONE -
INSANITY OR OPPORTUNITY

It was one of those days that if someone had told you what was going to happen to you that day, you would have told them they were crazy. And you would have been wrong, even though insanity was one theme of this day.

Twelve years had passed since the digits two and zero had driven the new world of computers to the brink of a collective heart attack. More than four years ago, the financial world had collapsed, and Americans remembered again why, in earlier years, a recession was called a "panic." It was a panicky time. At least the students in economics classes seemed to pay more attention for a semester or two.

This day was a beautiful Sunday afternoon. In late March, early spring-like weather brought the temperature to 70 degrees. Likely, more cold winter and probably snow would come before true spring, but this was a fine day to be enjoyed.

Charleston, West Virginia, the venue, is the capital and approximate center of West Virginia, a state of wondrous beauty and frustrating, grinding poverty. Our house is in the hills south of the Kanawha river, which is the southern boundary of downtown Charleston. The coal industry is all around us and, indeed, the Charleston professional community services the coal-producing counties of southern West Virginia.

This was my first opportunity to have a "sit" on the new porch that was part of an addition to the house completed late in the fall: the first great weather day with furniture. I was so far ahead in the work assigned to myself for the weekend that I had granted to myself a one-and-a-half-hour-early cessation of weekend work for entertainment and recreation of some sort. My wife and granddaughter were not asked to interrupt their activities because of my unanticipated gift of free time. Thus, I sat with the dog Teddi Rose and a book on the screened-in porch and turning in the indoor-outdoor chair, viewed the panorama covering three of four directions.

Having tried to start it the day before, I already suspected that the book, by a previously unknown author, would allow the author to remain unknown. So, desperate, I actually attempted to relax and take in the world around me. Ridge Road. Our house is one of only a few houses on either side of the flat, private road that runs on top of the ridge about a quarter mile to the house at the end of Ridge Road. On our side, the house is built on three levels down the ridge. About fifty yards below, at the bottom of the hill, is a row of houses and then sequential streets, houses, hills, and more neighborhoods. When this area completely greens, none of the houses will be visible from this porch or from the deck that runs down this northeast-facing side of our house. I own all of the land that I now behold, in my mind. And this self-satisfaction is all that is necessary since our house has no plans for governing, collecting taxes from, or pillaging these lands or their natives.

As I surveilled the panorama, Ridge Road extended to my southwest toward the dead end of the road that is a circle. The neighbor lady was just walking past my west side yard, and then a wooded lot which we own enough of to be a border against…aliens. We will be talking about the neighbor lady as we go along. She is at the early end of her evening range of walking. My guess is that she lives on the street that parallels part of our road but is below the ridge. She is somewhat younger than me and very personable and friendly. I sometimes see her when walking my dog, but her routine seems steadfast, even among our steady handful of walkers and dog-walkers.

Swiveling, Ridge Road comes back into view stretching beyond the north end of the house around a sharp curve in the ridge and to Smith Road: our public road access to downtown Charleston only five or so minutes away. Ridge Road is, of course, elevated and flat—terrific assets for walkers and for homeowners vis-à-vis both floods and snow in mountain country.

The curve was part of about thirty yards of Ridge Road which might be covered by a thick layer of ice for continuous weeks or sometimes months in the winter. Presumably, this glacier was a product of the cold, the wind at the crest of the ridge, and the relatively few daily hours of sun coverage. All Ridge Road residents, in order to interact with others during the winter months, were forced to traverse this ice patch of terror upon each exit and entry.

Each of us knew the danger as we attempted to control a vehicle on solid ice. The slope down the ravine was steep along these 30 yards, with a sufficient dispersion of trees that poor probability attached to a premature stoppage before the bottom. Indeed, death would be probable for all aboard. Probably fiery. What will you say to the family as the car slides over the edge backwards and begins the plunge to the bottom? Will it be inspiring or cowardly? Could it be a partial communication, abruptly interrupted, that results in a horrible miscommunication in your last words? Or, does it really matter?

On Ridge Road, we live with this nightmare scenario of the car and this ice patch for many days of each winter and more undoubtedly lie ahead this year. We know that the slightest inattention, or a temporary palsy of the wrist, could destroy our lives and those of our loved ones. Also affected would be the folks eating dinner in the houses below when the firebomb of a car literally rolls into their dining area. The fact that no one has yet endured such a tragedy only increases the perception that it will soon happen. It gives us all perspective, and a search for meaning, and probably builds character. On the negative side, and I am looking at it, we know that death may lie around the corner. Even the neighbor lady doesn't walk over the ice patch.

So, I re-focused on the backyard and side yard stretching below me. Buds on the trees would emerge soon, and then the greening. It has been a growth experience for a workaholic like me to even notice the greening, but every year of it brought me more joy. There were some upsides of age and experience.

If it were football season, this early hour off would not have been such a problem. But I was more or less forced to behold the dog, in peaceful repose on the floor several feet away. Teddi Rose Brookshire. I had come to name dogs after presidents, but the last two pets had been females— Wilson and Theodore Roosevelt. It occurred to me that the problem might soon be resolved or my definition might need to expand to Supreme Court justices, senators, and cabinet members.

Unlike our last, perfect dog Wilson, this particular cocker spaniel exhibited a host of psychological, behavioral, and perhaps spiritual maladies. She was a biter and hoarder. She literally bit the hand that fed her. Anything dropped on the floor was the property of Teddi Rose. It could be retrieved via bloodshed, or, we ultimately learned from a dog whisperer, by trading for a treat. Thus, knowing our own country does not trade for hostages, we rewarded the behavior that was unacceptable. Because this was a dog. And we were bleeding to death.

The dog's behavior had not really changed over the years, but <u>we</u> had adapted. We dropped less things, for example, and left less paraphernalia on low-lying tables. We became less choosy about which dropped items required retrieval via blood or trade. I hated the principle of a trade for stolen property, but if the dog had Chloe's report card, I threw a treat far away. Otherwise, the dog would seize the treat and then attempt to bite me before I retrieved the valued item.

(Parenthetically, I learned at some point that throwing a glass of water into the face of a dog will shock the dog into dropping anything. Unfortunately, one's dog begins to run away every time she sees anyone with a glass of anything. Or, you sometimes find yourself chasing your dog through the neighborhood holding a glass of water. This causes consternation for many neighbors. And there is Teddi Rose, who will drop the report card when doused with water, but then bite you once or twice. Hard. Because you threw the water in her face…and took her report card.)

The expense of this dog was also notable. We were constantly at our veterinarian because of her skin allergies. There was a big asterisk about her behavior in her file and a muzzle was always available. Her medicines were many and costly. Her medicated shampoo was many times the price of my shampoo. My grandmother would have had some comments about spending that kind of money on a dog. It would have been insane in her world. As an economist, I reflected upon the benefits and costs of this dog, and I thought some more about football.

My gaze then turned to the dark trunk and branches and crown of the tree that was close to me in this new view from the back porch. This particular tree had intrigued me before the addition of 20 feet to our three floors. In our old configuration of the house, the tree dominated the side yard view from the window in front of me as I worked in my downstairs office. When outdoors or in my office, the tree had a pull to it, an attraction.

With the addition to the house (which forced the removal of one of the tree's neighbors), I was seated ten feet or so from the branches. When it greened, the presence of this tree would loom even larger to anyone on the porch.

This tree had a head on it, with a proboscis pointed upward toward Ridge Road at the top of the side yard. With no green, one saw two trees, with the shorter tree a few feet up the ridge from the proboscis tree. While its height stopped just short of the proboscis, it provided branches that, when greened, produced a picture of a human-like head, nose, and arms reaching up toward Ridge Road, perhaps thirty yards above. The porch was just below the level of the road, and a gravel driveway had been added that was beneath the road and parallel to it. The porch, and my view, was also slightly below the crown of the tree.

Even with limited knowledge or recall regarding botany, it was apparent to me that the two trees were not of the same type, or species, or whatever it was called. But when greened, they would appear as one tree to the casual observer from the road or the porch.

"Hello, Michael."

I jerked to attention. It was clear, somehow, that this was a communication coming to me from the head of the tree that had been the object of my thoughts. It startled me just short of cardioversion because it felt so real. So, I did the courageous thing. I froze and was silent and waited.

"Hello Michael."

It was the same jolt of communication, and for whatever reason, I replied, "Are you talking to me?"

"Yes, I am ready to have a discussion with you."

"So, am I correct that you are the tree talking, or whatever, to me?"

"I am a tree."

There was a pause. I was thinking quickly about what to say next and how to say it. "But if this conversation is really happening, you would have to admit that a tree talking to a human would be a first-ever sort of thing. Which would cause me to think that you are more than an ordinary tree."

"This conversation is, indeed, happening and let us leave me as a tree."

I somehow knew that when the tree did not wish to have or continue a conversation on a topic, then the topic was not to be discussed. It is not clear to me how I knew this, but I did not push the tree. "So, how are we communicating? I am not talking. I'm just pointing thoughts at you. And I don't know what you are doing but I know your words."

"Directed thinking would be a sufficient analogy from your experience." The tree continued, "My question, for now, is whether you wish to have conversations with me from time to time? In units of your time, of course."

The tree did not seem to mind if I paused to digest what was being said. There seemed to be no expected cadence of question-and-answer by the tree, and I somehow sensed this freedom and required it. Let me use this pause to talk about what described the sound or sensation of the "voice" of this tree.

Of course, no words were actually spoken by the tree, but did I perceive a voice? Did the tree sound like some voice which could be used as an example—Charlton Heston, Whoopi Goldberg, or Peyton Manning? My difficulty is that it is only possible to describe what the "voice" was not, as I perceived the voice. It was not a voice from my hearing experience. It was not really a voice, as heard via the ear or remembered. Nor was it a thought directed at me by another, perhaps through a non-verbal communication. It was not any of those sensations, but something different from anything in my past that might describe it. There is simply no analogy which would be helpful.

Even more difficult to describe is how I could sense the equivalent of a non-verbal communication by another as a part of these words that were being somehow directed at me. If the words were accompanied by a human-like smile, or frown, or reproachful glance, I would know that. If there was a human-like change in volume, or modulation, or intensity,

I would know that too. An explanation is beyond me. One would need to perceive it in order to know, but once "heard," it would not be forgotten.

If I were to offer a word to describe the immediate impression that the tree's communication had on me, the closest is "compelling." Not exactly, but close. It was impossible for me to ignore the tree when the tree talked. One did not read, use an iPhone, or do anything else but listen when the tree talked. It was not so much that I felt compelled to listen, but rather that the thought of not listening did not occur to me. The communications felt as natural and as necessary to me as breathing.

There was never an instance of "false talking," either. I never thought the tree was talking to me but found that my mind was making it up. When the tree talked, it was clear to me. When there was nothing coming from the tree, I knew it. My own mind could not even fool me, as good as it was at fooling me. And there were times when I wanted to hear from the tree, but my wanting it did not make it happen.

Back to the conversation. It was clear to me that I would need to be the one breaking the pause. Imagine attempting to digest what was going down here while formulating a question. "So, if I think words to you that is good enough on my end?" Sometimes I knew that I was mouthing words at the same time, but rarely aloud.

"Correct."

"And I assume that we are speaking in the English language since I speak the English language, but just out of curiosity… could you be doing this in any language?"

"If you wish to change languages during a conversation, then I can keep up with you, but the only language other than English that you know is from Mrs. Hamm's Latin class almost 50 years ago, and you couldn't actually speak Latin even then."

That stunned me, but it did not hinder my query, "How did you know that my Latin teacher was named Mrs. Hamm?"

"Because I know everything about you."

"How much of everything?"

"I know all of it."

"Like you have read my resume or business website or high school yearbook?"

"I know all of it."

"Do you mean that you know all of the facts of my past?" The tree knew I wasn't finished. "Do you mean you know all of my thoughts, feelings, fears, hopes, dreams, and so on? Do you know what I'm thinking right now?"

"Yes. Actually I know much more about you than you do, because I know all of it, and you humans have no effective recall of most of what you know. And then there is your selective perception, biases, misclassified inputs, et cetera."

"So, are you basically telling me that you have sucked my brain?... And that you continue to do that anytime you wish?"

"'Suck' would be a poor description of what actually happens, because you still have your brain and it has not been affected by my appropriation of it. "Scan" might be a better term to the extent that you might have much chance to understand what is involved, anyway."

This stopped me. The tree talking to me knew things that no other human being knew. The entire and unvarnished truth of me. I felt violated, and vulnerable, and fearful. And this tree knew what I was thinking even as I thought it. Unless, of course, my mind was playing with me in a new and heretofore unexplained way. Thus, in this time, I came to face insanity.

Reflecting back, flashes about the possibility of insanity began and grew parallel to my first words with the tree. A first thought was that this imagined conversation was a temporary and harmless form of mental gymnastics between two parts of my brain. After all, much of my brain's time was spent arguing with itself. And I was in a relaxed and lazy-brained mode for the late afternoon, which facilitated such an intra-brain exercise.

But this brief interaction, so far, had not felt as if it were a process within my brain. It was, rather, something outside of me interacting with me. This feeling permeated the core of me. I do not know why, nor can it be further explained.

The result was my realization that nothing about this conversation was harmlessly without great consequence. The explanation alternatives to me were extreme. Either I was insane, or I had an opportunity to talk to something with shocking powers and no other human was (presumably) being given this opportunity. Insanity or Opportunity?

The knowledge that I had so quickly defined the disparate alternatives was an initial encouragement and checkmark in the "Not Insane" column. It seemed sane that a person having just spoken with a backyard tree was initially dealing with likely causes, such as insanity.

I knew that insanity did not run in my family. We had our share of problems and eccentricities, but no one had, to my knowledge, married either royalty or a cousin. No one was known to have had unusual relationships with trees.

On the other hand, I wasn't particularly well read in psychology or psychiatry, to my credit, I thought. What if there is a known and well-researched type of insanity involving men who, later in life, meet the equivalent of the invisible friend from childhood. What if I am another case study, first blooming? It probably has a name already, so that it won't be the "Brookshire syndrome." (No big deal, but I would have liked some credit for it.)

If there is not such a sub-branch of psychiatric disorder, is it because no one previously had the guts to admit it? Or, perhaps they have been shunted away to various institutions, or dealt with by a special branch of government agents. Perhaps they were prophets, poets, philosophers, artists, or songwriters, who are expected to speak about, write about, or create anything doing anything to anything, any time, for any reason, anyway.

Yet, I am an economist. A numbers person. Why would I sanely expect a once-in-humanity encounter with a talking tree? I have no artistic license to talk to a tree nor dominance of intellect that would make me a chosen spokesperson for anything. Nor have I ever had a particular fascination with, or interest in, trees. Despite many years of education, natural sciences, in general, and botany, in particular, were not on my list of topics to be further explored. I knew that trees had a trunk, roots, and branches... and needles or leaves, sometimes. Similarly, I knew that an automobile had an engine, a body, and wheels. If either topic became more complicated than that, other people needed to be involved. I knew nothing more specific than that about trees or cars, and I did not particularly wish to know anything more. A conversation with a tree would not be a scenario upon which I would focus. Did this really help me on the insanity versus opportunity decision? Probably not. But why a tree?

I knew the popular definition of insanity: doing the same thing over and over again and expecting a different result. But did that really help with my decision? I had not been repeating any thought or action involving my backyard tree and expecting the tree to talk to me. My expectation had been an hour on the porch, reading and occasionally talking to the dog. I had no expectation that the dog, or anything else, would talk back. My expectation of the environment around me was, seemingly, sane and normal and then the tree began talking to me.

The teacher in me was a stickler for definitions, and I had previous reason to know the internet and/or Websterian definitions of "insanity." I knew that it was not a technical term in medicine (that would be way too simple for a mind doctor). I knew it was an upset to a normal mental process, and I knew that talking with a porch tree was not normal. But it would not be normal whether I was insane or sane with an opportunity. I knew that insanity was a derangement in one who formerly had mental health. This said to me that a 62-year-old man without a history of mental illness <u>could</u> be struck down by heretofore unknown insanities: late-on-set insanity.

Perhaps the talking tree was the tip of the iceberg for me, and my insanity was real and would now progress rapidly. What was the progression: a talking tree, a singing dog, a laughing airplane? (I glanced at the dog but she wasn't singing. Good.) How far would it go? And if I were insane, then, by definition it seemed, none of these things would be extraordinary to me, beginning with the talking tree. They would only seem unusual to the people who took me away, locked me up, and talked to me in soft voices.

Also tucked into my definitional recall was the proposition that almost all insanity involves hospitalization. This was the first cognition that what others knew about, and thought about, my Insanity versus Opportunity debate might determine both the location and nature of my future life.

While the tree was patient with my thinking, I was substantially unsettled in attempting to choose between the alternatives. If only a new fact or relevant piece of information could point me in one direction or another, this would certainly govern my manner of proceeding. Wild ideas crossed my mind in this desperate state… ideas that embarrass me now. I considered, for example, that I might persuade the tree to go on television with me and discuss important topics for humankind. The flash of the evening news, the talk shows… it was a great thought. Yet, I knew that the camera would simply record the tree and me, staring at each other and saying nothing. The tree wasn't likely to say anything on TV. I knew he wasn't. Whether I talk out loud to the tree, or just stare at him, everyone will know I'm crazy. And it will be recorded and documented for replay and analysis. I would have no chance in the court system to stay out of a guarded place.

So, implicitly at least, I gave the nod to the opportunity (and sanity) option and charged ahead, by directly taking up the matter with the tree. This path to a solution had been my first impulse, because of a quick recollection that humans of the past, when faced with a similar situation, had asked what I was about to ask of the tree.

Deliberately looking at the tree's head, I thought to him, "Mr. Tree... I don't exactly know how to address you. But if you are real and you have been listening to what I have been thinking, then you would understand why I need to ask you for a one-time favor to me, so that I will know this is real and not insanity."

Silence from the tree.

"I was just wondering if, perhaps, you could show me a miracle: you know, something that could not be explained in human terms, that could not be done by a human, even the best and the brightest of us." Still there was silence from the tree, but I somehow felt he was listening and took license to talk further. It was one of those times when you hear yourself talking (or focused thinking, in this case) and simultaneously wonder if you are making an utter fool of yourself.

"It's not that I'm asking that you do something of benefit to me directly," and thought to myself, "although if you could help me win in racquetball more often, that would be really swell." Then, I realized that the tree had also heard the afterthought. I chastised myself, in thought, and hoped the tree might overlook my selfishness. "If you could just wiggle your branches, or raise the couch a foot off the floor, or make the dog dance on her hind legs..."

Silence. Then, "Does it occur to you that one of your family inside the house or anyone walking by on the street might see this miracle... and that this might end any chance of future conversations?"

"Well, if you ARE able to do any of these kind of things to help me with this pesky insanity issue, then I would just assume that you could easily handle those kinds of collateral issues, so that only I could see what-ever miracle you would do, and we wouldn't bother anyone else."

"And have you considered," said the tree, "that if conversations with a backyard tree are the cause of your insanity issue, then miracles that you perceive as performed by the very same tree are not likely to solve your problem?"

Actually, I was thinking that very thought but, unfortunately, I had taken the tree's participation in the conversation as encouragement to keep talking, "Yes, but a miracle or two would make a difference for me, I think. You could do something there in the side yard, just for example, so that only I could see it. Those bushes bordering the yard before the treeline, maybe they could move, or dance, or sing, or something. Or, the ground-hog and rabbits and deer who walk in that yard could make an appear-ance and do something... or clowns and a marching band... I don't really know... anything you could do?"

"No," said the tree. "That's ridiculous. I'm not showing you a mir-acle." And that was the last time the tree and I talked about miracles for a while.

From that time forward, I can tell you that my thoughts about insan-ity came less and less and, yes, I know this could mean that I was becom-ing more and more, shall we say, mentally disturbed. It felt so real to me that moving forward was not strongly questioned. Nor was there doubt in me, even at this early point, who was in charge. My ego was not small but, miracles or not, I was afloat in the tree's vessel.

If this was a grand opportunity for me as a human to ask questions of a powerful being, what question should I ask first? This was particu-larly important if only limited questions were to be allowed or if the time period for these conversations was very limited, I thought. And I therefore proceeded with the first important question that came to mind, "Could I just ask you a question that most of us are concerned about? It is I suppose a question under the topic of religion. Is there a life of some sort after a person dies?"

"First, you don't know enough about religion to be capable of a conversation which would be of interest to me. If I wanted to talk about religion, I would talk to your wife. She actually knows something about religion. Second, there are topics that you are not prepared to discuss with me. Your mind could not wrap around what I would say." Parenthetically, the tree's words, when you read them, might seem sharp, or rebuking, or even insulting. But when said to me, the nonverbal accompanying the words—whatever this nonverbal addition actually was—did not feel other than the tree speaking the truth as he knew it. There was no added punctuation to the words. Except when the tree chose to punctuate, and then it was very clear.

It was at this point in the first conversation that I erred. Instead of simply leaving the topic alone, my mouth leapt ahead without touching base with my brain, "Even some general direction from you could be very helpful to me. Could I just say a word—like Catholic, Hindu, Presbyterian, Atheist—and you could tell me "hot," "cold," "getting warmer," or maybe "red light" or "green light"?

Silence.

Have you ever said something with others present and wished your nose could crawl down and eat your mouth off? Hot and cold. Red light and green light. Could I have possibly said anything more stupid? A great human representative I was starting out to be. So, miserable, I waited.

"No"

That was ok with me. If he was willing to leave the red light/green light fiasco without further comment, then I was certainly ready to leave the topic for almost anything else. And the tree had one, final topic for this first conversation. Mercifully.

"We need to end today with the rules that shall govern our future conversations. The first rule is that I will initiate every conversation when I choose to do so and extending for varying lengths of time."

"Could I ask sort of a general question?

"Surely."

"Do I have any input into these rules… because there are certain times of the day…"

"No," said the tree, interrupting.

"Okie dokey, then," I mumbled, once again representing humanity with words of a sage conversant. But I just couldn't stop, "So this is basically your way or the highway, right?"

"An odd expression, but these are indeed my rules if the conversations are to proceed. Let me ask you, Michael, do you think I am bigger than you or that you are bigger than me?"

That was an easy question to answer at this point, "Based upon the scanning of my brain, alone, you are operating on a level above my pay grade." I was in the military just long enough to pick up an expression or two.

"Then that answers your question. The higher order always makes the rules. You as a human should know that. And while this reason is all that you need, a comment is that you have much more to gain from these conversations, with my rules, and more to lose if the conversations don't occur."

"More than you do, is that what you mean?"

"More to gain or lose than any other humans." He proceeded, "Rule #2 is that you CAN bring up any topic that you wish, but some will not be discussed. You may or may not be given a reason that you can understand, but that is the second rule. Are we clear on that one?"

"Yes." I felt like a freshman football player on the first day of summer camp. Or the prisoner after a long interrogation. By this point, I would have probably agreed to anything.

"Rule #3 is that you cannot initiate a conversation and expect me to respond to you in any particular time frame. You can sit out here on the porch anytime that you wish to engage me, but your wishes have very little to do with the timing of my response, in the time that you are using. Do you understand three?"

"Yes."

"Rule #4 is that you not discuss these conversations with any other human, at any time, under any circumstances. Let me point out that this rule enhances your own safety and freedom, which are important for our future conversations. While you have fears about insanity, others will be certain of it. Do you understand rule four?"

"Yes." I would have said "Yes, sir" or "Yes, madam" or "your honor" or some expression of respect, but I did not have a clue as to respectful tree greetings or appropriate salutations to a clearly superior tree.

"Finally, this is more of a suggestion than a rule, do not spend much time preparing for conversations, and attempt to avoid expectations about specific topics or specific questions at specific times."

Then he was gone. It was as if I felt him leave the conversation. No further response from me was appropriate or useful. I would wait for the next conversation. For the first time in a while, I focused on the dog, lying a few feet away on the floor of the porch. It occurred to me that every time the tree "spoke," the dog had raised her head off the floor or raised her head higher. Then, the head dropped when the tree ceased talking. My talking apparently made no difference to the dog. It was strange.

CHAPTER TWO –

PREPARATION

The analysis began that very night. Sleep was not easy. Four rules and a suggestion. What can and should be done to prepare for a coming series of conversations, within the framework of the four-and-one? First, of course, the one with the most wiggle room had to be the suggestion. The suggestion was that there be low preparation and low expectation about my ability to affect the topics of discussion.

Why was this one a suggestion but not a rule? It could certainly be that the tree knew that for me to not prepare for anything was an impossibility. Prepare is my middle name. (It is actually Leo, but my teenage friends made fun of that name so that I never tell anybody that my middle name is Leo. Prepare is better, but odd.) There might be no sanction if I engaged in excessive preparation for future conversations on unknown topics. At worst, I lose the preparation time, and I've already lost a decade-or-so preparing for things that never happened. Moreover, even if a low probability exists that my preparation will germinate in a major breakthrough of some unknown sort, toward my own welfare or that of humans, generally, the payoff could really be big. Or could the tree be testing me: to see if I will compulsively prepare, as is my nature, despite the suggestion? Why would he do that? I can't ask him. If he didn't want my input about rules, then he probably won't be excited about clarifying the suggestion, either. And it is not possible, surely, to control my expectations, because the probability that I may be able to pursue a break-through topic is greater than zero—that's a corollary of the suggestion. My fiduciary responsibility to humankind is to prepare for that possibility. Even a low probability times a great value yields the expectation of a great value. Knowing that I had a plan to exert some control over this situation, I slept.

In the next few days, I did not know, of course, when the next conversation would occur, but somehow felt that it would be at least several days later. I needed some time to focus but my life was of the billable hour and my workaholism was expected by me and others, so even a few hours of new focus were a big deal for me. I began with what I knew about problem solving: it always should begin by properly defining the problem. The problem seemed to be eliciting all the information possible from the tree, given the rules and my clear subordination to the tree in controlling anything. Moreover, I presumably needed to have some notion of the priority for information, as this would benefit humankind, of course.

Thus, in this role as information-seeker, I was to conjure, organize, and memorize questions to ask, if given the chance. It was presumed that little chance existed for nimbly sneaking pre-planned questions into discussions controlled by the tree. Either I would have an opportunity to ask important questions or I would not. My pre-thought would be useful, or not.

Since this preparation countered the tree's suggestion, it was obvious to me that the preparation had to be low key, in the least. There would be no PowerPoint presentation of issues and questions on the porch. This had to be mental only. I needed to prepare my mind for the asking of questions which might be addressed, even in the context of tree topics that were unforeseeable. Not unlike a cross examination at trial.

Thus, I began with a tool learned long ago and often used in management training—the six questions to be asked when approaching a problem. As stated in the Kipling poem, The Elephant's Child:

I keep six honest serving-men

They taught me all I knew

Their names were what and how and when

And where and why and who.

As important as Why questions felt to me, I seemed drawn to Who questions regarding the tree.

As the mental preparation for the next conversations unfolded, I found myself spending an hour or so a day on the porch: the venue for the first conversation. In retrospect, I'm not sure it occurred to me that this might not be the venue for all or most future conversations with the tree. There was not a rule or suggestion regarding the where of conversations. Most likely, I was so busy thinking about what I could finagle around the tree's suggestion that I was not thinking about obvious things which should have occurred to me. Thinking is a peculiar process.

A "first things first" issue, simply because of my time spent on the porch, was dealing with the family that shared the Ridge Road lot with me and the tree. Wife: Lynn, who had somehow stayed married to me for 14 years, was an accomplished professional and great role model for Chloe. She was a fashion and merchandising major at Virginia Tech, who had years ago entered the world of information technology and was a vice president of IT for our comprehensive, multi-campus medical center in Charleston. Very bright and intuitive. While I would be the first to say that my wife was near perfect in her spousliness, she does occasionally seem less than enthusiastic about my rare attempts at constructive feedback. I would never actually say this to her, however, out of an abundance of caution that such a comment might be taken as constructive feedback. Germane to the issue at hand, she would want to know what was happening on the porch and would not be an easy target for my deception. Fortunately, she was very busy.

Chloe: granddaughter and adopted daughter. The daughter of my youngest daughter, she had come to live with us when she was six. Now twelve moving into her teenage years, she was a gift to both of us. She was bright, perceptive, and perfectly capable of asking questions that I could not answer. The advent of teenagerism might help me here. She was decreasingly interested in where I was in the house or what I was doing. A talking tree might slide by if I was careful.

Thus, I resolved to be hyper-sensitive to those closest to me in all of my tree-related activities. The steady occurrence of time spent on the porch was made plausible by the newness of the porch. I could truthfully say that the value of time spent alone on the porch, once discovered, had come to be an activity that I enjoyed. The females knew, however, that I would not sit anywhere for thirty minutes or so without reading, watching, writing, or otherwise doing something.

In my own defense, it was known to me and the others that I was quite capable of focusing my attention for long periods of time on academic, intellectual, or consulting topics, but not without taking notes for myself or others. I had never spent as much as an hour with myself quietly contemplating God, for example. On the other hand, I had never spent that much time quietly contemplating Tennessee Vols football, either. It was therefore not acceptable for me to sit on the porch doing nothing, as the observer would behold me. Reading was the answer. I would read anything and would become lost in reading that which I enjoyed, just so the pleasureful reading did not significantly impinge upon my imposing work schedule.

If I was on the porch, reading material had to be with me. Even if the females were out of the house, they might surprise me with a quick return and find me on the porch sans readings; my cover would be blown. The notion that I would suddenly become introspective in my early sixties did not even seem plausible to me. Certainly it would not happen because of the availability of a porch. Only I knew, of course, that what it took was the availability of a talking tree.

Parenthetically, I was aided by the introduction of a Kindle as a Christmas present that year, an absolutely amazing device that electronically fetched books from the netherworld and displayed them electronically on a tablet. One could control the size of the print and the lighting behind the print and could ask for the meaning of words. The way it worked was great too. When Lynn was around, I sat in my TV chair, held the device in one hand and tapped it with increasing impatience. And I muttered to myself. Lynn came over and asked if I needed a new book. She then had the device display several alternatives and made the device provide me free samples. After making my choice, I grumbled and tapped again until Lynn came back over, skillfully tapped and swished and, after a few minutes, the book appeared. It worked like a charm every time. Motivation to improve my e-skills was low.

My practice was to carry the Kindle with me anytime I left my downstairs office after 4:00 or so. Occasionally, as a subterfuge, I would read from the Kindle in the family room to which the porch attached. Only by mistake would I enter the porch without my smokescreen device. Once there, the swivel chair was my choice, and I swiveled with the chair facing the outdoors, and the tree, so that the details of my Kindle usage were not easily observable from indoors. The primary objective was to have the Kindle open to a lit screen if someone came outdoors and to otherwise strike the general pose of a reader. The problem of cold weather would soon disappear and, except for the occasional thunderstorm, my venue for conversations was solid.

One other problem of family deception, which occurred to me even with the first conversation, was my tendency to mouth words, or even say words, when tuned into a conversation of the mind. It was a habit reinforced as an expert witness preparing for the "what if's" of possible question-and-answer vignettes in a coming testimony. In mental preparation and, most certainly, in coming conversations, I could not mouth or say words or exhibit communication non-verbals.

Persimmon. The tree was a persimmon tree (Diospyros virginiana L.). I didn't obsess over research, primarily because it would be a blatant disregard for the suggestion not to prepare, but for all I knew this was a unique tree with special characteristics. No, it was a persimmon tree. This was not a prominent tree among the mix of Appalachian trees, or in these parts, but not unusual in a forest or copse. It could be as short as 15-feet or as tall as 100-feet; mine was closer to 50-feet, eight or so times my height. The average life of such a tree at planting is 50 to 75 years, and I had no idea about the age of my tree.

The persimmon tree is identified by its crown at the top and general dome shape. The head on my tree also had a proboscis. The branches extend and turn downward. The bark is a distinctive block pattern. I casually walked by the tree in the early days to check this out. These trees, I learned, bore fruit after 10 years or so, with cultivated crops possible every two years and harvests usually in the fall. Ripe persimmons were noted to be sweet and delicious.

It occurred to me that it would be useful to know something about the neighbor tree that provided the outstretched arms of the combined shape. It was clear that this tree was not a persimmon. But this was deemed to be non-essential information, given the preparation-adverse suggestion and my fundamental lack of interest in botany per se.

Let us turn back to the substance of my ever-so-subtle preparation and to the magnetism of the Who questions. I knew only two things from the first conversation: the tree was thus far only describing itself as a tree and we both had agreed that this tree was bigger than me.

This was scant detail for moving forward. Who answers potentially affected why and how the two of us would talk, and what I would choose to talk about in what order. Most importantly, my mind simply could not easily move beyond the Who.

Perhaps the tree would respond if asked more specific questions, such as: "Are you God?" Even then, I would need to be mindful of the context around such a whopper question. How does one build up to a question like that? If only it was as simple as the task of the scores of lie detector operators, who had been carefully studied via years of television...

Are you a tree?

Are you a persimmon tree?

Are you God?

A really strong gut feeling told me that there is no easy or good way to ask someone or something if they are God. How much experience does the typical human have over a lifetime in asking that question?

It also occurred to me that if a direct approach at Who again failed, questions might be asked regarding the powers and/or abilities which the tree did or did not have. If I could ascertain what he could or could not do, this would be valuable insight toward the Who. It was a second-best approach, but a reasonable Plan B.

Why and When questions were important and needed to be asked if possible. Why was he talking to a human being? Why at this particular time in human history?

Some fleeting thought was given to the Whats of future conversations beyond this contingency planning if I were allowed to bring up a topic. It seemed clear that the tree could control all of the topics for conversation, but would he? I would find out.

At some point, I became comfortable with being prepared on Who and Why questions for the next conversation or any future conversation in which I was allowed to bring up a topic or otherwise ask questions. There was an expectation of a next conversation, but I certainly had no guarantee, or estimate, of how many conversations would occur thereafter. It also seemed likely that many of my questions would be answered if there were two-way conversations, even if they were on the tree's topics and none of my questions were directly asked. So, contrary to my natural tendencies of compulsion and obsession, I more or less stopped further thinking about that which could not be controlled. At peace, on the porch, I waited... and waited.

Through April, most late afternoons would include some time on the porch, reading or pretending to read. In retrospect, it was an exercise in "calling the tree" to conversation. I was ready. Despite a very clear rule, a resentment began to grow in me that the tree knew of my eagerness to talk but was apparently not affected by it. Who did this tree think he was, anyway? Realizing this question was the whole point of my anxiousness would calm me down temporarily, but it was a growing discomfort to have zero control over timing.

The time-on-the-porch pattern did offer some reward for this discomfort, however. Never had my watching of Spring been so systematic. Each day was a bit greener, more lush with Appalachian vegetation. The houses below me gradually disappeared, and my panorama became dominated by the serendipity of nature versus the infrastructure of man. The return of the animals was, of course, a part of this. In a 45-minute sitting, one might see many combinations of birds, squirrel, rabbits, groundhogs, and the occasional fox and coyote. And deer.

We had fought a small war with the deer in the early years of our life together here, my wife more than me. She loved to landscape and garden and was determined to grow a vegetable garden in the small section of flat land, just below Ridge Road and now a gravel driveway. The deer ate and trampled everything. Lynn became obsessed with internet remedies for addressing this deer problem short of shooting the deer, which was illegal in the city, anyway. One of my special favorites was lining the border of the vegetable garden with dog hair; the deer surely had a good laugh about that one. I remember the summer that the dog looked funny because she was shaved naked. We needed the hair.

Unfortunately, I was drawn into this war. A window in my basement office, before the addition to the house, offered a view of the vegetable garden and an outside door thirty feet from the garden. When other efforts failed, my wife turned to her least likely option for solving any problem and asked me for help. My assignment, during office hours, was to "Keep an eye out for deer in the garden." One thing quickly learned is that it is virtually impossible to keep one eye on the work in front of you and the other eye on the vegetable garden. My eyes simply do not work that way. So, when my left eye was focused on my work, my right eye was necessarily focused on the same work. Since my work actually involved thinking, long periods might transpire in which zero eyes were on the garden.

On one occasion, I was on an hour-plus conference call with my best attorney client. I watched three deer stroll up to the garden, eat their fill, and meander away through some of our flowers. Another time, hours must have passed while a vexing problem with data before me captured my attention. Upon finally glancing up, and outdoors, no less than five deer were observed standing in and around the garden. They had apparently been dining for some time, and at least two were sneering at me. I walked outside, knowing from previous experience that the deer would not scatter unless I walked within five feet of them and yelled. Arrogant they were. This time, 10 feet away, I aimed an invisible shotgun at them and loudly shouted, "Bang." One of them moved a few feet and resumed eating. The others just looked at me. It is likely that one of them said to the others, "This jackass thinks he can shoot us with his arms."

At that point, I pretty much gave up the idea that the war could be won. This was our Vietnam. It would be best for us to abandon the vegetable garden to the deer and remove ourselves from the contest with a modicum of dignity. Sometime later, Lynn also gave up, began to grow a few vegetables on a deck, and purchased our remaining vegetables from farmers, who apparently know how to deal with deer (in a manner that need not occupy my attention). The deer lost out too, of course. A terrific food supply simply disappeared for them. We would have given them 20 or 30 percent just to leave the rest alone. Yet, in their self-centeredness and gluttony, they had lost in the long run. Stupid deer.

A few years later, enraged suburban gardeners and taxpayers had the City Council allow bow hunting of deer in selected zones within the city limits. I had to believe that the first deer or so, thinking that they were protected in the city limits, had quite a surprise in early encounters with the bow hunters, and local deer arrogance would have been set back a metric or two. But word gets around. After awhile, the deer simply avoided the designated zones and further crowded into suburban gardens.

You will recall that I had the time for this kind of parenthetical thinking because I was waiting. Having sat in exactly the same chair in the same place on the porch, because that's where I was when the tree talked to me, it occurred to me that I might shake out a second conversation simply by a slight change in location. So, ever so casually, I sat in the sliding outdoor couch for a few days, then in the wooden rocking chair, then the other swivel chair, then my original chair placed elsewhere on the porch. It did not help.

While I didn't think my dress would make a difference, I generally wore, in my porch visits, the same jeans-and-something casual dress of the first conversation. Enough waiting caused me to continue to wear any business suits needed earlier in the day until I could have a dress-up on the porch. A show of respect, perhaps? No.

How I held my body also came to matter. For a while, I used the reasonably good sitting posture that was natural in reading, thinking, or talking. Then, better posture. Then, more relaxed to slouchy posture. Other body non-verbals were attempted to subtly suggest receptivity to conversation, in the context of feigned reading. It did not matter.

Where I looked, or seemed to look, was possibly important. Certainly, it was taboo to look directly at the proboscis of the tree or in any way to gaze or focus toward the tree. When I fake read the Kindle, it would be pointed at the side yard or back yard but not at the intersection of the two, which was, more or less, where the tree stood. Indeed, the fully-leafed branches almost touched the corner of the porch, and house. So, I could look up and view nature, as discussed above, and I was ever so close to direct visual and communicative contact with the tree.

Finally, I found myself attempting to use the topics, and substance, of my thought life in facilitating the timely resumption of conversations. For example, I posed myself in meditation toward the backyard while in a reading pose viewed from indoors. A meditative thought posture might indicate to the tree, who was surely monitoring my thoughts, an openness, willingness to listen, and perhaps humility that could beget a discussion. No.

There was then a set of respectful thinking, with a slightly bowed head. It was not necessarily aimed at respect for the tree but I looked at the couch, and I respected it; the screen on the porch, and I respected it; a big bug on the screen, and I respected it. Anyone would recognize my gushing out of respect. Nada.

A brief try was made at self-criticism in my thought life, which might again signal humility and also invoke pity. It would synergize with any redemption strategy that could be part of this. At some point, I was mentally begging. The waiting was killing me, and the insanity doubts were creeping back.

What if one were a devout Catholic, I thought, and kept returning to the little boothy dooger for confession but nobody talked back through the curtain. (Again, a long history with television shaped my knowledge of Catholicism.) Hopefully, one didn't really need the priest responding in order to keep this hypothetical Catholic from climbing out on a ledge.

Finally, "Hello again, Michael." The shock of this sudden re-emergence of the tree left me speechless for a bit, which is uncommon in my experience. The emotions stirred up were simultaneously relief, gratitude, resentment, excitement, and fear.

"Hello. Welcome back," I said.

"I only tuned in to part of your preparation. You really are the obsessive, compulsive, perfectionist type aren't you?"

"It is my preference to think of myself as task-oriented and a careful planner."

"You are fortunate that the suggestion was not a rule, and your last month was a poorly veiled attempt to start a meeting. This, of course, is counter to rule #3. You have a problem with authority, don't you?"

"Yes."

"How did you handle the Army?"

"Not very well." I could not determine if he was either angry or disappointed with me, and I didn't know him well enough to rule out sanctions or other punishment. It would seem that a brain scanner would easily be able to voodoo doll my various parts if he wished. I threw myself on the mercy of the Court because my options were limited.

"Yes. I have obsessed about a next conversation. It is not within my human capabilities to carry on as if you had never talked to me." When my brain caught up with my mouth, it occurred to me that I was subtly invoking sympathy for my flawed human condition and flattering the tree by at least implicitly acknowledging his superiority.

"Sympathy and flattery do not move me," said the tree.

Duh, the tree could read my thoughts. This relationship would be problematic. The smartass in me thought that nothing, technically, could move the tree because, well, he was a tree. It was not a good time for such thinking, but the tree had already heard me think it.

The tree surprised me here. "Mike, let us spend some time allowing you to ask questions, if for no other reason than they are obstacles in our path. Realize, however, that you simply cannot guide these conversations. Even if you were the smartest of humans, it would be like asking your Abraham Lincoln to pilot a rocket ship to Mars. So, ask."

I drew a deep physical and mental breath and said, "You did not wish to talk about it last time, but I must ask again. Are you God? Are you the highest power in existence?"

"Same answer. I am a tree, and you have already agreed that I am bigger than you. That is all you need to know for these conversations. A comment, however, is that this is one of the topics where too much information would blow your mind."

The tree paused, so I asked, "Do you mean my human mind simply could not grasp what you would tell me?"

"More or less. Your mind could literally explode. Either way, your mind would be a mess."

Tree continued. "Since we are not talking about religion, by the way, let us be more generic. If and when we discuss a highest power, refer to 'the Big.'"

"Is there a Big?"

"Well of course there is a Big. How could you possibly think otherwise?"

"But that is a huge deal. Humans have always struggled with whether or not a God... a Big... exists. You are asking me to simply take your word for it?"

"I'm not asking you to do anything. I am telling you, however, that there is most certainly a Big."

"With powers bigger than the universe as we know it?"

"With powers bigger than the All."

"What All?"

"All the rest."

"We are at the start of only a second conversation, and the reve-lations don't get much meatier than that one," I thought. It took a few moments to re-set myself.

"Then, if you are not the Big, are you a prophet or some type of messenger from the Big?"

"I am not a prophet. It is not my intention to discuss the future of humans or your future, in particular. It is enough to discuss human life now, without venturing into tomorrow."

"So, are there other trees like you, who can scan brains and talk to humans?"

"What do you think?"

"My guess is that you are the only one."

"Then there you go."

I pressed on, "Back through human history, has there ever been another tree that scanned brains and talked to humans?"

"Let's break down that question. Are you assuming that I know the complete history of tree-to-human interactions, which implies that I know all of human history?"

"Yes, that would be the assumption. Are you that big to know all of human history?"

"Yes. Bigger."

This was terrific news. I loved history. "This is sort of... off my track... but could I ask you questions about history?"

"Give me an example."

"Ok." What was the most monumental question that I could ask about human history? "Was Fidel Castro involved in any way in a plot to assassinate John F. Kennedy?"

"No."

"No, he was not involved?"

"No, I heard your example, and we aren't doing history."

This was a rebuke if I ever heard one, but he did not say it unkindly and neither were his non-verbals unkind. Nevertheless, I had just foreclosed all enlightenment about history. A wonderful human representative I was turning out to be. My apparent history error was of breathtaking magnitude.

There was more ground to cover, but I was digesting that if the tree was not focusing on either the future or the past, then our conversations would be about the present. The past and future would have been easier, and probably more fun; the present would likely be less comfortable. "Well, then, could you at least tell me if you have had discussions with a human before now?"

"No."

"Wow," I thought. There was another twitch of that nagging insanity fear. Yet, if the tree was speaking the truth, and I felt no reason to believe that the tree was untruthful, then the uniqueness of what was unfolding almost silenced me.

But I continued, "Is it important that you are a tree, versus a rock or a squirrel or anything else?"

"Yes."

"Why?"

"I can't tell you."

"Can you tell me why you can't tell me?"

"It is a Rule #2 item. Leave it."

Moving on, I asked, "If you had wished to do so, could you have scanned the brain of a human far away and began talking to that person, instead of me, like a political leader in Europe or a soccer player in Argentina?"

"Yes, I could begin many conversations with humans now, just as this could have happened any time before now."

"Are there any limits on what you could do, if you wished?"

"No, certainly not as you would be able to understand them. If you can think it, I could do it. So, the only limitation is in your ability to think, not in my ability to do."

"So, you could do miracles if you wanted to do miracles."

"That is redundant."

This tree could also resemble an English teacher, or a lawyer. "The power that you have, Mr. Tree, that is the most unsettling to me in our talking is that you can read my thoughts, maybe even as they are being formulated and before I can send them. It is difficult to engage in a conversation knowing that, and it makes me wonder why communication between us would be of real value to you."

"First, Michael, I do not read your thoughts very often. If one has the power to do a thing, one also has the power not to do it. There are occasions when I comprehend the etiology and formulation of what you speak to me, but this is rare. Secondly, your discomfort is because your knowledge of my abilities means that you must be rigorously honest when talking to me, and humans are not accustomed to rigorous honesty. This will become easier for you as we go along, and this problem for you will remove itself. And finally, you have already noticed that you are compelled to be honest in your communications with me, anyway. You do not need to know why."

"Then, let me ask, even though I believe I know the answer, do you identify with any race or ethnic group, in tree, or whatever, equivalents?"

"You economists have to deal with demographics, don't you? No, there are no race or ethnic identifiers of me."

"And gender," I asked, "it is difficult to think of you without masculine or feminine as an identifier, but I don't have a clue. I wouldn't know whether to use masculine or feminine pronouns in describing you. So, I have to ask if you are a male or female, or how that works out for you. And how do I deal with that one?"

"Gender is not an identifier of me, either. You can use masculine pronouns in thinking of me, however, because you will be more comfortable thinking of me as a man."

Political correctness aside, I knew he was right. Even better, if I was ever allowed to write about any of this, it resolved the mind-numbing he/she problem.

As before, I went at least one question too far. "And I would be remiss in not asking if you are some sort of representative of some group of beings in the universe who have power and knowledge and abilities that humans don't have...."

Interrupting, the tree said, "You mean, am I the scout alien from your science fiction movies? Why would I appear to you as a tree, versus a 3-headed snake or with an alligator head? Do you think I've come to you in West Virginia because my people eat coal?" There was not a hint of sarcasm with these words, as if he really wanted to know if these were my thoughts.

I said nothing.

"So, do we really need to discuss the alien issue?"

"No, the question is withdrawn." The tree could be sensitive.

I continued, "Then, let me ask: why are you talking to a human? Why now?"

Replied the tree, "You will have all the answers that you need when these conversations end, but we could speculate, I suppose, about the Why now? It could be, of course, that I am simply 'making my rounds,' as you might say it, to touch base with how a real live human is doing? What is he thinking?"

"But you just said this is the first time such conversations have occurred."

"That is correct."

"Then you don't touch base very often, apparently?"

"Not as you would look at it, in your time. There might be many ways of touching base, other than conversations, of course."

"So, that is the reason: to touch base with a human?" I queried.

"I did not say that this was a reason, but merely that it could be a reason."

This was a satisfying answer only in the sense that my professional life involved the precise use of words. The tree used his words precisely. It also was becoming more apparent to me that the tree had previously scanned the brains of one or more lawyers.

"It could be," the tree continued, "that I might need these discussions in making a decision."

"Can you tell me anything about this decision?" It seemed a natural response, so I was unable to stop, "I mean is it more on the order of terminating the human race, or more like giving humans more ear wax?"

"I didn't say that my purpose was making any particular decision. I said it was possible."

Clearly, the most that was to be produced from this conversation was a list of possibilities. I briefly pondered working with the tree, as we went through his list, on probabilities attached to each possibility, so that a weighted average might be derived as an answer to the Why Now? In a magical bubble of good judgment, I chose not to go there. If the tree had wished to give me anything beyond possibilities, he would have already done so.

"It may be that I need the energy of the conversations now, more than before," said the tree.

"It could be that even I don't fully understand Why now?"

"It may be that I represent someone else and am, more or less, following orders."

"It may be that I need to find humor."

That possibility was so different from the others, and so unexpected on the list, that I interrupted, "Do you mean that you have never experienced humor in your entire existence?"

"I don't understand it. If I were human, looking at what some humans are doing to other humans, I would more likely feel anger or sadness than happiness. But I don't know how to perceive the distinction between happy and funny, either. For the longest time now, I have watched humans laugh about disgusting and hurtful things, heard the jokes that are based upon the belittling of people or groups. But there is the laughing that humans do over what seems are everyday events, and it is spontaneous, and leaves those involved better by any measure, with no hurt to any other. It is my wish to understand that, to feel that. This humor, the dark and the light, is a human characteristic. It is not found among the deer or rabbits here around us."

Interrupting again, I asked what heretofore would have been a strange question to a tree, "Are you telling me that you have never laughed?"

The tree replied, "Of course, you know that I don't have a mouth, so I could not laugh audibly the way you do." The tree was struggling for the first time, "But I don't talk to you like other humans talk to you either, so it would be possible for me to laugh, and you to hear it. In answer to your question, No, I have never laughed."

Later recalling this admission by the tree evoked curiosity. How could this tree, with powers and capabilities far beyond my own, not know humor? How could I laugh, yet he could not? At the moment, though, sadness surrounded the words of the tree and that is what I felt.

On the other hand, the tree had come the closest to allowing my natural transition to a college professor mode. In this mode, lectures could be delivered on a variety of subjects. What I actually knew about the subject did not temper my joy of expounding, but it might affect the length of the lecture, and certainly its value. "Humor can be divided into a number of categories," I began. "Sarcasm, for example, is one of my favorites, and I can see how the casual observer might miss the subtleties of any particular sarcasm."

"No, no, no. I don't need a lecture on the categories of humor. Your brain and others have already been scanned for information, and I nevertheless do not understand this thing. Now may be the time for me to understand."

There was an awkward silence. The tree seemed to have ended what he wished to say about this, or other, possibilities on the "Why Now?" list. I asked, "Are there other possible reasons for your human discussions coming now? Is this the complete list?"

"Let us say," he responded, "more or less."

To me, "more or less" meant "no", but the tree said exactly what he meant to say, so I asked, "Is one of these possibilities the answer, or is it some combination of these possibilities...."

"Are we doing a multiple-choice test—all of the above, (a) and (c)?" He did not wait for me to reply. "You have a list of possibilities. A human life is a list of possibilities. That is the best it gets for you. Let us move along. One more question."

In retrospect I would have paused, for as long as the tree would have allowed me, to contemplate a "last question" to a superior being. Could this truly be the last question formulated by a human to a talking tree for, say, another four or five thousand years? Most certainly, my questions would be a rarity in whatever series of discussions which presumably the tree had planned. Moreover, the result of the Q&A session thus far had not exactly dotted the i's and crossed the t's of what could be learned here. Scholars could write treatises on the "last" question to be asked.

In fact, none of this interrupted my rapid formulation of the last question. The question said a lot about me, really, in that it was embarrassingly self-centered. "Why me? Why of all the humans on earth have you chosen to talk to me? While my ego is above zero, it is not <u>that</u> big. There are too many others: smarter, better, with more to offer. Why me?"

"If I gave you the answer to that question," he said, "the answer would lose its purpose." "Let us at least talk about some possibilities, however."

Another list of possibilities. At least I already knew to take what I was given without much of an attempt to elicit more. The tree was going to tell me what he was going to tell me and then he would stop.

"It could be," began the tree, "that you happened to move here, to the house next to me, and then you added the porch almost touching me, so you were the convenient and logical choice when I decided to pursue certain conversations. While I could travel to others, you were very convenient."

Speaking of self-centeredness, this one may have been first on the tree's list, but it was not at the top of my list already. Surely, something unique to me was a factor in this choice.

"It could be that there was a great lottery and you won. Or lost, depending upon how you feel about this when it is over."

"Then, how would you have literally positioned yourself to have discussions with someone else if someone else had won the game of chance?"

"That is easily done, but you need not dwell on how."

Neither of the first two possibilities on the list were particularly flattering, but it was merely a list and perhaps the tree was leading off with a not-so-subtle reminder about humility.

"It is possible that the path of mistakes that you have made over your lifetime was fascinating to me, and this could be important in the discussions that we will have."

"It could be that you have grown from at least some of this path and this is attractive for discussion."

"It could be because you remind me of me, a long time ago."

"It could be because of that sense of humor thing in your lineage. Your father loved to tell jokes all of his life, and he particularly liked to laugh at his own jokes. And you also love to laugh but spent many years when you could not laugh. Maybe you can tell me something that will help me understand."

"Remember too," the tree added, "that questions will be answered in the discussions to come, whether or not you can now ask them, or even envision them."

And he was gone.

CHAPTER THREE -

DIMENSIONS: BIG AND SMALL

By the second weekend in May, I was enjoying my porch hour occurring most late afternoons or early evenings, even while awaiting a next conversation with the tree. This one-hour decompression in the cadence of my day was good for me, I common sensically knew, tree or no tree. I learned to actually read the Kindle and wait for a conversation at the same time. This was quite a milestone in multi-tasking.

This good habit also meant that I would watch the unfolding of nature more closely and regularly through the spring. It was a beautiful place in the world to be and, despite the ups and downs of existence, I was a grateful man. And expectant. There is not a decent analogy for the anticipation of the next conversation with a talking tree, a talking tree of great intelligence.

I was swiveled around looking at the death curve one lovely Saturday afternoon, around 4:00. The ladies of the house would be off at errands for another couple of hours. An SUV slowly rounded the sharp curve traveling from downtown to home and, so few homes are down

Ridge Road, I immediately recognized the male driver as one of the newer residents of our street. It caught my eye because one of the other neighbors, in her sedan, was driving out of the neighborhood and on track to hit our new neighbor at the curve. But both drivers were being careful and paying attention so that the exiting driver easily turned into a side road, let the entering neighbor proceed down the road, both waved, and the car-of-courtesy backed onto Ridge Road and exited toward downtown. The obvious, and unwritten, rule was that the driver closest to the turn-in or pull-over area willingly became the courtesy car. Our new neighbor, being a very nice gentleman, had understood this from the beginning, as any nice person would assume was true with a one-lane road down the ridge. I looked forward to getting to know this new neighbor at least as well as I had gotten to know all of my other neighbors.

It had not always been true, however, that new residents learned this rule easily. We had enough turnover among owners that, in my time, there had been as least one jackass who did not learn the rule gracefully. Admittedly, it took awhile to realize that every driver needed to anticipate those stretches of the road where pullovers or driveways did not exist. So, one sped up a bit to reach an accessible area. If two cars met, at worst the courtesy car would have a short backup to the nearest passing-accessible area. This one guy thought the rule was that everyone else on the road should do whatever was necessary to allow his unimpeded progress up or down the road. He also drove far too fast for this curvy road with visual impairments and walkers, children, and pets.

Some of us talked about this guy and what was necessary, but I believe that all of the neighbors knew how to handle the situation. So, in my case, as an example, one day I had passed an accessible point and would have almost reached the next accessible point except the new neighbor gunned his vehicle and stopped in front of my vehicle. I was about ⅔ of the way between passable points, while he was about ⅓ of the way. Whereas he could have, at worst, reversed a few yards and temporarily driven into a side driveway, now either he backed up ⅓ of the way or I backed up ⅔ of the way. He clearly expected that I would do a curvy back-up for ⅔ of this distance.

To put this in perspective, in the Old West, and perhaps today in certain places, one of us would have gunned down the other. The legislature, however, had not yet mandated that all West Virginians not in a car seat be armed at all times, so neither of us was packing. While I had plenty of work to do, it was all in my briefcase in the seat beside me. There was no appointment or other, scheduled time confronting me. It was a terrific, Fall mid-morning. Obviously, the jackass was in a hurry to get home, for some reason, and then perhaps somewhere else, I supposed.

So, I shut down the car and began to work in the front seat. Didn't look up at him. Rolled the window down. It was clear that I was prepared to block his path for a while, because I could have gone many hours, enjoyed every minute of it, and been productive. I was actually prepared for the possibility that the jackass would call 911 and a Charleston police officer would come down our little private road and talk to me and the jackass about how it was a shame that we couldn't work out our differences. But after about 15 minutes, the jackass backed his ⅓ of the way back to the driveway, and I passed him and waved thank you. The real man in me was so proud of me as I drove by. It was the closest I came to storming the beaches at Normandy.

The guy learned the courtesy rule after one or two such encounters. He learned not to speed down the road too, but I can't tell you what I know about that one. At any rate, the jackass lived down the road two years or so and moved. Perhaps he came to know that none of us knew, or attempted to learn, his name but referred to him as "the jackass down the street who lives in the (previous resident's) house." Once you become known as a neighborhood jackass, it is difficult to change your image.

It should also be mentioned that he was not a large, bullying jackass, but rather a small, mouthy jackass. It is much easier for a neighborhood to deal with a small jackass on a one-way road. Said another way, smaller

jackasses may have more to lose from their jackassedness and statistically, therefore, one would expect the incidence of jackasses to be correlated with their size. The upshot of this, though, was that the Ridge Road
Golden Rule was preserved: be courteous to your neighbor so that, one
day when you are in an urgent hurry, he or she will be courteous to you.
It was a parallel to mutually assured destruction at the international level.

Somewhere in Charleston, about that time, my wife and granddaughter were having an SUV conversation between shopping and errands
destinations. I would not learn of the existence or nature of this series of
conversations until years later. This was apparently the first one, and it was
approximately as follows:

"Lynnie," said Chloe, "have you noticed that Pickle has been acting
weird lately?"

"Do you mean even more weird than he is anyway?" she replied.

"No, I'm serious. Weird… and it is when he's out on the porch, by
himself… and he is out there every day."

"Well, first of all, that's why we built the porch and I'm glad he is
leaving his dungeon of the office downstairs to read on the porch when the
weather is this nice."

"But that's not what is weird. What is weird is that some of the time,
he is not reading out of the Kindle, but just staring at it. He is really staring
over it, looking outside."

"That's great. Staring at the outside world on days like this is good
for him. He deals with numbers and legal documents all day."

"You interrupted me. When he is staring outside, he is talking sometimes. I can see his mouth move. It is like when he is driving and has some
stressful testimony coming, and he gets into imaginary cross examinations
with himself. Except he hasn't had any stressful testimonies coming lately.
And when he walks inside, he is thoughtful about something. What is up
with him?"

"Yeah, I've noticed all that. He is incapable of hiding anything. Nothing is going on. There is no reason for him to be particularly worried or stressed."

"And there is this one other thing. When he is staring and mouthing, it's not so much that he is talking to the outside… he is talking to the tree at the corner. To the top of the tree, not the middle of it. It's like he is talking to the top of the tree." She added, semi-jokingly, "So, is he becoming a danger to himself or others? Are these early signs of dementia?"

Lynn responded, "He's always mouthed words without realizing it, but I'll watch his porch behavior more closely. He is not becoming mentally incompetent as far as I can tell, but he has always been odd. We'll talk if we notice any further deterioration in his odd level. Deal?"

"Deal," Chloe replied.

Back to me, reading my Kindle on the porch. The rules, and the last conversation, led me to believe that the next conversation would be about a topic as yet unknown to me. Not a lot of preparation is possible for that, even for a major league control freak. It is interesting how one does not dwell on rules unless rules exist that are constraining, nor on one's control nature until one has no control.

However, I thought, there was one possible reason given to me for these conversations where I had something the tree wanted. I thus thought about humor. How is humor explained to a person (or tree) who has never experienced it? How situations can surely change: just a month or so ago, the probability was zero that my focus could become the teaching of humor to a tree. The notion that an economist would be called upon to teach humor to anything was slightly humorous. Sitcoms had been built around many occupations, even physicists, but demand-and-supply people were mostly only funny to themselves.

Then, the tree says, "Go ahead. We can talk about humor a while. I am still very interested in what you have to say about that." He said this in a way that felt as though a long time had elapsed, for him, since our conversation of only a few weeks ago. Time apparently was not the same for the two of us.

Mark Twain once observed that it took him three days to prepare for an impromptu speech, which a planning-perfectionist-type like me could appreciate. I had only noted the strangeness of humor among the reasons for our conversations, and I had most certainly not begun a course outline, the gathering of texts and readings, etc. This was very uncomfortable. How to start?

"Ok," I said, "let me start with a basic type of humor: a riddle. A riddle may not be intended for humor, but some riddles are intended to be funny." Something occurred to me and changed my stream of thought. "Wait a minute, a riddle is a question or puzzle...."

The tree interrupted, "I know the definition of a riddle."

"Yes, but I may know why you can't find humor. If I ask you a riddle, you already know the answer. You knew the question and the answer before the riddle was chosen and spoken. You already would know the punch line of a joke before I even chose the joke to tell."

"That would be a good point," said the tree, "but remember that if one has the power to do a thing, one has the power not to do it. So, it can be arranged that I can listen to your riddle and not know the answer that you will give me. My hearing of the riddle can be as if it were the first time for me. You need not know how this is possible, but assume this problem has been resolved. I still can't find humor. So, go ahead with your riddle."

"Let's start basic then: Why did the chicken cross the road?"

The tree actually hesitated a few minutes, as if he were formulating possible answers to the question, but then he replied, "I don't know, Why?"

"To get to the other side." A pause.

"That's it... to get to the other side? That is supposed to be funny and make someone laugh?"

"I'll admit it is not hilariously, back-slapping funny, but this is a first example…."

The tree, again interrupting, "It is not the least bit funny. Of course, the chicken had to cross the road to get to the other side, but what was the chicken's destination in the first place? Why was crossing the road even important? How did the chicken get to the road? Was a fox chasing the chicken? Getting to the other side might not be the best option for the chicken in particular circumstances. Many questions are raised, but what is funny?"

I tried. "The humor here is supposed to be that you consider the zillion possible answers for the question except the obvious one: to get to the other side. That is what is funny, at least in theory. And then there is the life lesson of the riddle: that sometimes we make things so complicated that we overlook the obvious."

"But who would possibly laugh at that? And does it occur to you that when you have to go to this much trouble to explain why something is humorous then it is probably not funny?"

"Let me continue. I know a hundred of these. Why did the dinosaur cross the road?"

"Why?"

"Because chickens had not evolved yet." Silence.

"Why did the chicken cross the road, roll in the mud, and cross the road back to where he started?"

"I don't have a clue."

"Because he was a dirty double crosser. Do you see how we can vary the funny?"

"I haven't yet heard a funny to be varied. Maybe you have to be a chicken or a chicken farmer to appreciate riddles, but you are not doing much for me on humor."

"Let's forget chickens. How do you know when an elephant has been in your refrigerator?"

"That doesn't even make sense, Michael. A chicken or an elephant can cross a road but an elephant can't possibly fit into a refrigerator. Is this about a very small elephant and a really big refrigerator?"

"You just need to ask 'How?' That's your role in the riddle."

"How?"

"Because you see elephant tracks in the butter." The tree paused briefly but did not smile a sliver.

"Michael, do you remember when I said a possible reason for our discussions was that you might teach me about humor?"

"Yes."

"That possibility is hanging by a thread about now. I am not moved by riddles. You must do a better job with this."

"Why don't I re-group and we'll try this again at a later time." Like never, I thought, but the tree probably heard me think it.

"Good idea," observed the tree, thoughtfully, for he had transitioned to what he wanted to discuss with me. "Let me ask you a question," he said. "When I say the word 'Dimension', what comes to your mind?"

That question surprised me a bit, although I really had no idea what the tree would choose to talk about or how he would begin. My pause before answering was also because, as a teacher, I made a big deal about students knowing definitions, and before a lecture, it was my practice to ensure my own knowledge and understanding of relevant definitions. Yet, my formulation of an answer meant a recall search unaided by Mr. Webster or Ms. Google.

So, I began, "My best, off-the-cuff definition is that it is a way of viewing the organization, in the extreme, of the universe…what you call the All. Any definition would probably have 'measurable' in it. The examples I can think of are measurable, or at least ultimately capable of measurement."

"Keep going. What else?"

"One observation which didn't originate with me, is that one learns a great deal about a person, or a people, by observing what they measure, and by the measures which they hold most important. In my world of economics, the notion of dimensions is as fundamental as the x-axis of length and the y-axis of height on a two-dimensional graph. We can use the graph in explaining to students the relationships between two variables, which helps them then understand relationships among many variables."

"So," interjected the tree, "What are the dimensions that you, and your human scientists, talk about?"

"Length and height are two of them. Depth is a third dimension that provides shapes -- areas that we can measure, like a cube. Ultimately, the shape of the All might be measured by these three dimensions, but I've got a feeling that it is not that simple." After a thinking pause, I added, "and time, I believe, is generally considered to be a fourth dimension. It is also measurable, backwards and forwards, and it can logically co-exist with the other three dimensions.

"Another dimension of the status of those four does not come to mind. My vague understanding is that in physics and other disciplines, more dimensions, and categories of dimensions, known and unknown, have been discussed. I recall that 'Super String' theory in physics is related to these other dimensions of the All, but I couldn't begin to tell you any details." I knew that my knowledge of string theory could have been from a careful review of scientific literature but more likely resulted from a science blurb in a magazine reviewed in some doctor's waiting room.

"But you are the one, bigger than me, who can scan brains and knows history. What is your definition of a dimension?" Of course, I assumed he was also planning to tell me, in due course, why this topic was important.

"Your notions of dimensions are good enough for our discussions now. Let's talk about the Small and the Big, and let us begin with dimensions which are already familiar to you." After a quick pause, "Do you see it crawling beneath you?"

I was unsure what he was talking about, but I looked down at the floor. "Do you mean the ant crawling across the floor?" Fortunately, it was the only ant in sight on the porch. If we had been indoors, my automatic reaction would have been to step on it. A thought must have struck me that the ant might somehow be important to the discussion, and I probably should not kill it.

The tree, of course, knew this, but he said, "Yes, let's talk about the ant. You and the ant. Let's talk about the Big and the Small, in dimensions that you can understand, of you the Big and the ant the Small. You do believe that a human is bigger than an ant, correct?"

"Correct," I answered, wondering where we were headed.

"Then, let us begin with an easy measure of the human-to-ant bigness: height. If the ant were standing up and you were standing up, what would be the ratio of your height?"

My pause in answering this simple question was embarrassingly long. This appeared to be a relatively short ant, but I had no idea about the average size of ants nor did I know the degree of accuracy that the tree expected. It was never my strength to measure anything against an invisible scale. There was also the issue of whether measurement was to be in inches or centimeters.

Even the normally-patient tree could not withstand the pressure of this silence so he answered his own question. "Centimeters would be easier, but assume that the ant is exactly one inch long, or tall. Close enough for our purposes. And you are exactly six-feet tall, so 72 inches. You are 72:1 bigger than the ant. And, by the way, you Americans should not wonder why other humans resent you, when you refuse to measure like everyone else. You were in field artillery and were forced to deal with meters and kilometers, and you don't remember a single conversion."

"I memorized the conversions but even then could not see them on the ground. Fortunately, no one ever let me near combat."

"So, Michael, the 72:1. Would you accept 72:1 as the ratio of your relative bigness to the ant?"

"Of course not," I replied, "for the obvious reason that bigness measurement must be about much more than inches."

"Do you mean other dimensions, other measures?"

"Yes."

"Would you accept the likelihood that whatever measurements that you make, there are other dimensions and measurements out there but as yet beyond the grasp of humans?"

"Yes, I would agree that this might be true but we humans, of course, use the current state of knowledge as best we can," I answered.

"At first blush, as you would say, considering whatever factors that you might consider, how far is the ratio above 72:1?"

"Very much above."

The tree suggested, "As in you are 720:1, or 7,200:1, or even bigger."

"My first thought in this judgment is that I would sacrifice the lives of 7,200 or 72,000 ants for one human life to be saved. That is a cliché response, I suppose, but it is my core thought about this. It is not obvious how one could have a limiting point to the size of that ratio on the 'I would sacrifice…' criterion. That's just the way humans think." Then, I added, "Well, most humans, I hope. There are some humans who seem to have a zero value for a human life, and an ant has a value above zero."

"Let us back up before we go forward. What do you remember about ants?"

Again I felt naked without Mr. Webster or Ms. Google or Madame Wikipedia but did my best: "They live in colonies, and they have a well-defined division-of-labor within each colony: certain ants do certain things. I think it is ants whose males live only a few weeks, and they may or may not get lucky and have an intimate encounter with a queen ant." I thought about the ant equivalent of my late Aunt Margaret saying at the male ant's funeral, "I told that boy if he went messing around with the Queen something bad would happen to him."

"That is more-or-less true," said the tree, "you also know, but don't remember…"

Interrupting, I asked, "You even know what I have learned but don't remember?"

"Yes, and what humans don't remember is a significant portion of what they have learned. You did have segments of entomology and general ant education in your earlier years, with random additions thereafter. You learned, for example, that many types of ants exist on earth, with a diversity of natures, and cultures, and characteristics which is comparable to the diversity of humans and groups of humans. There are, as you might say, good ants and bad ants, aggressive and passive ants, ants that willingly sacrifice their lives for other ants. You learned that ants teach skills and jobs to other ants. You learned that ants can form symbiotic relationships with other insects and plants in their environment.

"Ants are certainly better than humans at some things," the tree added. "If an ant left home base in a desert and walked for a day, the ant could find its way home. You, on the other hand, would not have a chance to find your way home. You can barely navigate with maps and street signs. A nomad would find your bleached bones amongst the shifting sands. You were also once intrigued in learning that because of the high death rates among foraging ants, older ants are disproportionately assigned that job. They are close to death anyway—an interesting insight into ant decision-making and ethics. You remarked that this solved the problem of funding social security programs for older ants."

"Now," continued the tree, "assume that you must use more criteria than the 'I would sacrifice...' standard in judging Man-to-Ant relative size. What criteria would you consider?"

"Again this is off the top of my head," I began, "I would consider many aspects of the physical and mental capabilities of both species, the roles and tasks that each could perform, or not, how they are able to interact with their environment, how they organize themselves into groups and societies—colonies for ants. Most important I suppose is their relative abilities in cognating. What are they capable of doing with their minds? What decisions can they make? Maybe it is non-cognitive characteristics like motivation and persistence. Also, I suppose, what emotions can they feel? Perhaps what kind of spirituality can they experience? With more time, I could pretty up a list of criteria, but is that enough to answer your question?"

The tree replied, "That is fine, Michael. Before your thinking goes further in modifying the 72:1 evaluation, let's look at you versus the ant from the perspectives of both of you." (The ant was crawling from object to object and would apparently play no active role in this discussion. A suddenly talking ant would not have been shocking at this point.) "Let's start with you—the Big in this relationship."

After a pause, the tree continued, "To what extent are you interested in that ant, its welfare, and its future? Do you view ants as good or bad, or is your viewpoint situational? How much of a typical day do you spend watching, interacting with, or thinking about ants?"

"These are rhetorical questions, right?"

"More or less. You can comment as you wish, but we are moving toward a destination," he continued, "Have you ever helped an ant? Have you ever harmed an ant when it was unnecessary, even to forestall an unlikely inconvenience? Have you ever killed an ant, or mass murdered an ant colony, just because you could?"

Here I had a boyhood recall, and it simultaneously occurred to me that the tree already knew about this incident. "I have a memory, when I was a boy, of burning an ant hill. It bothered me for a while afterwards... enough that I still remember it. Actually, I think it was Jerry Hinton's idea, and I was a thoughtless accomplice, but a jury would nevertheless convict both of us for first degree murder."

"So at least once, you were an evil Big in your own evaluation?"

"Yes, but I was a young Big. Never did anything like that again. Nor did Jerry Hinton, as far as I know."

The tree moved along, "Do you think the ant knows that you are up there, when you aren't moving around?" Does the ant perceive you as the most important large creature around it, or do you have the same importance as a chipmunk or a deer? Do you believe that even the smartest of ants has a chance of comprehending the size relationship with humans? Is there any chance that ants, over time, can grow their capabilities toward those of humans? Do you contemplate growing your own knowledge of ants over your lifetime? Do you understand what ants, collectively, do for you as a human? Have you ever contemplated thanking an ant for its role in your environment?"

The tree was pausing briefly between questions but I was not responding. My answers were "no," but the tree knew that, anyway. If it would have made the tree's mood any lighter, I would have straightaway carried an opened jar of Jiffy creamy-smooth peanut butter to the nearest ant hill as a good will gesture. But can ants eat peanut butter without becoming stuck in it? So many questions, and so few answers.

"Can you predict what will happen to the ant in the future?"

"Only if I was about to step on it."

"So, you could control its fate, or not? Do you care about its fate?"

"Well," I interjected, "now that you have caused me to think about it, I don't wish the ant any harm. I have a kind of live and let live attitude toward ants most of the time. As a practical matter, there is simply not enough time for me to care about, or take care of, all of the humans, either."

The tree said, "Let us now think from the perspective of the ant—the Small to you as Big. Can the ant perceive a man in any other way than poorly-focused vision, vibrations, and contact? In any other way does the ant think about you?... about what you could do or might do?... about why you do what you do?"

"My answer so far would be 'no.' I don't believe an ant is that big. Entomologists may be researching some of these questions, but I don't think that an ant's ability to think is comparable to that of a human."

"So, can an ant have values? Can an ant be grateful for anything that you might do, or not do? If an ant begins to climb a tree... this is not a chicken riddle... does the ant have any notion of the length of its journey? Does it matter to the ant?"

The tree was moving to a point, I sensed correctly, "You have at least focused on the relative size of a Man to an Ant, something that you would not have done otherwise."

"That is true."

"And you see the issues of bigness that exist between creatures, with a basic size difference of only 72:1."

"That is also correct," I replied.

"Let's get back to numbers. You have spent your adult life measuring with numbers. If you must measure on many criteria, not just the 'I would sacrifice...' one where you started, is the ratio more like 720:1 or 7,200:1?"

"Still bigger, I believe."

"Is it bigger than 72,000:1?"

"Probably, but once we go as far as 72,000:1, the attempt at measurement is so difficult, vague, and imprecise, that the numbers aren't very meaningful."

"Yes, but you have reached conclusions over your life when measurement was difficult? Would you agree that an appropriate measure would be somewhere between 7,200:1 and 72,000:1?"

"I suppose so. Not really knowing where we are going with any of this, I'm willing to accept a measurement closer to 72,000:1."

"That is good enough for our purposes. Somewhere between 7,200 and 72,000 to one. Closer to 72,000 to one. Seemingly, a broad range of high numbers, but all we need to proceed."

The tree actually seemed happy with himself. Almost relieved. His mood lightened moving forward, as if the hard part was over.

"Now," said the tree, "let us use you versus the ant as our foundation for Big-to-Small measurement, but view yourself as the Small. Let us consider the magnitude of that which is bigger than you, and let us talk first about dimensions which you already know."

This transition gave me the first confidence that the discussion was actually going somewhere: to a place that I sensed was very important to the tree.

"I need you to assume that the Big is now THE Big. You are an economist, so you make assumptions as naturally as most people breathe. Assume that the Big is bigger than the All, so that whatever are the size relationships we discuss, the Big versus Michael is bigger than that."

"Ok," I interrupted, as if the tree actually needed my permission to proceed. "Is the Big part of the All but also outside of it or totally outside of it, or what?"

"You are not ready to deal with that issue, but just stay with me here. Let's talk about length, which can also be viewed as distance. You are exactly 6 feet tall—the distance between the top of your head and the bottom of your feet. Do you recall the number of feet in a mile?"

"5,280," I answered.

"So one mile has a relationship of 5,280:6 to you, which reduces to 880:1. Let me remind you of some facts and measures that you learned at some point but do not recall. Your sun is 93,000,000 miles from your earth, so that the distance relationship to Michael's length is 93 million times 880 to one, would you agree?"

"Yes. I have a hand calculator and computer downstairs and can multiply that out for you," I offered helpfully. The tree paused, and it occurred to me how stupid was this comment. The tree did not require my computer to multiply large numbers.

"I do not require your computer to multiply large numbers," said the tree, but 93 million times 880 to 1 is good enough. Stay with me. You know, of course, that your sun is not the limit of the measure of the All as currently known to humans.

"You recall that a 'light year' is the distance that light travels in a year. Your scientists have measured this as almost 5.9 trillion miles. A trillion is 1,000 billion. A billion is 1,000 million. You would agree that one light year is many, many miles, right?"

"Correct," I answered.

"Approximately 300 billion stars have been discovered in your Milky Way galaxy, and this galaxy has been estimated to be 100,000 light years across. If the All were the Milky Way galaxy, how would we be doing in the All-To-Michael measure of relative length?"

"We would have a really big number relative to me," I admitted.

"And your scientists know of hundreds of billions of galaxies."

At some point in my education, I knew these measures, but they were overwhelming to me now.

The tree paused briefly, perhaps to allow the numbers to permeate my consciousness, but he was not finished. "Light years also bring up the dimension of time. Looking at the light from a star is also a look back in time.

"Your statistical time on earth, Michael, is 84 years."

I assumed that he was referring to a U. S. life expectancy table because I regularly used such tables in my work. One of my darkest days was when I mis-read such a table and noted that I had died two years previously. Nevertheless, out of an abundance of caution, I asked, "You are not telling me that I will die at age 84, are you?"

"No, it is not important if your actual experience is 74, or 84, or 94… for this discussion."

I briefly considered asking if he would mind telling me the actual length of my life, as this was an especially important factoid for me personally. There was not a chance the tree would have answered that question.

He proceeded, "Starting close to home, so to speak, your scientists have measured the oldest rocks in North American as 3.56 billion years old. If time is our measure, the All-to-Michael would be 3,560,000,000:84. Then, to put this in further perspective, human scientists have measured the age of the universe as 13.75 billion years, which is 13,750,000,000:84."

"Michael, how do these measurements compare to your 72,000:1 with the ant?"

It felt to be a rhetorical question, so I spread my hands apart, to non-verbally indicate, "A whole bunch bigger."

The tree asked, "Michael, these are dimensions and measures currently known. Can you comprehend these size differences of the All compared to you?"

"No, I really can't. I can hear or say the numbers, but I can't truly comprehend the bigness of the All compared to me. It is awesome, jaw-dropping, difficult to even imagine." I paused and continued, "So, is that the lesson: that the All, and therefore the Big, are so much bigger than I had previously contemplated?"

"Wait just a few minutes before wrapping up," answered the tree. "We are not finished with the Big versus Small discussion. We have only discussed dimensions that you already know—where you humans have made progress to advance the known to the end point which, of course, is the Truth. Indeed, you have far to go, and there are breathtaking discoveries that will occur to expand further your understanding of that chasm between what you know and what you have yet to learn.

"There are dimensions literally all around you humans on this planet that you do not know. Some of your best scientists have a label for this: the 'unknown unknown'. You therefore cannot measure them and certainly cannot even begin the journey of analysis and understanding. Furthermore, Michael, these dimensions may be parallel with your unknown dimensions but may also intersect the known. Scientists often label these intersections as anomalies because they have no other explanation.

"Let me ask you to do something for me. You see the space of a few feet between me and my neighbor tree. Describe to me what you see in the space between me and the other tree. Take your time."

I sensed this was important, if for no other reason than the tree was suggesting that the task should be unhurried and, by implication, thorough. Therefore, I took a breath, delayed my compulsion to speak too quickly, and looked upon the space between the trees. I looked vertically from the cloudy sky down to the ground and left to right—tree to tree—at each elevation. And then I attempted to do what the tree asked me to do, "At the top of the space," I began, "is the cloudy sky. Then, looking down in the imaginary distance between you and your neighbor tree, I see the tops of the trees in our adjacent forest—the ones that are taller than either of you. Then, you come into view to define the left hand side of the space and then your shorter neighbor defines the right hand side. And the foliage between you obscures some of the space between you. Were you even asking about the space above the trees or about top down?"

"Surely, you are doing fine. Keep going."

My thoroughness confirmed, I focused upon the space toward the bottom of the trees. "Then toward the bottom is the mowed lawn, extending to the left side of a short bush at the end of the cultivated yard, then some low scrub bushes, and then the bottoms of the trees in the neighboring woods beyond."

"There have been while I've been looking a few animals that appeared in the space. At least two birds flew by and a squirrel is foraging in the forest."

"Anything else that you see?"

"Not really. I could talk about various flying or crawling insects in the space, or the breeze that sways the trees occasionally, or the green color in the leaves of the bush. Is that enough of an answer?"

"You see Michael," said the tree, "it is no answer at all. I asked you about the space between the trees, and all that you have described is the space beyond the trees."

"But in the space literally between you, there is nothing but air, except where your branches and leaves touch and overlap. I know that air is something, of course. It is a mixture of gases, but I don't really see it, or at least don't know how to describe it."

"There are dimensions criss-crossing this space, and others like it, which are as yet unknown to you and other humans. Using examples that you would understand, there is enough in this space to power your city, or your country. It is not really that complicated looking back on it, after someone has discovered and others have analyzed. There is also enough here to destroy humanity, as you know it. The journey to the truth always has a dark and dangerous side. But you cannot begin to see that which you cannot yet comprehend. I am telling you, however, that the chasm between the Big and Small is incomprehensible in the dimensions that you know, and you know but a few of these. The truth is in the whole of the dimensions, and the matter and energy therein, so it should be no surprise that anything in your life might not be understood. To use one of your expressions, you are playing cards with only a part of the deck, a very small part.

"Let me ask you," the tree continued, "how does this discussion make you feel?"

I did a quick review in my mind, sighed a deep sigh, and said, "Small, very small… insignificant in the scheme of things. To use a fancy word: Nugatory… trifling, worthless."

"Let me comment on that. Small is good. It is very, very good. It is half of this fundamental. But Small in relationship to the Big is not the same as worthless. Small is worth a lot. And the source of this worth is the Big. A part of the bigness is that the Big is connected to each and every one of you humans. All 7 billion of you."

"Imagine that you had a connection with each of your 72,000 ants. You knew them since their creation, watched them do what they did. You knew where they were going, and why, can you imagine that?"

"No, of course I can't imagine that. There would simply be no time, as I know time, that this could be done…."

"Which is why we are talking about this enlargement to your picture of the Big, who is already unimaginably big in relationship to you. The Big is not constrained by your time or by any of the metrics in any of the dimensions that you know. He created the dimensions and weaves them together. So, the Big can do with the 7 billion what you cannot do with the 72,000. That's one reason why he is the Big and you are not."

I said, "But I really do not care, to be honest, about the lives of 72,000 individual ants. Apart from the time issue, they are just not creatures that are close enough to me, enough like me, for me to care about them individually."

"So you see still another enlargement of the Big versus you. This Big does care about you individually… about each one of the ants, too. It is not for me to tell you why. Or how. The surprise to me is why humans would be surprised by this. If you can imagine it, the Big can do it."

"This is not to say, Michael, that you are on a TV in the Big's control room being watched 24/7, or in my control room either. If a farmer plants corn, he does not sit in the field all summer watching it grow. There are other things to do. What one has the power to do, one has the power not to do."

"We start with the fundamental: an unimaginably large Big compared to you, the Small. Humans create their own misery believing in a Big that is too small or living as a Small that is too big, for the true gap between Big and Small has been appreciated by few. It might be tempting to think of humans moving close to the Big in some dimensions, but it is not true."

"Some humans," he added, "believe in a small Big versus themselves and in so doing ignore the expanse and complexity of the universe as humans currently understand it: the gazillion-to-one that is already known. Some see the All as so large and mysterious that it is maddening to consider, so they ignore the Big:Small relationship altogether. The subject frightens them. And there are some who contemplate the true gap between Big and Small but cannot accept a Big that is bigger than the All. An obstacle for them is how the Big started up. I can only tell you that humans and their scientists have far to go in understanding this one. Indeed, when they approach the correct answer to the start, they will be in the last stages of the journey. The start is the key to the end, and the two anchor the path."

"Please think on the Big and the Small, and we will talk further. This is the fundamental. You must accept the first thing first." And he departed.

CHAPTER FOUR –
COMFORT

By early June, the lawn and forest surrounding our house were as lush as Appalachian mountains could be. The steady improvement of landscaping was a project of my wife, and the border of our yard along Ridge Road was pleasing to the eye. With my regular time on the porch, I was often reminded of this gift, for which no effort on my part had been forthcoming. Economists called such a benefit at no cost a "positive externality." Who else would burden beauty with such an unromantic term?

This day on the porch I was reflecting upon technology, in general, and cursive, in particular. Yet another news story had appeared that cursive handwriting would vanish from American schools in the future, as e-technology only required keyboarding skills and the future world would be exclusively electronic. Moreover, voice recognition software would mean that writers would only have to say, not write, either cursively or electronically. Had the world gone mad?

Cursive provides the visual beauty of letters, words, sentences. A typed work is functional. It may be effective toward a purpose, but it is never beautiful. It does not visually inspire or enhance the appearance of a word, or motivate more words in a natural flow of the beautiful. The electronic word does not individualize the visual expression of words and thoughts.

The evildoers of electronic technology would point to the many who have abused cursive in their lifetimes. Certainly a teacher should have seen this carnage of cursive via the grading of papers. Indeed, past secretaries and colleagues might suggest that my own cursive was neither decipherable nor pretty. But it is beautiful to me, and I am a most important person in reading the words that I write. Moreover, I thought, while the cursive word might be ugly, the typed word is forever average in its appearance. The words that express our souls should at least be capable of visual beauty. And, finally, if God were to write a message to humankind in the sky, would it not be written in cursive? Who could possibly imagine God typing out the message on his personal computer? (It also occurred to me that I would see the cursive message written in English, and that this problem of differing languages would pose an annoying complication to sky-writing.)

What would the e-ristocrats of technology do next? Change the way numbers look? So, one is not 1, two is not 2, and 8x7=56 is no longer the keystone to the mastery of multiplication, passed down from generation to generation. Would they come after multiplication itself? My waking world was of words and numbers. Had the titans of technology no decency? no mercy? no sense of the natural order of things?

My mind was thereby triggered by cursive into a generalized, mental episode about technological change. The world of the last two decades seemed a whirlwind of rapid technological change, mostly wrapped around the electronic and inter-connected world: personal computers, software, apps, social media. The pace of change picked up everywhere -- in the world of work, the household, entertainment -- compared to changes in the world of my parents, the WWII generation. An everyday technological change that we shared with parents as I was growing up was television. We all knew how to use that technology, and neither generation was better at it than the other. After all, one simply had to be able to ambulate to the television set of the house and turn a knob to one of three possible channels. Substantial argument might exist among household members regarding this choice among three options, and losers had no alternatives for recording shows or using other TV sets in the household. The pace of change was steady but slow by today's standards, new technology was not difficult to learn or use, and the ability to use it did not divide us. We had issues of race, gender, poverty, and the Vietnam War to do that.

We didn't even have microwave ovens! I thought about how my grandmother, who lived with us, would have reacted to a microwave oven that had somehow been fit into our small kitchen. She might have spent some time simply looking at the new device, perhaps pondering its effect on the quality of food compared to more traditional cooking. She might have been resentful that the technology could have saved her much toil in raising her large family. Neither she, nor many, would have appreciated the acceleration of the pace of living which the microwave represented: fast microwaving, fast food franchises, the increased labor force participation by women and the accompanying need for time savers and a faster pace, and the stress of fastness.

It was ironic that I grew up in the more-or-less federal city of Huntsville, Alabama. It was the "Rocket City," where the German rocket scientists of WWII were ultimately located. I attended school and church with their children. One of the first "high tech" cities of America was emerging around me in the 1950's and 1960's, focused upon the rocketry of space exploration and defense. Whole industries were being created by technologies of Huntsville. Yet the micro world of Huntsville families was not directly affected by rapid change of life technologies. There was nothing comparable to the worldwide changes of the internet, personal and hand held computers and phones, and social networking.

Similarly, as a university student, my brief encounter with computer classes involved guardians of a mainframe computer who took my punched cards and, sometime later, gave me a paper output if the program "ran." There could have been elves in the mysterious back rooms doing all this work, and most of us would have been clueless. My computer-related training in field artillery was more substantial than in graduate school.

Not long afterwards, as a young university administrator, my colleagues and I (from human resources, finance, and IT) worked with large consulting firms on state-of-the-art software systems and data bases. The university would utilize these via a mainframe computer. Ironically, we used paper, and secretaries, in our working world, which was already dependent upon computers.

There was history, for me, of sometimes contentious meetings with faculty advisory groups. Many of these persons actually had a grasp of where technology was moving in the early 1980's. In one meeting, the faculty group was urging the administration not to purchase a scheduled replacement for one of our two mainframe computers, one serving the university and another for the medical center and hospitals. The same money, they argued, could be much better spent on a "distributed data processing" system with very small computers accessible to most employees of the university at many locations throughout the university. In a subsequent meeting of the administration members present in that advisory meeting, we had a good chuckle about that idea. So, we bought the replacement mainframe computer. The faculty, of course, were right. Perhaps these sorts of experiences tempered my enthusiasm for the acceleration of electronic and internet-related change which then unfolded.

One of my heroes in the struggle against these overwhelming changes in how one worked was a longtime colleague who taught graduate classes with me in an employee relations program. Let's call him Fred. His Ph. D. was in history, he was an expert on the history of work and workers in West Virginia, he was a great guy, and he was older than me. One day, I wandered into Fred's office, where he was staring at the personal computer placed on the desk of every faculty member several weeks before. Fred's normal, upbeat face was tired and despairful.

"They are actually going to require us to start using these things, aren't they?"

"That is pretty clear," I replied, "Next semester, you will be forced to submit grades from this contraption. They can post your termination hearing on that thing and if you or your friends aren't paying attention, you are gone."

"What are you doing?" he asked.

"I started regular tutoring by an expert about six months ago, so I am somewhere up the learning curve. I can't fight the wave." The higher tech people in my business world already thought I was a caveman.

Fred was pensive, sad. We did quick business, and I left. The next morning, my secretary said, "Did you know what happened to Fred yesterday?

"What?" I said, fearing some awful news.

"Not long after you were in his office, Fred walked into the Dean's office and retired, effective the end of this academic year. No one knows why. Do you know why?"

I knew but did not say. It was Fred's story to tell, but I knew why. Fred was a patriot! A leader of the resistance. He stood up to the overwhelming tide of change and said, "No, not me. I'm not going along, I retire." It helped that Fred's wife also had a good job, and Fred might have retired anyway. This was the late nineties equivalent of jumping on a grenade to save your buddies. Leaders resisting technological change are not well regarded, but Fred has become a folk hero to me. Fred and we lesser resistors may yet be proven right. But I was too young to retire, so I went along with the crowd. To my credit, I made certain that my progress with technology was one full step behind almost everyone around me.

Luck was with me in this regard as my own work colleagues lived and breathed the technological changes necessary to run our private business. My wife was also the chief information officer for our large medical center in Charleston. So, I travelled a long way on the expertise of others. If those people, however, die or otherwise forsake me before I die, my future could be hellish.

Lynn and I shared the common experience of working around medical centers and teaching hospitals, either as administrators or consultants. We had seen the reactions of medical doctors, and doctor-teachers, in the nature of their adaptation to the increasing rate of technological change in their working world. Some individual of every age group quickly embraced, and often led, the application of these changes. Yet, it was hard to ignore the influence of the doctor's generation on typical responses to these changes. As a doctor neared retirement age, the benefit/cost ratio of personally engaging in electronic charting in an office or hospital room fell sharply. Such doctors believed they should be able to continue cursive, or dictate drug orders, for example, to a machine and/or secretary. Never mind that the new technology provided safeguards for patient safety, particularly in light of dreadful doctor cursive. At the other end, younger to middle-age doctors, to one extent or another, had grown up with this technological change and with this pace of change. They were disappointed that the organization lagged behind the curve as they perceived it.

"Hello, Michael." The familiar greeting. The tree startled me from my thoughts.

"Hello. Welcome back."

"So you are bashing technology again?"

I was reminded of how creepy it was not to have the luxury of one's own thoughts anymore. The tree could run roughshod across my brain anytime he wished.

"Well, somebody has to do it. We see problems with the new technologies every day: massive computer theft and fraud, predators luring children into danger."

"Michael, you love the new technologies. What would you do without spreadsheets at work and the Adjust button at home?"

The tree had me there. In the early decades of my work estimating damages in civil lawsuits, our tool was a calculator, perhaps a programmable calculator. In complex, commercial cases, hours of sequential calculations might be made. Upon finding a mistake made early in the sequence, hours of re-calculations might be necessary. Personal computers and spreadsheet software eliminated this problem. A corrected error would automatically correct all related numbers in the calculation. It was a miracle.

The "Adjust" button on my financial software was even better. I was charged with the paying of (most) household bills, if for no other reason than alternative choices for my household contribution were even less palatable. One might assume that an economist would be meticulous and precise in supervising his finances, but one might be wrong. After dealing with amounts in millions and billions during a teaching or workday, small numbers may actually lose importance. Said another way, I hated the old, paperful check paying and checkbook reconciliation process. The new e-system ended with the stark reality of the monthly balance as my bank saw it versus as me and my electronic checkbook saw it. When the balances were the same, great! When they weren't, one could go through the drudgery of finding the problem. Or, one could click "Adjust"—it wasn't really a button. The Mike balance adjusted to the Bank's balance automatically. Next month, the process would start out o.k., and this adjustment was officially sanctioned by the software that allowed it.

Of course, I wasn't crazy in my use of the Adjust button. If the dollar differences were very large, I would be more likely to spend time checking for the problem, before I hit the Adjust button. And I have always monitored, mentally, whether the cumulative effects of my adjustments favored the Bank or favored me. It could certainly be expected that if the checking account actually had no money in it, someone from the bank would contact me. They always had before. They haven't yet, either, so the system must be working. Meanwhile, the Adjust button gave me peace. There should be more Adjust buttons in life. The tree knew how to pick his examples.

"But it is my nature to resist. I'm a rebellious type, and somebody has to tell the other side of the story. I went to high school and college during the Vietnam War. So, resistance is part of me."

"In fact, you resist some changes but not others and your choices of which to resist are puzzling to many. You are also not a rebel. You were in ROTC, Michael, and your wife thinks that you are the most predictable person on earth."

It is really difficult to converse with a tree who knows everything. The tree added, "You could be up-to-speed in important technologies easily if you would just spend the time, but you have chosen to be lazy. You are the three-toed technology sloth of your family, your university, your business, and your street, although you live on an especially smart street."

"Lazy? No one has ever called me lazy. Not very smart, maybe, but not lazy. My picture would be next to 'workaholic' in the dictionary, if anyone still used dictionaries. I work all the time."

The tree replied, "You are indeed industrious in many endeavors, Michael, but you are lazy in regard to this one. Don't fight the progress in tools. Fight for principles if you must fight, but don't place yourself on the wrong side of technology. You can try to aim technology, but don't fight it. Never backwards here, never go back. Remember, too, Michael, that your ability to pick and choose among technologies is waning. You'll either need to jump on the train here, or otherwise expect isolation and loneliness."

Wow, I thought, this was clearly a rebuking. The grateful receipt of feedback had never been one of my stronger points, but this call to technology was coming from a tree who was superior to me. This tree knew things that I did not know. He was taking this time to give me a message, so that I felt compelled to weigh the message. His words were, well, bigger.

Perhaps the conversation would have been more troubling for me, except that the non-verbals accompanying his words were not reproachful, or demeaning, or judgmental. By now it was clear that the tree could use non-verbals, or not, in communicating, and in this case, non-verbals eased my resistance to the change being suggested.

"I will try to do better," I said simply, and then I changed the subject. "Back to humor... I've been thinking about it. Let me try another joke." I could feel the tree groan, but he was a good sport about it, considering the chicken fiasco, and remained silent.

I continued, "There was a Ph.D., full professor of psychology doing research at a prominent, private university in the south; I think it was Vanderbilt. And as psychologists and sociologists sometimes do, he was studying insects to make inferences about human behavior. In one experiment, he took a spider, placed it on a flat table, and said 'Walk.' And the spider walked across the table. The professor cut off one of the spider's legs, put it down on the table, and said, 'Walk.' The spider walked across the table. The professor repeated the process of cutting off a leg and saying, 'Walk,' and the spider continued to crawl across the table. When there were two legs left on the spider, the Ph.D. cut off the next-to-last leg, put the spider down, and said, 'Walk.' Somehow, with one leg, the spider managed to crawl across the table. The Ph.D. researcher cut off the last leg, put the spider down on the table, and said, 'Walk.' But the spider just sat there. He said, "Walk,' but the spider just sat there. The Ph. D. concluded from this experiment that when you take a spider and cut off all its legs, it goes deaf."

I assumed the tree would say "Deafness had nothing to do with it. What kind of idiot was this Vanderbilt professor?" But he did not. There was a pause, and then he smiled. "You smiled. Didn't you. The joke actually made you smile."

"You know that I cannot smile. I'm a tree. A tree cannot smile." However, he did smile. I know he did, and the tree knew that I knew that he had smiled. One small step toward belly-laughing. "I will think further about the spider and, meanwhile, don't press your luck any further today." He obviously knew that I had two more jokes ready for delivery if the response to the spider was positive.

"I will return soon," he said and was gone. It was the only time in my memory that he hinted at when he might return.

The next day was June 7. I had been thinking about the coming of June 7 for several days, because one year before, my mother had died of cancer. It was only a few weeks after her diagnosis. Since the early morning, I had been thinking about her and how I missed her living with us in a household of many generations. It was a busy day of telephone calls and report writing. A focus on this sad anniversary was more-or-less deferred until my time on the porch in late afternoon. This was becoming a habit of my mind: deferring focus upon a topic until my special time.

It was a mid-80's day by late afternoon. Cloudless all day, bright, it was not ideal weather for mourning. So I settled into my chair on the porch around 4:00, holding my subterfuge Kindle, and was quickly lost in a journey of my own brain. There was first a review of three deceased relatives. I suppose this was a build-up to the anniversary focus of this day, but I cannot really explain what my brain does when it is let loose to meander.

The first was the death of my third wife, Darrance, when I was 44 years old and she was 37. Both her good looks and personality were most defined by the Italian in her. Dark, curly hair. She was one of the most contagiously happy persons to be around when she was happy, which was almost all of the time, but it was not fun for me when I made her mad. She had been an economics major and later took my courses for her master's degree. Later still we re-met and subsequently married. When a man is 37 and marrying for the third time, either he has been incredibly unlucky or there is something within him that is off-putting to a healthy relationship. Such patterns did not worry me at the time, however, because I was only 37, knew very little about myself, and worked hard enough to offset various deficiencies in me.

After a year and a half of a seven-year marriage, the migraine headaches from two occasions in her past returned. In my most guilty of self-pity moments, my thinking was that this return of migraines was triggered by my aforementioned deficiencies. After a week or so, the migraines did not come and go. They were there every day of the remainder of her life. She was eventually diagnosed with chronic cluster migraine headaches, which has been called the suicide disease. One week the headaches would be on the left side of the head, one week the front, one week she might, mercifully, sleep almost all of the time. On any day, she might have a few hours of reprieve, during which she would be out and about living the life that she would have otherwise had available. Some saw her in these periods and believed her disability was a fake, which was a hurtful addition to the pain and suffering.

Thus, I became a caregiver and lived a jumbled life of work and caregiving. It was a period of my life when I necessarily gave more attention to another person than to myself. This is not a bad thing but little recompense for an awful situation. Her illness was so rare in a female of her age that the medical experts had little data-based advice. Her diagnosis was never terminal, on the other hand, so that she could theoretically have lived to a normal life expectancy in her desperate condition. This also meant that pain medication could not be progressed in potency until an estimated time of death.

The fast-forwarding of memories included vignettes of 30-40 days in the hospital, facing pain, suffering, and possible death, and of the clinics and institutes. I remembered when we lost hope that her situation would improve, after we tried an experimental version of the new miracle drug and it almost killed her. It is a breathtaking loneliness that confronts a person who loses hope, and we both lost hope.

It was in this period that I learned to live one day at a time. The concept had been suggested to me, but I consciously tried it and later embraced it as the only path of survival. Yet, there were nights when I would leave the hospital thinking, "This was the worst day that she will ever have to endure and I will ever have to watch. Even if she dies, there can never be a day worse than this one." And the next day was worse.

Then she died. A few weeks before, after an ambulance trip and short stay in the hospital, she told me that this was a different hospital experience and that she felt differently than before… and that she would die soon. Despite her health, she took an opportunity for an airplane trip and long weekend in Myrtle Beach, South Carolina, where her best friend and brother would coincidentally be in the same location. On Saturday morning, she was taken to the emergency room and had lapsed into a coma by the time I was called. She was removed from life support three days later. An experience like that changes a survivor forever. Not necessarily for the bad, or not necessarily all bad. But different than before. There are impacts so profound that they are forever a part of who you are. It must be like time in combat.

My mind thereby moved to my father. He never finished his college education, which was interrupted by World War II. This would constrain him to lower tiers of management jobs, and it was a disappointment that weighed down upon him for much of his adult life. Yet, his work ethic was superlative. He was at his office at least an hour before anyone else. Later in his working life, he seemed to accept himself; he and my mother took up golf, as they say, and I believe he relaxed and enjoyed himself and his family and friends.

My Dad fought in two wars. He was in one of the later waves to invade the beaches at Normandy, and he was around the Battle of the Bulge. Then, a few weeks after joining an Army Reserve unit for the extra money, he found himself being re-trained and shipped to Korea. He was a transportation officer moving convoys around the mountains of Korea, and through the ambushes. I thought about what that must have been like. What love for the rest of us that men and women would somehow move past their fear and toward chaos and possibly death?

So many parents lost children and spouses lost spouses and children lost parents. What a sacrifice. My father lived through both wars without physical wounds, but for whatever reasons, he did not use the GI bill to finish college and, likely, law school. One considers how war diversions would have altered one's career trajectory, with that many years, at those ages, out of education and career experience.

My father taught me respect, although I never recall having a conversation with him about respect. He said, "Yes Ma'am" (when it was politically correct and meant for respect) and "Yes Sir" to every adult in all situations, every time, and he did so willfully, naturally. It was like breathing to him. Their race didn't matter to him and neither did their age. For a 16-year-old male in Alabama, white or black, who felt like a man, it was a real put-down to be called "boy" and an unexpected compliment to be sir' d. These salutations were just an indicator of the basic kindness of this man. He approached a person with respect and went out of his way to show respect until he had good reason to think or do otherwise. He would err on the side of respect, although some might call this naivete, but it is a good way to err and fine behavior to copy.

My father died in January 2007, after a relatively short fight with cancer. Only two months later, my son-in-law died. My thoughts about Jeff's death linked to my father because they were both kind and gentle souls.

Jeff died of sepsis: an infection that could not be stopped. He was a beloved father to Chloe, and she came to live with us when he died. There is a fond remembrance of Jeff and my father, which always makes me smile, even though the remembrance was linked to my Dad's last few years with progressing Alzheimer's. Until he was completely isolated by this disease, my Dad told jokes. Growing up, I remembered that he studied Robert Orben joke books for future public speaking, whether real or imagined, and when friends or family thought of my father, they thought "jokes." The problem for my mother and me, and for my grandmother when she lived with us, was that we heard the same jokes again, and again, and again. He was unfazed by our complaints.

There was a certain point when the progression of Alzheimer's had taken his short-term memory, even though his long-term memory was significantly less affected. Thus, he could remember jokes, including the punch lines, and often do a good job telling them. The difficulty for the rest of us was that his mind would produce a joke, and he would tell it. Then, he would tell the same joke again, because he could not remember that he just told it. He would continue to tell the same joke for all, or most, of the day. This was not constant, but it was irritatingly frequent, so that one would develop strategies for diverting his attention.

One spring, Jeff, my youngest daughter Nikki, and baby Chloe were visiting from California, and we flew my parents up from Alabama to join us. I can still picture most of us around the kitchen table, where we had been talking and laughing for a couple of hours, and someone realized that my Dad and Jeff were not with us. I found them outside on the deck. Jeff was told the joke-of-the-day, and he laughed. Encouraged, my father again told the same joke, and Jeff laughed. This had been on-going for almost two hours, and I realized that Jeff would have continued listening and laughing for as long as necessary until someone rescued him. It is a vignette that is a picture of what kindness looks like. Much was lost when Jeff died in the prime of his life.

And my mind turned to the anniversary of Pooky's death, my mother who had lived with Lynn, Chloe, and me more than four years. (Parenthetically, Pooky is an odd name for a mother. Her real name was Mary, and Mary was short: 4 foot, 10 inches short. There was, in the comics of her growing up, a particularly short character named "Pooky" and, sometime in the middle grades, her associates gave her that name, whether she liked it or not.)

Pooky grew up in a large East Tennessee family, with many older brothers and a twin sister Margaret. At some point, she learned to be a good sport, because her shortness made her a target. Yet, she was a skilled basketball and tennis player in high school and college, a head cheerleader, a teacher and girls' basketball coach, and a stay-at-home Mom for me.

Pooky had a signature laugh—loud and full of happy. In a dark theater, if she laughed, folks would know that Pooky was in attendance. It is perhaps unfortunate that my father's joke-telling and my mother's laughing were rarely connected, but this did not seem to bother either one of them.

She was a great Mom, and any toughness that I have came from her. It was a tough life being a Pooky, but she kept laughing. The 2007-2011 years with her in the household were a great thing for both her and Chloe. Pooky had a great-grandchild to love, and Chloe had two strong women as role models around her. I was raised with a grandmother and have appreciated what closeness with the older generation added to my life.

While remembering all of this, my mind turned to her illness and her death one year before. In the fall of 2010, Pooky showed some memory loss, which troubled her more than me. In January 2011, she turned 91 and who would not have some memory loss by age 91? But then her significant back pain began. Her doctor was a young gerontologist, in her first year of practice in the medical group of my own primary care physician. She started Pooky with stretches and recommended a new TV-watching chair to better support her ailing back. By late April, the pain was no better, so we returned to her doctor.

I related to her doctor the story of my father, who complained about back pain for many months before an MRI revealed widespread cancer. My message was that while it was unlikely this kind of lightning would strike twice in the same family, it would be great to proceed with an MRI and eliminate that possibility. She agreed. On the Friday before Mother's Day, the doctor called me and said that lightning had apparently struck twice in the same place.

Lynn and I told Pooky the MRI results and that further diagnostics or treatment likely held no benefits. I could feel her breath catch and sense her heart sink. She said, "Well, I've lived a good life." She didn't cry. Pooky was tough. I didn't cry, because I was my mother's son. We talked about Hospice and sat with her until she asked to be alone. When leaving that room, an aloneness struck me like no lonely previously experienced. Perhaps I was feeling what I feared she was feeling. Nothing could stop what was to happen. Acceptance is neither quick nor easy.

For only a few weeks, Lynn and I were caregivers. When the break-through pain medication was needed, I administered it. One did what one had to do, even if it was unimaginable before the crisis began. Pooky and I did not talk much about life, death, or other topics, even though I attempted to make myself available. This would be a regret of mine, but I did not have it in me to initiate such a conversation. Family and friends visited. We learned what the term "death rattle" meant, and she quietly passed away a few seconds after my oldest daughter Kristi had visited. We traversed the ceremonies of death.

One year ago. Now, the aloneness and separation returned, as my mind recalled Pooky. It is difficult to express feelings, especially deep-seated feelings, with words. Words are not feelings and feelings are not words. It is the attempt at finding words that is, I suppose, useful and therapeutic. Because we have to do something about the feelings. And words are something.

So, how did I feel about my Mother's death one year after? Sad and lonely, because I missed her, and to a large extent, these reflections were about me, not her. When both of my parents were alive, we shared many things, but a significant such thing was University of Tennessee athletics.

After every UT football game, watched in the stadium or on TV, I called them for a happy or embittered debriefing, unless I was simply too angry to talk. After the games of last Fall, there was no parent to call. For the previous four years, Pooky and I shared the special treat of watching together and sharing the ups and downs of football combat. We even watched the men's basketball team reach #1 in the nation, and the Lady Vols basketball team was always special. It was just me now: the only adult Vols fan in the family still around.

But I felt grateful, too. Her death had come relatively quickly, after a short period of pain and suffering. The hospice helpers had been a gift. I was grateful that the Mom-Son relationship had been a lifelong good one, capped off by four years in the same household as in my youth. Much was learned about Pooky, herself, and about family history, especially on those occasions when she had a glass of wine. There was gratitude also for the others in my life providing comfort that made the loneliness manageable, and diminishing. As I thought of my Mother, I smiled. If the remembrance makes one smile, happy is in there somewhere waiting to be freed.

Then, lonely again. I thought that such a lonely does not (necessarily) come the moment that the mind registers the death. It can come before or after. It is when one knows in his soul that this person is gone from him, that there is another hole in him. A cherished part of one has gone missing, it will remain missing, and there is absolutely nothing that one can do about this separation.

The finality of it all came from none other than Teddi Rose. Since Pooky's death, the dog-child who Pooky loved had many times every day entered her small TV room to see if she had returned. One day, the dog exited the room and looked up at me, standing in the hallway, with the most doleful look in her big brown eyes, and her eyes said to me, "She is gone... and she is never coming back, is she?" It was then that I cried, sitting on the floor with Teddi Rose, and we mourned our loss together.

My mind could not leave well enough alone. I thought about where Pooky was and what she was doing. Just because the tree would not talk about religion and the hereafter did not prevent my mind from going there. I humanly wished for her and all of those I loved 100 percent happy all of the time, whatever happy meant. And being the worrier that I naturally am, my mind stuck on the reality of not knowing, for sure, that my Mom was ok, was doing well.

In only a few moments, I was feeling sorry for myself. It is embarrassing to admit that one feels sorry for himself when it is someone else who died; it happened perhaps because the lonely and the worry were within me, but my natural self also searches for ways to martyr itself. As I was absorbed in such thought, the tree interrupted.

"I am sorry for your sadness, Mike. It is a difficult day one year after. But you had a wonderful Mother. She loved you every day of your life."

It occurred to me that the tree had known that he would be reappearing on this anniversary. I sat in his presence for a minute and then said, "Tree, have you anything like the parents or siblings or children of humans?"

"No," he replied, "but I have watched many human relationships, and you and your Mom were a good one. She told you the truth, among other things that she did for you, even when it was difficult for her to say and for you to hear, with the notable exception of Ice-Cream-roni."

I laughed out loud at that memory, breaking the somber mood. When I was young, they tell me, Pooky was consternated that other children loved to eat macaroni and cheese but I did not. Not a talented cook, even she could make macaroni and cheese. So, she began calling it "Ice-Cream-roni," and I could not get enough of the stuff thereafter. In my adult years, I would sometimes complain to Pooky that trust was difficult when she had so shamelessly lied to me in my early years about something as important as ice cream. Apparently, Pooky had taken such techniques from a psychology course in college, and she was unworried about any ethical ramifications of such knowledge.

"Have you ever lost something that you loved Tree?"

"I have lost many, many humans that I loved, Mike."

"Odd that he could love but not laugh," I thought. He heard me, of course, duh, and I believe that he very slightly smiled at this thought.

It surprised me that I then asked, "Can you tell me anything about Pooky that I have no way to know? What is she doing? How is she doing?" I thought that Tree had previously avoided some of the most important questions, like this one. Of course, he heard that, too; these conversations could be very difficult.

He paused for a noticeable time. "She did the transition that humans do when they die, and you and I are not talking about humans before birth or after death."

"But you are saying there is a transition at death to something else?"

"Yes, of course, from life to death, but that doesn't really help you, does it?"

There was an even longer pause, to the point of becoming uncomfortable. I did not know what to say.

"Mike," the tree began and he was choosing his words slowly, "You need not trouble yourself over your Mother or her welfare."

There was a longer pause. It was clear to me that Tree was finished talking, but my mind was processing the simple statement. My first thought was that these words could simply mean that there was nothing that I could possibly do to affect the post-death welfare of my Mother, so that it would make no common sense for me to anguish over that which I could not control. I thought that many such questions could be spun off from the statement, and clarification questions could take awhile. Yet, I also knew that he would not clarify. I just knew. He had said what he was saying.

I also knew that Tree's statement was not a manipulation of words that answered nothing. It was not only what Tree said, but how he said it. His non-verbals carried the assurance that Pooky was ok and would be ok. It felt as though this trouble was removed from my spirit, from the guts of me.

I thought to myself that is what comfort feels like. What more could it be? And I knew that this comfort would not have come if anyone else but Tree had spoken the same words. Because his words were, well, bigger.

Life brings enough troubles, and Tree had removed one from me. It was as close as one got to knowing what could not be known for certain. I felt very small compared to Tree, and that was good with me. Tree had departed, but the lesson had been learned.

CHAPTER FIVE -

THE CONFUSION OF CONTROL

It was a Sunday afternoon in early July. I escaped to the porch for some alone time and also, of course, the possibility that Tree might drop by for a chat. Sitting in my favorite chair, I scarcely noticed the verdant wonder of the forests around me. There was simply no time available for the beauty of nature.

We had just returned from 13 days on a business-and-pleasure trip to the western U. S. and Canada. Thirteen days out of my office. Quite possibly, part of me wanted to find some degree of catastrophe, which only I could resolve, resulting from my two-week absence. The large stack of files already collected from my office had been skimmed in the home office downstairs, and they awaited my detailed attention.

There were a few moments of thought, and a smile, about our time in California with Chloe's younger sister. But my mind had begun to swing to business matters days before. The pleasure and stress of vacation were replaced by the pressure and stress of work. It is easier to be a workaholic when work is abundant, and a ton of work awaited me. I gave a thought to a fact of my business life that perhaps applied to owners of most small businesses. There is either too much business or too little -- one extreme or the other.

In the new batch of cases received since we headed west was one that I would turn down, hopefully by email and not in a contentious telephone call. The lawyer didn't pay his bills within a reasonable time. He wouldn't pay them at all if it was not for his need that I show up for deposition and trial. He had already been told once not to contact me again. This was the typical, stark transition from the thoughtful world of an academic conference to the everyday world where I toiled. It reminded me that we were known—and sometime not used—because of our relatively rigid billing and payment rules. That made me smile. I loved rules, and our busyness and my proximity to retirement allowed me to actually enforce the rules, my rules.

There was a deposition by an opposing economist in my "stack" wherein my report and my professional accomplishments had been besmirched. My client attorney was wondering if these besmirchments were true. I happened to know that this kid opposing me had two years of experience, versus my own 40 years, and had apparently never read any of the relevant literature. I made a special note that if this case went to trial, my attorney would be ready to do some really swell besmirchments of our own.

The next two weeks would be awful, as I thought about it, but not for the catching-up in a business that I professionally and intellectually truly loved. There were two important cases coming to trial, and therefore to my testimony, in each of the next two weeks. The one late in the coming week had all of my preparation completed before our trip, for that is the way I rolled. This case might still settle before a trip to Memphis, and my presentation in this Tennessee wrongful death case should be straightforward with predictable questions in cross examination.

My main reason for not overheating about the Tennessee case, however, was the overshadowing vision of the scheduled Baltimore testimony a week thereafter. It was a potentially precedent-setting case and my testimony might affect a set of hundreds of similar personal injury cases. I was on the defense side of this case, and this set of cases, opposing several plaintiff economists. Preparations for a "first" testimony in such a case had been ongoing for several years.

This upcoming testimony had scarcely left my mind during any day of the trip. I knew, but did not dwell upon, the fact that 90 percent of my preparation work had already been completed, which meant that I could testify, without further preparation, 80-90 percent as well as my 100 percent "ideal." What happened on the porch was the beginning of the intense stage of preparation which would yield a 10-20 percent improvement and steal my mind from most other life activities. But I was all about that 10-20 percent difference, which is what made me a player in the big leagues of my niche of expert witnessing. Pressure was high from this time forward, but I had been in this place before and knew the steps to take through this period toward testimony. With most of my preparation already locked away, my mind indulged itself in a period of reflection on actors and their roles: my own attorney, the best around, but I always drafted the questions to be asked to me (most attorneys appreciated this, as did my attorney in this case); the judge; the plaintiff attorney who took my deposition and will cross-examine me; the plaintiff support experts and economists; my own foundation experts; the jury members to whom I would be talking. I was so lost in all of this that a gorilla could have seized Teddi Rose from the porch and it would not have registered.

My mind shifted at some point to what-iffing: a task largely put off until the end days of intense preparation, when testimony at trial is almost certain. What if various catastrophes happened with regard to travel and scheduling—a task less complicated because we were not in the academic year. I always did some what-iffing about my visuals planned for trial and whether any necessary equipment would be available and work properly.

My mind could not stop, apparently, and travelled to the extremes of what-iffing: in cross examination, what if the opposing attorney asks this question? How will I answer? And what if in response to my answer, the opposing attorney asks this question? What is my response?... and on and on. One could do this forever. At some level, I have always known that it was probably dangerous that I sometimes obsessed with myself in such a manner. On the other hand, there were times at trial when the what-iffing paid off.

I stopped. My countenance was intense, rigid, and stressed. I decided to think about something else on this beautiful day back at home on my porch. But the worry-and-fear button that directed my mind, under the guise of looking ahead, had already been punched, so my mind turned to personal health, an increasingly likely category of my thinking as I advanced toward the alleged golden years. On the horizon, in August, was a scheduled replacement of my left hip. Left versus right or hip versus knee may seem unimportant, but when it is your own left hip that is being medically targeted, this sort of detail becomes very important.

I was certainly <u>not</u> focusing on the miracle that I was still breathing and functioning in every way that I needed to function, and the wonders of medical professionals and pharmaceutical scientists who were prolonging the quantity and quality of my life. No, I was focused on the porch upon my left hip, soon to be replaced by an artificial left hip. I had already arranged to cover early fall semester classes for the intense physical therapy that I planned to undergo. But those things were not the problem. I had lost racquetball. Never again, said the surgeon, could I play racquetball, because of the abrupt starts and stops. Try a stationary bike for exercise, he advised.

It was gone. Never to come back to me in my lifetime. It was a big loss, and what I was losing spanned 37 years of my life. I played racquetball through four wives, two children, two grandchildren, and several jobs and employers. The game was always there for me and suited me perfectly.

It was good for me to beat on that little rubber ball. Yes, with most partners over the years, I lost more than I won, and I truly hated this. I am a really bad sport. But the exercise was marvelous in an hour, unaffected by weather, that could be tightly scheduled. It was suitable to a person who worked hard and maintained a fast pace. At any rate, I was thinking about my moving toward this surgery: my absence from teaching and testifying, the necessary time of physical therapy, and uses of down time. A personal trainer was probably a good idea for me thereafter. Unless someone was waiting for me at the Y to tell me what to do for an hour, I would use work as an excuse for missing trips to the Y. Fortunately, my mind did not travel to the horrors of surgery. I had become reasonably good at allowing medical professionals to do their jobs.

"I heard you what-iffing, Mike," said Tree, "and thought that it would be a good time for a talk."

"Hi, Tree, I have missed you."

"Let me ask. How were you feeling out here thinking to yourself about issues of business and health?"

I paused. Tree and I were jumping immediately into feelings, but it was a fair question. "Relieved in a way because it was an effort not to think about such things while on vacation. Now both myself and others assume my return to a normal state of things, wherein I can be a workaholic in both mind and deed. There is a feeling of moving back in control, of doing what I do as I've learned how to do it. And I also feel worried, stressed, mildly resentful, and tired all of a sudden," I admitted.

It also occurred to me that only a few years ago, I had stopped (overtly) working on vacations. Except in emergencies. This was not easy! I assumed that Tree heard these thoughts. "I occasionally worry about the stress that I bring on myself by being an obsessive, compulsive perfectionist, but it is my natural way to be. Maybe when I retire in a few years, my Self will tone itself down a notch."

Tree asked, "Are you comfortable when you are the Mike of the last little while alone on the porch, thinking the way you were thinking?"

This, of course, made me recall our last conversation, and I replied, "Feeling in control helps me with the trouble of contemplating chaos, but it brings me troubles too."

"Would you like me to help you with controlling people, places, and things better?"

"Yes, of course I would."

Tree seemed to think a moment. "Since Teddi Rose is out here with us, let us experiment with your dog. Do you desire to control Teddi and her behavior better, and with as little struggle as necessary?"

I glanced at Teddi, who continued to raise her head when Tree was speaking. "That would be a great place to start. There is a long and troubling history with this dog and our inability to control her."

"Then, tell me first how, and how well, you control the dog's behavior to meet your objectives now. What would Teddi Rose do if you told her it was time for a bath, for example?"

"That's easy. She would begin to creep and then sprint through the porch door and living room to her large wooden crate home in the next room. Then, she would huddle in the back of the crate, so that I would face a biting risk to make the bath happen. Same thing if I said, 'Let's go see the Vet.'"

Tree observed, "So, at a time when you really want to exercise control—for the dog's own good—you have little control over the dog. Tell me, how is it that Teddi Rose ever takes a bath?"

"Well," I began, "one does everything possible to trick the dog until she is secured to her leash and then, resignedly, will follow the human down to her basement bath. So I don't do anything stupid like mentioning the B word, or walking toward her with my glasses or watch already off or my long sleeves rolled up. It is important to act exactly as if you are leashing her up for just another walk outside. The dog has a talent for detecting subtle changes which portend a bath. To begin with, the dog knows when it is 'time' for a bath, even though we don't have a consistent day of the week. Somewhere deep down, the dog has to know that she is filthy and beginning to stink. So she is on guard for the very event that is designed to preserve her as a family pet. One cannot approach her either too happy or too sad. For example, to move toward her singing 'it's a beautiful day for a walk in the park' would not, and did not, work. Like lightning, she was in the back of the cage. We don't have a park, and Teddi Rose apparently knew that."

"And what if she beats you to her cage?" asked Tree.

"It was one of my great feats of problem solving," I said proudly. "We have a cushion, of course, on the floor of the cage that exactly covers the cage bottom and can be easily removed for washing. If I pull out the cushion in one continuous motion, she sits in front of me to be leashed. She hasn't yet let the cushion slide beneath her, keeping her at the back of the cage. The look on her face is priceless after a cushion-pull happens, and before she collects her wits, I have her down in the sink."

"Basically then, you use a combination of deceit and superior force," said Tree. "Not to mention the generous allotment of treats that you give the dog for performing mundane acts," he added.

"That would be an accurate summary of where we are with Teddi Rose, yes," I admitted.

"Let's begin our experiment with Teddi Rose by communicating and controlling her to stand up and focus her attention upon us. You need not and cannot use voice commands, or other sounds or gestures. Neither can you think deceptions, threats, or promises of rewards at her. Keep your willful projection on the dog's head until you have accomplished your objective. It is a relatively simple process but does require practice. Let me do it first, and then you try."

There was a brief pause. I heard nothing from Tree and experienced no communication between Tree and Teddi. The dog, whose head was already raised, stood up and aimed her body and her line of sight directly at Tree's head, even though she could not see Tree's head from the back of the porch. She remained standing up, frozen.

"O.K., Mike, you try it." Teddi Rose laid back down with her head on the floor and still aimed at Tree.

At this point, I was very enthusiastic about what we were doing and what Tree was attempting to teach me. It occurred to me, however, that I had very little experience in communicating with, marshalling, or focusing my inner forces toward anything. I had rejected several suggestions by others that meditation would help me, for example. Yet, I would do my best. The words "stand up and look at me" were thought toward the core of my brain. These words marched in and any other brain topic was pushed aside, except for breathing and heartbeat function of course. I avoided the temptation to prematurely unleash these words toward the dog, as I assumed the force of the words would need to build up in me until it could no longer be held within. And finally, I stared at Teddi with piercing eyes and released my thought directive. Having learned the value of follow-up in little league baseball, I continued to vector wave after wave of willforce at Teddi's head.

Nothing. After twenty or thirty seconds of this effort, the dog still lay prone, looking at Tree. My effort was redoubled (a curious term learned from politicians). I could not recall focusing this intensely on anything, and projecting focused commands was a new one for me, at least with this kind of conscious force. My face was turning red…

"Stand and Look At Me

Stand and Look At Me."

my thought beam commanded. The dog stood up and turned around to aim toward me.

I was elated. Then, Teddi lay down with her head on the floor. Her brown eyes regarded me casually.

"Good enough," Tree interjected, "now let us have her walk to us and Sit Pretty." Of course, Tree knew everything. Sit Pretty was one of the tricks that our canine behavioral and developmental consultants had successfully taught Teddi Rose. Her behavior never really improved, but she liked to do several tricks for marshmallows. Sit Pretty was my favorite, in which she sat up with her front paws in a particularly adorable position. I gave her extra marshmallows for Sit Pretty.

"I will do it first." Again, I detected no communication between Tree and Teddi. After a moment, the dog stood up, turned and walked to the porch screen touching Tree, and did a Sit Pretty. She remained in the Sit Pretty, looking up at Tree, and facing away from me.

My turn.

"Walk to me and Sit Pretty." I pictured the simple vignette in my mind. That picture would need a powerful percolation of the will to reach sufficient force for the sendoff.

"Walk to me and Sit Pretty," I said to the depth of my mind. It was a pulsating force, pushing all else out of the mind, but "Walk to me and Sit Pretty." The picture, the words, pounding, mounting pressures. This must be what a volcano feels like before it hurls forth. Then, I let it go, whoosh, guided by my laser eyes at Teddi's turned head. After many seconds of my forceful beam, the dog continued to Sit Pretty for Tree.

"Tree," I asked, "can you tell me what I'm doing wrong? Any more guidance that you can give me on how to do this? Tips? Anything?"

"What you are attempting to do to communicate with and control Teddi Rose is ok for this experiment. But you must do what you are doing more intensely. Harder, much harder. Redouble your efforts."

So I did. The conscious buildup of will that ensued was unique in my experience.

"Walk to me and Sit Pretty.

Walk to me and Sit Pretty."

The beating of the Telltale heart was nothing compared to this. I willed Teddi to turn toward me, and I focused intensely on the picture, the replaying vignette. All of me grew tense, clenched fists, rapid heart-beat, blood pressure up, red moving into my face. When I could no longer contain the force of my will, it loosed itself, and my laser eyes guided the forceful missile to target.

While I strained with the pulsating rhythm of force impulses cata-pulted forward, the dog did not flinch. She would not even turn toward me, much less walk to me and Sit Pretty. Frustrated, I attempted to once more increase my efforts. Another redoubling, I knew, would likely cause me to pass out, throw up, or worse. Wave after wave hit the pooch's head...

"Walk to me and Sit Pretty.

Walk to me and Sit Pretty."

Teddi Rose stood and turned around toward me. She looked at me. I did not pause in my efforts.

"Walk to me and Sit Pretty." After a second, she trotted to her orig-inal position on the porch, aligned her body toward Tree, and lay down. She then raised her head, looked at me, and smirked. It at least looked like a smirk to me. Deflated, I stopped the effort.

Tree said, "You can't do it, can you?"

"No. Not unless you can give me more tips, training, or magic... or I can revert to deceit, treats, or threats...this is apparently not going to happen. The dog is not walking over here for a Sit Pretty."

"That is it then, now you have it," advised Tree.

"Have what?"

"Mike, you can't talk to a dog... and even if you could talk to a dog, Mike, you cannot control a dog. Absent reward or punishment, if Teddi

Rose comes over and sits pretty for you, it will be a breathtaking coincidence. But that is really not the point."

Tree stopped talking and, after an elongated pause, I reluctantly offered, "Ok, what is the point?"

"That you can't control other people, either. Not dependably, anyway, and certainly not without deceit, coercion, or treats. You can't do it, Mike. You just can't."

Defensively, I pointed out, "But you did it. Twice. So, there is a way to do it."

"Let me remind you of our first conversation," Tree explained matter-of-factly, "of course I can do it. I am Tree. You are not. I can do things that you cannot do. No need to feel singled out here, Mike. Humans have a very limited ability to control other humans, places, things, and events. That which cannot be controlled is large and noteworthy; that which might be controlled by a human is relatively small."

I was, frankly, out of sorts about what was going down here. "Why didn't you just tell me what you wanted to tell me? Why this thing with the dog?"

"Because the 62 years of experience that you have in unsuccessful attempts at control have not done the trick, as you would say. Further steps were necessary and Teddi Rose was available."

My mind reflected on what had just happened, I glanced at Teddi, head down on the floor, and I began to laugh. It was a good, honest laugh, a laugh at myself commanding the dog. I was 100 percent duped. It had not occurred to me that Tree was setting me up.

Tree, however, had not smiled nor joined in my laughter. "Tree," I said, still laughing, "don't you know that what you did with me and the dog was really funny? The way you sucked me into doing what I did. It was very well done. A real step in humor for you."

"It was not meant to be a laughing event. This is important for you. We need to discuss control." Suddenly, he softened, and asked, "but it was funny?"

"Yes, it was. But important truths can also be funny, and funny things are sometimes important, I suppose." It was a clever turn of phrase, I thought, but had no idea what it meant.

"Let me ask you, Mike: what is the center of you?" Tree was instantly serious. It struck me that he sounded less rhetorical than genuinely interested in hearing my answer.

It was not clear to me what Tree was asking. "Do you mean what part of me feels to me as my center—my brain, my gut? Or do you mean people, or principles, or feelings?" This was not a question which had been anticipated, but little about me and Tree had been anticipated.

"Let me give you some thoughts which may help," began Tree. "Mike, your center is located wherever you feel it to be. The center of you is where you reach for extra when extra is required. It is what everything is collapsing toward when your world is falling apart. It is where your happiness and gratitude reside. Your center is the source of your direction; it tells every part of you where you are headed and provides energy and momentum for you to be on your way. It is your landmark, your lighthouse that guides you.

"The center of you dominates your thoughts and behaviors, in ways that you may realize and in ways that you don't. When you deviate far away it pulls you back, like a personal magnet. It is what you think about when you awake in the morning. You may center for the good or the bad, as you conceive them. And your center can change. It is an important characteristic of humans. Their center can change. Until the last breath, the center can change."

I thought for a minute and then loosed a stream of thought. "I assume we are still not talking about religion, right?"

"Right."

"Ok, there are the people I care about, family and friends, that are, at least sometimes, at the center of me. There are values at the center of me—as basic as a sense of right and wrong. Feelings are the center of me, sometimes, from sadness to joy. I have memories that feel at the center of me." I stopped and pondered the question, "These are what come to mind... is this what you were asking me?" It would have been impertinent, at this point, to ask why he was asking me, but I thought it and he probably heard it.

He replied, "Yes, I heard your answer. But none of those things are the center of you. Mike, you are the center of you."

That was a stunner. An unexpected slap in the face. Feedback had not been foreseen. "Me?" I exclaimed, "Do you really think that the very core of me is self-centeredness?"

Tree soothed, "Yes, but my statement is not to be a rebuke. It is simply a description."

"But if there was one thing about myself that I have consciously attempted to reform, to remedy, in the last several decades, it was my self-absorption." I continued, "because it was certainly true in the past. Can't argue with that. Are you telling me that I am no better?"

"I did not say that. You have made progress and you are less self-centered than previously."

"Because I actually do things for other people, without expecting anything in return. And my focus on, and caring about, others has gone up, not down."

"All true," said Tree, "you have made progress."

"Are you telling me that my progress is dwarfed by the size of the self-centered mess where I began?"

"I would not have used those words. You have your periods of others flashing through your center, but as a generalization, you are what you are thinking about when you wake up in the morning. You are always on your mind."

"Are you planning to tell me who else should be somehow placed in the center of me? Who or what should it be?" I asked.

"Almost any other human than you in the center would be an improvement for you. Your life would be lived better and more easily. Although it depends upon who is in your center and why. It provides no benefit if your replacement human is centered for idolatry, or envy, or resentment, for example. If your centering is for helping or caring, then you have gained over yourself as the center of you. And, of course people change, people disappoint you, people die."

"The best of living comes to you when the Big is the center of you, Mike. Whatever face you place on the Big, that is the face that you should see in the center of you. If not always in your center, because you are human, it should dominate the core of you. It is for your own good that you would replace the center, and all of our talks to come flow from this replacement of your center.

"You can't grow toward yourself, Mike. You are as big as you will be. But in the direction of the Big, your path tilts upward. Whatever the obstacles or triumphs, you are moving toward that which is bigger."

"But what does my center have to do with control?"

"It has everything to do with control. Because the center of you is, most often, you, the confusions of control harm your everyday life. They make your life more difficult than your life has to be."

"You are bigger than me Tree. Are you suggesting that I place you in the center of me, that I become a human with a tree in my middle?"

"Why would you settle for me," the Tree answered. "It is the Big, not me, although you could do worse than a tree in your center. It is an improvement over where you have been, with you as your own center."

"What, then, do you suggest that I do with the controlling, self-centered person that I apparently am?" It was a reasonably honest question, with a whiff of denial and a whisper of self-pity.

"On a daily and sometimes hourly basis, be conscious of your ability to sort, and willfully attempt to improve this ability to sort as you go forward. Sort that which you cannot control from that which you might control. The first stack of people, places, things should be large, and the second stack small. Over time, as your sorter develops, the first will grow noticeably larger, and the second smaller. Do this until you sort as naturally as you breathe?"

"Where does it go, all this control I am giving up? Because there are things that must be done, and planned, by <u>somebody</u>, even if it is not me."

"That is easy to answer but difficult to actually do. You give it to the Big. Hand it over. Let it go. You do not need it. You will live better without it. And those around you will be grateful that you gave it up. You will, if you are diligent in this task, also come to see yourself as smaller, and the Big as bigger.

I thought that simply remaining a control freak would likely be much easier than this late-in-life change in my natural self. Hearing that, Tree added, "Life becomes easier too. This is all toward an easier life. I would not be with you to make life more difficult."

There was a pause. I contemplated. Then, Tree added, "You are struggling with this, because it is at your very core. And let me not mislead you. This will not <u>be</u> easy for you even though the direction is toward easy. The people, places, and things change, and the confusions of control never disappear. To make it a special challenge for you, Mike, we both know that you begin with a past as a management trainer, which was a nice sideline for you professionally but added to your toxicity. You <u>taught</u> the subject of control to other humans, and planning, and goal setting, and evaluating the performance of others. Do you remember what you taught them? Do you remember monkey traps?"

I smiled at his knowledge of my past. Aspiring and existing managers were taught that they had four basic tasks: to plan, to organize, to direct, and to control. The control task involved setting standards for work and productivity, creating systems for measuring actual performance, and developing mechanisms for moving actual performance back (up) to standard when necessary. A commonly used example was the heating and cooling system in a home. The resident set the desired temperature (standard), and a thermometer measured the actual temperature. When a deviation occurred, the heating or cooling kicked on to move the actual temperature back to the standard.

The subject of control also related to what we taught about planning, with the setting of goals and the formal and informal evaluation of performance against the goals. One could not be a manager if one could not effectively execute the control and planning functions. Chaos would ensue. My own teaching, I reflected, permeated myself, although it also seemed that I was born with an affinity for control.

The "monkey traps" story was added to my trainer repertoire via an isolated article read somewhere that was not written for purposes of management training. It was more likely written as self-help or self-improvement advice. In parts of Asia and on certain Pacific islands, for example, monkeys were the most readily available source of meat. Humans developed a simple trap for catching the monkeys. Rice or some kind of treat was placed inside a gourd or coconut through two holes cut just large enough for the monkey to reach inside.

When the monkey's hands wrapped around the treat, he made fists, and he could not pull his fists back out of the two holes. Since the gourd was securely fastened to a tree or large rock, the monkey was trapped, unless he simply let go of the treat, unclenched his fists, and ran away. But the monkey would not let go. Even as he watched his executioner return with a club, even as he died, he would not let go. As I reviewed the story in my mind, I realized that Tree heard me think it.

"Yes," I finally said, "I talked about control and planning and goals and evaluation, and monkey traps, as a trainer from my late 20's into my mid-50's when I lacked the time. When I talked about monkey traps, though, I don't recall that it was particularly under the topic of control. It was more about the difficulty and pain of letting go of failing projects or methods. It was about the reluctance to change or innovate. It was a reminder of how we hold onto the familiar even in the face of terrible consequences."

"Well then, you were short changing your own example," Tree said. "It is a lifelong chore for you, much more than a management task, to avoid control when it is not necessary. And to realize how little control that you really have, so you don't waste yourself on that which you simply cannot control. The consequences for you have always been toxic. It is an unforced error of your mind and nature that can be changed.

"Even when good judgement and good intentions require you to attempt control, you must hope that the good outweighs the harm. Your natural self is the monkey here, and you have quite a journey before letting go feels natural to you."

Tree continued, "Your controlling mind previewed your next month -- the testimonies coming in Court. How much of what will happen in that courtroom do you actually control?"

I replied slowly, "Well, first of all, there is more than a 50 percent chance that any case will settle before trial or be continued to a future date."

"Then do you only pursue a 30 or 40 percent control-and-worry routine, instead of a 100 percent version if the event is near certain?"

"No, I probably fret, plan, and prepare at the 100 percent level until 100 percent drops to zero."

"How has this 100 percent mindset worked for you so far?"

"Well enough that my business and reputation have steadily grown."

"And at what price?"

I knew that he already knew everything about me, and the answer to any question he would ask me. It was a soul-searching question, but I knew the answers. "The intellectual challenge of estimating human life values has always been fascinating, and the field changes rapidly so I am always learning. But it is hard on a person who thinks like me not to be fearful of failure and anxious about any chance of a mistake. This I must hide, of course, which only makes it worse. So, I must will myself to appear confident and in control, through the most stressful of cross examinations."

"You force yourself to pretend to be relaxed. One of your human psychiatrists could write a thesis on that one."

I smiled, briefly, "There is no question, Tree, that I pay a price for my controlling and perfectionist nature. Maybe the heart disease and even thyroid problems. Certainly, a price is paid in the time that my mind is occupied, and my body stressed, even when I am with family and friends and my mind should be there with them."

"If you could drop whole sets of worry, like if the judge may hate you, or if you could lower your level of perfection and control, in general, what is the chance it would hurt you?"

"Some chance, but probably not much."

"When something goes wrong in a testimony, how many times could you have anticipated it?... with more what-iffing, perhaps?"

"Only a handful of times. Usually, it was something I was not told, or too bizarre to anticipate, or just bad luck. It was rarely something that I could have controlled."

"Controlling harder and better did not work with Teddi Rose either, did it?"

"No."

"Mike, the benefits are not worth the costs to you and those around you. Dial it back, lower the level, think yourself smaller, and let go of that which was never under your control, anyway.

"You have already shown that you can make progress here in medical matters. For whatever reasons, you have learned to give up control to the medical experts who keep you going. This has been a help to you, and you would agree that your life is easier because you have sorted this one out of the dominion of your control.

"Mike, let me ask you another question. As a trainer and teacher, what did you say about expectations?"

That was easy. I spilled out words repeated many times, "Management theorists and textbooks emphasize the importance of high expectations, as a manager, for yourself and others. It is the self-fulfilling prophecy. High expectations exert an independent influence toward high productivity and results. You and others somehow fulfill the prophecy. The same for low expectations influencing low results. And before you say it, yes, these high expectations are discussed in regard to control, standards, goals, performance evaluation, and planning. They go together."

"So does the toxicity go together? How have the high expectations worked out for you?"

"I think that it drives me to work harder and better. I think that it also influences others, but this is less clear and less certain from my experience."

"And at what price?"

"It is a pressure on me, and I'm sure on others. It weighs upon the soul. It causes anxiety and sometimes fear. I know what you are saying about toxic...."

"Then, let me suggest that you begin the process of dialing back your expectations. When you must do the chore of setting goals, do it and immediately begin the process of letting go of expectations in your own mind, in your center. Do not allow expectations much space in you. And if you must expect, then expect that you will simply do the best that you can, in the circumstances of your life. Others too."

"What you are saying, Tree, is heresy to the motivation freaks," I observed.

"Lowering expectations of the mind is a companion of giving up control. It is an equally difficult, lifelong process of awareness and improvement. But the payoffs are equally great. Don't spend more of your life setting yourself up for agony when you are imperfect, or turmoil when others are likewise. Yet, there need be no toxin in doing your best, nor poison in hard effort, nor drawback in human competition. Your mind need not make life more difficult than it is, and living smaller in your own mind paves the way for living easier with this human problem."

I ventured, "There are people who perceive that they have <u>less</u> control than a human naturally has. I know such persons. What about them?"

"Indeed, there are both the oppressed and the depressed, as examples. The first are prevented from the level of control which a human rightly and naturally has, such as control of their own thoughts. The oppressor can be a government or a member of the family. And the illness of depression can burden a human spirit with the illusion of no control, a terrible despair.

"That is not you, Mike. Their struggle to a better life, to a safer zone, also begins with the small and the Big. It is the path out of the struggle. It is a centering on the solution, so that the storm subsides."

"This is much to think about," I said simply, "I will try."

"I know that you will," said the Tree, which was surprisingly encouraging, and I felt him leave me.

CHAPTER SIX -
THE DEATH OF FOOTBALL

By mid-August, the hip operation had been postponed for at least the Fall, and I was enjoying an August 15 on the porch. Tree remained green and beautiful in front of me. The first cool nights and early mornings had come, as hints of the autumn ahead. A few yellow leaves had appeared on some of the maples in the backyard.

Tree visited me briefly that day, as I sat on the porch, and he was an every week visitor from then through October. The frequency of visits during this Fall was the greatest of any period over our relationship, although most were short and often involved brief discussions when Tree might actually ask me questions. A significant portion of our Q&As involved football, and I would learn that he actually was watching all or parts of NFL or college games with me.

August 15 is a day that I have remembered since age 14 in Huntsville, Alabama. This was the day that two-a-day practices started in Alabama high school football. Let me describe those practices. Hot. It is very hot in the deep south in August. Humid. This is when water crowds out oxygen in the air. Intense. It seemed that the battles for which we prepared were harbingers of the course of world history. On the August 15 of 1967, I said to myself, between practices, that I must remember and cherish all future August 15s for as long as I would live. My football career was ending in the fall of 1967, two-a-days would never face me again on August 15s, or any other day. No matter what else was happening in my future life, I had to be happy that it was not two-a-day football practices in Alabama. And I never since had forgotten to find this joy on subsequent August 15s of my life.

As I thought this, Tree said, "Hello, Mike. Congratulations on another August 15. You have actually created your own holiday in remembrance of the tough times of high school football. Do you give yourself a gift of some sort?"

"I give myself a mental and emotional gift of gratitude all day long, as I revel in what I'm not doing in two-a-day football practices."

"Why did you play football if you cherish the end of your playing days?"

"Well," I began thoughtfully, "first of all, I loved playing football, and baseball, and basketball - - the three sports of my growing up. We played sandlot ball, baseball the most. It is my enduring remembrance of life as a boy in Huntsville: playing ball from morning to whenever we were required home. Lunch was an annoying interruption, except that we were starving. Only a flat piece of ground was required; we could improvise, and our stadiums were easily converted from baseball to football, or vice versa. Money was not required. Adult supervision was not necessary and, indeed, was discouraged."

Since Tree seemed intent to listen, I continued, "It was a wonderful growing up Tree, all about playing ball. When my friends and I didn't play ball, we watched it or talked about it. Pro players, and college players, and even local high school players were our heroes. Likely my first introduction to envy was in imagining what it would be like to be one of them."

At some point, I interrupted the flow of the discourse to ask, "Tree, football is always great to talk about, especially this time of year, but you know all about me. You know, I suppose, everything there is to know about football. Why is it of interest to hear me talk about things that you already know?"

Tree answered, "Because what one has the power to know, one has the power not to know. I have chosen not to know about American football or about you and football. The topic was saved for you and me."

This seemed a bit peculiar, but the Tree had his reasons for what he did, so I continued, "Then came organized ball: various levels of little league in baseball, church league basketball, and 5th and 6th grade football. Apparently most folks thought that organized head-knocking among youngsters should not begin before age 10."

"So, this was tackle football?"

"Where I grew up, football meant tackle football by age 10. I happened to have the toughest 5th grade football coach ever. He had been a college player and was an offensive guard on the local semi-pro team. I remember what seemed like hours of head-to-head tackling. Another guy tackled me straight-on, and then I tackled him. Same idea for the fundamentals of blocking and of running the ball. It is possible that I thereupon began to learn courage but will never know for sure.

"Lots of Dads were there to watch the late afternoon practices. Most of the watching Dads, including my own, had played football, and almost all Dads watched and talked about football. Dads and sons were all about football, even by 10. It was a glue that held them together, a common language, a culture. It caused pressure and discord in some such relationships, but I think was a good thing for most of us. Many of our Moms too were great sports fans and wonderful supporters.

"The winning I liked. Starting with the Fifth Avenue elementary school football team, the winning part of competition was a feel-good thing. We were the class of our league and won the city championship. Our practices were sufficiently rigorous that games were a relative walk in the park. Our coach never considered punting. We either scored or fumbled to end our offensive possessions.

"We won the junior high school championship and had an undefeated season, too. Then, on to big time Alabama high school football. At most schools, football was clearly above basketball, baseball, and track in the pecking order. We had over 100 guys on the squad. Competition was intense for playing time, and playing time required a year-round commitment. The conditioning program between the season, spring practice, and the next season was in some ways more dreaded than practices. In other ways, though, we were relatively fortunate. Only a few years before, some coaches withheld water during practices to promote toughness.

"Our next door neighbor had the honor of being Benny Nelson's uncle, and my fifth grade teacher was Benny's mother. Benny was an All-American halfback for Bear Bryant at the University of Alabama. One weekend his friend Joe Namath visited Huntsville with him, and they spent approximately one hour and seventeen minutes at the house next door. Joe Namath was already a legend as he prepared for his senior football season. Only Bear Bryant himself and George Wallace were more discussed among Alabamians. We did not have the courage to go next door and meet Benny and Joe, but I held bragging rights for several weeks simply because I had been so close to them. Within a year, my Uncle Frank, who didn't care for football, would question in amazement why the New York Jets would sign Joe Namath to a $400,000 contract because, 'all he could do was throw a football.' My Uncle Frank just didn't get it."

"So, I played football, Tree, because that was what most male teenagers who had any athletic talent whatsoever did. Schools had been integrated, on a token basis, when I was in the sixth grade, but the first African American player competed on the Huntsville High School Crimson Panthers football team when I was a player. As a matter of fact, we played the same position. His name was Rick Gilliam. What courage he had, but that is another story, Tree ... an important, other story."

Tree and I had such conversations weekly, it seemed, as the NFL season and the first college games began. Tree was briefed on the basics of football development—youth leagues, junior high, high school, college, and pro. He was an enthusiastic student learning the rules, the strategy and tactics, and the terminology of the game. His questions and comments were wide-ranging.

It was the first NFL Sunday night game, I believe, when the females had gone to bed early, and I had relaxed on the porch at halftime. Tree had been watching the game when he asked the most surprising question, "Why do you keep a score in football? Couldn't you play exactly the same game without keeping score?"

Only a few times in my life have I been speechless, without a ready answer. In fact, I prided myself on prompt and decisive answers even when the question was unclear or entirely beyond my store of knowledge. While not responding, I thought "Geez ,Tree, give me a break, do you really need me to answer that question?" But, of course, Tree heard that, and it felt to me that I had hurt his feelings.

"Because the whole point of playing the game is to win it."

"Really?" said the Tree genuinely. "So the players will not know if they are enjoying the playing of this game until they know whether or not they have won the game? Isn't it too late by then?"

"Well, no, not exactly…"

"Could not a team be declared the winner by some other means than a score?" Before I could reply, "And does the winner always play the game better than the loser?"

"No, bad luck and bad referees can lose the game for the more deserving team," and I knew that this had been particularly true for the noble lads of The University of Tennessee football team in recent years. "But there has to be some sort of scoring to determine a winner."

"Why don't the fans at the game take a vote on who played the best overall and one team is declared a winner."

"Because the home team would always be the winner."

"Then," reasoned Tree, "on average, every team would win half the time. Isn't that what happens anyway?"

This was becoming more difficult than explaining economics to a 5-year-old, but he wasn't finished. "It seems to me that if football is such a terrific game then the intrinsic value of playing would make keeping score unnecessary. What happens if the teams have a tie score when the game is over? There is no winner if the teams tie, correct?"

The game was back on in the other room, but I could not be so rude as to walk out on the conversation. I despairingly answered, "Actually, it is more complicated than that, Tree. There was a time when pro and college teams could tie. Now, in the pros there is a 15-minute sudden death period."

"You surely don't mean they kill some humans because the teams tied?"

"No, no, no. It basically means they continue playing for 15 minutes and, more or less, the first team that scores is the winner."

"And what if the score remains tied after 15 minutes?"

"Then the game is a tie."

"But you said that one team had to win?"

"Well, actually that is true in the playoffs toward the championship. They keep doing the 15 minute periods until someone wins because someone has to win."

"Why?"

"Because no one could win the championship unless winners advanced through the playoffs to the Super Bowl."

"Why couldn't the fans somehow vote on the team that had played football the best during the season?"

"No, no, no, that would not work."

"Then why not let the sportswriters vote for the championship team? They are supposedly experts."

I paused. "Actually, Tree, that is how it was done in college football for most of my lifetime."

"So the winner of one particular game might not be the champion?"

"Correct, but the Win-Loss-Tie records of teams would be critical to the vote."

"You mean the team with the best record would be the champion?"

"Not necessarily, and several teams could have the same win-loss record."

"Can college teams tie?"

"They could until sometime in the 1990's, but now there are special rules if the regular game ends in a tie."

"So, how does it work?"

I sighed, "Tree, it is really complicated. The next time a college game ends tied I will come out here and give you a heads up."

"You are telling me that teams could tie and there was a big vote to determine the college champion. But now teams can't tie and there is no vote, right?"

"Close, there are votes by sportswriters every week but the championship is settled by teams playing and one winning in special games at the end of the regular season."

"And how are the teams chosen that play in these special games?"

"There is a vote."

"And is the final winner the team that plays the best football in these special games?"

"Not necessarily, remember luck and referees."

"And does this forced scoring and winning result in general acceptance of the country's college champion?"

"Not necessarily."

"Then, I still don't understand why you keep score. The score doesn't change how the game is actually played."

Tree was beating me into submission, but he gave me the path that I needed. "Yes it does, Tree. The game is played according to the score as the game progresses. The play-by-play tactics of the game are heavily affected by the score. That's why we keep score. In fact, much of the post-game discussion by fans concerns how coaches and players responded to the particular score at particular times of the game." It may not have been the only answer or the best answer to why we keep score in football, but it was good enough for us to resume watching the game. There was no way for me to know at the time that keeping score would re-emerge later as an important topic.

A few days later, Tree asked, "If you were happy to quit playing football after high school, why have you been such a diligent fan of football for all of the years since then?"

It was a reasonable question, and it prompted thoughts which had previously occurred to me. "You have to understand, Tree, how the culture of football, in general, and of Southeastern Conference (SEC) football, in particular, affected boys and young men in the deep south. In my growing up years, there were no big league professional teams in the south, for any sport, until the Milwaukee Braves baseball team moved to Atlanta in 1966. I was entering high school. So, the fan focus was on one's college football team of choice. Most southern fans had not attended college, but their allegiance to Alabama, Auburn, Tennessee, or other teams was undiminished by their educational attainment."

"And you were a Tennessee fan living in Alabama?"

"Yes, and that was not easy, particularly since the University of Alabama was a perennial contender for the national championship. The year in high school that Tennessee beat Alabama, my decision to avoid obnoxious gloating may have saved my life.

"By the way, southern boys <u>did</u> closely follow pro sports. Having no pro team in or near one's location, however, meant that a kid had to actually think about the teams that would be the recipients of their affection and idolatry. Methods of choosing varied. Because of my emerging fear of being less than perfect at anything, I simply chose teams that were the closest to perfection at the time. Thus, my own pro favorites were the New York Yankees in baseball, the Boston Celtics in basketball, and the Baltimore Colts in football. I can still name the starting line-up for the Yankees in 1962. Left-hander Whitey Ford would be the pitcher. To be another Whitey Ford was my earliest ambition, or Sandy Koufax of the Dodgers as a second choice.

"I was also a news junkie by age 12 -- reading the papers and watching the news. George Wallace's Alabama, as the civil rights movement unfolded, was the object of scorn and ridicule by the national press. This hostility outside of the south toward Alabama was, of course, a source of pride and a rallying point for some Alabamians. Southerners were also vulnerable to an institutionalized inferiority complex -- that Americans elsewhere were somehow smarter, or otherwise advantaged, and therefore more likely to succeed. It also exists in Appalachia as a burdensome, self-fulfilling prophecy. Everything that a news-junkie kid saw or read about Alabama, it seemed, was negative, except for the University of Alabama football team, coached by Paul 'Bear' Bryant. They were the best in the entire country, respected by all Americans who knew football. They were our collective self-worth."

"But the south has changed, Mike. Big cities have pro teams, the economy has lessened the lags behind other states, and many more forms of entertainment and leisure exist now. Is football still more important to southerners than other Americans?"

"Yes," I replied, "from my own observation and experience, football, certainly at the college, high school, and youth levels is a more important part of life than elsewhere. Not everyone, of course, but many southerners carefully follow their university's recruitment of high school players; they can tell you height, weight, number of yards gained, tackles per game. It is a year round deal, and there may be only a slight abatement of football discussions when football season ends.

"And you need to know that posturing and the manner of talking to others about football becomes an art form that one learns in youth and grooms over the years. It is particularly important in talking with a fan of the current week's opponent."

"I don't know what you mean," said Tree.

"Let's assume, Tree, that Tennessee had scheduled a breather game for the coming Saturday. They were to play the Fighting Flutes from the Rhode Island College of Fine Arts. Our coaches, players, and any fans encountering the press or a Flutes' fan would say, 'If we don't play our best game on Saturday, the Flutes will beat us. They have their entire team back from last year. Despite some early season setbacks, they have dramatically improved in every game. The size of their offensive and defensive lines is being discussed across the country. Their quarterback Fabian really came into his own as a passer last week. Our young men are certainly taking this game seriously.'"

Tree responded, "Those are very nice and complimentary things to say. Seems as though it is good sportsmanship. Why is it difficult to learn how to say pleasant things about a football opponent?"

"Because it is a total lie, Tree, and everyone knows it is a lie. Our fans know that. Their fans know that. The sportswriters know that also, but they are apparently obliged to publish the official, lying commentary of our coach. Then, they might report something more truthful, but it is in their own interest to promote the possibility of viewing excitement come Saturday."

"What would happen if you or your coach spoke the truth?"

"That would be awful," I began. "The truth would be something like this: 'In retrospect, we should not have scheduled such a poor excuse for a football team even as a laugher game. We may win by 100 points. My only concern is that one of our key players might be hurt in warm-ups or running to the locker room. The Flutes have all 33 of their players back from last year, when they posted a 1-11 record. They won a game by forfeit. This year they are 0-4 and 0-2 in Eastern Rhode Island conference play. Their margin of loss closed dramatically in last week's game, in which they scored their first points. It is amazing the Flutes can compete at the college level with offensive and defensive linemen averaging less than 210 pounds, but they are still trying. Their quarterback, Fabian, completed his first two passes last week, for minus 3 and 6 yards, before breaking his arm. My challenge is to keep my young men from belly laughing as they review the films of the Flutes' games.'"

"Surely, you could soften the truth from that?"

"Not really, Tree, the truth simply cannot be said. One must lie, in this circumstance and many others. And the lie must be properly nuanced. It takes years of practice," I instructed.

"Let me just ask, what would happen if some nicer version of the truth were said by a Tennessee coach or fans?"

"Then we would be upset by the Flutes. They would beat us."

"That doesn't seem possible, given what you said about them."

"It doesn't matter. It is an immutable natural law that if you say anything derisive about an opponent, they will post it on their electronic bulletin boards and thereby beat you."

"Why?"

"I don't know. It is an immutable law of football. Maybe came from Bear Bryant. But this is the nature of the knowledge that surrounds the game of football and its culture. New knowledge may cease early in adult life about language, math, and science, but not about football!

"To a true fan, Tree, a football game is, or at least may be, the ultimate drama to be viewed by a human. Movies or TV shows rarely beat a great football game. Extremes of joy and sorrow will be felt, feats of unimaginable athletic talent might be witnessed, the thrill of victory or the agony of defeat may hinge on one fluky play, or a flash of football stupidity by a coach or player, or the misplacement of a ball on the field. Courage may be seen, and sometimes good sportsmanship, but the intense struggle for one more point than the opponent knots a fan's stomach until the game ends… unless it ends in a tie, but let's not go into that again."

Sometimes in this series of conversations Tree's questioning was annoying, but, in retrospect, the subject matter of his inquiries was refreshingly impossible to predict. For example, he asked after one television game, "Mike, why does each team have eleven players on the field, versus 10 or 12? Eleven seems to be a strange number to choose. It is two more than baseball and six more than basketball, but that doesn't explain anything. How was eleven decided?"

"I could guess, but really have no idea Tree. It has always been eleven, and it has not been a common subject of discussion among either experts or fans."

"So," Tree began, "why not let the defense have one more player than the offense, since they have no idea what the play will be or which direction it is heading?"

"That's not a crazy idea," I responded, in order to give Tree some encouragement, "but that would stifle offenses, lower points scored, and would not be popular with a fan-ship that generally prefers offense and scoring."

"If close games are preferable to watch, why not give a team behind, say, 20 points or more at halftime, or perhaps a 12th player in the second half?"

"No, Tree, they couldn't do that."

"Why?"

"I don't know."

"And Alabama," Tree said, "why not make them play with 10 players and give the other team 12 … at least until somebody starts to beat them occasionally?"

"That wouldn't be fair, Tree." I responded brightly, "But life isn't fair after all. You may be on to something here. That idea has some real merit." I hoped that he would pursue the idea because he might actually find a way to make it happen.

One afternoon, he had questions about the names of positions. If the quarterback is so important, why is his position only given 25 percent of the worth of a fullback and 50 percent of the worth of a halfback? And how does a tailback fit into this measurement system? Why are some tackles allowed to tackle but some tackles not allowed to tackle? If offensive tackles can only block, why aren't they called blockers? And what are guards actually guarding? It is my recollection that he had an unusual affinity for centers, and I believe it was because "center" made sense to him. An unbalanced line really bothered Tree.

Another day his questioning was about points. Why 6 points, versus 5 or 7, for a touchdown? Why do you add one point thereafter? Is it because that is one of the few times that a foot actually touches the ball? But, then, why would running and passing the ball the same three yards bring two points? Why don't they award points for a really great punt? Why not award at least a few points if the offense ends up only an inch from the other team's goal line?

"Because it is a game of inches," I said automatically.

"Why?" he replied.

"I'm not sure." Indeed, I was less certain about everything.

"And who decided on three points for a field goal? Why is it three points if kicked from the 1-yard line, which is closer to the goal than the one-point kick after a touchdown? Why not more points the further away? Why two points for a safety? What does 'safety' even mean?" And on and on.

After one game, he was fascinated with punt returners. "So, if they hold a hand up in the air, then everyone knows not to hit them because when they catch the ball, they can't advance forward, right?"

"Yes," I replied, "called a fair catch."

"Has anyone ever hit the punt returner, anyway, really hard when he doesn't expect it?"

"It is rare, but I've seen it happen. Either the tackler doesn't see the fair catch signal, or he just chooses to possibly kill the punt returner, anyway," I answered.

"Then how does the punt returner not think about that possibility when he makes the signal and is waiting to catch the next punt. How does he ever catch the punt knowing that could happen?

"I don't know, Tree. Nerves of steel, I guess, because they almost always catch the ball." Then, Tree surprised me.

"There would be a 15-yard penalty if the player actually hit the punt returner anyway, right?"

"Right, and they might throw the player out of the game. I'm not sure about that."

"If they did that, though, on the very first punt and certainly if they did it on the first two punts, wouldn't the punt returner, or his replacement, be very likely to fumble one or more times thereafter? Thirty yards in penalties, versus recovering the ball one or two times, is an attractive trade-off, especially if you have your two worst players do the deed."

"No, you wouldn't do that Tree. I don't ever remember seeing something like that happen."

"Because a team never commits a penalty except by accident."

"No. I can't say that, Tree. Often a player knows he is illegally holding, for example, but hopes a referee will not see him."

"And the coaches know about this?"

"Yes, sort of, more or less."

"Then the only special thing about hitting the punt returner is that it is so out in the open, so obvious?"

"That and the punt returner might be killed. Still, it might work, at least in the short run. If winning were really everything, then you would expect to see it more. Same for roughing the quarterback.

"Except the other team would do it back to you," I added.

"Is that the reason?" asked Tree. "Another 'mutually assured destruction' reason?"

"I'm not really sure of anything anymore," I admitted.

On another occasion, "Which is worse: losing a close game 50-49 on a last second field goal, or being blown out by a clearly better team 50-0?"

"Yes," I said simply.

"What do you mean, 'Yes.'"

"Yes, both are worse. They are differently worse, but they are both worse than winning. Please don't bring up ties. I've been to both places, as a player and a fan, and they are both worse. I can't explain it better than that."

One conversation that I remember was deeper, more philosophical. Tree had watched with me a surprising Tennessee win in the opener, a win over a small team, and then a defeat by the University of Florida. Tree observed, "You know, Mike, for you as a fan, winning is a good thing but moves quickly to worrying about losing. Your joy in winning is not as great or long-lasting as your misery over losing. Why do you do it? And since a 50:50 win-loss record must be the average, long-run, for all teams together, why do you Americans do it?"

These are questions which I had asked myself on several occasions, always after losses. "It is a great question, Tree. Let me talk about 1998, because the answer begins and ends with 1998. Do you remember me in 1998, when I married Lynn just before football season began?"

"Yes, I remember," and Tree smiled, "but tell your story again about Tennessee and the 1998 football season. You like to hear it, yourself."

"It was the year after Peyton Manning left for the pros and there-fore the most unexpected of years to win a national championship in the many years of my fan-ship. 13-0. We beat Florida State in the first national championship game...at the Fiesta Bowl. My new wife pointed out that from the first game I had screamed, whined, and worried my way through the season, seeming to squeeze much of the fun out of winning. What was I to be like when Tennessee started losing? (She would learn the answer to that one later.)

"The fact of the matter, Tree, is that I loved every bit of the 1998 season and 1999 championship game, as I look back on that season. It was perfect. Every up and down, every coach, every player was as it was supposed to be. Every game, before or since, which ended badly, was somehow made worth it because of 1998. Even if never seen again in my lifetime, that season, that championship game, was good enough to make all of the collective agony of fan-ship worth it."

"But you agree that this is not particularly logical?" Tree asked.

"I agree, but you have to be for something in your life, Tree, that is beyond the month-by-month or the year-by-year -- that is somehow bigger than you."

"I can understand the concept," Tree interrupted, and we both smiled.

On another visit Tree asked, "It is so easy to watch a football game on television, why would so many fans actually choose to go to the stadium? The expense, the traffic, the discomfort in very hot or cold or wet weather... Why?"

"Those are the reasons why I only use my football tickets and drive to Knoxville one or two games a year." I reflected a moment and continued, "I can only speak of big-time college football games, having lived in a pro-sized city for only a couple of years. A big-time college football game experience is magical thing, Tree. It is unlike any other kind of day. If one is lodging in the site city, whether for the home or visiting team, it is a two- or three-day experience, depending upon the travel distance. All hotel lobby, restaurant, stadium travel, and related time involves interactions with your fans and the other team's fans. Remember, many years of training are required to master the communications that ensue. Most conversations with own-team fans involve negativity, what-iffing, and worry. Only amateur football fans are arrogant and unaware that arrogance, alone, might ensure a loss. With other-team fans, we have already discussed that all conversation is tactical, and the truth may require artful manipulation.

"Everything about the environment, the campus, the stadium is carnival-like. The stadium viewing of the game is truly different from at home – for better and worse, but different. Assuming good seats and weather, a football aficionado can focus on any piece of action on the field, not the choice of views by the television decision makers. The focus can be watching a particular receiver run a route, or a blitzing linebacker, whatever. Football is a team sport, Tree, and so is fan-ship. The common experience of fans viewing their team together magnifies the thrills and slices the agonies. You really ought to go to a game with me," I started, and then conjured the picture of Tree and me walking into Neyland Stadium. "That would be quite the sight." We both smiled.

"On the other hand, the long TV timeouts are excruciating for stadium fans. The special referee with a red hat, who stands on the field during such timeouts to prevent play, is much despised by all stadium fans, especially in lousy weather, and he surely must be wearing a facial disguise and using a fake name. Obnoxious, drunk fans can be a problem, but some persons are naturally obnoxious and do not require intoxicants. I also sympathize with females at crowded games, because of their large space requirements versus men in urinating, and the resulting bottlenecks. At big-time football games females must monitor their intake of any type of liquids or suffer consequences that are unimaginable. At any rate," I concluded, "it is an experience that has been a cherished part of life for me."

Tree changed the subject, "Just out of curiosity, how would you and fans like you reallocate your time if there were no football to watch or talk about, either at a stadium or on television?"

I almost laughed. "What a dreadful topic to think about, Tree. You are talking about a substantial amount of time in the fall and early winter for me and fans like me." Yet, I attempted an answer. "There is a first thought that I would spend more time with my family. In my case, neither household female spends significant time watching football with me, nor talking about football, nor caring about football or the outcome of important games. We nevertheless have a certain equilibrium in the household that accommodates my watching of football in my man-cave downstairs office. The absence of football would clearly disrupt that equilibrium, which has worked out rather well from my perspective. And it is not at all clear whether the busy wife or almost-teenager granddaughter are seeking more of my time.

"To my credit, their needs and activities take priority over football," I thought and I remembered taking Chloe to a birthday party during a Tennessee-Alabama game-of-the-week. This sacrifice was made easier, however, by the odious score at the end of the first quarter of play. "So, this re-allocation of time would unlikely be a big one in my situation, Tree, and I suspect that football families would face widely disparate circumstances in moving to a new equilibrium of interactions." I was briefly struck by the thought of spending my reallocated time watching more of the television typically viewed by my female housemates – fashion runway shows, cooking competitions, home fix-ups, Hallmark Christmas movies. That simply was not happening. I would rather eat liver.

"Another option, of course, is to spend more time working. Some persons either don't have the option of more work time, or they do not wish to spend more time doing what they already hate. As a self-employed professional, this option is available to me. But I am already a workaholic, and no friend of mine has ever suggested that <u>more</u> time working would be good for me." Tree also heard my economics brain speculating on the effects of such re-allocations on national productivity and economic growth. More time would be available for productive work, surely, but what about the devastating morale effects on a large segment of the workforce?

"Football fans could shift some of their time to watching other sports. Pro baseball and basketball have grown cold to me, except for dutiful viewing of the World Series and NBA Championship series. Perhaps college basketball could begin a month or so earlier, but that would only help me if the Tennessee Vols had ranked mens or womens teams. The lady Vols future is highly uncertain with the heartbreaking departure of Pat Head Summitt as coach, and Tennessee men come through one or two years out of every ten. Some fans might shift time to gymnastics, track and field, swimming and diving, car racing, animal racing, et cetera."

"What about soccer?" interjected the Tree. "Would fans shift from American football to everybody else's football?"

"Some might, but not me and I suspect many others… unless, of course, a child or grandchild was playing."

"Why?"

"Because the only thing my football and soccer have in common is that they are both played on a flat surface. Besides, 'offside' in soccer is absolutely impossible for a football fan to understand. I think soccer officials either call offsides at random or when they think the wrong team is about to score."

"What else?" Tree asked.

"Other hobbies or new hobbies are possible, I suppose. More racquetball would have been great but for the hip problem. Lots of people here hunt, fish, hike, canoe, and pursue other outdoor activities. I did outdoors in the Army and didn't particularly like it. And even if I wanted to begin hunting, which I don't, I would need a gun of some sort. But my wife won't let me have one. She thinks I would be a danger to myself and others."

"Because you are unstable?"

"No, because I'm a klutz who can barely be trusted with a pencil sharpener." I continued, "And to wrap this up, I could re-allocate time to self-improvement activities: religion, spirituality, exercise and health, meditation. More reading is likely. Yes, I could definitely increase my leisure reading. More art, music, and culture are possible, but unlikely. I could also spend more time in charity or civic work, or generally helping others, and I would like to believe there would be some time re-allocated here."

"Thank you," Tree said.

"But why did you ask that question? Do you think football is too big a part of my life, Tree?"

"I didn't say that. It is part of my learning about football and its effects." Of course, he didn't really answer my question, but Tree chose his words and his topics carefully even if I didn't understand them.

In retrospect, it is surprising that we did not talk more about other topics during the period of frequent meetings. It was a Summer Olympics year, for example, and we had one retrospective discussion after they had ended. Tree was knowledgeable about the Olympics, in general, and particular competitions, events, and athletes. He again asked questions about scoring. "Does a country win with total medals, or gold medals, or gold plus silver? If a country doesn't actually "win" the Olympics, then why does anyone keep a medal count? Does #1 in the medals count cause the people of the world to like Americans more or less? Does a high medals tally mean that a nation has the best athletes, or just the most athletes, or the largest financing? Doesn't anyone ever talk about medals per capita?" As I recall, the Tree also observed that humans had some strange habits in how they kept score.

It was also a presidential election year, with intense campaigning surrounding our frequent conversations. As a news junkie, anyway, I was particularly full of it -- politics -- in the months before a pivotal presidential election. It was a time in which my chosen conversations would gravitate to the political, even before football. Yet, Tree and I did not discuss the various political campaigns, or candidates, or issues.

Perhaps it was my own fault, because it would have been great to talk with Tree about the elections. Moreover, conversations with the Tree might have revealed some Tree-like insights into which party and persons would prevail. The problem was that as soon as the thoughts were thought, Tree knew them. He made it known to me that we would not be discussing either present or future politics. Tree neither brought up politics nor gave me any opening to do so. I have never understood why. It was a disappointment, but it was not for me to go there. Tree was bigger than me.

So, by the end of October, on the porch in late afternoon, my mind returned to football when Tree showed up for a chat. After exchanging pleasantries, I asked Tree the question which had burdened my mind. "Tree, why in our last talk did you ask me what I would do if there were no football?"

"Mike, you know that we are not talking about the future in general or your future in particular. Knowledge about the future is a line that humans cannot cross. You are not made for that."

"But you have made me afraid, Tree, that football is somehow going away. Was that the real reason for the conversation?"

"I cannot talk with you about the future. It would be a contradiction in the natural order of human existence. If a human were to know facts about the future, then the future changes, and the facts are no longer true."

Yet, I persisted. "Please, Tree, I cannot stop obsessing about this. I'm not asking for knowledge about myself, or my family and friends, or the Dow Jones average, or the evolution of the universe... just football. Could you find some way to tell me about the future of football?"

Tree hesitated. Then, slowly he mused, "I suppose that the future of football could be discussed with you if I also take action to ensure that you cannot act upon or share the knowledge."

Out of my anxiousness, I mumbled, "I assume you don't mean that if you tell me, then you'll have to kill me. It is not quite <u>that</u> important for me to know about where football is headed."

Tree ignored the comment and continued, "but while it could be handled, Mike, you need to realize that humans don't time travel forward for good reasons. You really do not want to know what is out there. It is bad enough that humans know about history but often ignore it."

"Please, Tree. Just this one time, this one topic. And then you can erase what I know or do whatever you need to do. No harm done. Just once?"

"Very well," said Tree, "but remember that you pleaded with me to do this." He questioned, "Do you only want the bottom line, or the long version of the story, or something in between?"

"Something in between." I could feel dread rising in me, since the brief preamble did not seem encouraging.

Tree began, "As a preview, Mike, your football dies out in your country. American football dies. That is where the story ends."

This was, as they say, a gut punch. The air wheezed from my lungs. A combination of panic, disbelief, and despair engulfed me. I could not speak. Tree was apparently not concerned about giving me this bad news gently.

"The issues of continuing with football," Tree intoned, "divided the nation. They set family against family, spouse against spouse, child against parents. They divided Americans by age, education, gender, and by race. They differentiated them by place – South versus North, coasts versus middle."

"The path to the end was played out at all three of the levels: youth through high school, college, and pro. The entire structure of football imploded."

In my bewilderment and anguish, I blundered, "Was it CTE? Did CTE kill football?" I was referring, of course, to chronic traumatic encephalopathy, and the increasingly publicized effects of multiple head injuries.

Tree replied, "CTE was a rallying topic to be sure. I know you have some knowledge of CTE. Remind us of the high points."

"I have followed what has gone on with CTE, more or less, because of my professional work in litigation and my love of football. I recall that research into the effects of repeated head trauma began in the 1920's and that early publicity centered around professional boxing and what was called punch drunk syndrome. A handful of U.S. research centers have studied CTE intensely since at least 2000, and their major source of information has been autopsies on the brains of football players, especially former NFL players. My recall is that they can't yet detect CTE in living persons but that researchers are working on it."

"What else?" Tree questioned.

"I know the effects of CTE can be terrible, and that they may result from repeated concussions or even repeated blows to the head which fall short of actual concussions but occur over years of playing football. The symptoms of brain degeneration include problems with mood, behavior, progressive dementia, movement, and coordination; also, suicide, maybe Parkinson's and Lou Gehrig's disease (ALS) may result from this cause.

"I know that research issues are the obvious ones. How many hits to the head, and over what time frame, results in how much probability of a player later suffering from CTE and its effects? How does the likelihood of bad effects change if the beginning age of tackle football is increased? What equipment changes, rule changes, or other actions might reduce the incidence and severity of CTE that are somehow considered acceptable?

"And I know about the lawsuits by former NFL players against the League for failing to protect players from concussions and these various health effects. Much of the substance, as I understand it, involves the League's failure to warn players of these health effects and, in fact, its actions to hide or distort the information which they had on CTE. So, the full disclosure of information is a basic issue as this litigation moves forward and, at any rate, estimates of the medical and care costs of coping with these effects keep going up."

Tree and I exchanged some more information on CTE, and then Tree continued his prognostication, "But, Mike, the CTE controversy was only the latest and most publicized part of the increasing focus on the violence of the game. Children, teenagers, college athletes, and pro players die, become paralyzed, and are otherwise maimed every year. The publicity of such circumstances grew exponentially and was likely fueled by the publicity surrounding CTE. The opponents of tackle football emphasized violence as the defining characteristic of the sport."

It was simply impossible for me to listen any longer, because the discourse about the future could not stand unchallenged. "Tree, 'violence' is really inappropriate as a description upon which the future of football should hang. Football is aggressive, and it is certainly a contact sport. One needs a certain toughness to play and, yes, it hurts sometimes. Players can be injured, but, Tree, the purpose of football is not violence. Violence implies some evil motive to exert force, like a violent crime. That's not football. The word is unfair."

Tree replied, "I am not attempting to debate what is fair, but at your request, I am pointing out that increasing numbers of Americans came to think about violence and football. Since you mentioned intent, however, you do agree that players attempt to hurt other players, right? To 'put the hurt on them,' 'rattle their cage,' 'lay them out,' 'knock their butts off' and other such expressions. It is not to kill them, or permanently maim them, necessarily, but maybe to put them out of the game, or make them fumble? Quarterbacks, punt returners, and receivers are especially targeted, it seems to me.

"So, there is planned violence, Mike, but check the various definitions of violence. Terrible force can be applied to a player, maybe by several other players, regardless of intent. A former player with dementia has the disability, just the same, if all of the blows to his head were absent malice, or bad motive. The violence of the blows does define the game. It is the brand that the NFL promotes. Much of what you fans debrief about after a game are skilled escapes from violence or survival despite it. This is where conversations among Americans increasingly turned, Mike. That is what I'm telling you. So, do you wish me to continue?"

"Yes, please," I said dolefully.

"As you know, deaths and serious injury have always occurred in football – from the youth to professional levels – apart from CTE. Such occurrences in the future were met by worsening publicity that was generalized to the sport, itself. Even responses, such as concussion protocols, were continuing reminders of the negatives of the game.

"Indeed, the responses by football to the uproar over the violence in football created another path of the sport's decline. Changes in the rules of the game and limits on the amount and nature of contact practices, as examples, ignited vigorous debates over the Powder Puffing of the American game. Opponents of such changes in the game – as you played it, Mike - used substantially more vulgar words than Powder Puffing. Fans had different thresholds for when the powder puffing process crossed the line of powder puffication when football was no longer worth their fanship."

While Tree was not attempting a debate, it was very difficult for me to simply listen to these revelations without responding. Because football was such a significant part of my past, and my heretofore planned future, this felt as though it was a personal attack by unknown others on a cherished part of my life. "But surely, Tree, these future debates did not only focus on what some believed to be the negatives of football. Surely others discussed the negatives of <u>ending</u> tackle football.

"There are negatives resulting from the disappearance of tackle football to boys and young men, or to adult football fans for that matter. What is the cost side of the benefit/cost analysis of ending football? Do young men re-direct their aggressive impulses to crime, or other anti-social or unwholesome activities? Do problems of drugs, alcohol, and obesity become worse? How do adult fans deal with their loss? Do their re-allocations of time and energy, in net, make society better or worse?"

Tree replied, "Yes, of course, these conversations occurred, and such trade-offs were discussed. I have already told you how these debates ended up, however. Have you heard enough or do you want more?"

"I'll take more." It was like insisting upon hearing the details of one's impending demise.

Tree continued, "So, at the youth level, parents and guardians controlled the decision to allow boys to play tackle football. As concerns about the safety of football became more publicized, research also aimed at whether delaying the beginning age of tackle football would substantially reduce long term health effects: delaying to age 12 or 14, and, arguably, to ages at which too little time was left for learning even a powder puff game. Or, so late that good athletes had already moved to other sports."

"Then a federal judge took a page from previous rulings about filtered cigarettes and forced helmet manufacturers to include a label, 'There is no safe tackle football.' Parents, then, would face a decision to allow a child to play despite focus on possible harm.

"Middle and high schools had more difficulty funding tackle football. The costs of liability insurance skyrocketed; so did the cost of padding, helmets, and practice equipment necessary to meet rising safety standards. While universities and the NFL might afford such costs, a growing number of youth leagues and school systems could not. School board meetings were notable for discussions regarding the continuation of tackle football, and organized protests against football periodically occurred. Then MAVIS was formed and its effectiveness in publicity and lobbying followed the path of MADD."

"MAVIS?"

"Mothers Against Violence in Sports. And their aim was to take out tackle football first, before moving to other sports. They measured the drop in high school football players from one million downward as their benchmark of success. They were very successful in their endeavors, and football declined in importance from the bottom up."

Tree paused. "Please keep going," I said softly.

"At the NCAA level, the public opinion debates first turned political. Liberals, in general, came to the position that tackle football had to be ended by legislation, if necessary, while conservatives defended football without significant changes. Oddly, conservatives began to use the term 'American football' to emphasize the importance of the sport to the national culture. One either supported the playing of this American sport or one did not, and such persons were barely American. It became a badge of honor, on the other side, for most faculties to advocate dropping football, despite a loss in alumni giving.

"Rule changes were many and varied and often involved the separation of players in space. The theory was that players who touch each other less probably hurt each other less. No one could find the right way to limit contact in practice without increasing injuries in games because players were not adept in avoiding injuries from contact.

"Issues of politics and regulation came to a head with the contentious enactment of the Brady-Manning legislation, defining roles for federal, state, and local governments…."

I immediately interrupted. "You mean Tom Brady was in the House and Peyton in the Senate?"

"That is more detail than is necessary. You don't need to know which Brady or which Manning or who was in the Senate. Nor do you need to know whether ex-quarterbacks were in Congress or were publicized examples of the effects of CTE."

"That is an awful thought," I thought.

Tree continued, "College coaches and administrators came to worry about football liabilities as medical doctors had earlier learned to worry about medical liabilities. All of their other problems were also magnified by the organized resistance to tackle football -- coaches' salaries versus faculty salaries and paying players for their time, skill, and risk, for example.

"The death of football also proceeded place versus place, and indeed it inflamed region against region. The northeastern and western coastal states ceased college football first, and their congressional representatives pushed for a national ban on the sport. The rest of the country generally disagreed, and southern states particularly supported the status quo in football.

"The National Football League, while its new player foundation began to crumble, was obviously a focus of the debate because it had worked for decades to own Sundays, along with the prime time of Mondays and Thursdays. It was a huge and successful industry, and the media sub-industry provided 24-hour focus on the league. The players' union had its own debates about practice limits and safety-related rule changes versus the puffication threshold that would destroy the profession of American football. The African American community also had a special debate ongoing, as professional football had been a disproportionate ticket upward. Intense debates occurred within the Pro cities, and one particular puffication led to near-riots from Boston to Los Angeles.

"The continuing publicity over CTE and other ramifications of violence also increased the intensity of other NFL problems, such as taxpayer resentment over the costs of new stadiums, the overexposure of televised games which hardened the resistance of non-fans, player salaries and ticket prices, and social protests by players. The league spent large dollars on safety-related technologies and changes, but the magnet system in newer, smart helmets was found to cause its own brain injuries. As some would say, the NFL just could not catch a break."

"So, the NFL actually closed down?"

"Yes, it did. Tackle football ultimately ended, even in the south."

I was devastated. "Tree, tackle football may have played a role in the greatness of my country: in the strength of our military and the competitiveness of our businesses."

Tree replied, "Yes, the conservatives arguing for the football status quo also turned at the end to issues of national security. Two problems raised by anti-footballers made it difficult for footballers to win such an argument. Number one is that the Israeli's don't play American football. Number two is that women do not now play, nor have they ever played, tackle football."

I was even more devastated. My moribund countenance would have been a picture to remember. Thoughts ran through my mind of life without football. The moment felt surreal. I could not form words.

In the silence of my misery, I felt a sound that was heretofore unknown to my senses. It was deep, hardy, resonant. It was rolling, like a belly-shaking laugh. It <u>was</u> a laugh. Tree was laughing, belly laughing.

So I started laughing too. I don't know why. Nothing we were talking about was funny. But this laugh of Tree was laughably funny, and

I could not stop my descent into belly-laughing. He laughed at my laugh, and I laughed at his laugh. Tears came to my eyes, and it remained unclear what was so funny. Then, it dawned on me what was so funny.

"You made all of this up Tree. Football doesn't die out," I muttered as Tree was unsuccessfully attempting to end his laughing.

"Yes, Mike, I made up the story," he said with pride and then converted to what must have been a Tree chuckle. "It was an experiment in humor -- whether or not I could actually do humor. And if making someone laugh is the objective of humor, then the experiment was successful. We both laughed a lot.

"This was really fun. I have never done fun, so it is new to me. But you should have seen you. About to cry. It was difficult not to start laughing before I finished the story."

"But you are now very joyous," said Tree, "and laughing still. What kind of humor was it that I just did, Mike?"

I laughed some more about what he had done to me and Tree also laughed again. "Bullshitting," I replied to him, "the common term, at least from my upbringing, is Bullshitting. You just bullshitted me, Tree, and you did it very effectively."

"A rather crude term for a category of humor," Tree observed.

"It is the planned telling of an outrageous story. It is untrue by definition, but done for the purpose of humor. The funny lies in the ability to convince those hearing the story that you are telling the truth, until either you confess what you are doing, or laugh, or they figure it out. It is a funny of gullibility."

"I at least like Bullshitter better than Liar," Tree observed.

"It is all about the intent, Tree. But most humans cannot do this type of humor very well. It requires knowledge of the subject, verbal ability, and self-control. Ironically, I myself am a rather good bullshitter and really enjoy doing it. But I have never seen it done better than you just did it.

"How long have you been planning this?" I asked.

"For the last few months while I watched you watch football, and listened to you talk about it. You are way too serious about it, Mike. Football is very high-stress entertainment for you."

"Well," I laughed a bit more, "you, as they say, 'sucked me in' to your story. It did not occur to me that you were making it all up."

After a moment of reflection, I added, "You know, Tree, that in my own defense, you are a bigger-than-me entity who knows things that I don't know. So, you really have an unfair advantage over me as a bullshitter. You could likely pull off something like this again. The problem is that I often need to know that what you are saying to me is not bullshit, or I could never take you seriously."

"Yes, you make a good point. Now that I have moved past a humor hurdle, I will not do that to you again… probably."

"I should have known, as a labor economist, that football could not be ended because people could be injured or killed playing it. Various occupations have varying probabilities of serious injury or death. It is not just the playing of football that is risky. Many occupations are risky, and economists measure the wage premiums paid to persons for working in these kinds of jobs. So long as someone is not withholding information on the nature of job risks, people can make their own decisions."

After a pause, I said, "And Tree, I should have said before that football simply runs too deep in families for it to be ended. As my Dad's Alzheimer's worsened, our last topic of coherent conversation was Tennessee football and basketball. When Pooky lived with us in her last four years, much of our mother-and-son enjoyment was Tennessee football and Peyton's Indianapolis Colts. Football could not be ended in America. There are too many American stories like this one."

Tree had said nothing. This made me nervous. It was not funny. "You told me that football would not die, right?"

"Mike, I told you that I made up that story about the death of football." After an awkward pause, he added, "We are not talking about the future, Mike. It was a joke."

"But then we are right back to where we started, Tree. You know what happens to football and I don't."

"Yes, that is correct. You only want to know good things about the future. The future doesn't work that way, Mike. Trust me: you don't want to know about the future of football or anything else."

"OK, Tree," I surrendered, "I don't want to know." I did want to know, however, and Tree knew that I wanted to know. Lessons about football are especially difficult to learn.

CHAPTER SEVEN –

FEAR AND ANGER

Approximately one year after Tree's coming out to me, I was seated on the porch with my walker and crutch after the hip replacement. The spring was blossoming and beautiful, but the allergies accompanying spring in the mountains weighed me down. My last physical therapy session at home had just been completed, and a few weeks of visits to the therapist were ahead. I would renew teaching shortly, and I would begin to work with a trainer to institutionalize a new pattern of post-racquetball exercise.

Barack Obama had begun his second term. In this year, the first resignation by a Pope in 600 years would occur, a new leader in North Korea would take over, the 50-year anniversary of John F. Kennedy's assassination would be marked, and evidence of cannibalism at the Jamestown Colony would be revealed. There was no apparent pattern to these news highlights, although conspiracy theorists would likely suggest some linkages.

My mind was reviewing a tape of my few days in the hospital. The highly recommended surgeon may have been clinically marvelous but was an arrogant ass and had not bothered with a post-surgery visit. Yes, some doctors were not pleasant people.

I was reminded of my experiences with doctors as a young administrator at a large medical center. There was a prized surgeon who threw a scalpel at a surgical nurse, apparently in a gesture of negative feedback over her performance. The nurse believed that the knife whizzing by her ear was an inappropriate response. The ensuing controversy lasted almost a year and was only resolved when the surgeon was reprimanded and promoted to management.

A hospital might actually run for a while without doctors, but not without nurses. My recent experience was with nurses more kind and patient than stressful circumstances would seem to dictate, which was also true for most doctors and other hospital staff. Indeed, the rhythm of hospital life still intrigued me, as it differed from the routines and flows of relationships outside the hospital bubble. One could see, hear, and feel the raw emotions of anger, fear, anxiety, worry and, on the other hand, compassion and gratitude. Having not actually lived in a hospital work environment day to day, however, I could only guess at the transition issues into, and out of, this bubble on a routine basis. Customers and visitors provided a wide-ranging mix of pleasing or unpleasing characteristics and temperaments.

Tree had visited only once, briefly, since football season. The purpose of that visit escaped me, although he basically said he was checking on me. Checking what? I resolved to ask him this question the next time that I was with him, but he was there.

"Hello, Mike."

"Hello Tree. It is good to see you as always."

Pause.

"I found your second PT session to be painfully amusing," Tree said, and I believe that he smiled.

Michael Brookshire

I laughed. "A good choice of words, Tree." It wasn't funny when it happened. When the physical therapy people snatched me for my first PT session, on the afternoon of my surgery, my first observation was that they were a bit hasty and they could return tomorrow. But after the PT session, the surprise was that the pain was not that bad. In session two the next day, exactly the same movements brought agony even to a tough guy like me. The difference, it was explained to me, was morphine, plain and simple. I had it in #1 but not in #2.

"I learned to be really skeptical when they do something to you the second time. And I learned to know what drugs I was on before showing off my rehabilitation prowess."

Turning serious, Tree said "I came to talk about negatives today -- to get them behind you -- starting with fear. Are you up for that?"

We, of course, were going to talk about his topics, but any other topic besides me and fear sounded more appealing. So, I attempted a deflection, "Can I ask you a question first?"

"Surely."

"The last time you came, it was not with a topic. What determines whether you come with a topic?"

"That's a fair question. You need some time to practice. To incorporate what we have talked about into how you live. Or at least time to make a start of it."

"I assume you mean, for example, am I lowering my daily level of control freakism?"

"Yes."

"And am I?"

"Well at least you are thinking about it."

"But you could monitor me without actually showing up."

"True," and he added, "Sometimes I just need to stop what I am doing and come to see you."

He made me feel special. "Tree, what do you think of humans, generally? Not me, but humans as a species?"

"You are avoiding my topics, but we will get there. Why do you ask about humans generally?"

"Because you are bigger than me and bigger than the biggest human. So, you are my only chance to receive a bird's eye view, so to speak."

Tree hesitated momentarily and then said, "If I were to choose one of your words to describe my view of humans, it would be 'diverse.' Humans are diverse."

I interrupted automatically, because of my deficient listening skills, "Do you mean their differences by ethnic group, race, sex, age ...."

"No, no, no!" Tree interrupted back. "You think like an economist. That is not what I mean. The circumstances of one's birth start the diverging and, of course, differences by race, gender... by genetics... begin there. But the human start ranges from incredibly rich to poor, advantaged or not, loved in a household or not, in a peace or in a war. And the issues of how children grow aside, the diversity of ambition, or not, is notable in itself, and the growth that occurs or not, from the beginning to the end."

Then, Tree told a joke, "A little girl comes home with her first report card, and her proud dad takes it from her. She has made one Satisfactory and four Unsatisfactories, and the daddy is stunned speechless. The little girl says, 'What do you think the problem is Pop – environment or heredity?'"

I chuckled. "Haven't heard that one."

"I know. I checked that first."

"So, you told your brief joke to illustrate a point?"

"Not really. It was reasonably close to the topic, and I'm looking for opportunities to practice my humor skills." He continued, "In the time that we are speaking, some humans will show great love and compassion while others pursue murder, and mayhem, and cruelty. Kindness exists with brutality. Generosity with selfishness.

"The emotions that dominate particular humans at particular times produce large diversity in human actors, beyond circumstances and traits. Humans dominated by fear and anger are interspersed with others who have found purpose and gratitude.

"Think, Mike, of a human world where this diversity was not the defining feature. Watching 72 humans would be the same as watching one human 72 times. Nothing differs, nothing changes. If one is angry, they are all angry. If one is happy, they all would be happy. If one is ruthless, they all are ruthless."

I said, "It occurs to me that Earth could be the diversity experiment and some of those other scenarios could be playing out elsewhere." This was really a question that I was asking. "It would seem that a diverse humans' scenario would be more interesting to the viewer, although an all-angry experiment might be an Action/Thriller drama."

"Experiment is not what the human experience is," Tree responded. "You are approaching boundaries in our conversation which we will not cross. There is a reason for the human experience, but it is beyond your capacity to understand. Recall the ant, you, and the universe. But think about the common sense of it, Mike. Why conduct an experiment if one already knows the outcome? Since the Big has free movement through your time, he can always know an outcome if he chooses to know it. He could control every aspect of human life, but he chooses not to do so. His interventions are relatively few. What the Big has the power to do, he has the power not to do."

"Why?" I asked.

"Why indeed," Tree replied. "It is what it is."

It remained in my nature, I suppose, to ask one question too many. It was worth a shot. "So, Tree is there any light that you could shed on where humans are headed … on what will happen to us?"

Tree answered, "Let's see. We could talk about global warming and the great continental fires, or nuclear weapons, or the collapse of Pennsylvania and West Virginia into a great hole that sucked Ohio down with it and caused earth to wobble toward the sun, or the invasion by aliens dressed as cocker spaniels."

"O.K., Tree. I got it. You are not telling me."

"That is correct. Did you learn nothing from the football discussion? Don't ponder the future. Keep your head in the day. That is the start of living smaller, Mike. It is an easy and obvious way for taking the bads out of your existence and making room in the middle of you for the good that makes you joyful. Live in a small time, not a big time. Live in the day, not the day before or the day after, or the year, or the lifetime. Your stage must be set in the same time unit that the earth dictates, because the rewards of living smaller, which we will discuss, are unlikely to materialize if you choose to live outside the day."

The concept of living one day at a time was familiar to me, you may recall, because I hunkered down to live this way as a caregiver in a dispiriting situation. Even then, it was very difficult to tether my galloping brain to one day. And I was at least vaguely aware that mine was a survival application of a broader concept. I asked, "How am I doing, Tree, as you see it, in living in the day?"

Tree plunged ahead as if he had expected my question, "Let me ask you some questions, Mike. In a typical day, do you spend some of your time troubling about the past, whether a bad memory from the past or an error from yesterday that might indicate that you are less than perfect?"

"Well," I began.

But Tree interrupted, "You don't need to respond. I know the answers to these questions."

Then, he continued, "Do you spend significant time, in a day, pondering the future? How much of this time is planning, which might be productive, versus worry that is useless and brings you down? How much of the unproductive time pondering the future involves events, people, or circumstances over which you actually have no control? Is your mind more easily drawn to worry than to gratitude? What expressions are on your face when you ponder either the past or the future?"

Tree paused briefly between each of the questions, and it was apparent that we would not be dealing with these questions if my score on the answers was a good one. Uncomfort enveloped me, and I said, "Am I worse at this than most other humans? Other people live in the past. Other humans worry; other humans plan ahead."

"Yes."

"What do you mean, yes?"

"Yes, you are worse."

"Oh." I have never liked the word "worse" when applied to me, and I queried, "Is that really such a bad thing?"

"Yes."

"Oh. So what do I do to improve myself here?"

"You make improvement an important goal for yourself. Daily. To live in the day and value the day. Behavior is goal directed, so that over time the change in the middle of you will be accomplished.

"Mike, treat the start of the day as if it is the start of a new life, and attempt to value it as such. At the end of the day, work hard to be thinking about the day. After a while, the middle will follow along. Your mental departures from the day will lessen."

"What about planning, Tree? You know that I spent years teaching and training managers about the importance of planning. Organizations and people must think ahead."

"Certainly, many humans are determined to do this," Tree replied. "You may need to allow time in some days for planning, but be jealous of time spent planning. Do it, know that you are doing it, and then push yourself to let go of it and move back to the day."

"But if I let go of it, what if I forget about it in the future, as a guide to what I do?"

"We are talking about <u>you</u>, Mike. Little chance that you will forget the plan. It is much more likely that you will obsess over it, day after day."

"Also, Tree, in a fast-paced and rapidly-changing world, it is really difficult to separate out the time frame of today," I offered professionally.

"You can do this, Mike. Deal with a day's worth of change, today. A day's worth of trouble. A day's worth of serendipity. Any more than a day's worth is unnecessary and brings you down."

"You know Tree, I live a good life now, at least compared to most of my past life. And I am accustomed to it. Is fundamental change in how I operate really going to make me better, or happier?"

"Yes. You don't know what a happier life feels like because you have never been there. As you come to realize a day as if it were a life, you will know that you are making progress, for example, when you begin to see wonders of the first time."

"What do you mean?"

"Do you remember the wonder you felt the first time that you saw the ocean, or a big city, or a picture of the universe? Or the first time that you hit a home run, or caught a touchdown pass, or fell in love, or accomplished something that once seemed impossible?"

"Yes," I mumbled, "the first time only happens once. It is special."

"It only happens once until you begin to value a day as a lifetime. The wonder of the first time happens again and again. It will be impossible not to experience this happiness."

"Meanwhile, you will need to trust me on this." He anticipated my thought, "because I am bigger than you. Living out of control, and into the day, sets you on the path that you need to follow.

"This is not for me, Mike. It is for you. You can live the rest of your life the hard way or the easy way.

"Let us move on, because your progress here allows you to remove negatives from your life, but this is not guaranteed. There is much to think about and do. Are you still with me?"

"Yes." I replied, more certainly than I felt. Tree had a pull to him, so that I did not consider opposition to where he was taking me. This is difficult to describe, and I didn't truly appreciate the strength of this magnetism until looking back on these conversations.

"There are emotions and feelings in humans," Tree began, "which drag them down. Great benefits will accrue to you in your future days as you remove from your middle these forces that make your life uncomfortable. This conversation begins with fear, and its cousins anxiety and worry. You had occasion to focus on these topics in your career, which is unusual for an economist or anyone besides a psychologist or psychiatrist, correct?"

"Yes," I said, "in my couple of decades as a management trainer and team builder, individuals and small groups would sometimes discuss such topics. I learned enough to likely be dangerous, but it was my job to facilitate discussion, not to teach anti-anxiety techniques or diagnose worry maniacs."

"And tell me the difference between fear and anxiety," said Tree.

"But you already know the answer."

"True, but it will freshen your focus to speak some of what you know, before we talk about you."

I was not enthusiastic about applying any of these topics to me, as theoretical discussions were much easier, but I dutifully began with the basics, "Fear is located in the present. If a bear is chasing me down Ridge Road, I feel fear of a very negative outcome. Anxiety is a more generalized, negative feeling about some threat or discomfort perceived in the future.

"Modern man has carried more fear into our days than is necessary. Bears don't chase us very often anymore, at least not around here. Modern life also means large and growing problems of anxiety, which afflict many of us. Anxiety disorders are epidemic in developed countries. But there are still plenty of humans who live in daily fear, of starvation for starters."

"So, in your 62 years on earth, Mike, how many times have you discussed your fears and anxieties with another human?"

"It would depend on the particular fear we are talking about, but fear and anxiety discussions are not common among men from my experience. We largely pretend it is not there. At least I came to know at some point that instead of being fearless, there was fear and anxiety spread all over me."

"But you nevertheless have not talked about it with others very often?"

"Only about fragments, probably in small doses, and likely by happenstance," I admitted.

"Then let us talk about fears or persistent anxieties that have troubled you," Tree directed.

"Tree, you already know everything about me...."

"That is true, but you do not know everything about you, so pick a fear."

"Well," I began, "probably the easiest for me to talk about is one that I first remember. Cows. I have a fear of cows. Or perhaps, more accurately, a persistent anxiety about cow situations that might confront me in the future."

"Just to clarify, it is cows, not bulls?" asked Tree.

"Yes, cows, dairy cows."

"And it is not fear of a herd of dairy cows on the side of a country road but of being alone with one cow in a closed barn, right?" Tree inquired.

"Yes, a mean cow. I have never thought that all cows are evil." Just as it was occurring to me that Tree had become a psychiatrist, Tree said,

"At the risk of sounding like a psychiatrist, tell me the story of the grandfather and the mean cow."

Sigh. One had to assume Tree knew what he was doing. "I was around age four, I think, and we were on a visit to my grandparent's small farm in Jonesborough. East Tennessee. More specifically, there was a barn, primarily used to hang and dry out tobacco – the cash crop for a retired county road commissioner. The barn contained one milk cow, unless the cow was out in a small pasture. I had watched my grandfather milk the cow several times.

"At some point in the visit, I freed myself from supervision, walked around the hog pen, and for whatever reason, entered the barn. Perhaps I had some vague sense that I did not have permission to be in the barn alone but did not recall hearing a specific prohibition in that regard. I had not been specifically prohibited, either, from standing in the middle of the highway. Parents can't cover everything, and kids can do foolish things.

"I did remember to latch the barn door shut, because that instruction had been given to me and was, in fact, my only known duty while in the barn. It was dark in the barn, with little light filtering through the cracks in the walls on an overcast afternoon. I walked many, tentative steps into the barn while my eyes adjusted to the dimness, and then I saw the cow. Standing faced toward me, untethered, less than eight feet away was the cow."

Tree was allowing this monologue, so I finished, "Tree, it wasn't just a cow. It was a big, mean cow. Its face looked, well, really mean, and its hostility was aimed at me. Tree, I'll never forget the big, dark, piercing eyes of the mean cow. In that moment, it became clear that the cow intended to kill me, a hapless four-year-old boy in the wrong place at the wrong time.

"To my credit, I did not choose either of the first two options of the freeze, fight, or flight options in a fearful situation. Fighting the cow, of course, was impossible. Freezing was out, as the cow had already seen her victim. There was no time to run out of the barn door after unlatching it, as even a slow cow would have been well along in devouring me as I raised the latch. But there was a ladder ten feet to my side, which extended to a small loft. Somehow, I made it to the 7th or 8th rung of that ladder before the cow could react to my surprising speed and kill me in whatever manner that dairy cows typically kill small humans. There was little time for such analysis, but the cow did not attempt to climb the ladder. The standoff continued for an eternity of a few minutes until the startled grandfather rescued the wailing grandson from the murderous cow."

"My view of cows has never been the same. It took years for the nightmare of the mean cow to dissipate. Anytime that I was particularly close to a cow – at a county fair, for example - my heart would race, I would sweat, my throat would constrict."

Tree interjected, "What has happened to you when you have walked into a barn, since the mean cow incident?"

"Nothing, because I have not walked into a barn since then."

"Never?"

"Never. Believe me, I would remember. Why would I voluntarily walk into a barn knowing that a mean cow might be in there waiting for me? One should learn from his experiences. The next time, there might not be a ladder. And no one, not even the Army, ever required me thereafter to walk into a barn. The really good news, also, is that it is almost impossible to wander into a barn by accident. One would almost deserve to be cowed to death."

"Your continuing strategy, I gather then, is to simply avoid barns, and thereby mean cows in barns, through your remaining days?"

"Yes, Tree." I said confidently, "Avoidance. That is my strategy. It has worked so far. I am almost never burdened by my mean-cow-in-a-barn fear. It is simply not happening a second time."

"So, in your reading about fear, is that what the experts say to do... avoid?"

"Of course not. You and I both know the textbook answer is to face one's fear, examine it, yada yada."

"But that doesn't apply to you and the mean cow?"

"No, this is a situation easily avoided in the normal course of my remaining life. There is no need to face it. My sincere belief is that confronting this fear will not make me a better person."

Tree paused for what seemed to be a minute. "Mike, you need to find the opportunity for some time alone with a cow in a barn. This is not even your most fearsome fear."

Rather than make a firm commitment to a cow encounter, I again attempted a deflection. "What is surprising about my childhood period is that fear and anxiety about a nuclear annihilation were apparently less of a problem for me than was the fear of cows. I was still in elementary school during the Cuban missile crisis and living in the U.S. rocket city. The possibility of a nuclear war was so fearsomely awesome that I think it froze us into acting as if the threat was not there, or at least that it could be ignored in daily life. Some argue that applies to climate change today."

Tree did not respond to the diversion but did allow us to move on. "Talk about another fear, in your top three fears," he prompted.

"I really don't want to do that, Tree, because future avoidance is even more important for the next one." Yet, I proceeded because, once again, he was basically the one in charge. "Height. I am very much afraid of height."

"And narrow that down a bit," Tree suggested.

After a moment of thought, I responded, "Not afraid of airplane height or in any way of air travel. But I am terrified at the thought of ferris wheel height, and I would very reluctantly look down from a building, even a one-story building. The primary reason for my dislike of horseback riding is that horses are too tall. I could probably do a Shetland pony but that would really look stupid."

Tree asked, "How did you manage to survive military training?" He knew that I had wondered about that myself.

"Beats me," I replied, "so much of the confidence courses had to do with jumping off, sliding, or rappelling down from high places. I think my survival had a lot to do with the fact that the Army really didn't give me much of a choice."

I mused, "If the confidence course had instead emphasized crawling through small spaces, possibly snake infested, I would have been at much less of a disadvantage."

"Really?" Tree asked.

"O.K., probably not. I am also afraid of snakes." Then, I said, "I was about to say that the origin of this phobia is unknown to me, but, as I think about the cow incident, I can recall my horror at realizing how far up the ladder that I had climbed, beyond the cow's reach. My grandfather had to climb up and uncling me from the rungs onto which I had frozen.

"Tree, maybe that is the source of this lifelong fear of height."

"Then if you can get past the cow problem, within a year or so, you could be in a sky-diving club," Tree offered.

"Very funny," I muttered.

"When you actually did these height-related challenges in the Army, did it not boost your confidence regarding height issues in the future?"

"Not one bit. The facing-your-fears stuff is much overdone. And, like cows in barns, avoidance throughout my remaining lifetime seems to be a good option. My mind and spirit are not dragged down by my fear of height when leading a life unlikely to require climbing, jumping, or floating."

For whatever reason, Tree moved on, "Ok, Mike, now talk to me about the third one." No reason existed for me to say, therefore, that the third one was fear of failure. Tree sometimes skipped steps in a conversation when in pursuit of a point.

"Sometime in my thirties," I began, "my lifelong fear of failure became apparent to me, and I have thought about it since. Not obsessively, I think, but from time to time. It has been a part of me since my earliest recollection about school and organized sports. And it was extreme. I was, or I became, a perfectionist. Any chance of a significant mistake, or of being #2 in anything when #1 was possible, produced fear and anxiety in me. The anxiety of not being a star player if anyone else my age was a star player is a feeling that I can remember. In academics, I found a place to be #1, or close. That, and student politics, sustained me through college and workaholism also helped in an early, successful career.

"But everyone fails, and in retrospect, I am unsure if the occurrences of failures or less-than-perfection performance were as troublesome as the persistent anxiety about the future. Also Tree I don't know the origin of this fear of failure problem. There is no memory of pressure from parents, for example."

"Except for your fear of reading in public," Tree interjected, "with that example of your fear, you came to know an origin, correct?"

"Yes." This topic from the past had certainly not been anticipated.

"Then talk to me about reading in public," Tree instructed.

"By sometime in junior high school," I began, "it was apparent to me that reading in public, notably in a classroom, was a frightening event. When called upon to do so, I stumbled haltingly through the task, while my heartbeat raced, I began to sweat, and my throat constricted. Particularly perplexing was that no such problem occurred when I simply spoke in public, whether in class discussions or in front of a group. In fact, speaking in public was central to my career.

"In high school and college, I would go to great lengths in avoiding public reading. This included the memorization of passages that could be said in public under the guise of being read. Speaking with notes or from an outline also did not seem to bother me, only reading. Avoidance of this problem became a persistent concern for me, but ad hoc occurrences could, and did, occur. My physical reaction to the situations did not improve.

"As it happened, I attended a high school class reunion and was in a conversation with a female classmate, who was almost always in common classes with me from elementary through high school. I cannot remember how the topic originated, but she asked me if I remembered a particular teacher from elementary school. The teacher had us alternatingly read passages from books, and she criticized us - sometimes made fun of us - for our mistakes made in reading. Since then, my classmate said, she had been unable to read in public.

"I did not remember this teacher or these experiences. Perhaps it had been blocked from my memory. I can remember being truly wide-eyed at that revelation. It explained, at least to my satisfaction, my lifelong trouble with public reading."

"But this awareness did not make the problem disappear for you." Tree stated.

"No, I learned quickly that the same physical symptoms continued to make such events frightening. So, my anxiety over future events did not diminish much."

"Yet, you now freely read in public. That trouble is of the past, true?"

"Yes, I believe so." And, anticipating where Tree was headed, I continued, "There came a time when I found myself in a safe, small group, where I ultimately shared this puzzling difficulty. Later, in the group, I began to read. The negative reactions and feelings simply left me, and this change transferred to other public settings."

"Somewhere in that story is a lesson for you," Tree noted. "Would you not agree?"

"Yes, I replied, knowing that any such lesson would be unlikely to stretch into my riding a horse, for example.

Tree asked, "And you would agree that we are only talking about fears and anxieties that you know about. There could be others?"

"That is, of course, possible," I agreed.

"How do you think you are doing in dealing with fears of failure and imperfection, or your level of daily anxiety, in general?" Tree asked.

"I actually believe that good progress is being made. One reason may simply be aging. But toward the end of my professional career, opportunities for public failure will begin to drop off quickly, and that will be a happy outcome of retirement, I think."

Tree pressed forward, "Talk to me for a few minutes about you and worry."

He knew the answers but, again, I complied. "My father was a Hall of Fame worrier. I got that from him. Genetics or environment, whatever, I have carefully planned for the future but worried a lot too. Sometimes it felt as if I could not have a good day. If it was a bad day, it was a bad day. If it was a good day, I spent much of my time worrying about bad possibilities in future days… and it was also a bad day."

Tree returned to a self-assessment, "Do you perceive that your level of worry is staying about the same, increasing, decreasing?" I paused for too long and Tree added, "What would your wife say if I hypothetically asked her that question about you?"

I smiled. That answer was easier. "She would laugh at me if I suggested that my worry level had significantly diminished. My own rating would give me some progress."

It is my belief that Tree chuckled at this comment. It was an eerie sound but akin to his belly laugh. "There is really good news for you here, Mike. You still have plenty of room for improvement in moving fear and anxiety and worry out of yourself."

That is very good news," I said without conviction. "So, you are saying I have things to do, changes to make, actions to take?"

"Yes, it would be wonderful for you. And it all fits together, by the way. It begins by living smaller, out of control and into the day. This is a good start to driving away fear, anxiety and worry. Opportunities will arise for you to practice removing these troubles as the troubles of life nevertheless occur. We can both watch you apply yourself here over the next while."

Then, Tree transitioned once again, "While we are discussing negatives which bring you down, let us discuss anger, and its brother resentment. You have the same background definitions and basics as you did with fear, am I correct?"

"That is correct, Tree. Related to training and working with small groups and teams. It has also been many years ago, and I have never been an expert on the subjects."

"Remind yourself of what you know," required the Tree.

"Anger is a negative, intense, and uncomfortable emotion which is a response to a perceived threat or hurt. A resentment links to both fear and anger and is a strong indignation at unfair treatment – of oneself or others. Some call resentments refried anger, and they may go on forever.

"Anger is a common emotion among humans but becomes harmful when it is too great or too frequent. It triggers facial expressions which are not pleasant, physiological responses that are not good for the body. I recall that, unlike fear, anger doesn't improve the ability to respond to a problem but decreases effective thinking. Anger can be passive, like evasiveness, or aggressive, like bullying and selfishness. In the extreme, it can become rage and can lead to violent and criminal conduct. Suppressed anger, under the surface, may also be very destructive for a human.

"I remember about resentments that they hurt the resenter, who feels them, but rarely disturb the resented. The person resented generally could care less and, thus, this downer has zero helpful purpose. Yet everyone, they say, has resentments."

"Let's talk about the survey that you took a few days ago," Tree said.

I should have seen this coming. Sometime recently, I had been read-ing an article about anger in men. Perhaps it was a scientific journal article or one of those state-of-the-art health magazines that one reads in doctors' or dentists' offices. "You didn't, by any chance, set me up with that anger diagnostic survey, did you Tree?" I thought.

It had not been my intention to discuss these survey results with anyone, or with Tree. "The survey was a long listing of possible situations in life, which the reader would rank 1 through 5 as to anger that would result – 1 for "very little" to 5 for "very much." So, there was a pencil handy and I actually took the assessment and added up my score. The many situations seemed obviously tilted to 4 and 5 responses and, indeed, my responses were 4's and 5's… mostly 5's. Then I looked up my total score in the interpretation section."

"And what did that tell you?" Tree encouraged.

"It had cut-off scores diagnosing the degree of one's anger problem. If you were above the top cut-off score, it basically said that you were a danger to yourself and others and needed to turn yourself in at the nearest correctional facility or psychiatric emergency room."

Tree interjected, "Your score was noticeably above the top cut-off score. The look on your face when you realized that was priceless." Tree seemed to begin a low-grade laugh, somewhere between his odd belly laugh and a mere chuckle. "So again, what did it tell you?"

"It suggested, of course, that the survey was for amusement only, probably never tested for validity, not peer reviewed in scientific journals. Low scores by readers, of course, would discourage further reading. I and other readers had been set up for a false, or at least highly exaggerated, revelation. Having said that, all of those 4's and 5's left me unsettled."

"Your surprise," said Tree, "was because you do not believe that you have a significant problem with anger issues, or resentments. Is that correct?"

"I certainly believe that I have worked through some anger issues. I don't feel angry very often. Yes, you are basically correct that anger doesn't seem to be a problem for me."

"Do you remember any of the situations used in the survey?" Tree asked. "Do you remember the one about being in a ticket line and someone cuts in front of you?"

"Yes."

"And you responded with a 5?"

"Yes, only because I couldn't respond with a 6. Everyone would put 5 on that one," I insisted.

"Mike, you not only put a 5. You also know that you would be the most likely person in the line to say something to the line-breaker."

"That is true, Tree, but that one is a particular pet peeve of mine," I defended.

Tree continued, "Then there was the one – you are seated in a restaurant, 15 minutes pass, and you still don't have service or a glass of water. And you did another 5, correct?"

"I'm sure you are correct. Fifteen minutes is a long time, Tree. Again, most people would say 4 or 5."

"You don't believe that some people are moderately angry 3's or others were actually enjoying their conversation and are, at most, an annoyed 2?" Tree asked.

"Maybe," I answered, "some people are ridiculously patient."

Tree said, "And when you are around such people, Mike, you often feel angry, don't you?"

"Well, yes."

Tree continued, "There was the one about being in a dispute with someone, who calls you a stupid jerk. Again you are a 5?"

"And again, most people are a 5. I couldn't possibly be any angrier than the average man."

"Mike, did you know some people would actually laugh at being called a jerk…"

"It's the 'stupid' that makes me mad," I interjected, "the 'jerk' would only reach 3 or 4 because it is entirely possible that the person could be correct about that one."

Tree continued, "or ignore the remark, or walk away."

"Well those other people are not me, Tree." And then I grimaced at myself for contributing to the point he was attempting to make.

"Then, the one about you unpack a gadget just purchased and it doesn't work. Another 5."

"I could probably have gone to a 4 on that one. No product is 100% reliable."

"But 4 is much anger."

"Yes."

"Let's talk about some of the driving-an-automobile situations. Those made you so angry that you placed a 5 on the next item because you were still mad about the driving one… every time."

It wasn't clear if that comment was true or was a small joke, but he did not stop, "The one about you are driving at 50 mph, exactly the speed limit, in a no-passing zone and the car behind you is right on your bumper. A 5."

"That is actually dangerous, Tree, so it is a bit of righteous anger."

"But, Mike, you are most likely to be the one on the other person's bumper."

I sighed, "I was a 5 on all the driving ones, I think."

Yet Tree was not finished with examples. "You accidently make a wrong turn in an unfamiliar parking lot and someone yells, 'Where did you learn to drive?'"

"Of course, that would make me really angry."

"Even if you realized your mistake?"

"Yes."

"Some people, Mike, would laugh at themselves, or shout or signal an apology, or simply be more anxious about their confusion than angry about the remark. Or, they might shout out 'Nebraska' or 'South Dakota' in response."

I made no comment.

Tree moved on, "Mike, you had zero 3 or less responses. Don't you think that is odd?"

"As I said, the questions were biased toward angry responses."

"Then let me move beyond the survey. Speaking of driving, you commonly – to your credit, Mike – allow cars to merge or turn off a side street in front of you, when to do otherwise would force the driver to wait on someone else to be kind and generous."

"Yes, I do that."

"But then you expect them to wave a thank you at you for your kindness, correct?"

"Yes."

"When they don't wave, you are angry, correct?"

"Yes, I get over it, but this at least momentarily angers me."

"Partially because you always wave at the kind person."

"Yes, always. 100 percent of the time. My father taught me that by example."

"And from your experience, Mike, what percentage of other persons wave a thank you when you are kind to them?"

"Maybe 20 percent." I could feel my jaw tighten. "Higher outside of urban centers and in the south, generally."

"So, you continue to let drivers in front of you and 80 percent of the time, you are rendered angry?"

"Yes."

"And has this 2 of 10 become lower over the years?"

"Not really."

"Does it make you just as mad today as it did 10 or 20 or 40 years ago?"

"Probably. I can't help it. I wish when they didn't wave thanks, I could at least put them back where they were before my charity."

"The 2 of 10. Do they make you smile?"

"Not particularly, but there might be a flicker of appreciation that someone did something that I do all the time."

"Have you ever expressed anger at inanimate objects? Thrown things at television sets during athletic contests? Whacked some part of a personal computer when you can't accomplish an e-task, or because it is too slow?"

"Yes, you know I have done such things, but I think actual aggression has diminished over time."

"The last time you whacked a computer was yesterday, Mike."

"It was just a tap, but it made me feel better," I replied. This line of questioning was making me uncomfortable, but Tree had one more example.

"Mike," he began, "am I correct that you unconsciously make up, and play out, vignettes in your head of persons that you know, or don't know, doing things that make you angry, so that when you realize consciously that such an episode is occurring, you end the scenario angry. In other words, Mike, when there is not enough anger around you anyway you are capable of manufacturing imaginary anger?"

"Yes, that happens, but not often."

"And usually associated with extreme stress?"

"Probably," I guessed.

"Do you think average persons, or average men, do this?"

"I have no idea." Then, I added, "Ok, Tree, I am slowly perceiving here that you believe I have a much bigger problem with anger than might have previously occurred to me."

He didn't comment. He simply began to laugh. That is rude, of course, but in fairness to Tree, he apparently could not hold it back any longer. It was a hearty laugh in the indescribable range of his laughing sounds. That also made me angry, but in my consternation and indignation, I began to laugh too. Laughing at oneself is a good thing even if the journey there is long and circuitous.

When Tree stopped laughing, he said, "The middle of you is packed with stored-up anger and while your rate of packing away anger has slowed in recent years, you are still a net packer… adding to your own misery. Mike, do you remember the day in elementary school when you came in second in the voting for head patrol boy?"

"Yes, now that you remind me," I replied.

"Do you know why you remember, Mike?"

"No."

"Because you can't let it go. It made you angry then, and it makes you angry now. You resented the guy who won the vote all through school. You played football with him but never liked him. Yet, you never said a word about it to him, not then, not ever. Mike, it was head patrol boy, not even senior class president, although that is another example."

"My remembrance of this is that he voted for himself. I couldn't get past that."

"But, Mike, you also voted for yourself, correct?"

"I don't remember. OK, allow me to assume that anger is a more significant problem for me than heretofore imagined. Is there anything that I can really do about it?"

"Yes."

"And doing something will cause me to live a sufficiently more comfortable life that would make any pain of changing worth it?"

"Yes," Tree insisted. "Mike your middle needs to shed anger and unpack it. You could not hold so much anger without fear in there too and that much anger means accompanying resentments. There is much good to fill the space in your middle as you drive out the negatives. The day brings a day's worth of trouble, but you needlessly carry so much more."

Tree added, "Mike, if it were not worth it to you to change, would I have brought this discussion to you? You must trust me on this because…"

"You are bigger than me," I finished, and smiled at Tree. It was true, though, I did trust him. "Just for the sake of discussion, what would you suggest that I do Tree about all this anger that I allegedly have?"

Tree paused briefly and then said, "You must live life each day without adding to your store of anger and, at the same time, you must begin to unpack what is there. Some of these changes may not be easy for you, Mike. You will need to stop driving automobiles except in emergencies. When riding with others, you will need to wear a blindfold and keep your mouth shut if possible. It may be best for everyone if you mostly stay at home. And when you are at home, you can't watch football on television… probably no sports but certainly not football. You can't watch news shows, either. You will need to stay away from news."

The football comment froze my pacemaker for a few seconds. I should have known better, but it was, again, how he said the words matter-of-factly. No hint of exaggeration. My mouth could not have formed words if my brain could have delivered any. After a frightening pause, he did, indeed, chuckle in his odd way, and I relaxed, tentatively.

"That's where you are headed if you can't find some perhaps less extreme measures to make progress here. So, calm yourself. You are not that important. Stop taking yourself so seriously. What you are angry about is either currently unimportant or likely uncontrollable. You are a smart guy, Mike. Do something, learn how to meditate, something. And you need to begin to work on driving immediately because you are a mess on the roads."

The discussion was wearing me out. Before I could focus on the picture of change in front of me, however, Tree encouraged me.

"All you do toward your fear and anxiety troubles also drives out anger. All of the living small in your middle, out of control, being careful with expectations, in the day… all of your improvements here will also help you shed new anger and resentments.

"As for the unpacking," Tree continued, "there is much to do. You will need to spend some time finding what is there and releasing it. You can do this, Mike."

He continued, "In that anger assessment article, do you remember the four characteristics of angry men?"

"Yes, that was also unsettling to me: perfectionism, excessive competitiveness, difficulty adapting to change, and … ah …"

"Difficulty relaxing," Tree helped.

"Yes, and we both know, Tree, these are primary characteristics of me. It is feeling burdensome to behold all of this," I said.

"I point them out to give you four other areas of work which also help you avoid this burden of troubles. They are also measures of your progress."

"And how much time will it take me to make progress in all of these things we have talked about?"

"You are the expert here. What is the life expectancy of a USA male at age 62?"

"To age 82 or so," I replied.

"That should be just enough time," Tree said.

CHAPTER EIGHT –
GROWTH

It was early August of 2013, before football season, and Teddi Rose and I were on the porch. The temperature was a mild 82 in early evening. Sunset approached soon. The ladies would not return from a Michigan trip until morning and combined with the nice weather, it was great porch time.

My thinker was hyperactive and wide-ranging on this particular evening. I can remember obsessing, again, about directions in the mountains of Charleston. For my many years of residency, east often seemed as if it should be west, and vice versa, and north seemed as if it should be south, and vice versa. When our local TV personalities placed a map of Charleston, properly oriented toward the north, before the camera, it made sense to me. But I could neither see it or feel it on the ground, as I now looked directly west, where the sun would set, to the right of the direction of the road down the ridge. I could not reconcile the screen with the ground, which is frustrating.

It is also unnerving. You may recall that I was trained as a field artillery officer. One of the most important lessons from my training at

Fort Sill is that, regardless of the particular type of artillery piece under consideration, it is important that one points it in the proper direction. And I could not feel the directions of my own small city. An overlooked serendipity of American history is that the U.S. government chose not to send me into combat.

As was usual, my thoughts turned to Tree. Only one conversation between Tree and me had occurred on the porch since the fear and anger discussion. It was a quiet, checking-in-with-you visit from early summer. I had more-or-less agreed to address several enhancements to myself, and it was clear to me that I was being watched. Even in a couple of months, I felt, some progress was being made.

A first priority for me, thanks to Tree's less-than-subtle feedback, was anger. Within that category, it was anger while driving. Tree's implied threat of taking away my driving privileges made an impression on me, and it did not seem farfetched that he could do so, one way or another. My first impulse upon addressing the topic was bookstore-and-internet research. Plenty of material on aggressive driving and road rage was available.

There were more survey and other questions about self to address. I knew that Tree would remember every single one of them. First, though, it was troublesome that the most likely raging drivers were male teenagers or persons with certain psychological disorders. Great, I thought, either I'm a male teenager who never grew up and/or I currently have a mental disorder – my self-advice was to not pursue exactly what type of psychological disorder(s) disturbed me.

The unnamed icons of this subject matter also suggested that aggressive driving was most likely to turn into road rage if the individual was under stress in other areas of life. Duh! Was some young academic person promoted or tenured as a result of this breathtaking research?

My mumbled responses to various diagnostic questions reinforced my notion that if this is a problem area for me, it is a non-severe problem. For example, did I honk the horn often? It depends on what is meant by the word "often." Not every day. On the other hand, there are fewer horn-worthy events every day in Charleston versus, say, Manhattan. Important, I thought, is that most of my honks are instructional in nature. They are intended to help fellow drivers realize that the light had recently turned green, or to understand the meaning of a yield sign, or to remember that the left lane was created to be a relatively fast-moving passing lane. Moreover, my occasional honks were a quick tap on the horn. Rarely would I engage in a substantial, full-throated honk, and this likely resulted from unusual stress in some other area of my life.

Do I tailgate or flash my lights at a driver in front of me who I believe is driving too slowly? Rarely, but, yes, sometimes. Of course, most of the time it is possible to pass such a driver in a reasonably short time, and I am not so obnoxious as to honk and pass just to make a statement about slow driving. Unless I am under unusual stress in some other area of my life. Thus, the drivers at whom I honk are simply being reminded that a colleague driver wishes to go faster than 12 miles per hour, and, in this sense, is also instructional in nature. Any self-restraint with such honks came from embarrassments in the past when the person being passed was a neighbor, friend, boss, etc. This is one of many reasons for avoiding eye contact with other drivers.

Do I regularly drive over the speed limit or try to beat red lights? No. Not regularly. First, 3-5 mph over the speed limit is an enforcement limit, after which one becomes increasingly likely to be pulled over. It is assumed, therefore, that speed limit, for these purposes, really means 5mph greater than the posted speed limit. Secondly, my belief in having exceptionally bad luck is intense. My assumption is that when I disobey a traffic law, my car is disproportionately likely to be pulled over. When stopped at a traffic light, at the bottom of a long hill leading toward my house, I will take my high-performance automobile from 0-55 mph in a few seconds, then tap the brakes lightly and continue up the long grade at 55 mph, the enforcement speed limit. It gives me pleasure to look in my rearview mirror at the gaggle of drivers left far behind. I don't know why. Indeed, it seems odd to me that the other drivers of high-performance vehicles don't do what I do when driving from the river up the hill toward home.

Finally, do I ever use obscene gestures or otherwise communicate angrily? Fortunately, obscene gestures don't include throwing up both hands in a "Where did you learn to drive" gesture. Angry language was commonly spoken for no apparent reason, since I usually did not have a passenger and the offending driver could not hear my instructional suggestions or rhetorical questions. This one made me feel badly, however. It was embarrassing, even when unusual stress existed elsewhere in my life. Yes, I might have a problem.

On a brighter note, there were questions about the quality of my driving, as I might stimulate aggression from other people like me. My self-assessment was that my own driving was darn near award-winning. Then, there was a three-day period of two testimonies in two different cities that were close enough for driving to be the sensible transportation.

Driving into the first medium-size city after dark, it occurred to me that one piece of technology that I really liked was the invisible lady who talked me through directions from the interstate highway to my hotel. The problem for me was that I do not see well at night and, in particular, have a difficult time reading street signs to verify the invisible lady's directions are being followed. Particularly at intersections, I would necessarily slow down before either turning or proceeding. With light downtown traffic, this was not a large problem. The large problem was the burly, late-teens guy driving behind me in a souped up, jacked up silver truck. For some reason, he was heading where I was heading, but he apparently did not need help from the invisible lady.

Then, I made the mistake of initiating eye contact with the young man via my rearview mirror. His facial expression indicated that he found me and my vehicle to be troubling.

It was clear to me that this young man had one or more psychological issues and therefore fit the profile for an angry road rager. As predicted, this stranger stayed on my bumper as I periodically slowed, and he gunned his mammoth engine. It was difficult hearing what he was saying, but he likely did not represent the local chamber of commerce welcoming me to town. Finally, he roared around me, and I could more easily hear "old" in the list of descriptors which he shouted at me. A bit ruffled, I proceeded to the hotel wondering about this hostile treatment. But it could not be denied. I saw me in the eyes of that angry young man, and it was not attractive.

Two days later, in the Queen City, my testimony was completed in the early afternoon of a sunny, summer day. Upon exiting the downtown parking lot, I was confronted, perhaps for the first time, with a machine showing and talking to me about how to pay and exit. This newest replacement of humans with technology both repulsed and terrorized me. The glare from the sunlight made the directions on the screen difficult to read. I did a couple of erroneous insertions, then I dropped my credit card and, as I opened the door to reach the insertion point, the same, basic mistake was again made. Eye contact. I made eye contact with the driver of the car behind me, who had been watching me. He was a thirtyish, well dressed, professional type, driving a red BMW convertible, top down, who struck me as having the unjustified arrogance of a young trial lawyer. Without malice of expression, and in a calm voice, he said to me, "Why don't you go back to Mayberry?"

The gate opened and I drove away. Didn't see that one coming. The guy would only have known about Mayberry and The Andy Griffith Show via reruns, whereas I had watched in real time. No one in Mayberry – the mythical, not-very-diverse town in the North Carolina hills -- ever drove a high-performance vehicle of the type that I was driving. This guy was another angry man, probably under unusual stress in some other area of his life, who seemingly enjoyed making a comment that was unnecessary and disrespectful. It made me feel a bit better knowing that I had never done anything like that. At least not exactly like that.

Driving home, I resolved to try two suggestions gleaned from somewhere, and a month or so of early efforts had since ensued. The first was the use of a pause, at the beginning and the end of each driving event. It could be brief and mental-only, obviously, when others were with me. The pauses were about awareness, because the first step toward solving a problem is to be aware that it exists. I know that much from my trainer days and had coincidently been interested in the effective use of pauses. So, the goal was to somehow focus upon each driving event as an opportunity to improve my attitude and behavior. It also would help my ability to focus on the act of driving per se, as my mind tended to wander away from the driving task.

An important question becomes what one says or thinks to oneself during the intro and ending pauses. Is the pre-driving pause simply a reminder of the problem, or does it become a pep talk of sorts? My first inclination for a pep talk was, "There are people out there who would kill you. Be careful and drive defensively." Reluctantly I realized that such a pause would do nothing to address my own anger problem while on the road. My intro had morphed into something like, "This driving event will be a test. Chill out. Do not drive aggressively or react angrily to those who do. Find a way to make peace, not war, with other drivers." It was a work in progress, and I had already realized that this pause did not include those persons, not driving, who designed highway and street repair and construction projects without thinking of me first. The drive-ending pause was a quick debriefing pause to reflect upon the completed driving episode. It could be a simple, "Good job," if angry and aggressive driving had been avoided.

My fundamental difficulty with pause-related improvement was remembering to pause. I was a busy man, after all, with much to occupy my mind. My first day was one pause (before drive 1) out of eight pause opportunities in that day, which was only realized the next morning. Change was not easy for me, and I was now an old dog attempting to learn new tricks.

The other idea, when a triggering event occurred, was re-framing, a skill that women as a group had learned long before men, from my observation. The goal was to quickly re-frame an event as a different event or, even better, as an event with a story behind it. I had successfully reframed one construction zone, for example, as if I were an undercover supervisor counting how many persons were working versus not working. The count was pleasantly surprising, although I almost ran over one of the supervisors while counting. He dropped his doughnut. Unfortunately, there was a second construction zone on the same trip, and my mind did not successfully re-frame the second delay which stretched before me.

Reframing with a story had also been attempted a few times. It held some promise, but it wasn't clear to me that these attempts at diverting my own anger were entirely healthy. On my third morning, after an intro pause, I was driving to an early meeting on the interstate around the north side of the city, minding my own business and observing the enforcement speed limit.

The southbound lane dumped traffic into the left of my lane, and a southbound driver would need to maneuver rightward across two lanes to take the first exit. Lots of interstates were bottlenecking through a narrow river valley in the mountains. Most drivers in my lanes, who knew about this challenge for merging drivers, were as cooperative as possible to facilitate their passage. I sensed a driver to my left travelling very fast, and he honked, as if to forcibly enter my lane.

I made the same mistake, again. Eye contact. This guy's face was contorted in a rage, and he was apparently screaming at me. He was around me quickly, caused the driver to my right to brake urgently and swerve, and the crazy guy drove off the exit. My first reaction was to think and/or express negatives regarding the offending driver. The man to my right was saying something, and he held up one arm to me in the universal signal of "where is a cop when you need one?"

But what if I had misinterpreted the maniacal face? What if it was desperation or anguish? Because he had a medical condition and was hanging on for the emergency room, which was indeed located off that particular exit? He had looked to be badly constipated and perhaps was having chest pain. Or, had he just been notified that a relative was in that very emergency room? Perhaps it was his identical twin, from whom he had been tragically separated at birth and recently reunited.

My trip ended before the story could be properly concluded, but neither an aggressive word or deed had been forthcoming from myself. A small victory perhaps. A week or so later, I was atypically caught in rush hour traffic moving from the river up the long grade toward residential hills. In fact, I was boxed in behind the stereotypical little old lady, who was driving approximately 43 mph even as traffic cleared in our passing lane, versus the 55 mph enforcement speed limit. It seemed an eternity that this lady crawled me forward, but somehow it struck me that this was a test. What I did not do was honk, not even one tap, nor did I utter harsh instructional words. Even as such things were considered, however, I formulated the plight of the widow, who had only recently been forced into driving by the untimely death of her 91-year-old husband. And in that short time, she was already the victim of a carjacking by mountain cultists and a near-miss by an airplane making an emergency landing on the highway.

A problem, of course, is that I might be carried away by this reframing thinking and forget, for example, that I was still driving. This story-thinking might not be good for me, in general, but the point is that attempts were being made at progress on the anger front.

It was dark now, but the dog and I were in a zone. My thoughts turned to my last encounter with Tree, for there had been another interaction not on the porch. I don't know why I had thought that Tree would not travel with me beyond the house. I knew he was more than a tree. But I did not think he would follow me to a courtroom testimony in Baltimore.

At just before 9:00 a.m. on a Tuesday morning, I was seated in the back row of the audience rows of a Baltimore City, Maryland, courtroom. At some point, the judge would instruct the clerk to fetch and seat the jury, there might be other, brief matters before the court, and then I would be the first witness of the day. My mind was moving through the last stage of preparation for direct and then cross examination. No last-minute checks of my report, of the visual 8 x 11's to talk through with the jury, or of anything else was necessary. These chores had been accomplished several times over. This was about the how of my testimony, not the what. It was finally not about worry or doubt, but rather about thinking myself up in confidence for this big event. Confident, but not cocky. My voice could not tremble, my hands could not shake, and I most certainly could not sweat.

"You would relax more completely," said Tree, "if you would think yourself smaller, not bigger."

My startled gasp was sufficiently loud that three persons seated a few rows in front of me turned and eyed me briefly. "Not now," I thought, "please not now."

Of course, Tree heard this, and I could sense his feelings being hurt. His thought-voice was a stereo all around me, so that it was impossible to know where Tree had located himself. He said, "I'm just trying to help, Mike. Relax, you have been doing this for almost 40 years. You have a complete set of visuals, and all you need to do is talk the jury through the visuals. You could do this in your sleep, and the other attorneys don't have a clue what to ask you."

I was watching the judge speaking with the attorneys from both sides at the front of the courtroom. The screen for my presentation partially distracted my view. This courtroom had not yet been upgraded with a so-called Elmo system, whereby 8 x 11 pages, for example, could be displayed on small monitors in front of the jurors, judge, lawyers, and witness. "Thank you, Tree, but I really have to go."

"Oh, do you need to go to the bathroom again before you testify?"

My name was called to testify, and I thought to myself as I stood up and began walking toward the front of the courtroom, "No, Tree, I did not until you just brought it up, but now I do. What else could happen?" Yet, I did not believe that Tree would follow me to the witness stand and disrupt my testimony. Surely not.

After being sworn as a witness, I was being seated in the witness stand and making my first eye contact with the jury. "Tell the judge good morning," Tree whispered.

My stomach dropped, but I said in a small voice, "Good morning, your honor." I had never done that before, nor seen it done by a witness. The judge, who had seemed cold and distant, looked at me in surprise and replied, "Good morning, Dr. Brookshire." The jury had not heard me, but they saw the judge say good morning to me and smile. She had not smiled at anyone before me.

"Nice touch, Tree," I thought at him, "that worked out. Now, please let me do this." A junior attorney was seated by the overhead projector and ready to place the transparencies on the screen in tandem with my testimony. My belief had always been that jurors cannot see or understand calculations and numbers spoken into the air, such that enlarged charts and power point slides were critical to their having confidence in me about the dollar damages.

For some reason, the lawyers again huddled in front of the judge, who turned on the "white noise" machine so that the jury could not hear the discussion. Sitting next to the judge, I could hear the arguments and was none too happy with the subject matter. The lawyers retreated and mine gave me a doleful look. The judge switched off the noise and announced to me and all present, "Dr. Brookshire, we will proceed with the testimony but the visuals cannot be used or admitted into evidence. Let's move this equipment out of the way." Momentarily, her head morphed into that of an evil cow.

"Holy crap," I thought inartfully, "She can't do that. I've never seen a judge throw out visuals. Maybe one or two, but not the entire presentation set." Apparently, she <u>could</u> do that because the screen was being disassembled and carted away, an awful spectacle for the jury before my testimony had even begun. What was I to do? My lawyer was avoiding eye contact. Would he even ask me the questions as previously planned? I felt very small and helpless. The only strategy that had come to my mind was faking a heart attack.

Then, Tree whispered into my ear, "It will be ok, Mike. Testify as if the visuals are on a screen before the jury and say what you had planned to say." So that is exactly what I did. My set of visuals was in front of me and my lawyer's questions were matched with the visuals.

It worked out pretty well, requiring a bit more time describing sources for some numbers which were on the invisible visuals. As jurors realized what I was doing, they seemed to perk up at the unusual undertaking and a few were amused by the effort. The opposing attorneys objected but had an extremely difficult time explaining the basis for their objection. Her honor overruled the objection, and I liked her better.

Cross examination was not affected by the absence of visuals. At one point, the opposing attorney made a backhanded inference about the integrity of expert witnesses. He, of course, had built his case on expert witnesses. "Don't respond to that. Let it go," Tree whispered.

"I know that, Tree." I thought back, annoyed. Except that I did not think it. Apparently, I mumbled the words toward my left ear. The judge asked me if I was alright. We proceeded, and I was soon released from the witness stand. Tree and I had not visited since. The outcome of the case was a good one. Retirement would come in only a few more years.

Teddi Rose and I left the porch for our evening poop and tinkle walk. The night sky was magnificent with stars and constellations; there was only a sliver of moon. We walked on a dark private road and were largely shielded from the interfering lights of the city. After returning, I departed from a ritualistic viewing of television and returned to the porch with a hot tea and my Kindle, thinking. Since my discussion with Tree about Big and small, stargazing held more interest and wonderment. I had come to think more often about science and scientists, who journeyed into the great unknown of the universe, and my reading had increased about scientific fields other than my own.

Some group of astronomers somewhere had claimed there were more stars in the universe than there were grains of sand on all of the beaches of the earth. Wow! One had to wonder who actually counted all that sand, but the point for me was the unimaginable size of the scientific challenge.

One reminder of what I knew but had forgotten stood out regarding the scientific progress of those concerned with the cosmos. The universe is growing at an accelerating rate, while our ability to "see" the light at the frontier of observable space is not. Our state of knowledge, or at least observable knowledge, is actually decreasing as lights of distant galaxies move beyond the frontier.

Another reminder was the key scientific assumption that the physical laws defining the universe we can see also apply to the universe that we cannot see. What if this assumption is wrong? What if it is badly wrong?

What if beyond the horizon, giant space creatures are being formed from matter and energy? Wolves, perhaps. Space wolves. What if they tire of grazing on galaxies beyond the horizon and cross the horizon chomping inwards? What if humans are sensed as particularly tasty treats for space wolves, and they are headed our way? What if we cannot see them coming because they travel in a dimension as yet undiscovered? We simply don't know. After all the advances in knowledge regarding the universe and matter, and time and motion and energy, space wolves are possible. The notion is farfetched, perhaps, but until 1971, we weren't sure that black holes existed either.

It seemed that everything I was learning and remembering impressed me more with what we did not (yet) know versus what we did. Starting with one of the notions that I knew about physics -- the principle of uncertainty from the German physicist Heisenberg. The act of measuring affects the measurement, so that we are always uncertain about the results of the measurement. The principle also applied to the research of social scientists, like economists and psychologists.

Neither are scientists certain about what human consciousness means. From mathematics to medicine, biology and chemistry to geology and oceanography, so much was unknown. This made me feel scientifically small and gloomy. Were scientists, including social scientists like me, important in the cosmic scheme, with a journey of countless generations ahead for the uncovering of the ultimate truth?

Tree interrupted these thoughts, and it was as if we had just walked out of the Baltimore courtroom. "See, Mike, one of your worst fears -- a judge at the last moment shatters your expectations of how your testimony would occur. Yet, you were well prepared and, regardless of the circumstance, you did the best that you could do. You did not have a heart attack, fake or otherwise, nor did you tremble or sweat. So, stay small and be calm. You are merely one actor playing one role in a much bigger process."

"Did you set that up, Tree? Just out of curiosity, are you staging learning exercises for me?" I queried and thought to myself that I could have done without that one.

Tree ignored the thought and replied, "No, but I knew it was coming and decided you might need some help." Then he said, "I have been watching your road rage improvement efforts."

"I am at least working on it."

"Indeed, you are. Any changes that you can make in how you approach your life on the streets are very likely to be good ones. Keep up your efforts and there will be a day, looking back on it, that you can perceive fear and anger leaving the middle of you."

Tree observed, "But you were contemplating weighty topics of the state of human knowledge ... of science and scientists. Can we shift to you and how you might grow your middle, as space begins to open up there?"

I hesitated and then asked, "Can we talk about scientists first?"

"Surely. We can do that for a while. It actually relates to our discussion anyway. You are dejected about how far the process of scientific discovery has yet to go in uncovering the Truth. Is that correct?"

Recalling our early days together, I thought myself again to be a representative of humankind, facing a Q & A of potentially large importance. It is surprising, in retrospect, the detail that I could remember about this conversation, and others, with Tree.

"Let us back up a bit," Tree said. "To discuss science, we must talk about growth, and to talk about growth, we must discuss change. As it happens, Mike, you taught the topic of managing change. Remind the two of us what you know about change."

There was never much question about who was in control of our conversations, and I complied. "Change is a process, best described in reference to something of importance that may be changed through time. In management classes, this might be the level of morale and productivity in a particular work group at a particular time. As an economist, I might draw a two-dimensional graph, with the vertical axis representing higher and higher levels of productivity, and the horizontal axis is time. More simply, one can think of some level of productivity as the level of liquid in a cup, perhaps a measuring cup."

I paused, Tree said nothing, and I continued. "For an individual, I suppose, we might be measuring the level of happiness or fulfillment at any time. This level is subject, at any time, to down-pressures and up-pressures and we assume, to start, that the Ups and Downs are in equilibrium, counterbalancing each other. Then, we make a change to improve our happiness, or a change, positive or negative, is imposed from our environment. What predictably happens immediately after a change is that things get worse; the level goes downward. The Downs overwhelm the Ups. We battle the downturn to stop it and then turn it around. If a planned change, we hope to reach a new, and higher, level than before. That is why we made the change. The example is taking a lesson… a promising basketball player who finally reached a coach who begins to improve the fundamentals of his jump shot, or her jump shot. In attempting to shoot differently, the young athlete likely misses the basket entirely, but the investment ultimately pays off. This is difficult to appreciate, however, when one cannot hit the basket. And, of course, some changes are obstacles to be overcome, and great effort is required to reach the same level as before the change."

I finished, "And life is a dynamic process, with many changes, in different stages of this process, ongoing all of the time. Life is about change. It is all about change."

"A good summary of the process," Tree interjected. "While you favor significant change in the world, Mike, we have previously discussed your aversion to almost any change affecting you personally. At least that is what you say."

"That is correct, Tree."

"But the change process is what it is?"

"Yes."

"Mike, growth is the highest order of change. For humans. It is an application of the change process. A group, or a person, attempts to push the level, of happiness perhaps, upward, but up-pressures and down-pressures exist and are encountered along the way. There is a flow of changes to be worked through and, at worst, there may be monumental obstacles to growth. Growth pushes through obstacles toward increasing happiness, if that is the measure.

"Or in the case of humans as a group, Mike, and turning to scientists, the level of good being sought is in terms of the Truth, to the final and ultimate answers to every path of human inquiry."

I asked, "So what, exactly, are we measuring that the human race and its scientists are pursuing?"

Tree responded, "In pragmatic terms, that you would appreciate, how about our measuring, at any time, the percentage of Truth known. The top-of-the-scale, of course, is 100% Truth. In the purest sense of scientific inquiry, that is where the scientists are heading.

"Scientists are about growth, Mike. They are all about growth. What further do you wish to discuss concerning scientists?"

"Well, back to where we started, if the gap between humans and the Truth is so incredibly large, is the work of any scientist worth the effort? Can one person, or one research effort, make a difference in this quest for knowing all there is to know? Did Einstein, for example, jump us up five percentage points, or was it just a tiny movement?"

"Sorry, you are not yet ready to understand the answer which I am not giving you, anyway. But I liked your Professor Einstein. He thought often about the Big and the small. It was a pleasure to watch him think."

"You knew Albert Einstein?"

"Never interacted with him, no, just watched.

"Mike, why does this matter to you: the length of this gap between frontiers of human knowledge and the Truth?"

"Because much of my career has been as a teacher and researcher. It is important that what one does matters. And if there is little chance of reaching the conclusion in one's lifetime, or in many successive lifetimes, how do we motivate ourselves?"

"Yes, scientists are important in the scheme of things. It is in the nature of humans to grow, although this is difficult to see in the actions and inactions of many. Scientists, or any humans pursuing Truth, have the yearning abundantly. They share a burden and a responsibility, especially those at the vanguard, pushing the frontier outward. For when time is welcoming for great leaps forward, someone must be at the starting line ready for the race."

"Then, may I ask how far along are humans in this 0% to 100% Truth continuum?"

"Humans are certainly above zero. But realize that humans haven't identified all of the dimensions yet. There are things you don't know that you don't know."

It was unclear if Tree meant this to be encouraging, but he heard me think that he was being none too specific, and I asked, "What about our rate of growth toward the Truth? Is it increasing?"

Tree replied, "It varies through time, but there have been short periods of time when the rate of growth for humans pushing forward was remarkable."

I said, "Let me try a related question. Is there some, describable place that, when found, will mean that humans know it all? Know 100% of Truth? And would that mean that humans know as much as the Big knows?"

The mood turned somber. I could sense it. A somber vibe heralded importance. Tree answered, "Mike, the Truth and the Big are the same. They are the same place. As far as a human could understand the answer, they are the same. This, of course, is debated among humans, but I am telling you, Mike: When 100% Truth is found, so will be the Big."

Sensing this as a whopping big revelation, in and of itself, I continued, "So does that mean humans would be as big as the Big?"

"Whoa, Mike. Even if I thought you could possibly understand the answer to such a question, I couldn't answer the question anyway. Out of bounds." Then, he added, "let me give you some bad news and some good news about the gap between humans and the Truth… and the Big. The Big is growing too, Mike, not standing still. And, yes, that could mean that the Truth changes. How could you expect otherwise? You humans have much to learn about both immutability and infinity."

"Then, humans and our scientists could not possibly close the gap. That dampens my spirits further. Perhaps because it feels uncomfortable not to have an end, or ultimate victory."

"And then there is the good news," Tree interrupted, "think about rates of growth. The Big controls rates of growth of himself and humans. The Big can converge the rates of growth, moving two paths to a common place at his discretion. Of course, knowing today's Truth tomorrow doesn't do it, because by tomorrow the Truth may change. But be assured that the Big can handle such details. Unimaginable progress by humans is possible in a very short time, when one door is unlocked and many doors ahead have been left ajar. Yes, it is possible that humans could reach 100% Truth."

"Then what would happen, if humans reached Truth, 100% Truth in your scale of Truth?" I asked.

"That is an excellent question, Mike. What would happen, indeed? Do humans, and their scientists, really wish to reach the Truth… the end of growth?"

"And that implies we are as big as the Big?"

"Don't hold your breath, Mike, waiting for that to happen, but think of all that you would lose if it did, beginning with comfort."

"This is much to consider, Tree," I said slowly.

"Plenty of time, Mike. You have the rest of your life and possibly much more."

That was a tantalizing statement for follow-up, but I knew we were finished on this topic, at least for now. Sometimes Tree liked to mess with me, perhaps for the fun of it.

"Turning to you, Mike," Tree moved along, "assume that you are successful over time in removing from the middle of you what holds you back… what brings you down. Like fear and anger. As your middle opens up, what do you add there? What do you grow?"

Tree continued, "You are the scientist of your own life, Mike. It is up to you to push the bounds of what you know and what you are, obstacles or not."

"But some humans grow and some humans do not grow, so it is not exactly necessary to human life; it is not oxygen," I said.

Tree added, "And some humans grow themselves through great obstacles. It is a diversity of CAN and WILL. Some humans, for whatever reasons, physical or mental, cannot grow. Or their capacity to grow is limited. This is very sad. Then, there are humans who could grow but do not choose to do so. It is a different level of sad, a foreclosure of what could have been."

And as I was about to comment, Tree finished his thought, "You have no choice, however. You must grow, Mike."

"Why must I grow?"

"Because I am bigger than you, which is all of an answer that you need right now. Trust me."

Slightly changing the subject, I said, "Ok, Tree, just to put this in perspective, how do you think I am doing in growth, however you would be defining personal growth?"

There was an awkwardly long pause, which made me uncomfortable, and Tree replied simply, "Not very well."

This was stunning feedback. Tree must have momentarily confused me with someone else. I asked in bewilderment, "Tree, I worked hard through school to a Ph.D.; then I researched, published, and taught. I have always loved to read, almost anything, and to learn. I'm a news, politics, and history junkie. How could you think that about me?"

"Yes, Mike, in your almost 63-year history, you have generally exhibited continued growth and steady growth, with notable spurts here and there. But notably confined to selected areas where you like to grow.

That was in the past, Mike. Lately, not so much growth. You are decelerating. In calculus, you have a problem of the second derivative.

"You have a choice. In your remaining life expectancy of twenty years, do you grow and live 20 more years, or do you relax from growth and live one more year, 20 times?"

Tree stopped, clearly waiting for my answer. My impulse was to answer quickly, but this was not a simple proposition. Teaching was losing its fun after all these years, and I was not particularly anxious about its cessation. I would miss much of the work of an economist estimating economic damages in real life cases, but not the stress of both travel and testimony. I was ready to accept deceleration of activity but wondered, myself, how a perfectionist workaholic could do that successfully.

Tree responded to my thoughts. "The way you do that is to reaccelerate. Add and grow in the middle of you. As you push out fear and anger, there is much room available in you for adds and grows. If all of your buckets of fear and anger departed from your middle this moment, little would be left growing to fill the void. Your psychological ribs would collapse into your psychological innards."

I sighed. "Ok, Tree. What do I add to me and my life? And to what do I grow?"

"It is not for me to tell you. If I gave you the answers, the questions would lose their meaning."

I thought, "Then why did you bring it up in the first place, Tree," and Tree heard that.

"Mike," he offered, "I am willing to give some general advice if you wish and would be pleased to discuss what you might do. Whatever you add or grow, set the direction of your efforts toward the truth, as you believe it to be, toward that which you admire, which is in the same direction as the Big. And a large advantage of the Big in your middle is that it is not then you that is in the middle. You cannot grow toward you, Mike. You are already as far as you can go."

"Ok, what else can you tell me?" I asked.

"Generally, add others to the middle of you as you choose what to add and grow. Others moving in is a terrific way to move you out of the middle of you. Fear and anger are self-centered and bring you down. Their replacements need to be other-centered, in one way or another.

"You need to embark upon experimentation with the new, develop an openness to change. All of the new that you sample will not work out so well but that is how change and growth work. Change is not particularly comfortable in the downturns, as you have suggested, but your status quo has a value which rapidly diminishes. You owe a renewal of your growth to yourself and others. It is how you pay back. It is how you pay forward. It is how you find the truth that you were meant to find."

"But after all the years of working, don't I deserve some period of time to rest and relax, before embarking on this mission that you seem to foresee for me?"

"Do you really wish to talk about what you deserve? Also, after about one day of rest and relaxation you would be a rudderless mess. What I am suggesting to you is a gift, not a chore, and it is time for you to accept the gift. Now."

It was obvious that I should let the "What I deserve" comment pass. Tree knew everything about me. It had been a poor choice of words.

Tree continued, "You don't need to have a personal planning retreat to begin thinking about what you might do differently, and then begin to make changes a bit at a time and see how they fit. You could think about how you might change how you typically spend your time. Or, what adjectives do others who know you use to describe you? How would you like that to change over the next twenty years until your statistical death?"

The analysis of how one spent his time reminded me of a time management exercise from my training days, but I was familiar with its potential value. "Ok, Tree, let me talk about how I spend my time and how that might change. But this is off the top of my head stuff."

"That is fine," Tree replied. "This is about starting out. From my observation, starting is a necessary first step in growing."

"Family time would be the first choice for increased time. But I'm not sure that immediate family are seeking that from me. Lynn has a large job herself plus many other priorities, like parenting Chloe. Chloe receives all the time she will give me, but she is entering her teenage years and time with me will have lots of competition. When she can drive and chauffeuring ends, that time together will decline. In what I suspect will be years that proceed too quickly, she will leave for college, hopefully a great university like Oxford or the University of Tennessee."

My next thought was that I could increase time spent in activities of hedonistic pleasure, but I couldn't think of anything specific. It felt as if Tree was glaring disapproval at me. This alternative seemed to perform poorly on the "others" criterion, unless there was a group hedonistic pleasure activity that I might try. Wisely, I moved on.

"Eating, sleeping, grooming, exercise, dog time: staples of a typical day," I said. "My first thought is that time spent here is about right. Even the dog does not seem to desire more time and, because I am the bath person, she avoids me when she senses herself dirtying. If anything, here, I would increase exercise. The hip replacement ended racquetball and tennis; the weekly personal trainer plus home stationary bicycle riding don't replace that intensity of exercise, but they bring a new circle of friends and acquaintances. And regular exercise allows me to eat a daily allowance of ice cream and peanut butter, which may be the fundamental motivator of exercise endeavors."

Tree was not interrupting, and I thought about mentioning an increase in time spent in civic and charitable activities. These possibilities did not excite me for the short run, at least, with my work schedule. On the other hand, I also thought about the considerable time spent on sports watching but did not believe that reduction in time spent here would be feasible or appropriate. Tree heard all of these thoughts, of course.

"Tree when I have thought about what I would do with my time, as I semi-retire and retire, more time reading always comes to mind. Reading consumes much of my time in a typical week now -- most for business and professional reasons, but as much as possible for entertainment."

Tree interjected, "Your increase in reading for entertainment. What kind of books?"

"I will pick up and read almost anything, but a typical book of choice -- by an array of authors and their progeny -- might involve a secret, joint effort by the Russians and Chinese to, say, weaponize weather versus the USA. They are working out of a secret headquarters in Pyongyang, North Korea. An elite group of 20 American super-soldiers, headquartered in a bunker under the Rose Garden, infiltrates North Korea, overcomes the hundreds of inept guards at the secret headquarters, and destroys the enemy capabilities. First, however, they cleverly find a way to scorch Moscow and flood Beijing for a month or so to teach both countries a lesson. We have no casualties. I like books like that, Tree."

"I suppose increased hours in that kind of reading do not grow me much," I mused, "and it is not more time involving others. There are apparently a few men's book clubs, probably in New York City and Portland. I can't think of anyone I know to call who would seriously consider such a socialization involving reading and discussion. Perhaps I'm underestimating the men I know, but I doubt it."

Tree and I were silent for a while. My mind was futilely searching for Adds. "It seems as though you have much room for the new in your future, like the skydiving club we discussed previously." Tree smiled, but the comment was not remotely funny to me, because I did not know what Tree might say or do next.

"Well," I began, "more than once in my history someone has asked me if I had ever considered meditation. You did, yourself, as I recall. Maybe that would be a useful new activity, although it would not seem to be other-directed."

Tree commented, "Well you would need to begin with yoga on your way to meditation. You might be surprised as to how other-directed is this process. So, this may be a good Add for you. The fact that people who know you would gasp in surprise is a reason to try it."

"And I could concentrate on making new friends and being a better friend. That feels good to me as an Add for my time." It occurred to me that this discussion made me feel as a kid in a candy store picking and choosing.

"It has been suggested that I might actually learn how to use social media. My wife and grandchild would be convinced that a zombie had taken over my body if I all of a sudden showed interest in doing this. I do have great concerns seeing persons who spend way too much time on their social media gadgets and activities. But this would certainly shake up my status quo."

Tree moved along, "Let us talk about descriptions, adjectives used to describe you. If I asked people who know you well, what words would they apply to you?"

"Workaholic would likely be one of the first descriptions. Probably self-centered; task oriented; intelligent, hopefully; jackass possibly; perfectionist; obsessive compulsive…"

"You can list good things too, Mike."

"Tree, those are the good things," I replied. Tree knew that, I was sure, but was apparently still working on sarcastic humor.

"And how would you like those to change over your future?"

This required a pause to think, as it was a query without precedent in my memory. Slowly, I began to talk about possibilities. "An easy word that comes to mind is happy. Why wouldn't anyone wish to behave so that others would say, at his funeral perhaps, "Mike was one happy dude. Even when he was being a horse's ass, he seemed to be darn happy about it. Died with a smile on his face. Despite everything, he found a way to be happy."

Tree said nothing, so I finished, "Happy is so general as a description, though, it is difficult for me to wrap my arms around happy. I am more sure about how sad feels than I am about how happy feels to me. It is not clear to me what actions on my part would increase my happy rating. For sure, it is almost never used to describe an economist. Has any economist ever given a happy speech? When every single economic indicator looks great, we spend all of our time prognosticating on which bads are surely to break through somewhere. They call it the dismal science for a reason."

"Then leave happy alone for now, Mike. It may be that aiming at happy is not what you need to do, anyway. If you make other changes in the middle of you, happiness will find you."

After a pause I said, "There are descriptors of people that are admirable in persons, generally, but just don't turn me on for attention anytime soon. For example, charitable and generous are very nice designators of a person, but retirement will mean that income goes down, not up. Unless my ship comes in." This would be surprising, I thought, since no ship had been sent out.

"Forgiveness is another one. That's not high on my list simply because it's too hard. Particularly forgiving oneself.

"Then, grateful. I admire grateful in a person. Oddly enough, Tree, I believe myself to be above-average on this one. It is a part of me that has grown." Mentally, I prepared for Tree to bring me down a notch.

"Oddly enough," Tree replied, "I agree with you. It is amazing that a human being with so much fear and anger could nevertheless be so grateful."

Tree had no further comments, and I moved on. "There is an attribute, Tree, that I have greatly admired in a few persons whom I have known in life or other persons whose behavior I have seen or read about.

Kindness. It would be a wonderful thing to have others think about you: Mike is a kind man."

"Would some persons who know you say that now?" Tree asked.

"No, I don't think so. It would not be an adjective that I would attach to me either."

"What is your definition of kindness, Mike. What does the word mean to you?"

"I cannot remember actually looking up the meaning. But kind people seem to have a will, a motivation to make others feel less alone… to feel worthy of attention, and comfort, and love. That would also apply to kindness toward oneself, I suppose.

"And a kind person does what he or she does expecting absolutely nothing in return. Otherwise, it is a trade, not a gift. It would be very difficult for me to sort out past kindnesses on my part from actions that either pay back or create a debt. However I was living that caused others to think of me as kind would be a good way to live. It feels right to me. It is not clear to me what actions would be involved, but that is an Add."

"What else?" Tree encouraged.

"There is another word, perhaps a fancier word of sorts, which I have admired as a state of one's mind, or perhaps their inner self. Equanimity. And I have looked up that word before. It describes a mental calmness, a composure, an evenness of temperament, and it is usually framed as the ability to exhibit these characteristics in regard to a bad or difficult situation.

"A small problem is that equanimity is a noun, not an adjective. People exhibiting generosity are generous, but exhibiting equanimity does not make one equanimous, or perhaps equanimitous. It is little things like this that drive me crazy about English. So, I could never be described as kind and equanimous, and I do not particularly wish for bad things to happen to me so that equanimity might be demonstrated.

"It would seem to me, though, that however I was living that people would describe my reactions to life events with this word would be a good way to be living."

"Would you have been described with this word when facing difficulties in the past?"

"My equanimity rating would be all over the place, depending on which situation we were talking about. It is something that I don't think describes me but I would like to add this. Again, I really do not know what to do or where to start."

Tree interrupted, "Opportunities will present themselves in life, of that you can be sure. Your plate of Drops, Grows, and Adds is more than enough to begin. I will be around as you proceed, and we can talk if you like, but you have all the time you need: statistically, twenty years."

It was not clear if that was a life expectancy joke of some type, but I quickly replied, "Most definitely, Tree, we need to talk. I can't do this alone." But Tree had already departed. By this point, I immediately knew when he left.

CHAPTER NINE –
TRUDGING

Over the next three years, my goals, thinking, and actions were substantially different than would have been expected absent my year and one-half of interactions with Tree. The journey is perhaps best described as a trudge, which is a word many use as a difficult, burdensome walk. But it means to walk purposefully, and, although the three years from August 2013 to August 2016 were sometimes difficult, they also had a good share of challenge, reward, and fun. And they held purpose, albeit given to me by Tree, which in its simplest form was a happier life than one absent the trudging.

It must be said that I had my doubts, when pursuing various changes in me, about whether the benefits would be worth the costs. Either one followed the outline set by Tree or one did not. Tree was always assumed to be around or near, so that significant deviation from the path would not go unnoticed. Of course, he even knew when I was <u>thinking</u> about an easier, softer way. Tree's influence never felt oppressive to me, on the other hand,

and my occasional doubts and hesitancies did not approach rebellion over the new directions.

Indeed, Tree visited regularly over the period, either on the porch or, sometimes to my consternation, in other venues. Our conversations were shorter than before, and less philosophical. They were generally related to my trudge, and the unpredictable appearances by Tree were an important encouragement, and fine tuning, along the way.

The family, of course, traveled with me through the progression of life. Lynn retired from her CIO position but for most of the time was semi-retired by an employer which did not want her to leave. She used freed-up time on Chloe, friends, and keeping me and the dog out of trouble. Chloe moved from middle school to high school, and her claim to our time and attention always topped any list. Mid-way through this period, in May 2015, I retired from teaching; forty years in higher education was enough. My fulltime attention vocationally became my consulting business, although time was certainly freed up with the cessation of faculty work. Tree steered me toward use of this time in accelerating my growth, versus, I suppose, sloth or hedonic pleasure.

A parallel issue continuing over these three years was how my relationship with Tree might remain undetected by my household family members or others. As my relationship with Tree became more comfortable, the chance that I would slip up in my cover-up probably increased apace.

The recounting of 3-year highlights generally follows a chronological sequence, although overlapping activities require me to carry a subject to a stopping point before changing topics. The first organizational thought which I recall was that select activities regarding anger and fear, for example, be continued and expanded before any significant focus turned to Adds and Grows. Space in the middle of me first needed to be freed up.

There were important threads, however, which ran throughout the three years and across specific efforts at Deletes, Adds, and Grows. These were the fundamentals of thinking myself smaller, at least with reference to a Big and an All, of realizing the limits of my control, of lowering my expectations, and of living a day at a time.

Tree gave me little choice in being mindful of these themes, perhaps because he knew they differed so dramatically from my life-learned beliefs and habits. He invaded for 14 consecutive days the sanctity of my morning shower, the place and time of my brainful beginning of each day.

My long-held habit had been to arise sufficiently early each morning, typically 5:30a.m., to allow an hour-and-a-half of the leisurely acceleration of cognition before a start of an externally oriented day. First was the obligatory walking of the dog, which varied from one to ten minutes depending upon the state of her excremental systems and her wonderment over the front yard, which had been virtually the same yesterday. The local newspaper was fetched, TV news turned on, and first coffee was Keurig'ed. The function of the ensuing 45 minutes was to enjoyingly drink my first daily cups of coffee while doing what news junkies do. Little productive thought was expected and little occurred. This was a preparation for my time in the shower stall, the small space where daily cognition came alive.

Imagine my surprise when one morning, after a few minutes of pondering, thinking, and planning in the shower, Tree began to critique me. I couldn't see him, of course, but it was as if he was either standing outside the shower or perhaps sitting on the closed toilet seat. "No, no, no, Mike," he began, "your daily thinking is already large and in charge. If you wish to live a small day you must start the day thinking small."

Tree's sudden appearance in my most private of time startled me, and it was somewhat uncomfortable to be stark naked beginning a conversation with an unusual bathroom spirit. With shampoo in my eyes, I reviewed my thinking and, truly, it was all about me and the tasks and obstacles facing me in the coming days. A frown had already formed from this review of loathsome consulting deadlines.

Tree continued, "The easiest way to think yourself smaller is not to think of yourself at all. Begin with thoughts about others whom you care about or whom you know to have troubles larger than your own. Or focus upon that which you believe to be bigger than you and your small size in relation thereto. The ant and you and the universe."

Thus, it began. Fourteen days of training in how to begin a day. Tree had a captive audience, whose listening and thinking abilities were waking up but whose talking abilities were barely engaged. We thought together about my smallness, in relation to almost anything, and about how little control that I actually possessed over people, places, and things.

We reviewed expectations, too. It was not simply to identify what I expected to happen, and then to lower it or re-frame it as either more realistic or less negative. Tree also sought to take expectations away from my forecasting, so that the day I was entering simply held fewer expectations and more mystery: as the day truly was, for a small human with little control. Even in these early days, I could feel the lowering of frustration and anger, for there is no difference between actual and expected when expected does not exist. Whatever happened, my aim was to do the best that I could toward what felt to be the right thing under the circumstances.

More than anything else in this two weeks of visits, Tree worked with me to filter away those thoughts, and especially those worries, that did not involve the present day. Events planned for next month were out of bounds, as were thoughts of the weekend or even the next day. While pondering of times past, regrets especially, occurred, less of these were problematic at shower time. Yet Tree spent time rooting out remorses, guilts, and shames which underlaid the dawn of my day, and he encouraged me to postpone these to following days. It seemed that one would thereby postpone such thoughts forever, after they appeared for quick acknowledgement and processing. One way to exalt the day is to think of no others, and Tree started me on this practice. On some of these mornings, the water was turning cold when my day was begun again.

On the first of the fourteen nights, I was lying in the early repose before sleep comes, which had been a time that I habitually troubled myself with thoughts of the future and of the past. Rarely were these positive thoughts. Tree pointed this out, as a matter of fact, as he whispered to me from somewhere over the bed. Lynn was already asleep; she regularly retired an hour or so before me. Tree made this end-of-the-day visit for the same period of two weeks. He encouraged me to reflect on how well, or not, I had stuck to the fundamentals which I was endeavoring to embrace. I remember him, in this time, as much more the cheerleader than the critic. And that was what I needed because none of the fundamentals were consistent with my past, with the self which came naturally.

After two weeks the visits ceased. But at every shower and sleep, I knew more about what to do and not to do. My natural self did not change easily or swiftly but my mindfulness of the attempted changes in me grew. There was a momentum which I came to perceive. Whether my morning and night development was a continuing gift from Tree or was a natural result of my diligent efforts was a question, but the growing, smaller me suspected the former.

Early in the trudging years, the combination of efforts to purge my anger in general and my road anger in particular was an obvious use of my time and effort. A single event interrupted the momentum of these endeavors and added an obstacle to the path forward.

It was a gorgeous mid-morning in late fall, cloudless with a bright, cheery sun dissipating the morning chill. I was returning from an early deposition downtown, driving up the long grade from the river into the hills of residences. With my mind on the completed testimony, I had forgotten the start-of-driving pause. Yet, traffic was light on this short drive home and little chance existed for a road anger scenario. Imagine my surprise, therefore, when a police car appeared behind me and gave one burst of flashing lights and siren, directing me to pull over onto the ample, paved shoulder.

The police officer parked behind me was checking with Charleston dispatch control, or whatever it was called, to ensure that my vehicle was in no way "hot." I knew this not from experience but from a lifetime of reading about, and viewing, a wide range of crime stories, and ceaseless efforts of police and prosecutors protecting me and the rest of the public. While obtaining my driver's license, registration, and proof of insurance for the conversation to come, I reviewed the limited possibilities for illegal transgressions on my part. I had changed lanes without signaling in antic- ipation of my left turn just beyond the summit of the hill. There had been nary a vehicle behind me to see such a signal. Surely not that?

I double-checked the inspection sticker – a previous bust – but was ok there. Because I hit the brakes so fast upon seeing the policemen, my exact speed at enforcement siting was unclear to me, but my foot pressure on the accelerator was habitually consistent on the oft-traveled trip home.

When the police officer stepped out of his car and approached my side window, I was struck by the youth of this baby-faced male. Probably just out of the police academy. Could be his very first stop. Is that good or bad? Probably bad.

"Sir," he said, "Do you know why I pulled you over?"

A trick question. Not what had been expected. In my exasperation, I told the truth, "No, Officer, I don't."

"You were driving 55 miles per hour and the speed limit is 50 miles per hour on this road." He pointed to a speed limit sign two feet in front of my car, as if that was necessary.

What I wanted to say was "Exactly, 55 is 5 miles per hour above the posted 50 miles per hour speed limit, and I was within the 5 miles per hour leeway before enforcement action is taken." But that would have been beyond even my stupidity threshold. I wondered if this five miles per hour enforcement buffer was no longer (informal) state law, or if they had ceased teaching this concept at the police academy, or if the officer had been sick that day.

It was important to proceed carefully. I apologized, "I'm sorry, Officer, there is almost no traffic and I apparently didn't notice being a few miles over the posted speed limit."

"Yes, Sir. Exactly five miles per hour over the legal speed limit, ten percent over."

"Was there still an enforcement buffer?" I thought, "but they changed it to a percentage buffer and didn't tell anyone? Would he tell me the percentage for future reference? Prudently, however, I did not argue, hoping that such reasonableness would at least nudge the officer toward a warning in lieu of a ticket. Of course, officer discretion could also have been eliminated.

Then he wrote out and handed me a ticket for a speeding violation with real dollars and real points toward a 10-point limit. So, there was no reason not to say, "I thought that you might give me a warning since there was almost no traffic and I was only 5 miles per hour above 50."

"Sir, how long have you been driving this road?" he asked politely.

"A long time."

"And, Sir, how long has the speed limit been 50 miles per hour?"

I wanted to say, "Since long before you were born," but I said, "For a long time."

"So, warnings haven't done much good with you, have they sir?"

I was not happy with this young officer, but his logic was difficult to refute. I accepted the ticket, paid it, and from that point forward, on that road, I have never exceeded 53 miles per hour, or six percent above the posted speed limit. True, 52 miles per hour would move me below five percent – if that is the new buffer – but I choose to live on the wild side of five percent.

One of the pillars of my belief in the justice system, broadly defined, had been shaken, and my resentment over this complicated my attempt to lighten the road. I continued, nevertheless, to focus upon start-and-stop-of-driving pauses and perceived some progress in habitu-ating these mental bookends around driving events. An obstacle was that when I was most pressured, apprehensive, hurried, or discontented, I was most likely to forget the starting pause, and these were the most likely mindsets to bloom into road anger.

A memorable scenario was a driver who flew past me on the inter-state around the city. I was early-morning cruising at 63 miles per hour, or five percent above the posted speed limit, while my estimate for the speeder was 83 miles per hour, which my mind automatically converted to a 38 percent margin above post. Only in Miami would such an enforce-ment margin be allowed. Reframing failed me, as I watched an SUV in front of me quiver at the force of the fly-by. It was unsatisfactory to think that the offending driver had overslept and was rushing to unlock the front door of the coal mine, or to deliver the canary. I found myself casting out anger of word and thought. My mind sought reckoning and punishment, even if such thoughts were unbecoming for a smaller self. Something else was necessary for progress.

Within a few days, my pondering had led me to a new possibility of dealing with troubles of automobile life. A mythical Charleston Central command and control center, with which I could be in real time contact while driving, came to exist in my mind. Perhaps the encounter with the young officer had sparked the idea. I could transmit my reporting of road events to this nether-switchboard and bring closure to a matter in a way which reframing had not. Since this was make-believe, there was no radio protocol to break, nor anything to be learned about crime codes or num-bers, follow-up activities after reporting, coordination with others, etc. I imagined myself as a more-or-less auxiliary officer, whose role largely ended with incident reports and appropriate comments. Communication equipment did not clutter my vehicle, nor weapons, nor a heavy metal screen separating me from a prisoner in the back seat. Apprehensions, arrests, and prisoners were the concerns of others; neither lawyers nor arrestor's remorse affected me.

So, for example, if the incident of the 83 miles per hour driver occurred again, I could immediately be informing Central, via my hands-free technology, that a dark-colored 4-wheel car, Ohio license NUW423, had just passed me doing 93 miles per hour near mile marker 2. (As an aside, West Virginians believe that drivers from Ohio are exceptionally unskilled and troublesome.) The miles-per-hour enhancement would ensure a swift and overwhelming response by enforcement officers and was logically parallel to the enforcement limit buffer for speed limits. The license number and mile marker were, of course, invented but accuracy was unnecessary, and random detail might be added at my discretion.

Occasionally, I would add an offense code, like a 323 or a 27, although such numbers were more important back in the early police shows of my youth. It seemed to me that, logically, number 1 would be murder, so most of the time the agitation which prompted my reporting in the first instance warranted at least a double-digit code number.

In the rare instances when passengers were with me, my thought communications to Central were abbreviated and with less detail. "See the car in front of me weaving from lane to lane. Illegal 42s and 276s likely in the vehicle." Central knew my exact location and could see the offender through my orbiting camera system. It was superfluous to know that the offender was likely to be charged either with a 42 or a 53 for consuming way too much of the 276s. Nevertheless, I sensed the suspicions of the ladies as I quietly interacted with traffic difficulties, replacing previous diatribe with barely perceptible mouth movements and the occasional, satisfied smile.

There were times when I likely abused my reporting powers, primarily by reporting incidents which might fall short of the threshold of a state code violation. Thus, a number would not (yet) be assigned and the incident reported under the miscellaneous code 99. These code 99's could only rise to a "stop and hassle" response by enforcement officers, but not fines or imprisonment. Drivers who did not allow me to merge onto a main road, for example, might warrant a 99 call, especially when I was under stress in some other area of my life.

Never did I carry on a conversation with any of the persons at Central. That would have meant that I was crazy, and this entire exercise was purposeful, not crazy. Yes, likely comments back to me from the folks at Central were sometimes imagined or considered. That is very different from an actual, imagined conversation between me and Central. As an example, they might have said, "Good job on the license number of that 93 mile per hour vehicle. Great alertness. Good eye." Or, there was the time when a seemingly nice lady signaled me a bird for easing my way in front of her. Not illegal, perhaps, but I reported her for a 17 "disrespecting a public official" and recommended that she be placed in the public stocks in front of the courthouse (actually it was a bicycle rack); Central said that they accepted my recommendation.

To my credit, I thought, good and positive reports were also sent to Central. I once commended the Mayor and City Council on the paving of a particular road, and Central promptly passed this along. My most common compliment involved the one or two out of every ten drivers who waved thanks when I was somehow courteous to them. Theirs was an under-rewarded population of goodness in society, so that I regularly reported such persons to Central as time allowed. My understanding with Central was that many of the persons would be pulled over by one of our Thank You officers and presented with a reverse citation and a special bonus-and-hotel package. One had to be prudent in these positive reports, on the other hand, because both the Thank You officers and the driver bonuses had been frequent targets for budget cuts.

And so my driving efforts proceeded. At some point I recognized that vignettes involving great anger previously might now result in entertainment. Tree was not effusive about my progress here, but he did not attempt to stop me. I thought it was a step forward.

Tree did not abandon his interest in football during the almost half year when it was annually played, but we both avoided discussing the future of football. We would more-or-less watch together several Tennessee Vols or Denver Broncos games each year and, just as I did with my friends, would debrief on these, WVU, Marshall, Bengals or Steelers games. A drawback, however, was that Tree would remind me of the anger, angst, and frustration which football fanship, especially, brought to my in-season life.

It could not be denied. Off season, I talked and complained about the past and coming season occasionally, but an uncomfortable lump of fanship pressure did not occupy the middle of me. Truly, the football season could be 60 minutes old, and I was already fuming about performance, scores, bad luck, referees, etc. Neither could it be denied that good feelings from watching a sport that I loved, or from winning games, did not match the negatives of losing games, in either duration or intensity of feeling.

The Vols football team was middle-of-the-pack in Southeastern Conference standings over this period. They won some big games but lost a bunch too. They did not defeat Alabama, which is gnawingly irritating, and lost once to Vanderbilt, which is even worse. The team was not good enough to seriously pursue a championship but not bad enough (yet) to fire the head coach and start over (again), so that a championship might someday be within reach. One would have thought that these "middle years" would have been a good time to confront my fan anger syndrome, but progress here was middling.

A new strategy emerged by coincidence. One Saturday, I had a Chloe-related midday event which easily took precedence over a Vols game televised at noon and largely overlapping the other event. The opponent was a ranked, and significantly favored, SEC opponent playing at home. Not a problem. I simply set the TIVO to record the game. Only a small chance existed that I would learn the score during or after the game, assuming reasonable precautions not to listen to a radio, or turn on my iPhone, for example. Soon upon my return home, I would go downstairs to my man cave/office and watch the game without commercial interruption.

Unfortunately, we stopped for milk on the way home, and, of course, I saw a friend in the store who knew me well enough to remember my Tennessee fanship. He said from across the aisle, "Your Vols really pulled one out at the end. Congratulations!" I smiled and said something like "there's always next week," because football etiquette requires the deflection of good news or compliments. The way I really felt, however, was two opposite ways simultaneously. A paradox. Angry, because my plan had been to watch the game, with all of the curiosity, wonderment, and thrill of not knowing the final outcome. Happy, because I knew the outcome and it was unexpectedly delightful. The happy swamped the angry in quick course, and I walked into my man cave high fiving myself, which is awkward but oddly joyful.

Thus, I watched the replay in its entirety, knowing the final score, the one-point margin of victory, and the victor throughout. It was a memorable and thoroughly enjoyable experience. We were down 13 points at halftime. It should have been much worse given our dubious game plan and poor execution. Yet, I was unfazed at the turnovers, blown opportunities, blocked punt, and the general absence of any reason to expect an upset win. Confident. Cocky. After a fast-forwarded halftime, I eagerly anticipated an exciting second half.

Not so. With 10 minutes remaining in the fourth quarter the Vols were behind by 10 points, the other team had the ball, playing in their stadium, and it had begun to rain. From my decades of experience as a Tennessee football fan, and because of my generally pessimistic outlook in the face of uncertainty, I recalled many instances of my team losing a lead in the fourth quarter but held less recall of against-all-odds comebacks in the fourth quarter. Yet, I remained a chill dude, for a man of my age. The thought only lightly crossed my mind that my convenience store friend might have been confused or had cleverly set me up for a cruel joke.

Then, the game changed. The defense of the Vols rose up to give the offense the necessary opportunities to close a two-score gap. A recovered fumble and onside kick helped also. First, a field goal hit the side bar but fell through for three points. I held my racing heart when the ball bounced, and I already knew the field goal would be good. We scored on a pass play as time expired in regulation play. The Vols would obviously kick the extra point, and the game would proceed to overtime. Tree might show up, because he loved to hear me explain the rules of overtime in college football.

But wait! The Vols lined up to run a 2-point play to win, not to kick a one-point conversion and move to overtime. "No, you can't do that!" I shouted, jumping to my feet. Then, I realized, Duh. No team in college football has ever faked a 2-point play, shifted, and kicked a 1-point extra point. So, there will be no overtime. If Tennessee runs this 2-point play, they will succeed, score, and win, because I know they win by 1 point! Sure enough, Tennessee ran a rather basic off-tackle play, which had not gained as much as three yards in the entire game. Our tailback scored standing up, as the opposing players showed surprise as well as the agony of defeat. Apparently, our opponent had anticipated a trick play from us, and we fooled them. Brilliant, although if we had a trick play we would have already used it. It was such a wonderful moment, a great feeling, a testimony to the goodness of fanship.

The next week was another big SEC game, against the number one ranked team. I watched the game, as normal, in real time. The opponent beat us badly, at our homecoming, in every aspect of the game except the marching band. They joyously and unnecessarily ran up the final score on us, an insult which we would surely repay sometime later in the century. The viewing experience was anger-ful from the first play, a touchdown, until I turned the game off midway through the fourth quarter. Knowing the final score ahead of time would have stopped me from watching even one second of this odious debacle and from carrying a new layer of anger and resentment through the weekend and into the week ahead.

An epiphany of sorts struck me that very evening. As a fan in the 21st century, I had an option to consider besides the real-time-viewing status quo: Guaranteed Final Result viewing (or not viewing): GFR, the "Giffer" method. It helped being a Tennessee fan living in West Virginia, because the GFR method required a fan to schedule GFR viewing at, say, 7:30 pm after a real time 4:00 start of the televised game. One would have pre-planned extra recording time in the event of lightning or overtime, which might delay when one ascertained the final score and made their ex post viewing decision. In the time gap of the actual game, the Giffer fan would typically avoid learning anything about the course of the game, although GFR viewing offered many alternatives in what information was disclosed, and when.

Upon learning the final score, and victor, a range of actions might ensue. In the case of the one-point comeback win, the decision would require no thought; watch the entire replay, sing and dance. If there were a one-point loss, just the opposite way with a comeback by an opponent we were supposed to beat, I would delay watching the replay while considering whether watching the game for the thrill of sport and competition outweighed actually seeing the final result, about which I had been warned. None of these replays have yet been watched, but it remains possible. In the case of a blow-out, humiliating loss to an opponent, whether expected or not, I deleted these recordings to avoid the annoyance of saving them until the next cold day in hell.

It occurred to me that the Giffer had simply not been available as an option to previous generations of football fans. Somehow, everyone but me had overlooked this obvious, deliberate use of current technology. For once, I was at the vanguard of innovating technological change. Surely, the landscape of social activity among fans not actually attending a game would diversify. Giffer parties might be scheduled for like-minded fans, at least some of whom might wish to lessen the in-season knot of anger in their middle.

The party start time could be anytime from the true start of the game to the assumed end of the game. A half-Giffer of course would begin at the scheduled start time of the second half. Guests would check all electronics at the door and pledge not to seek any knowledge of what was transpiring in the game as they ate, drank, and were merry.

Everyone would be told the winner and final score at the same time, after some leader watched a post-game show from a bedroom. This information sharer would need to be considered trustworthy by all guests, because he or she could really mess with a lot of folks if so inclined. Again, variants of the party might involve more information – halftime score, yards gained, overtime or not. Then, a pause would ensue while guests made their own decisions, already having obligatory social involvement out of the way.

Phase 2 of the party would thereupon begin in front of one or more screens. In the happy event that all of the guests favored the winning team, which won a close one, the guests would likely remain, most for the duration. If they weren't unhealthfully bound to fanship, the GFR method would not have been appealing in the first place.

Given knowledge of a loss, some guests would leave or leave early. This would be understood by all Giffer enthusiasts. One screen could be for psychologically well-balanced persons who could view the loss and continue to socialize and have a moderately good time. Another screen could be set aside for the drunks and really bad sports, who were often the same people and were driven home in a special Bad Sport SUV. There were many options but, again, the technology enabled choice in both party design and guest behavior. As yet, I have kept a lid on this innovation for both individual and group activity. And, back to the point, Giffer viewing or not decreased my in-season anger.

In regard to the NFL, Peyton Manning was now quarterbacking the Denver Broncos, and I was an (unlikely) Denver fan. It also became my practice to Giffer view some of these important games. After Peyton's

Super Bowl win, early in 2016, and his retirement, GFR viewing became less important, because I did not have a dog in the hunt, or at least a big dog. Tree and I discussed favorite teams and players, so that both of us had favorites but football anger was moving out of me. I still watched many games, and I enjoyed them relatively stress free.

Tree pointed out in a conversation that, especially for me, the opposite of anger was patience. Almost anything that I would be doing to increase patience would also reduce anger. Theoretically at least, this inverse relationship also flowed in reverse causality. This mattered -- and I agreed – because no one, who ever knew me, believed that my assets included patience. Considering anger-reduction as resulting from patience-improvement was a daunting way to view the challenge.

Tree and I also discussed my own belief that I was more patient, or less impatient, in my world of work than anywhere else. Perhaps it was because I was more comfortable in that world and in that role, more confident, less fearful. Perhaps it was because I perceived that I had more control of outcomes there?

In truth, I always was a relatively good producer of services in society, but a near-awful consumer of goods and services. My producer life was the exception to my being disdainful of, fearful over, and anger-inclined toward other transactions and interactions between me or my family and others. My lack of patience in these involvements held much capacity for improvement.

For example, the consumer experience which I desire involves my general understanding of the good to be purchased; discerning the correct category of store – jewelry versus hardware; traveling to the location; interacting with store personnel as necessary; making my selections; paying; and returning home. Only one retailer continued to fill that description for many years in the new millennium, my men's clothing store. Then, the store went under. I was likely one of their last good customers. By 2015, I looked around and had missed a couple of decades of technologically related change in the methodologies of these transactions, which were apart from my world of teaching and expert witnessing (where I kept up in one way or another.)

My wife knew, because I kept telling her, of my sincere desire that she avoid predeceasing me. Left alone to deal with the world, I would starve in only a few days. Or I would need to be in an assisted living facility at age 65 for functional dementia. Or worse. She and my teen-age granddaughter shielded me from most of this new world, probably because it was easier at the time to do it for me than to teach me how to do it. Also, I did not desire to learn how to do it. Back before Tree.

Yet, there were more instances each year when I was forced to deal with this rest of the world for one reason or another. There was the time, for example, that I had to deal with my bank-issued credit card. Let me back up and put this episode into perspective. Especially when Lynn moved from only dealing with my health insurance carrier for me to also dealing with Medicare and Social Security, she began to assign To Do's for me that she thought I could possibly handle. One was dealing with my dentist's office on my own and my multiplying doctors' offices on my own. While email correspondence with such offices became easier and more common for many, I eschewed these mechanisms in favor of dealing with humans over the telephone. Thus, the move to automated options in lieu of a human voice answering a provider's phone lead me into a world of automated intelligence, a breeding ground for fear, anger, resentment, and impatience.

Sometimes it was easy. The first option was scheduling. With minor encouragement from my family, I could realize that this was my option, hit "1," reach a human who was all about scheduling, transact my business, and accomplish the objective. Nothing, of course, is that easy, or at least remains that easy. It became increasingly difficult to reach a human person via the maze of options, and then the person might or might not have been able to communicate with me, and they might or might not have been the person who could give me the necessary information, make the necessary decision, remove the mammography from my bill, etc. Then, one might be placed on hold for someone else who would never answer, if they ever existed.

A memorable breaking point for me was the aforementioned credit card error on my monthly statement, which was sufficiently large and obvious that even a poor consumer like me could not miss it. Having just remarked about the free time I sometime found since faculty retirement; it was suggested that pursuing this bank error be my project.

The error, I believed, was apparent from the bank's own monthly statement and verifiable using past statements. The total of the detailed purchases for the month fell far short of the total monthly purchases shown elsewhere and used to calculate interest and the balance due. Either the bank needed to identify the purchases omitted or credit my account to correct the error. So, I called the toll-free number provided for "assistance" and was connected to a continuing loop of five options. None of the five options seemed close to either dealing with an error on my credit card statement or connecting me to a human. So, I moved through the sub-options to each option and still had no path toward my objective.

The realization struck me that the bank had developed a system wherein the possibility of error by the bank was not allowed. Amazing. While still avoiding email, I assembled a snail mail cover letter with a few documentation pages from the bank statement. A snail mail letter was sent in reply informing me that someone would call me. He did, but he had little to say. Instead, he listened to me quickly talk through the documentation of my problem and my desired solution. Then, without other comment, he said someone else would be calling me. No one called me, but I was sent a letter requesting me to re-send my documentation, which I did.

The matter remains unresolved. The point is that any progress on my part in regard to anger or patience was despite the appearance of a new, angerful environment. It was a sign of some mindfulness on my part, perhaps, that I did not obsess even more about the de-peopling of assistance to customers. My natural self would have created an ample layer of anger simply considering the possibility that companies estimate the dollar exaggerations or errors that someone like me will tolerate before making their life more miserable than they are making mine. I would see a huge conspiracy to pad profit margins and/or meet budget requirements via targeted approaches to different consumers, about whom they know everything. Fortunately, I did not think this way anymore, mostly, with regard to navigating this changing environment, and Tree and I sometimes discussed and assessed incremental improvement, or setbacks.

This made me mindful that thinking myself smaller would help me here and lowering my expectations to simply doing the best I could reasonably do also helped. I had no special status in the order of things to better treatment than others, which was also subject to the whims of chance or perhaps higher intervention. The use of a deliberate pause before and after a call-with-options experience began, and I would occasionally consult with Tree on how to deal with these situations.

No external interaction was more formidable to me than a trip to a large supermarket, and clearly among my reasons were fear of failure and anger and frustration about shopping challenges which exposed my inadequacies. The end of such a process of consumerism is most relevant to patience: standing in line to pay. There were some rare days in which I could not avoid a supermarket experience, as when my wife was sick. Thus, on a particular Friday afternoon, notwithstanding all of the difficulties and stresses encountered from the start of the shopping experience, I found myself in line to pay. The use of a pause before an impatience-triggering event had actually crossed my mind while in the parking lot and, again, as I surveyed the line of persons in front of me and glared at the section for self-help paying, the technology of which I feared and abhorred. Moreover, the 10-items-or-less line held no promise because I either had no items or eleven or more. I don't know why. It was akin to my bad luck in choosing the slowest moving line.

"You chose the shortest line, Mike – three people in front of you – because a lady with overflowing groceries just paid and the next lady with two packed carts is just beginning. So, every other line will move faster than your line. This is not rocket science."

"Hi, Tree," I thought back to him. The location of Tree's voice was not clear to me, but he was somewhere close by.

Tree continued, "Why do you view the persons ahead of you as hostile obstacles, whose goal is to make your shopping experience uncomfortable? And why are you in such a hurry that you view them as delaying some time-critical event later today?"

"I don't know why I set myself up like this to be angry and discontented. I have nothing to do that is especially time critical," I admitted.

"Then chill yourself, Mike, relax your jaw, unclench your fists, take a deep breath, and attempt patience." Tree then told me about the lady now checking out with her two full carts. She was my grocery queue nightmare. Two carts full, lots of coupons, and she was chatting up the checkout clerk like a lost brother. The clerk himself was enjoying this rambling chit chat which clearly was slowing the process. He was a slender, old guy with black hair combed straight down over his eyes and a large, bulbous nose dominating his face.

"The lady is a retired nurse, very shy, never married. Friday grocery shopping and Sunday church are the social highlights of her week. She likes this clerk and always picks his line. It took them six months to begin talking to each other and now they probably overdo it."

"No kidding, Tree," I thought.

"Talk to the guy in front of you, Mike."

"Why?"

"Just do it." This sounded more like a directive than a suggestion so I did.

He was a friendly guy, an EMT for the fire department, who was working with a special first responder group to follow-up with drug- overdosed persons revived with Narcan and steer them into some type of treatment. In his early forties, I would guess, he had raised two daughters as a single dad – one now at West Virginia University and the other about to graduate from high school. An urban hero was this man.

I continued to talk with him while he checked out, and I thanked him for what he did in his job for the rest of us. The old clerk guy did not have much to say to me, but he was quite efficient. Someone else bagged me, so to speak, and I was out of there. Not a bad experience at all. I simply forgot about my natural impatience. Signs of progress....

Concerning the fear in the middle of me, a memorable episode from the trudge sprang from my choice of cow as the least difficult pathway forward. It was very unlikely that harm would come to me simply from being alone in a barn with a milk cow. Setting up such an encounter is not simple, however.

One cannot easily sneak around the farming property of others searching for a cow in a barn. What if there were many cows in a stranger's barn, so that they could attack from all sides? What if they alternatively had an urgent group moo which brought the farm proprietor running with a shotgun? How does my family explain at the funeral what I was doing in that barn? Moreover, one cannot simply knock on a farm door requesting cooperation with a fear-reducing bovine meeting.

I certainly could not ask my wife, her family, or close friends for help with this process. They would be very unlikely to find the mental soundness in a late-in-life meeting with a milk cow. A guided tour of a large dairy operation would fail to address my particular fear. My answer came via a practicing psychologist whom I had come to know well as a friend in a weekly discussion group and who had a large family scattered around central West Virginia.

Serendipitously, my friend David and I became engaged in a discussion about his family and their wide-ranging vocations, interests, and life stories. His cousin Ron was a few years older than me, was wounded in Vietnam and awarded a disability pension, and soon thereafter inherited a 50-acre farm in an adjacent county. He said that Ron was one of his favorite cousins, whom he visited every couple of months, and who was one of the most consistently happy guys he had ever met. Ron had never married. He had no kids but lots of friends. Ron also grew his own vegetables, which he shared with others, and always kept a milk cow in his barn.

I took a really big risk telling David my grandfather-and-cow story, and of my recent determination to face a cow alone in a barn and conquer my unusual phobia. He asked why now, and I said it was a long story that was best not discussed. He let it go but mused that a psychologist could not argue with facing one's fears. He said that he would arrange a meeting with cousin Ron, who would be happy to show me around the farm. "But I'll tell him something like learning to milk a cow was on your bucket list for the year. That is unusual but the truth is even more strange, and we first need to get you on the property."

"I don't want to milk the cow, just look at it."

"Yeah, I know. You will have to figure that out. Cousin Ron is a great guy. I'm sure that you can find a way to pull this off." The meeting was set at 9 a.m. the following Wednesday. Tree encouraged me not to back out, so I found myself driving on rural county roads listening to directions from the talking lady. Lynn and Chloe had their own activities on this late summer day, and I often dressed in jeans to go to my office in the summer.

The mailbox address and entry driveway were easy to find, with the talking lady's help. I was far from significant civilization. Yet, two cars pulled out before I turned in. City cars, not trucks; a middle age man, and a twentyish female driver. A busy farm. The wide gravel driveway extended for almost 100 yards to a modern-looking, ranch-style house, and Ron was sitting on the front porch drinking a coffee and waiting for me. It was

9:00 a.m. Vegetable gardens occupied land to the left of the driveway, with some well-tended flower gardens on the right. Seemed unusual for a bachelor farmer?

I parked in front and met Ron. He was about my height, with a scraggly beard, gray and white like his mop of hair, and wire-rimmed glasses. His weathered face was dominated by clear, blue eyes that seemed to sparkle with mischief. I declined coffee, too nervous to hold a cup, so he put his down and walked me around to the back of the house for a quick tour. In the back was a garage-sized building facing to the side and, just beyond, a large, fenced-in area containing a barn, several smaller sheds, coops and many chickens, a pig pen with a massive hog therein, and some pastureland. We walked into the fenced area, and he pointed out the fallow fields just beyond and then cultivated fields of corn. These extended to Ron's own mountain, which was thickly wooded and ended his property.

After 15 minutes or so of friendly conversation, Ron got to the point, "David tells me you would like to milk a cow sometime in your remaining life, and this is your lucky day." I had been dreading this conversation.

"I don't really need to learn how to milk a cow," I said tentatively, "as much as just being around one for a few minutes in your barn there."

His eyebrows arched up in surprise, "So you just want us to walk in there and look at my cow?"

"Well, really I need to be in there alone with the cow."

"While you are in there alone with my cow," he hesitated, "what are you going to do with my cow?" Some alarm appeared in his otherwise calm demeanor.

"Just look at her. That's all." And Ron grew quiet.

This was not working, I sensed, and I could not effectively recall any of the deceptions which I had mulled around in considering how to get in the barn.

Before anything more could be said, Ron laughed merrily and said, "David told me the whole story -- your grandfather's cow and your late-in-life attempt to deal with it."

I was embarrassed but Ron was actually making this much easier. "You probably think I'm crazy?" I asked.

"Eccentric maybe," he laughed, "but it will make a great story for my friends and neighbors. I'll give you a new name to protect your professional reputation."

He continued, "Let me go in there with you to meet Bessie – yeah, that's really her name – and then I'll leave the two of you alone for a while and wait outside... just in case you start to mess with Bessie and she tries to kill you." He laughed again and said, "Just kidding, but don't walk behind her. She could kick you into orbit if, for some reason, cows simply don't like your looks."

Before entering the barn, however, Ron ascertained that I knew almost nothing about cows, and he proceeded with a well-organized lecturette on the topic. In twenty minutes, he cow-educated me about Holstein cows, like Bessie, how long milk cows give milk, and how birthing and milk production inter-related. He told me what would happen to Bessie after about another year of milking; there is information about the food supply that city people do not want to know. He told me about mastitis, and lameness, and infertility. Then, Ron briefed me on the health and welfare issues affecting the cows of many large dairy farm operations. His description of the lingering emotional issues for cow moms and calves separated at birth choked me up inside. Turns out, Ron was a committed cow rights advocate, despite what he had plans to do with Bessie. By the time he said we should go in the barn to see Bessie, my attitude about cows was already changing.

Thus, Ron guided me through the barn door, latched it, and flipped a switch turning on various lights throughout the barn. There was a loft but no ladder; two stalls had half-doors which I could jump over in case of attack. Bessie was standing tethered loosely in front of a feeding trough, and she turned her head to watch us as we entered and walked to a few feet of her right side. Bessie was white with large black spots. She had an udder, one of the few things which I knew about cows. Ron talked to her softly and lovingly, as I did to Teddi Rose, and he introduced Bessie to me, explained my story to Bessie, and asked the cow to be nice to me. Bessie glanced at me with soft brown eyes that seemed to convey both understanding and pity.

While he talked, Ron stepped up to Bessie and softly stroked her neck and shoulder area. After a while, he had me standing there doing the same. What does a stranger say to a milk cow? How was breakfast? What's up before lunch? How's it churning down there in those two stomachs? So, I just patted her and mumbled.

Ron left and closed the door. I continued to stroke Bessie, and I was feeling pretty darn good. "I appreciate your time this morning Bessie." What a stupid thing to say, I thought, but no one would ever know. After five or ten minutes, it was done. There was nothing else to do or say, except, "Goodbye Bessie. Thanks." And I turned and walked out the barn door.

Ron was smiling. "Are you fixed?"

"Yes, I think that I am fixed." We toured and talked a bit longer. Ron was a self-described old hippie, having lived a counter-cultural lifestyle both before and after his soldier days. He invited me to come back with David for some social time, and I agreed, without any idea of how persons socialized on a farm. We walked around the open side of his garage, and a shiny, newish Jaguar was parked there. He could tell I was surprised and said "The car is named Bessie, too. I always name my car after my cow. Trade cars and cows at the same time."

"Whatever you do here, you must really do it well to afford a Jaguar," I exclaimed.

Ron smiled, "An uncle of mine suggested a terrific business model to me shortly after I inherited the farm and it has worked very well. It funds my cars and vacations."

"I don't suppose you have ever shared your business model?"

"No, if it was shared, it would no longer be terrific."

We shook hands, and I drove back down the driveway. As I turned onto the county road, an SUV entered the driveway. This was a Grand Central Station of small farms, and Ron was not affording a Jaguar growing corn. Regardless, cow fear was gone. It was a wonderful day that Tree and David had worked out for me.

Other fear-facing opportunities were by-passed during these years, however. Horse riding opportunities were readily available but not pursued. Jumps or flips off diving boards were another option for facing height fears, but diving boards were quickly disappearing because of lawyers.

My expert witness career continued so that the fear of failure potential for cluttering the middle of me was still around. There would be one more testimony trip involving Tree during this period. It was in the dead of winter, again to Baltimore City, with an afternoon layover in Charlotte. By this point in my life, there was little appealing about business travel. It was even difficult to read my leisure book during airport waits because of the perfectionist pull toward continued review of my files until my testimony occurred.

By an hour before departure time out of Charlotte, the gate area was packed. "Quit your obsessive review of your notes and read the spy book on your Kindle. You are already prepared at 100 percent of perfection and you may implode if you don't put those files away." It was clearly Tree, but the voice was somewhere else in the gate area.

I surveyed the crowd around me. Many people were standing because no seats were available, except one open seat against the outdoors windows. Why was no one occupying this seat? I placed my files back in my briefcase, leaned back, and then closed my eyes. "So, you are travelling with me," I thought at Tree, but he did not reply. In a few minutes, I opened my eyes, glanced at the ticket desk, and noticed that the vacant chair had been filled. An older man was reading a newspaper suspended in front of him but seemed to be staring at me above the newspaper. He was a slender, older gentleman wearing an overcoat which extended to the floor. His hair and facial hair obscured his eyes and ears, but he had a noticeably large nose. "Is that you over there, Tree?" I thought in the man's direction.

There was no reply, and I looked around the gate area and then closed my eyes briefly. When I looked again at the man, he had vanished, and the seat again was conspicuously empty. It occurred to me that I might finally be succumbing to the pressure of my work and losing my mind. The trip to Baltimore proceeded without incident, my attorney took me to an early, working dinner, and I returned to my hotel room for further perfectionist preparation.

Tree began speaking to me as I sat at the desk overlooking Baltimore's Inner Harbor. He was either on the bed or hovering around or above it. Tree then led a discussion with me about my peculiar blend of fear, high expectations, and perfectionism. Within a few minutes, we were both laughing at me. To prove a point, Tree gave me a quiz about the case – plaintiff's birthdate, highest annual earnings, IQ scores – and I answered perfectly. So, we watched a movie together. Before leaving, Tree said he wouldn't be around the next day but that it was time that I learned how to do this stuff on my own. He said he was headed for Albuquerque. It was very difficult to ferret out Tree's attempts at humor from the truth.

The next morning, from first coffee through testimony and return home, I felt as if Tree was around, but he did not communicate or appear. The judge was bald, cleanshaven, and plump, which encouraged me, and neither the opposing attorneys nor anyone on the jury resembled any image that I held of Tree. Also encouraging. The testimony proceeded and ended, and it had been the lowest level of stress on a testimony day in memory.

I didn't think about fear of failure. I didn't think about me at all. Just my luck that when my profession was finally becoming easier, I was about to retire and leave it. Yet, rarely had a day felt so uplifting.

Time passed very quickly. Before I could dwell on my faculty retirement, it happened. By summer 2015, half of my working life -- of students, and colleagues, and teaching – was behind me. The finality of the change was bothersome, but it was time to move on. Two weekday evenings during the academic year, preparation and administrative and advising time, and research and publication chores, driven by ego and perfectionism, were no more. With Tree's encouragement, I contemplated new dealings with others, combatting my natural impulse to claim the new time for myself.

An early thought was that my group of acquaintances was sufficiently large that expanding acquaintances was not my first priority. Deepening the relationships already established did resonate in me, and the easiest way to start was with immediate family. Lynn and Chloe, of course, had not been briefed on the Tree-prompted quest of Deletes and Grows. They showed no obvious desires for relationship deepening, and it occurred to me that deepening conversations would be warily received and the development of joint action plans to be pursued was unlikely. So, I kept my control-oriented mouth shut about a grand design for our future. I made known and attempted to live my availability and, again as suggested by Tree, focused upon watching and listening. Nothing dramatic happened, but both persons seemed to enjoy the frequency of when I would tune in to them and often do what they wanted to do. It was in this way, for example, that I spent time viewing an array of cable offerings about fashion, cooking, and remodeling homes. These were not as entertaining to me as football, but less stressful, and the family moved along together into high school.

Fertile ground for deepening was the discussion group which I had reluctantly joined years before and, as previously noted, had helped me with the fear of reading in public. It required an effort to listen and watch intensely as others talked, in lieu of the heretofore emphasis on talking and preparing to talk. Tree suggested that I come early, stay late, and spend time listening and talking one-on-one. My volume of personal phone calls changed from nothing to something. Knowing others better sometimes meant spending time with them, perhaps helping them, and increasingly dwelling upon their problems and concerns. This one-on-one deepening required mindfulness and consistent effort. But not a lot of effort, really, not compared to the new, good feeling in the middle of me.

Two male friends of mine had been friends of my late wife, and we occasionally had lunch over the years or otherwise were together. We began to have lunch regularly, every couple of weeks. It became an important part of my schedule. Inevitably, we became very close by virtue of this frequent contact. This deepness of relationship with others was uncommon in my past.

Exercise increased a bit with the removal of faculty time. Two days of gym time each week, usually with a trainer, continued, and I was able to work up to 30 minutes on my home stationary bike every day. In a related move, my cable news watching time was restricted to this 30-minutes each day, exactly at the end of an afternoon. While exercise may have been a "me" activity, it eventually became apparent that my current regime held a great advantage over the racquetball regime of 37 years. Racquetball fed the excessive competitiveness in me. It involved scorekeeping. The new regime was compatible with where I wanted to go – happier. And another set of acquaintances and possible friends were other gym regulars with whom I could interact while masquerading as an old jock.

Learning time increased as teaching time ended, perhaps part of some circle of professional life. More time was spent on learning how to use technologies of communicating and, well, existing in modern times. The effective integration of business and home computers, and both with my iPhone, was a marvelous efficiency and enhancement to my working from home. Many apps were learned and some mastered, but my females were so good at this stuff that little advancement happened, for example, in making travel plans, shopping, or hailing drivers when out of town.

Social media usage was also all around me in the household, and relevant information, posts, pictures, and video segments would be shared with me, while requiring nothing from me in the fetching of information. With encouragement from Tree, I spent some time reading about pros and cons of time spent on social media. My platform for evaluation was Facebook because writing and reading posts were more likely for me than sending pictures, making quick comments about current events, or learning on YouTube how to repair something.

Being on the darkish side of the digital divide meant sometimes participating in a human grouping where everyone else was using mobile devices to read – Facebook, for example, to text to others, and even to research information related to the group conversation. One could argue about whether they were a bit rude or I was simply a dinosaur, but it was clear that the others were not likely to join me in the past.

The meaning of "friend" in the social media context struck me, in contrast to my own notion. The friendship that I valued and sought was far deeper, as information, thoughts, and feelings shared were <u>not</u> for possible consumption by a larger public. There was also a worry that users of social media tended to become less patient as their usage increased, addicted to fast information, less able to delay instant gratification or consider the long run. Less patience and more anger was not my intended direction.

On the other hand, the availability of speedy information, on an awesome breadth of subject matter, and with communication networks heretofore unimaginable, had great appeal, and my past improvements had yielded some high payoffs. Search engines were becoming a toy for me to scratch itches from my curiosity which heretofore had been unreachable at a reasonable time and cost. The vast majority of the inquiries which I had begun to make, when time allowed, had no potential payoff except the reward of truth seeking. An early recollection involved a question first asked to me by Chloe circa age seven. I did not know the answer to her question, and half-hearted attempts at gathering relevant information had yielded nothing. But now that my comfort level with software applications had sufficiently advanced, this question which periodically vexed me could rather easily be addressed.

Why doesn't Goofy have a last name? Mickey has Mouse. Donald has Duck. Virtually every other cartoon character has a last name. If Mickey and Donald set the mold, it should be Dog. Goofy Dog. Was it a lack of alliteration that nixed this one? Then why not make him a gangly goose? Goofy Goose? My mind pursued many avenues of perplexity.

Easily learned, via the new technology, is that Goofy's character began in 1932 as Dippy Dawg, and it was occasionally given as Goofus D. Dawg. For a while in the 1950's, Goofy lived at the address of George Geef, which was presumably his formal name. These were exceptions, however, to an almost ninety-year life as Goofy – one-name Goofy. How much did it weigh upon Goofy in his moments of reflection, to ponder why his pals the mouse and the duck had solid, reputable last names but he did not?

Finally, in a 1992 cartoon, Goofy's diploma was read by a narrator as that of "Mr. G. G. Goof," but this was another, brief diversion from one-name life. What was Disney attempting to hide about Goofy? It does not seem to be that difficult. Dog. Goofy Dog. He is at least as much a dog as Mickey is a mouse and Donald is a duck. Cannot anyone at Disney recognize the mental harm that this inconsistency and confusion brings to someone like me?

Thus, the new technology gave me heretofore unrealized access to relevant information. But not really an answer to the why question. Perhaps others, alerted by this easy availability of information, will rise up and demand that someone finally does right by Goofy. Or perhaps I am the only soul consternated by this injustice. Even the simple is complex.

One focus of learning time, begun late in this period, was Eastern philosophy, beliefs, and practices, religious and otherwise. Books, internet research, and yogaish friends informed me, and any notion of my being widely or well-read was smashed. The focus on the inside of me was welcomed, and it was a great reinforcement and encouragement that so much of my learning was compatible with where Tree was moving me. There was so much to ponder about activities previously taken for granted: breathing, eating and drinking, assessing the calmness, or not, of my mind. Possible paths were delivered, away from fear and anger and toward kindness and equanimity. An early concern was my vision of a future conversation with my wife as I transitioned into vegetarianism, the elimination of coffee, daily meditation, and the occasional, new posture (asana) adopted for watching television. She would likely react to such topics, coming from me, with concern. It was clear she didn't believe that my intention to "try out yoga" was for the benefit of stretching my aging body.

Indeed, it was surprising to me that I found myself in a yoga studio at a beginner's class. I would learn that the others had several sessions behind them and seemed to know basics not readily gleaned from my reading. The others did not resemble my age or gender; they eyed me warily until I began to meet their expectations. While they were arranging their bodies in the basic, sitting position, I was circling my mat like a dog, contemplating how to move my body to the floor. There was nothing basic, or easy, about what was then asked of me and my body. My replacement hip and weak lower back were particular obstacles. Once the instructor, whom I knew and liked, attempted to help me by gently pressing down on my butt with her foot so that I might lie face down, flat like my fellow students. She stopped after realizing that as my butt moved down toward the mat, my head rose up off the mat in tandem. Apparently, this was because of a Peronie's disease of the spinal column, which would need to be overcome by my mind and body.

Before leaving, I was able to watch some of an advanced class, in which the fluidity of movement was impressive. The image formed in my mind of my high school football coach warming us up for practice with postures, breathing exercises, and the occasional mantra. This would have evoked a full belly laugh, except that my unyogalike body hurt in virtually every hurtable place. Tree would not allow me to quit after only one session, so the adventure continued.

Meditation interested me, and I determined to read up on the how to's and pursue this on my own. This was, more or less, my past approach to a new endeavor. It did not work out well. Even assuming that I could have arranged my body, mind, and environment into a proper starting place – which was difficult enough – my mind would need to be cleared out of stuff. My mind would not clear. Once I felt close to a beginning but Teddi Rose interrupted with an urgent poop request. Thus, the Eastern part of myself limped forward but such pursuits, themselves, were heretofore unimaginable.

By the summer of 2016, I was falling into a rhythm of mindfulness and effort regarding Deletes, Adds, and Grows, which seemed to consume any available time but also caused time to pass very quickly for me. Three particular topics of the summer were memorable.

The first was my generalization of the value of Pause. Tree and I agreed, in one porch conversation, that my natural self was pauseless. I charged ahead even if in the wrong direction. On the one hand, my professional activities had caused me to value the effective use of the pause: as a teacher and a trainer, to ask a question to a group and then pause for a response; as an expert witness, to pause after a question and then respond decisively. On the other hand, pause was not evident in my conversation style – pauses to listen, for example. Also, my management activities would have benefited from more pausing, especially if associated with more thinking. The pause notion was helping me with anger, and it seemed certain that more and better pausing would be positively correlated with more patience. Thus, my resolution was to generalize my use of a pause between stimulus and response, between thought and action, between first impressions and a reframing. It was my Boomer generation which sped life up, except in comparison to the generations thereafter, and it seemed important that I bucked the trend and began adding speed bumps to slow me down.

Active listening was an important part of my management training programs on communications. I knew the literature, the value, and the technologies. Don't interrupt. Ask clarifying questions. Pause after they finish and before you begin. Consider the speakers' point of view. Resist adding your opinion, when unnecessary. Et cetera. And I agreed with all of this, but none of this had been applied by me to me. I don't know why. So, my mindfulness was cranked up here. Tree was most encouraging of these efforts.

My negativism needed to be addressed: another staple of my natural self and a promising delete. Improvements in fanship activity enlightened me here, and these were reinforced by random psychology readings on the 3:1 greater impact of bad emotions over good. My resolve was to avoid bad in cognition and deed. Do no harm. Pause before you say something that will require three goods to amend. I read and watched less news in my typical day. My hope, also, was to become more easily positive and to look for the positive, the pony in there somewhere.

Implementing such changes in me was painfully difficult and slow. The old dog and the new tricks. It sometimes seemed a whack-a-mole process of frustration. This is the arcade game where moles appear at random in various holes and the player uses a mallet to whack them. My mindfulness expansion was producing so many moles that consistent progress vis-à-vis any particular mole seemed elusive. Interestingly, I increasingly found myself muttering to Tree, as various efforts were made, even though we were not in conversation at the time. This helped me not to quit.

Tree gave me particular encouragement in a porch conversation bookended by the summer Olympics beforehand and the advent of school for Chloe and football season for me. We were discussing my efforts and my uncertainty about progress. "On the anger front, I feel progress in reducing and avoiding anger in the present. But nothing has been done to address the ball of stored-up anger that must be somewhere in my middle."

Tree observed, "Your progress may be better than you think it is. Your expectations are too high for fast progress, and you are notably impatient. But you are working on these too. Let me encourage you that as your inflows of new anger diminish, that heavy burden of stored-up anger… and resentment… begins, at least, to melt away. Aim at improvement, not at perfect. As you trudge toward a solution, the problem may go away."

"Do you think smaller of yourself than before?" Tree asked. "Have you lowered your opinion of what you control versus what you don't? Is your mind better contained within the day?"

I began to slowly nod my head affirmatively, and he continued, "I believe so too. Your recent recognition that active listening might be a recipient of your attention made me chuckle." He smiled, "You have great potential for improvement here, and your listening more and better would surely relate to smaller, and less in control. And to kinder."

"Can't say that I am a kinder person yet. I feel softer, more chill, more of the time and that feels good."

Tree said, "But, Mike, let me point out that you are kinder to yourself. Those good feelings that you have, and bad feelings that you are not experiencing, show that. You feel less alone in your middle, even as there is less of you there."

"Thank you, Tree. You lift my spirits."

"The really good news here is that excellence is not required. There is no scorekeeping system at play. All you must do is try."

"Got it." It was a good end to the conversation, on a positive note. So, we previewed the coming football season, and he forced me to again describe the college rules for tie games after regulation play. It always made him laugh.

CHAPTER TEN - CONTEMPLATING OLD AGE

My attention to changes in the middle of me did not cease in the fall of 2016, but it lessened. For reasons that I can identify, and perhaps some that I cannot, my focus was diverted from the day that I was in to the contemplation of my remaining days ahead. This became an obstacle to my progress and proved difficult to dismiss from my thoughts. For several months, I was stuck in the contemplation of old age.

A most obvious trigger was my September 11 attainment of age 66, when I chose to begin receiving Social Security retirement benefits for "normal retirement age." Oddly for an overthinker and compulsive planner, little thought was given to the possibility of delaying the receipt of benefits to age 70, with an increased monthly benefit thereafter and through death. It was a choice ripe for economic analysis. Yet, my illogical negativism pushed me toward thoughts of my untimely death (before my statistical life expectancy of age 83.2) and, with my luck, grossly untimely. If death occurred before my age 70, zero dollars in benefits would come my way, despite my lifetime (forced) contributions. If relatively soon after age 70, the higher monthly benefits would not approach the age 66-70 benefits that had been given up. This risk could not be tolerated. The government would not have its way with me. Receipt would begin immediately upon age 66 normality, even as contributions into the system from my consulting income continued. The income redistribution built into this system did not bother me, except that the feds could more efficiently and transparently accomplish this through the progressivity of income tax rates. These details aside, the point is that my mind necessarily turned to future ages and years. The dispassion of life expectancy issues to an economist was greatly eroded when the old age and death under consideration belonged to me.

In retrospect, it is a bit surprising that my age 65 beginning of Medicare eligibility had not triggered my old age contemplation. But Lynn had graciously assumed the tasks of dealing with the federal government and making Medicare Part B decisions, so that no death-influenced decisions weighed upon my mind. The transition was as seamless for me as dealing with the government, and change, could possibly be. Moreover, my diverse array of health issues, while short of life-or-death concerns, caused the government to begin significant spending on my behalf. This evoked a dubious satisfaction that the government was finally spending some of its money specifically on me.

In addition, retirement decision-making had been initiated more than a year before, when I decided to retire from my faculty position at the end of the 2014-2015 academic year. Fall 2016 was my second football season unaffected by academic work. Only occasionally had I missed teaching, but facing a second retired year, nostalgia for my past work with students troubled me. There was no going back. While employers received the benefit of probationary periods to judge new employees, a probationary retirement period had not been an option for me at the end of employment.

This first retirement decision also pointed me toward the more important decision, affecting workload and income, of when and how retirement from my economic consulting business would occur. Until I decided otherwise, this work was more than a full time job, and much of the faculty time freed up a year before had simply been reallocated to this (thankfully) thriving business. Lawsuits, and thereby expert witnesses on economic damages, seemed immune to business cycles affecting other businesses. I lived in a great country, and the blessings of liberty in our courtrooms had been good to me.

My older colleagues testifying across the country, who had entered the business with me in the 1970's or early 1980's, had generally chosen not to retire, or seriously think about it, while still going strong at age 75 or older. Balanced against the rewards of continuing this work, including the mental rewards of meaningful work, were the costs of engaging in work that could be extremely stressful. How would you like to work for trial lawyers, with rules enforced by judges, who were also lawyers? Sigh. A part of me wished to cease such work sometime before my death, so that a relaxing alternative lifestyle might be enjoyed. This, in turn, triggered a self-awareness that relaxing was neither a habit nor a skill for me and that I was having difficulty picturing a happy, alternative lifestyle. Tree-induced changes notwithstanding. My younger partner and I had discussed how a phased retirement for me might work, but no beginning date had been considered. Again, any such thinking necessarily involved my older age and progression toward – hard to simply ignore it – death.

Even by the mid-age-60's one noticed the upturn in acquaintances and friends who died or who struggled with serious health conditions. In the fall of 2016, I was witnessing two close friends dealing with cancer and complications, in one case, and ALS (Lou Gehrig's disease) in the other. Both men were younger than me and, except for their primary diagnoses, healthier. How does one not think about older age and the unyielding possibility of death at any time?

Moreover, by age 66, one notices that he is being treated differently than before. The differences are increasingly difficult to ignore or accept. Some are institutionalized. For example, automatic qualification had occurred for a double-dose of the flu shot each fall. Thus, if the cock-tail did not fit the particular strain of flu in my nostrils, it was doubly too bad. Also, my primary care physician automatically promoted me from annual visits to twice a year. By now, I knew that we had plenty to talk about in these more frequent visits. This is assuredly not the type of visit with another person that one wishes to run long because of the number and complexity of agenda items. Worse is when persons one does not know volunteer to let one see the doctor ahead of them, but at least this had not happened to me yet.

Persons around me had begun to talk in lowered voices. I was more likely to ask them to repeat themselves. It is possible, I considered, that the problem had existed for some time but that I did not give a hoot about what anyone else was saying. Now, with my enhanced attention to active listening, the problem manifested itself. I finally had my hearing checked, but to the surprise of everyone, this was a rare health exam that I passed. Rather than celebrate, my thinking turned to the alternative explanation that others had conversations about topics not intended for me to hear, such as the topic of me. Creeping paranoia. Or worse, a speaker did not need me to hear because others in the room were the targets. Invisibility.

From my experience, persons around me of less advanced age had difficulty adapting to my needs and sensitivities. It is not cheering to announce one's 66th birthday, for example. Most others will automatically smile and say something like "Congratulations." Then, they are in trouble thinking of their next, follow-up comment.

This follow-up is not difficult when aimed at a 6-year-old or a 12-year-old. It is something positive that relates to the child's attributes per se or attributes unusual "for his age." If the attribute is maturity, then the child is precocious. Only a precocious child would know what this word meant, or how to spell it.

It is not so easy to follow up with the 66-year-old. The younger adult might use, "You can't really be 66 years old." How does one reply to a comment like that? "Yes" or "Why would I make it up?" What I did find to be a satisfying response was, "So what age did you think I was?" They will laugh to buy time because you have really changed the momentum in the conversation. They must then guess at least ten years younger than 66, and they must choose some, awful stereotype of age 66 males that Mike does not (yet) exhibit.

Your younger friend might say, "Your mind is as quick as ever." Ask him or her for a couple of specific comparisons as examples. Thanks for reminding me where I am headed. Clearly, you have dismissed any possibility that my mind could quicken further. Postcocious is not even a word. "For your age" is not the positive qualifier that it was in childhood.

Persons who are older might be expected to be empathetic and more experienced with handling age sensitivities in conversation. Not so. The older guys in my gym were more likely to respond to any health complaint with a comparison to their related health status of this joint, organ, or gland in detail. "If you think it is bad now... "is their theme. Why would they do this to a kid like me? They should exude hope for my future, not extinguish it.

Back to my doctor and his team of nurses and diagnosis coders, all of a sudden, and for no good reason, these persons begin to regularly ask new questions. One that is particularly irritating is "Have you fallen in the last 6 months?" As it happened, I had recently fallen off my stationary bicycle, but I am darn sure not telling them about it! Someone will take away my car if the stationary bike is that much of a problem. And saying "I can't remember" is the worst possible response to any question. This is particularly true if your spouse has told your doctor of your failure to open the garage door before backing out in three of your last five attempts.

Much to my dismay in a late September visit, I learned that my physician had recently attended a gerontology seminar. "Hurray," I thought,

"This is just dandy." Among other new questions, he asked if I could count backwards from 100 by sevens. I said yes and gave him a challenging look. He explained that this question was to establish a baseline for the remote possibility of future cognitive problems. I replied that I would do so but asked if he first would count backwards from 100 by eights, as an example. He was actually older than me, and I assumed that he would have been practicing up on sevens. He dropped the topic and has not remembered it thereafter.

So sensitive had I become that the Silver Sneakers program of my university insurance, which now paid my gym membership, made me more resentful than grateful. How long did it take some marketing wizards to think of this term for my cohort? Silver, it is assumed, is because of the silver in one's hair. How insulting would that be for older, bald persons of both genders? With all of the racial divisions and issues facing the country, one would have thought they would have stayed away from colors. Did the geniuses brainstorm alternatives... Wrinkled Raincoats? Sagging Socks? "Sneakers" was even worse for a manly man. John Wayne never wore sneakers. Ray Lewis never wears sneakers. Peyton Manning probably doesn't wear sneakers.

Watching TV commercials further reinforced the pounding of age into my consciousness. Then the nether world learned of my age from apparent hacks of the social security system, so that only age-related ads popped up on my screen. In a typical screen viewing day, in return for a modicum of entertainment and information, I endured, for example, endless advertisements for a dizzying array of prescription drugs. Many of these drugs were for conditions that had only come to my attention in recent years, because I only recently had attained older age milestones and either an older friend or I had reason to learn about the condition. These advertisements allocated significant time for lawyer-inspired detailing of possible side effects. Why would they not be required to tell us the ratio of persons helped by the drug versus laid low by these side effects? 10/1 versus 1/10 is important information.

Competing drugs for erectile dysfunction were my side effects favorites, and it is my belief that the four-hour erection warning was invented to increase sales. A prescription drug commercial might be followed by ads for Raisin Bran cereal, soups, ointments, diets or dietary supplements, or cruises. If Raisin Bran's appeal was that it was good for me, why would the maker not also jazz the product up a little to make it more fun? How hard would it be to add a snap, crackle, or pop? Or to create a Tony-The-Tiger-like mascot: Ronnie the Racoon of Regularity? Then I might view nursing home commercials featuring actors in their fifties who had been only slightly aged-up. These were often followed by commercials for lawyers fighting against rampant nursing home abuse. Reverse mortgages ads make me smile because I imagined the consternation of heirs when they learned that Daddy's only asset had passed away along with Daddy. That was how Daddy afforded his annual adventures to raise a little hell in Branson, Missouri.

For all of these reasons, my one-day-at-a-timing was disrupted by unproductive and generally depressing thoughts. Even Tennessee victories in two important Giffer games could not ameliorate this negativity. By late September, I was choosing to read up on these topics, and my injurious thinking became more organized and systematic. It was a serious relapse to my natural self before Tree began his efforts on my behalf, and Tree was unavailable to mitigate the damage.

A labor economist is inclined to read, and sometimes research, articles and statistics on "older workers," their retirement transitions, and even post-retirement income and other household statistics. One Friday afternoon on the porch, looking at my Kindle, was consumed with such thinking. Life expectancy, of course, is a powerful statistic and a healthy life expectancy measurement had also been developed. I reflected that some would argue that my healthy life expectancy had already been passed, because of my various health problems and the arbitrary questions and classification protocols for "healthy." At least one researcher had concluded that for men, life after age 75 was not worth living. If so, the gradual rise in life expectancies was nothing to be excited about.

A new measurement of "prospective life expectancy" was gaining favor, in which old age might be measured as beginning when one was 15 years from the end of their statistical life expectancy. Thus, if my life expectancy at 66 was 83.3, then I had two more years before old age struck: a meager period of unbridled, statistical joy. Plentiful data were available on all sorts of bad stuff that would statistically plague me in the years ahead. If I made it to age 85, for example, my probability of having some form of dementia would be about 50%. Swell.

The postwar baby boom meant a large cohort of Americans moving with me through silver/golden years. Various dependency ratios of non-producing adults versus working adults implied that youngsters needed to start working a lot harder. The boomers strained health care and social services, and many boomers facing retirement were in precarious financial circumstances. Almost 60 percent of working Americans had no money in a retirement account and no defined benefit pension. Americans were not great savers.

Factoids that I once would have ignored came to conquer me. One scientific study had shown that significant calorie reduction in rats could extend their life expectancy by 50 percent. I am not a rat. Is someone thinking of applying this research to people like me? "Calorie reduction" is not a term which is attractive to me. Perhaps the takeaway for humans is to go after the skinny rats first because the fat ones will soon die anyway. Even in my negative thinking, I could quickly discern the meaning of research data.

An October porch session was coincidentally prompted by morning research in a doctor's waiting room, where I had ample time to read an entire issue devoted to aging men and their body systems and parts. One of the research themes was that parts which one would like to stay flexible did not and parts which one would like to stiffen up also did not.

Digestive system. One expert observed that an older's life is built around bowel movements. Little romance or encouragement is found in such information, which sadly seemed very plausible to me as a generalization. I had already scored in this category with diverticulosis. Rules were provided for both bowel and urinary behaviors. This was an older man's equivalent to learning to count at a young age, except much less uplifting.

Bones and joints. My entry into this category had been with the hip replacement. The priority line-up for future joint replacements was set in my mind.

Cardiovascular. The good folks at the Cleveland Clinic had given me significant post-doctoral training in this medical specialty. I learned why undiagnosed hyperthyroidism had likely caused my heart to temporarily stop on a series of occasions; thus, a pacemaker had been installed many years earlier. A heart ablation had been attempted to cause my heart to beat in normal rhythm versus atrial fibrillation. This involved two wires moved up from the groin to the heart, one with a camera and one with a torch. Any more detail would ruin the mystery for those enjoying this procedure in the future. I now took a separate drug for proper heart rhythm. While I rarely troubled about the heart attack possibilities in regard to my cardio life, the thought of a debilitating stroke was fearsome.

Eyes and ears. Graves disease resulting from thyroid difficulties had moved the muscles around my eyes, so that my 20:20 eyes pointed in different directions. One operation had failed, and prism glasses restored 2-headed persons to a single head. The possibility of blindness gave the stroke risk some competition on the front lines of unhelpful thought. Skin. My body remained covered up with this material and that was all I wanted to know. Leprosy had a low probability of striking me, but that had also been true of Graves disease.

Exercise was a recommendation that was body-wide in its beneficence. And dietary recommendations were ubiquitous. In general, the olders' metabolism fell to 60-70 percent of its previous level, and calories needed to be reduced in proportion, so: grains, nuts, broccoli, cauliflower, beets, other vegetables and fruits, no meats (or only fish). Dairy products were not recommended, and I had a stabbing anxiety that some future doctor might pick up on the implications for ice cream. My best-case meal would be salmon and honey nut Cheerios, with tons of water. A call from a client mercifully ended this agony.

In another session on the porch, a few weeks later, I had just finished some pro bono training on change and motivation. Two concepts, which represented obstacles to one's positive motivation, stoked my age-related thinking and related dolefulness. There are two tragedies in life – one is that we fail to accomplish our goals and objectives. The other is that we do. While Mike the trainer pulled some positive suggestions out of this model for his audience, Mike the porch thinker did not.

The second was that the future life view of the young is like looking out over a great plain, extending to the horizon. There are no fences. The options, opportunities, and paths forward seem boundless, even though choices and circumstances that fence one in may begin at an early age. By age 66, it was difficult to see the plain because of all the fences. One could spend hours dwelling on closing horizons and lost opportunities, and I did.

Finally, the last of colored leaves was disappearing in mid-November, and I was standing on the porch drinking coffee. The ladies of the house were on a weekend trip, and on this sunny Saturday morning, my thinker began to think. How would my aging affect the changes that had emanated from my discussions with Tree? Where was Tree?

"Hello, Michael," Tree interrupted. "Sit down. We need to talk." Growing up, my mother would only call me "Michael," or even worse "Michael Brookshire," if she was preparing to harsh me for some transgression. Nevertheless, I was very pleased at Tree's return.

"Welcome back, Tree. I have missed you," I said, glancing at my watch.

"Your 10:00 conference call just cancelled," Tree assured me, "we have all the time that we need."

He then admonished me, in a tone of controlled exasperation. "Mike, what were you thinking?" My mother also said that when my behavior was exasperating. He continued, "Why have you been doing this to yourself? You had been making steady progress out of your past and into your day. Then you moved out of your day into this obsession with future possibilities which are off-putting. While you have been engaging in this mental tour, you missed a beautiful fall, out here in your own backyard. You missed details of family and friends -- and football. You have stopped even attempting to meditate. And, you have forgotten your pauses in driving. Not a single report to Central has been made in the last month. You are missing days again, Mike. Days that are forever gone."

He paused, and I agreed with him, "Everything you say is true, I know that. It was not my wish to have these thoughts bring me down, but they are stuck in me, or I in them. To my credit, I at least recognize that this old age and death focus is holding me back. We need to talk. I need your help."

"You don't get a lot of credit for recognition. This has not been subtle. You are even doing reading and research on the topic. So, not much credit." I sensed, however, that his tone had softened, and he may have smiled.

"Let me be sure that we understand each other. You want me to indulge with you in your recent departure from progress living in the day? You wish me to be a co-conspirator against the foundation of smaller?"

"But only to talk this through with me. I did not realize these anxieties, these fears within me. You would be the first to suggest that I face my fears." Then, I added in a poor attempt at humor, "It far eclipses the cow-in-the-barn problem."

"Very well, Mike," said Tree, "I will listen to you if your objective is to place these thoughts to the side, so that you may move forward again.

You were likely to overthink these thoughts at some point, and we might not be around each other in that future time."

"Where are you going, Tree?" I asked in alarm.

"It is not my intention to go anywhere," he responded, "but there is always the possibility that you are."

I thought about Tree's statement for a few moments and simply replied, "Oh." Then, "I'm not sure where to begin."

"Why don't you talk through a scenario of your remaining life that is a best case – a really good scenario? At least lay a positive on your table of expectations before you load it up with gloom."

This had not been anticipated, and very little of my recent thinking had been positive. My first thought was that my status quo for the past several years had been darn good, and Tree's suggestions had made the last years of my life even better. A scenario of more of the same would be terrific.

"A good scenario for my future would begin with good physical health until the moment of my death. My current conditions would not go away, but they are being handled well enough presently. If they don't worsen and nothing is added, I would be more than satisfied with such a future. And if this could end with an expiration in my sleep, or like my Pappaw, that would be grand." My father's father at age 89 took no prescription drugs and had rarely been sick when he walked to the downtown of Jonesborough, Tennessee and had a fatal heart attack on the steps of his bank.

"The next foundation of a positive scenario, Tree, would be that my mind would stay sharp and clear to the end. Like my mother and her mother. Unlike my father's Alzheimer's or his mother's thirteen years in a nursing home. Then a steps-of-the-bank ending."

Tree wasn't interrupting so I continued, "Third, family and friends would need to cooperate by avoiding death, serious health problems, or significant calamity; thus, they continue as family and friends. New friends would be welcome, and relationships could deepen. So that I remain connected. I am not alone."

"Next, that in my scenario the days ahead have meaning to me and to others. That I feel self-worth. Of course, Tree, within the context of my smaller and more humble self. I would like to accelerate my learning of new and different topics, with time freed up from my final retirement. The blank to fill in, Tree, is what new work or charitable activity fills up my time?"

"You, of course, have already considered some alternatives," Tree said, "so what are your current top three alternatives?"

"I need to think more about alternatives unless I expert witness myself to the end. But, since you asked, the most viable alternative is to write a book or two – about anything but economics. If an intriguing topic popped up, this would give me purpose. Or, if we are brainstorming best cases, I might begin to write a newspaper column, featuring satirical but thought-provoking commentary on important political and social issues of the day. This would require us to actually have newspapers in the future. Better still, I become a stand-up comedian, or the equivalent for an older joker, a sit-down comedian."

"Interesting choices, Mike. Do you notice the common thread running through them? It is the opposite of smallness." He said this with mild sarcasm, but not harshly.

"And also, no world wars, plague, or famine," I added. "Yes, I know my ego looms large in my alternatives for a new direction but this is, after all, a mental fantasy, which ends my 20,000-foot view of a really good scenario."

"Why not," Tree asked, "assume this scenario and get back into the day? You've been assuming professionally for over forty years. This is your chance for a big payoff."

"I would like to do that,Tree, and perhaps I can, but that same economist in me always thinks about probabilities, and the probability that a near-perfect future will happen to me is very low."

"So, you trade a great possibility for a probability which is itself a collection of miserable possibilities?"

"Well, I wouldn't frame it that way, but I would like to talk through with you the troubling thoughts which have seized me."

"OK. Go ahead. I am listening," he sighed.

"Just to organize this a bit Tree it occurs to me that three categories of what lies ahead of me can be separated out, in terms of thoughts that pull me down. First, there are issues of aging per se. Since one always ages, it is the olding years ahead that weigh on me. Then, there may be a dying period, absent sudden death, which is distinct from olding. And finally, of course, there is death. I can't think of death without thinking about what comes after death, so death and after is the third category."

Tree interrupted, "I do not want to know how many hours you have spent preparing this presentation, do I, Mike?" He sighed again.

"No Tree you do not."

"Some of what you wish to talk about is out of bounds for us, Mike, but go ahead and talk. What are the olding issues which burden you?"

"My first thought is about loneliness. However many years or days that lie ahead, I do not wish to be alone in the world… to feel lonely."

"Yet, in our time together, you have spent most of every day – good days, you say- alone," Tree observed.

"Yes, I have thought about that, but I am alone by choice. It is solitude to work, and think, and even attempt to meditate. And to read for learning and leisure. Lonely is not how I feel. The circles around me: household, close family and friends, are there to the extent that I want them, almost all the time. My solitude rests on that foundation. Absent these feelings of connection, there would be no solitude. Only loneliness."

"These feelings of connection have only come my way in recent years," I explained. "For most of my life, I felt lonely; in a crowd, or a group, or by myself. It is a feeling which overwhelms even hope."

"So, where I am now, Tree, the best feelings of connection and support ever, could only get worse in olding. The worst of the worst is if I'm in the dying stage. The thought of feeling alone then is a dreadful possibility."

"By the way, Tree," I added, "the end of football in my olding would make me feel lonely. Just saying, for what it is worth."

"You are amazingly well prepared for an off-the-top-of-your-head commentary, Mike."

"I did have lots of time waiting for you to show up Tree," I countered, and then realized the comment was a bit testy. Tree fortunately let it pass.

"Then," I said, "there are all the possibilities for a decline in my physical health. This also involves the fear of how I die, if my preference for sudden death is not attained. Simply put, it may hurt. It may be hard to watch or to think about, as I am doing now. The scenarios of decline and death are endless."

Tree volunteered, "Apparently, you have attempted to think through as many as possible."

"Nonworking joints would be a comparatively small problem, except for the obesity and cardiac consequences, but we have a menu of serious difficulties, like heart failure, cancer, blindness," I continued, unfazed by his comment. "With my luck, a low probability disease or event could cause suffering and death: a terrible pandemic, or even a bad flu season; a car wreck, maybe at the death curve; a severe reaction to a vegetable-borne pathogen.

"And there are multiple offshoots to think about in the various scenarios. Is the dying period short or long? Is pain and discomfort not so bad or really bad? Am I fighting or in palliative care? This is a lot to brainstorm if one lets oneself do it… which, of course, you do not wish to encourage. Indeed, I have not travelled to these mental places until the last couple of months."

Tree asked, "How much of this thinking is useful to your present self, beyond prompting exercise and a better diet, for example?"

"There is only so far that I'm willing to go, by the way, in regard to diet. Red meat, ice cream and peanut butter are not negotiable at this time."

"Until the first heart attack?"

"Yes. And in answer to your question, none of these thoughts are useful to me. It is my hope to be rid of them."

"Moving along, Tree, the scenarios of physical decline are not worse than possibilities of mental decline and suffering. My clear and sharp mind would no longer be so. Dementia and Alzheimer's are dispiriting to deal with in others. Usually close family. Some might say that it is worse than being the patient. But I am discussing me, and I know such a path is possible for me. My father and his mother did have this fate. My mother and her mother did not."

"As bad as these thoughts are, in themselves, they also link to such equally worrisome topics as nursing homes. Every time I hear a comment about memory loss, or make a joke about it myself, I think about my father and his mother. Then, I think about me. Do I wish to know, if it were possible, if Alzheimer's is likely to befall me? No. Plans have been made for my family, so that is not a factor. Thus, by the time someone first hassles me about losing my memory, I hope to forget about it immediately."

"Tree, there are other mind-related possibilities in old age which I have observed. Bitterness. In my olding, will I turn sour, hateful, bitter, and will I be mostly quiet about my extreme discontent or mouthy? This is not out of the question for me if forced onto a broccoli and beets diet. Perhaps some olders are actually acting out their revenge on the rest of us. So, I would join the 80 year olds who drive 40 miles per hour in the passing lane of a 55 mph enforcement zone, just for the purpose of hearing the honks and screams of the impatient humans behind."

"Are you still with me, Tree?" I asked.

"Yes, I am hanging onto your every word." He said this matter of factly, without sarcasm, but Tree was still working on his attempts at humor.

"Next, Tree. Will I have self-worth?" Will my life matter to me and others? Or will I simply be waiting around for the death train? Especially after my last retirement, if I retire, will past accomplishments sustain my self-worth? Or can I find other activities to feel purposeful? People who know me are concerned about how a workaholic can satisfactorily fill up his time. As am I. There probably needs to be something to phase into – the novel writing, the sit-down comedian work. Perhaps, the various television networks will realize their need for an olding correspondent. They have political, legal, medical, and other experts. Boomers should demand a specialist in olding, who expresses the olding point of view. I could do that."

"It occurs to me," I added, "that the irreversibility of processes and events in olding is a thematic drag on one's morale. It is very difficult to re-start or re-do. The chance that an olding correspondent position would open up after I left my business is, well, small... especially one providing reasonable accommodations for my actual and potential ailments."

"And there is the related issue: will I continue to learn and grow in my olding? Will I come to know more of what you know and I don't? Will I know more about the Big? Will my curiosity stay with me? Could it increase? It would be troubling to 'top out' at age 66 in what I know and what can be learned."

Tree interrupted, "Mike, you are not even close to finished, are you?"

"Not really."

"So, let's take a break." It was not clear to me why Tree needed a break, but I walked the dog, ate a sandwich, and returned to the porch. It was a perfect afternoon in November: crisp, a cloudless sky.

"I'm here," Tree said.

"Moving along," I intoned, "thoughts of my losing my independence are very troubling. The topic overlaps others, like bodily and mental decline. It is true that most of my time is spent in the confined space of my home office. Yet, I can read what I want when I want, or I could drive to Knoxville on a whim for whimsical purposes. I can live where I want. I can work for pay or otherwise. I have the mental ability to criticize any politician, at any time, for anything, with either exclamatory phrases or complete sentences. The fear of losing these freedoms of independence is both that I lose the ability to do something and the dread that someone else will do things for me or to me.

"Losing my driver's license is on this list. It could happen if my vision worsens, or if the authorities make an example of me for disrupting traffic via slow driving in passing lanes. Or my loved ones could fool me into believing that I have never owned a car, while sending the car to a nephew in graduate school. I, myself, was involved in one of these maneuvers. It is not that I leave my home to drive elsewhere very often, but that is not the point, Tree. There may be a time that Lynn is unavailable, and I have an urgent need to see one of my body parts specialists, or drive to a football game and receive a distinguished alumnus award at halftime, or attend a fundraising fashion show for charity. All of that would be gone. And the goneness is not reversible, unless I have hidden enough cash in my underwear drawer to buy a new car. Sadly, driving a car would cease when I had finally developed the emotional maturity to handle driving a car.

"Losing independent living, in a residence of choice, is the greater fear, particularly in a scenario where my wife has left me for a younger man who can sing and dance. I might be there with dementia or without, requiring little assistance with activities of daily living or lots of assistance. Again, such a move is irreversible. Rare is the headline that a John Doe emerges from a nursing home at, say, age 85 better than ever and ready to return to his work as a sit-down comedian. Do such places elect officers? Maybe I could finally be president of something, intervening on issues of pudding and the comparative strength and softness of alternative adult diapers.

"It would seem," Tree said, "that anything you might be doing now to accept life as mostly beyond your control would help you, whatever your future scenario happens to be. Just saying."

My response was to push forward. "Financial security after retirement and throughout olding is not the concern for us that it is for so many boomers, not to mention most of the olders of the world. Lynn and I were fortunate to receive good educations and earn income large enough to save for retirement. Coming from a modestly middle-class family, I did not feel 'privileged' but compared to most of my worldwide age cohort, I am certainly so."

"You feel some privilege guilt then. Your thoughts are combining guilt and fear now. They go so well together."

This was the closest Tree had come to outright sarcasm, but it held a twinge of lightness. "What occasionally troubles me, however, is that various scenarios could render my family penniless. These scenarios are unlikely, but possible. It makes me feel both guilty and anxious to even think about them. Yet, I could copy my grandmother with 13 years in a nursing home at an expensive level of care. My pacemaker rendered any purchase of long-term care insurance for me impossible, so 13 years would easily make my fear a reality. Or it is possible that a rare disease might find me, which can only be held at bay by an orphan drug produced for only 19 patients in the US… at $999,999 annually per patient. With dementia, I might be scammed. The specialized school for older persons to learn the ins and outs of being a broadcast news correspondent might be fake, for example. And this is only the thinking about me, versus the extra worries of difficulties for family and friends."

"Are we wrapping up now, Mike?" Tree asked.

"Two more, Tree," I answered. "There are miscellaneous bad obstacles and scenarios that could affect me; they may not be categories but are possibilities which I have thought about."

"Miscellaneous bad things?" Tree asked, in a more-or-less incredulous tone. I believe he sighed once more.

"Yes, like the obvious ones – world war, famine, plague, the planet burns up. Several thoughts here. I am too old to be recalled to active duty unless the Army badly needs old economists. Geezers die first in most famines and plagues. If I need to fight for, hunt, forage for, or grow food, my goose is cooked. Or not cooked, as the case would be."

"Also, some thoughtful nerds warn of a coming technological singularity, in which artificial intelligence is able to improve itself and, more or less, takes over from humankind. It would be unlikely that I would even see this one coming. Or, what if a spin-off of the eugenics movement targets older people, who are no longer deemed useful? What if they particularly target retired economists? What if 50 percent of the 65+ males are required to be eliminated, and a University of Florida graduate heads up the selection committee? Once again, unlikely but possible."

"Finally, Tree, another phenomenon bothers me, regardless of how good or bad my future scenario happens to be. I can't know how many days that I have left, except statistically, but however many, time seems to fly by faster and faster. My Mother told me this would happen. This means that I am moving too fast into the olding where all of these possibilities are lurking."

"Why do you believe this speeding up of time occurs?" Tree asked. He added, "You have already researched the issue."

"As it happens, I have read some random articles and postings on this time-passing-faster perception. First, though, there is a good reason, I think, that time has seemed to pass by swiftly for me in recent years. My business has been good, and its workload has been very high. With Chloe, my family life has, happily, been busy. Then, there are the changes I have been attempting. When I am focused on a case or writing a journal article, I may look up and two or three hours have passed. Time has disappeared. Being less busy, or less productive in some way, is not a path which I wish to take in slowing down time. Less hectic would be nice. Less stressful? Definitely yes. But not less full of meaningful endeavors.

"One science-based explanation, which makes some sense, is an analogy to two parallel train tracks, with two trains passing in opposite directions. One is my train and represents my brain perceiving, processing, storing, and retrieving mental stimuli. All of these processes slow down in olding. The passing train moves at the constant speed of chronological time. Yet, if my train slows down, the passing train appears to be speeding up. My ideal response, of course, would be to eat enough fish and carrots to prevent my train from slowing down. "

Tree was silent, and I moved to a conclusion. "One other phenomenon is notable to me and is based upon my observation of Teddi Rose and previous dogs. When Teddi has sensed a trip to the vet, hidden in her cage, but been retrieved and leashed, she is then in a great hurry to be placed in the car and leave for the destination which she dreads. She is drawn like a nail to a magnet."

"They say that anticipation of either something bad or good slows down the perception of passing time, as in working by the hour in a monotonous job watching the clock for quitting time. Or as a kid waiting for Christmas. If this is true, then it would seem that dread speeds up the passing of time. When I choose to think about olding, dying, or death, it is like looking at the mythological Sirens. I am drawn to my end, faster and faster, hypnotically, irreversibly. Like a nail to a magnet."

"Mike," Tree asked, "if you touched a place on your body and it really hurt, what would you do about that?" It was a surprising question.

"Go see a doctor?" I guessed.

Tree replied, "I was looking for 'stop touching it there!' If your mind is not locked upon some dread of your creation, the magnet does not operate on you."

"Yes, that feels to be true," I agreed.

"How do you predict that your future scenario will likely go, Mike? Your most likely scenario?"

I thought momentarily and then began to lay the qualifications for my prediction, "Well, it is impossible to predict, but… "

Tree interrupted, "That is the point, Mike. It is all that you need to place these thoughts aside. You have laid your possibilities out here. They are piled up on the porch. You have little control over the goods and bads ahead. Do not live another day obsessed by the future you cannot control. If time speeds up for you, keep the quickening of time constrained in the day. You can do this, Mike; you have let go of more difficult things. Then, return to the path you were on. However long that you have, live it deeper and wider."

"I am feeling better, Tree."

"Good. Are we finished for now?"

"No, no, I was not finished. While we are on the topic, can we talk a little bit about the value of life… or of one's own life. It has also troubled me in the last few months. If at the end of one's life, what would be one's own view of his life's worth, based upon what criteria?"

"We cannot talk about how the Big values human life in general or your life in particular. It is out of bounds for a discussion. The topic crosses the line into religious discussions, where we cannot go."

"But you can listen, Tree," I entreated. "It is helping me to express these thoughts that have been troubling to the middle of me. How I think about my own value, to myself and others, perhaps to society, affects how I live today… and why I live, until my end. It is not simply relevant to what someone might say about me in a eulogy, although that is one way that I think about my value or meaning in life."

Tree hesitated a moment and said, "Very well, Mike. I will continue to listen."

"Religion aside," I began, "a first candidate for a value of life, which seems to be close to the same thing as the meaning of life, is a value in dollars. A value in dollars or any other unit of exchange. Perhaps because I am an economist, this possibility of human value must be dealt with first and placed somewhere.

"You already know, Tree, that economists have methods for valuing a human life. This has been a controversial topic in regard to estimating damages in death and serious injury cases: the value of the enjoyment of life, itself, beyond more straightforward losses of earning capacity, household services to the family, or medical costs from the injury."

"And you have written books and articles on the topic, Mike. Does that trouble you?"

"No, the willingness-to-pay studies, as they are called, have had many purposes, and are probably only interesting to a small set of people. But they are a starting point of valuation. To make a long story short, an academic study might isolate the wage differences between more and less risky jobs, in terms of average, on-the-job deaths annually. 10,000 workers, for example, might pay $10 million in total wages given up in order to work in a safer job, whereby one life per 10,000 workers is saved. Since no one knows which one of the 10,000 workers will avoid death, the $10 million value derived from U.S data and statistical analysis is a value for an anonymous, statistical life."

I was attempting to be brief, since it felt as if Tree's mind was wandering away. "There are several other types of these studies, as with what consumers will pay for smoke detectors in terms of one life saved. $10 million per life is a reasonable, average value of a U.S. life as we approach 2020. Many of these studies were prompted after a 1981 executive order by President Reagan imposed a benefit-cost test on new regulations proposed by federal agencies. The upshot was that safety-related agencies, such as the Occupational Safety and Health Administration, needed to justify their benefits in terms of lives saved, but a dollar value per life needed to be attached to the estimate of the number of lives saved. Various agencies have since used different values for a statistical American life. If a new administration or agency head lowers the value of life that is in use, the relevant safety standards become more lax, and vice versa."

"Most American courts have rejected the use of these dollar benchmarks, for the primary reason that they are not tailored to the specific plaintiff. This is part of the reason Tree that I don't think these studies mean much to what I am after here. Even if an average $10 million value was significant as a value of life, it would nevertheless be an average. My own observation has been that humans have a wide dispersion around any average value. It reminds me, as I say this, Tree, that it is not clear to me whether it is an absolute value for me that is on my mind, or a value relative to others.

"Can I say one more thing about dollars, Tree, and then I'll move on?" I asked and paused.

"By all means," Tree replied, as if he were genuinely interested. This was appreciated and encouraging.

"There are plenty of specific dollar values attached to a human life, but I'll pick net worth as a representative value. The dollar value of assets less liabilities, and the size of assets, in itself, might reflect a productive life for society and for others. It could mean that a business owner, as an example, produced a good or service valued by society and paid good wages and benefits which financially supported many employees and their families. On the other hand, drug cartels support many employees, and the net worth of their leaders may be very high (and untaxed!). Persons who do well in legitimate businesses may lead private lives of great harm. Thus, dollars might be one measure of admirable activity in life, or it might not.

"Never have I heard dollar values from a person's balance sheet of assets less liabilities rattled off in a eulogy, nor listings of financial help to others, charitable contributions, etc. It is unseemly, but it is also misleading for life value purposes: was it earned or inherited, is it mostly the lottery win, were taxes paid, how has it been spent, etc.

"But there is another reason that dollar values don't seem to me very important. Dollar values are generated from a world of trades. When I think back over my life, it is rarely a trade that is remembered – or remembered with a smile. Rather, it is the gifts. What I gave to others, expecting nothing in return, or others gave to me. Seldom are those gifts expressed in dollars. They are more likely in terms of time, and attention, and support.

"So, Tree, I will leave dollars now. They are unfulfilling on the topic of life value. After all, I was a human before I was an economist. If it turns out that money and power actually are the measure of life value, it would be a great surprise and disappointment to me and the masses.

"A balance sheet of one's activities in life nevertheless seems a useful tool for measuring life value when looking backward from the end of one's life, even if the comparison is not dollar assets on the left-hand-side of the ledger versus dollar liabilities on the right-hand-side."

Tree interjected, "Ok, Mike, but listen to yourself talk: your mind is now in a future day reflecting on past days. If being out of one-day-at-a-time was a crime, you would be locked up for a while."

"I know, Tree, let me try to talk myself out of this mess. The dollar assets/dollar liabilities labels must be replaced. It could be a life ledger of "good acts" versus "bad acts." Or "right" versus "wrong." Or "helps others" versus "hurts others." Many issues arise when a human attempts to think through such a valuation, and yes, Tree, you know that I have recently engaged in such thinking. Is it only acts that make the ledger of life, or do thoughts count? Is it what we intend or what actually happens that counts, even if by accident or luck? How does one add or subtract? Two rights might cancel one wrong, but it depends on the magnitude of the particular rights and the specific wrong.

"How do I know if my concepts of right and wrong are the correct ones, and, religion aside, isn't the Big, as one understands the Big, the source and arbiter of those matters? Have the seeds of right and wrong been implanted in me, or correctly taught to me? Or, what if I have been exploring the world with a false map? My valuation of what I brought to the world versus what I took away would be incorrect and meaningless, because rights and wrongs were not correctly identified.

"I also have no idea how vocational successes or failures find merit on the ledger, versus actions affecting family or friends or community. Do job titles matter – teacher or nurse versus warlord or false prophet? Can one's value in one area of life cover a miserable performance in another one? Some of these topics are discussed in eulogies, although the information provided tends to only be good-sided, with participants free to think about the other side if they wish."

"What is the chance, Mike that you will be able to resolve these ledger valuation problems in your remaining lifetime?

"There is no chance."

"And what does that suggest to you?" Tree asked.

I did not wish to answer that question and moved on. "Or the value and meaning in life could be how we grow in a lifetime, and we have discussed growth before. Is that the measure of our value, our meaning?"

Tree, of course, did not answer the question, but he waited for me to continue. "Perhaps this by-passes the issue of what is our value – accomplishments, good acts – in the sense that whatever determines value is to be grown over a lifetime. Baseline value, by whatever measure, at birth or age 12, or age 20, might not matter very much per se. Life is about growing our value, our meaning. It is where we end up compared to where we started.

"Yet, like other possibilities for life value, it is not simple to wrap one's arms around. Is it only our results that count, or are intentions and efforts of value in themselves? There is the complication that two persons might begin in exactly the same place, but one has relatively smooth sailing through life while the other faces great obstacles. Then what counts, so to speak, is where one ends up compared to where one started, with consideration for the number and magnitude of the obstacles which they faced.

"From my experience, humans very much value growth in themselves and others – presumably the growth of what we believe to be good versus bad in a human. We love rags to riches stories, those who grow from bad to good, those who reach their full potential despite daunting handicaps and hurdles, those who are knocked down but come back better than before. But babies and children die, Tree, and growth as a life value would seem unfair to them. Others might begin in such dreadful circumstances, or face handicaps or hardships of such magnitude, that it is difficult for me to imagine how their growth could be compared with those more privileged and lucky. Issues of metrics and scoring are mind boggling."

Tree felt to be listening attentively but was not communicating. I continued, "Without talking about particular religions or religious beliefs, is the value of life what we believe about the Big? About what death means and what happens after? About how we are supposed to live? About what is right and what is wrong? Religion and religious virtues commonly make obituaries and eulogies, not simply life facts, accomplishments, and deeds. Again, all sorts of issues arise. Is it lifetime beliefs, beliefs at the end, or growth of beliefs through a life of obstacles? What of the deaths of the young, or sudden and untimely deaths – how does that work? Is it beliefs only, or a weighted score of what we do versus what we believe? Is valuation based upon how strongly we believe, how we hold to our own beliefs despite hostility or oppression? How is the consistency of our deeds to our beliefs factored into a valuation? What happens if we are steadfast to our beliefs over a lifetime, but we were wrong, and a different set of beliefs were the true map for our journey?"

"Is it helpful, Mike, to delineate these possibilities, issues, and questions when no answers will be forthcoming?"

"Yes, I think it is, Tree. Please bear with me. My list is about finished," I promised.

"Very well."

"Or is there a specific attribute that if one finds it, and keeps it, and demonstrates it in thought and deeds, one has value, or added or special value? Perhaps it is as simple as finding happiness in life, but there is substantial debate about what leads a human to be happy, what keeps him there, how to measure it. A life of service to a Big or to others seems a noble attribute, although measurement remains a problem. Or is it knowing and accepting oneself, or acceptance of the universe and its ups and downs, in general? Is it compassion, or generosity? Is it gratitude... is it moving through the challenges of life with more gratitude than fear? If it is patience, Tree, I remain in serious trouble."

After another pause, but no comments by Tree, I moved toward an end. "Then, there are obvious possibilities for the valuation of a human life, which must logically be included on the list. One is that human life has no value or meaning or purpose, so that no set of thoughts or deeds or beliefs or attributes matter in the scheme of things. It appears to me that there are plenty of humans around the globe who believe this, or at least act as if they do."

Tree interrupted, "While it is not my intention to pursue a two-way discussion, if this possibility were true, I would never have come to you. It would have made no sense, either in your realm or my own."

This was an encouragement that Tree might begin to shed some light on these matters, but I recognized that Tree heard this thought when I thought it. Of course, he probably knew this thought before I thought it.

I concluded, "Or perhaps at the other extreme, the value or meaning of human life, in general or mine in particular, might be so profound, or otherwise beyond human comprehension, that one would be a fool to waste time on such matters." My thoughts had run dry. I stopped talking and cast at Tree what must have been a pitiful look of confusion and frustration.

"Ok, Mike," said Tree, "One comment. It is not wrong, and entirely human, to think about such mystery from time to time, in your days ahead. Growth for you means that you find some answers, and reduce Mystery, at least to your own satisfaction. Even as you chip away at Mystery, your twin chore is to accept the Mystery which remains through the end of your human time. It is also true that if you were simply given answers to Mystery, your life would lose meaning. Having said this, Mike, you need to return to the day. Be jealous of time when your mind travels to the future."

After a pause reflecting on those comments, I said, "Thank you for listening to me." He had made a comment despite his discomfort over discussing these topics, which gave me the impetus to re-open a topic from our early conversations. "And finally, Tree, there are my thoughts of death and thereafter."

"Mike, you know that religion, in general, and afterlife for you, in particular, are off limits for our discussion." It was a rare moment when I had known what the Tree would say.

"I need to ask a question, Tree, whether or not we proceed. Are you implying that religion is not important?"

It was a bit of a surprise that he promptly replied, as if he had anticipated this question. It was easy to forget, when deep in conversation, that Tree held the power to know any or all of my questions that were coming.

"No. On the contrary, religion may be all that is important for you and other humans. Yet, it is not the subject of our discussions, and I cannot discuss even the reasons why this is so. You will recall that this was one of the rules."

"But Tree, my understanding of the nature of the Big affects how I think, and how I live, before death. It also affects why I live. Even if you simply listen to my thoughts, it will help me… our talks so far today <u>have</u>

helped me!" I knew that this statement was genuinely true. Talking to that which is bigger than you is a comfort that other humans cannot provide.

"I will continue listening for a little while more then, Mike," Tree said, "so long as our purpose is that you set these troubling thoughts aside."

This was my purpose, and I do not recall a motive of somehow eliciting a Big Reveal from Tree on the life-after-death topic. He clearly was dampening any such expectation.

"On the subject of death itself, Tree -- the moment, the hour, or the day of death -- you would know the name of Woody Allen, correct?"

"Of course. He is an American comedic philosopher. I like Woody Allen. He makes me laugh, now that laughter has become an option for me. Woody Allen said that he was not afraid of death, but he did not want to be there when it happened. What about Woody Allen?"

"Actually, it is the quote that you just said. I mostly agree with that. At the appointed time of my death, it would be great to be missing, tardy, or at recess. Yet, people and their loved ones have had beautiful and meaningful experiences on their death day and moment, from what I have heard and read.

"A thought, Tree, is that anyone thinking about the meaning of life would necessarily think also about the meaning of death. It has occurred to me that death for humans, throughout human history, has never been an imperative of inadequate space for each generation of humans who might continue living. As we have discussed, there are plenty of stars and solar systems out there. A lack of space for humans is not the problem. Rather, it is a lack of suitable transportation and logistical support which has been the limiting factor. The Big is big enough, I suppose, to have provided these answers if he wished. For whatever reason, we have the death moment, and it is, after all, only one moment out of all of the moments of life."

Tree then made a comment. "Yet, it is the existence of that moment which gives your life all that is good in life. It allows humans to be grateful, even if they don't deserve it." After a brief pause, he added, "Mike, you are not harboring some illusion that your thinking or talking will result in the cancellation or postponement of your personal death moment, are you?"

"That would be too much to expect," I said sadly, "but what happens after that death moment has been really messing with me lately, whether we place religion aside or we place religion front and center."

Tree did not respond, so I proceeded. "If I continue with a listing of possibilities which occupy my thoughts of late, one is that death has no meaning except as the ending date for a personal chronology. Death is simply the extinguishment of life. Afterwards, there would be no consciousness. Nothing. Nothing for an eternity... although eternity loses meaning if there is nothing after death. I suppose it is possible for life to have meaning even if death and thereafter hold no meaning. Further, a Big could nevertheless exist absent anything after human life. Religion aside.

"This is not the worst alternative which I have imagined, Tree. Nothing means no reward. If, in a day, I attempted or succeeded in good works, there would be no possibility of afterlife bounty. But it means no possibility of afterlife punishment, either. Eternal nothing is better than eternal punishment.

"If I <u>knew</u> that this was true – nothing – would it affect how I live the remainder of my life... with no reward for good nor punishment for evil ... would it cause me to live my life differently? I do not believe so, but at my age, most possibilities for licentious or riotous behavior don't apply anymore. It also seems difficult to accurately see in oneself how much of his net good over bad in life is because of possibilities for reward versus punishment, compared to how he would live while moving toward nothing.

"Certainly, many humans believe there is nothing, or they at least act as if they do. A problem for me, religion aside, is that I can't put religion aside. Indeed, if the true answer is nothing, humans would require a re-appraisal of religion itself."

"Can we move along from your thoughts about nothing to your thoughts about something?" Tree asked.

"Surely," I said, "one possibility after death is a looping of the human soul back into another round of sentient life. My daddy, the amateur comedian, had taken a course in comparative religions. What he took away from Eastern thought was a prediction that he would be reincarnated as a bull in Montana. Since no one wished to encourage my father by asking about his thought processes in this regard, it was never clear to me if he considered this scenario as a positive or negative looping toward an ultimate destination. Even if this bull was well fed and had unusually attractive cowmates, it would be mighty darn cold.

"Religion aside, how would the Big make these assignments, or judge when looping might end? Could humans continue to grow if human episodes were spaced between animal or insect assignments? What if my next assignment was as a University of Florida football fan? What depravity in this life could merit a loop like that? Or, what if I started out as a University of Alabama football fan, who is now being punished as a University of Tennessee football fan? What an awful thought," I shuddered.

"Mike," Tree asked, "without regard to your next assignment, would you wish to start your human life over again?"

"I have actually thought about that, Tree," I answered.

"I am not surprised."

"No, I would not wish to live through again some of the things I somehow lived through, but I would love to stay exactly where I am right now for a long, long time – no olding, no dying, no death or after. This cannot happen, which is the point of having this discussion."

"Then, Mike, why don't you go ahead and talk about what frightens you the most?" Tree seemed to know that I was beating around the bush, and of course, he knew the thoughts that had been hidden from others.

"My anxiousness is really about the alternatives, after death, of judgment and the outcomes of that judgment. I am afraid of a Big who is primarily a scorekeeper – a Big of judgement based on a life score. And that primarily troubles me because judgment makes little sense to me absent a resulting reward or punishment, although it is possible that there could be judgment only for the sake of judgment, or toward some other purpose unknown to me. A judgment based upon my score might lead to punishment.

"This would not be quite so terrible if the punishment was a bad assignment for my next looping back through life because it would be temporary. A poor soul might have a gig as a bull in Montana, but hope would remain for an ultimate reward. This leaves me at the possibility of the worst future punishment -- punishment that is eternal.

"One of my favorite sayings, Tree, and I don't know the source, is that nothing too good or too bad lasts too long. Yet, eternal punishment is an awesome exception. So, Tree, what if my punishment is really bad and lasts forever?"

"Mike when you leave one day at a time, your mind quite literally goes to hell, doesn't it?"

"Apparently," I mumbled and continued. "There is a related thought Tree, which troubles me almost as much as eternal punishment that hurts. Religion aside, the notion of a Big who casts one into an eternal fire, for example, does not fit for me. It seems inconsistent with the seeds of right and wrong in the middle of me. If that is the nature of the Big, it shatters the image that I would emulate. It seems that the Big would be bigger than that."

Tree said, "Mike religion aside, what are your thoughts about how scoring, judgment, reward, and punishment might work? We both know that your mind has wandered here over the past few months."

"Well, religion aside, I have many questions but few answers. And plenty of unanswered questions remain even if I do attempt to reference a particular religion.

"All of the issues that we talked about in how humans value a human life… about how humans keep score. It only becomes more complicated and uncertain when one turns to how the Big keeps score – if he is indeed a scorekeeper – and how he judges based upon that score. It is a reasonable assumption that what goes on is above my pay grade and incomprehensible to me.

"But what criteria are important to the Big in a life evaluation? Are they few or many? Do they have the same weight or are the weightings very different? So, then, what is the reason for the weightings? Is there a strong, positive correlation between my good-versus-bad criteria and weightings and those of the Big? Or religion aside, is there some big act or virtue or accomplishment, whatever, that most humans and I are missing… which the Big weighs very heavily, so that humanity may have missed the boat?"

Tree was neither commenting nor shutting me down, so I continued, "Scoring. Even if the criteria were known, how does the Big actually keep score in the various categories? More importantly, is the life value judgment based on an absolute standard of total points, so that there is a Win/Lose cut off at, say, a score of 80 on a 100-point scale? 100 being perfect? And would the Reward/Punishment decision be as simple as the 80-cut-off score? Binary, like a toggle switch? Therefore, 80 would bring the same rewards as a score of 99. A score of 79 would mean the same eternal punishment as a 1. Or are there different levels of reward in the reward place and, truly, special places, much worse than average, in the punishment place?

"Or is the judgment a relative judgment, based upon the scoring, however it occurs, so that the top, say, 40% of scores are rewarded, and the others punished? Absolute versus relative judgment would seem to be a big deal, notwithstanding the choice of a cut-off score. My gut feeling is that the notion of competition with others in such an important, eternal matter, is not to be desired. It makes me nervous. Perhaps because I'm worried about how I will do in the race. But I have the same kind of problems, I suppose, with an absolute score."

"Mike," Tree said, "keep in your mind that humans were made and oriented toward complementing each other. Competition is a choice for humans, not a necessity of their middle. Moreover, you are the scorekeeper here, Mike, prompting your own troubles about scoring, and winners and losers. Finish your thoughts. I am still listening."

"And if there is a hottest part of Hell, do persons like me go there simply for having these thoughts or asking these questions? Whatever, another thought concerns what the punishment is really like. I have mentally reviewed some alternatives, and I have a worst-case fear. What if eternal punishment is to wake up from death, so to speak, fully conscious – as humans know consciousness – and completely alone? What if eternity is conscious aloneness?

"My thoughts are not only on the punishment side, Tree. I do have positive thoughts about a reward judgement and what it might mean, and my questions here are many but happier. Do we continue to grow, Tree? Is that a big part of reward, that we continue to grow toward Truth… all of it? At the other extreme, I suppose, is that the reward is to know all there is to know -- as much as the Big knows. Is that reward? Then science ends. Then faith is irrelevant. Or is the reward a horizon of new possibilities and dimensions of growth which are unimaginable to me? Could there be space for growth that is, literally, cosmic in its proportions, or even better? These are exciting thoughts, especially if all of my dogs and most of my relatives are back with me and growing, too. Will there be football, the cherry atop the chocolate sundae of reward? That is a rhetorical question. I can't handle how competition and scoring would work in reward football. At least the college tie-breaking rules might disappear, along with the red hat referee for TV commercials.

"Ok, Tree, I'm finished." The sun was setting atop Ridge Road, and a beautiful sunset was soon to unfold.

After a noticeable pause, Tree said, "You are human, Mike, and it is certainly true that you humans keep score, judge, reward, and punish. Whether you need to emphasize it as much as you do is another matter, but we will not go there.

"What lies ahead of you, Mike, and ahead of each human, is the Mystery toward which you must grow and also must accept… and, finally, Mike, that you must come to cherish. The Big is there, the Truth is there, all ultimate beauty is there. The last scenario that you want is the elimination of Mystery. Do the next right thing today, Mike. That is your solution. If you will live in the solution, these troubles will go away.

"And a last comment, on the nature of the Big. In a list of descriptors of what he is and what he does, judgment and punishment would be far down the list, as a human might possibly understand the list."

This was a revelation, which was of staggering importance to any human who troubled over the visage of a scorekeeping, punishing Big. I was compelled to attempt one, follow-up question. "What would be at the top of that list, Tree, if I could possibly understand it?"

"What do you think, Mike?" Tree asked.

"I was hoping for love, mercy, and compassion," I replied.

Tree did not respond to my comment, but he smiled at me. It was the most warm and wonderful smile, a smile of immense kindness. I had never felt less alone.

We talked about football for a few more minutes, I thanked Tree, and he left. I had learned nothing for certain, but everything that was good for me, about that which I did not need to know.

CHAPTER ELEVEN -
A MIRACLE PARADE

It was Thursday, January 26, 2017. I remember the date because it was the 40th birthday of my youngest daughter Nikki. We would hopefully talk on the phone, Charleston to California, later in the day. Some thought was probably given to how old one was to have a youngest daughter turn 40.

We had been through extended cold weather and periods of snow for two months, but this day was clear, bright, around 65 degrees by the mid-afternoon. Chloe was in an after-high-school activity until 7:00 or so, and Lynn was in and out of the house. My work was over for the day, and, wrapped in a warm sweater, I pulled the cover off my favorite porch chair and sat down with my Kindle. Nippy… that was how my grandmother would have described the briskness of the temperature. Having a discussion with Tree was not expected, but always possible. We had not talked since olding and death.

Since that discussion, however, the troubles of projection into the future had left me. My return to trudging within the day brought back some progress. Neither Lynn nor Chloe believed that I was really attempting to meditate daily in the solitude of my office. Clearing my brain of distractions was proving to be surprisingly difficult. My half-hearted attempts at finding a mantra which fit my essence were complicated by the elusiveness of an identifiable essence in the middle of me. If I had an essence, it was very difficult to pin down. In frustration, the ladies of the house would sometimes be regaled with seemingly spontaneous chants, which they found aggravating after a while and certainly diminished their confidence in my seriousness of purpose.

I found myself thinking of Petula Clark, having watched an entertainment news special on her latest comeback attempt as a pop icon now past the age of eighty. Good for her! The height of U.S. popularity for this singing Brit was the mid-sixties: my high school years, when one felt compelled to know something about popular music to at least meet minimum standards of cool. My total lack of music appreciation at birth had remained unnurtured, but the music of Petula's songs was snappy and upbeat, and I could actually understand her British-clipped words. So much was I enamored with Petula that I actually memorized the words to her top hit "Downtown," which were sometimes mumbled aloud as others sang Beatles' songs. This was intended to leave the impression that I knew the words to other popular songs, which I most assuredly did not.

In fact, my primary remembrance of music from my high school years concerned the culture-shattering U.S. tour of the Beatles. My 10th grade football teammate Chuck Avery somehow obtained tickets for their concert in Atlanta. He told the coach that he would be missing two practices to attend the concert, despite our help in brainstorming many plausible lies that might have saved Chuck's life. But Chuck told the truth, experienced the Beatles, and only spent a week or so practicing with the fourth team. His courage had been unimaginable to me, and Chuck became a folk hero of sorts. Of course, Chuck was a really good football player, and our coach really liked to win. It would have been swell to miss a couple of practices to sing 'Downtown' with Petula, but I was expendable and would have been killed as an example of the limits to self-expression.

Teddi Rose diverted my attention. She was barking at three deer walking slowly through the cemetery to disappear over the more graded slope down the other side of the ridge. Teddi was not a courageous dog vis-à-vis other animals: other dogs, cats, mice, groundhogs, etc. She was only barking aggressively because she was in the air, on an enclosed porch, 100 feet away from the deer. When encountering a deer on our walks along Ridge Road, she would fail to see the deer, even if it stood a few feet from the road. Then, when we were a safe distance past, she would look back and bark once. She would receive undue praise for this minimal act of heroism, and the balance of nature on the ridge would be maintained without significant disruption.

Over $400. The bill from Teddi's visit to the vet earlier in the day was more than $400. Her skin allergies and their treatment made the high cost of pet doctoring particularly astonishing.

We had paid thousands of dollars for unrelated ear and knee surgeries. And she had just entered her dog olding period when these expenses would only go up. My economic subconscious was calculating the likely lifetime costs for this dog, as I watched her chewing on her leg. Pet health insurers had not looked kindly upon Teddi's medical history, so that was not a viable option. Moreover, a recurring and troubling thought beyond the costs per se was that children in the world were starving and millions of humans had no access to health care, while my family was spending this kind of money on a pet dog.

Tree interrupted, "Mike you can find more trouble thinking than other humans walking into a combat zone."

"Hi Tree," I said happily, "It is good to see you." I remembered to resume my Kindle-reading pose, focusing outward toward Tree. His rebuke felt as a mild icebreaker, and I looked forward to a conversation.

"Since you brought it up, Mike, your lifelong disinterest in music, and lack of knowledge and appreciation of the musical world, is indeed embarrassing."

I thought it was not a bit embarrassing to me, but he heard that.

"Why would you shut out such beauty from your life? This needs to be on your Add list. Start learning the words to at least one more song than 'Downtown.' The national anthem doesn't count. And it would not hurt you to allocate some time each day to relaxing with music. Maybe as prelude or epilogue to your valiant attempts at meditation." Tree sounded sarcastic.

I promised Tree that some kind of effort would occur in this direction. At least he was not talking about horse riding and skydiving.

Tree continued, "And you are inventing hypothetical pet health scenarios and estimating future Teddi Rose costs. Have you considered discussing with Lynn and Chloe the benefits versus the costs of Teddi?"

"No, I know what they would do. The conversation would quickly be turned to their evaluation of the benefits versus the costs of me. The clear message would be that benefit/cost analysis was not in my own interests as a discussion topic. They would laugh and laugh in their extended evaluation... and, besides, I love the vexsome little creature. I would even give up peanut butter a few days each week if necessary to purchase her fancy shampoo."

"The point is that your mind is still successful in carrying you into the future. Have you forgotten our football discussion?"

This was taken as a rhetorical question, and I did not respond. Tree then surprised me, "But you caught me on a good day. We can talk about the future for awhile if you wish."

"Really?" I asked, excited, because this was a 180-degree reversal from his previous position.

"Why not? Pick a topic."

So, for a joke, because he would never answer such a question, I asked, "What will be the value of the Dow Jones average on September

11, 2023?" The answer, of course, could make me quite wealthy if I am still around in 2023.

Tree responded without hesitation, "An answer would require that the Dow Jones index actually exists on September 11, 2023. But the Great Devaluation, and its aftereffects, rendered the Dow Jones measure meaningless."

"What do you mean Great Devaluation, Tree?"

"Mike, you really do not want to know any of the details."

He was wrong. I wanted all the details. Looking into the house for a pencil and pad, a thought struck me. "Tree, you are doing it to me again aren't you?"

"Why, whatever do you mean?" he answered, and I perceived that he said this with a polite smile.

"Bullshitting me, Tree. You are making up wild, provocative stories about the future to reap enjoyment and humor from my anguish, should I be so foolish as to be sucked into your story. Like you did with the death of football."

"Mike, I told you that my particular story about football was not true, but you still do not know what is true about the end of the story. So, what is bullshit and what is not? That is an important characteristic of the future, Mike. You don't really know for sure. Even if I laugh." He paused for a few moments and added, "Do you wish to end our conversation about the future?

"No," I answered quickly "let's do it." Why would I forsake even the possibility of true prognostication about the future? "For my own good," had been Tree's previous answer, but would this opportunity ever be provided to me again?

"Back to the Great Devaluation," I ventured, "Can you tell me what the percentage reduction was to the value of whatever was devalued?"

"No. That is the last thing you want to know. You would worry constantly until the time the devaluation actually occurs and would be none the better for all of that worry. Unless, of course, I am making this one up." He was still smiling and seemed to be enjoying himself.

Then, Tree abruptly changed the subject. "Speaking of the high cost of veterinary bills – and the unbalanced distribution of income in your country – imagine how expensive Teddi Rose, and successor dogs, will be after the luxury taxes go into effect."

"What luxury taxes?" I said.

"The luxury taxes imposed upon those who spent their money on things that lots of people viewed as luxuries.

This was difficult for me to believe, but Tree continued, "There will be a time when significant numbers of your fellow citizens, and politicians, come to be concerned about the government's debt. Another set of your people become increasingly angry about income distribution, as the gap between haves and have nots widens. Then, the balanced budget amendment passed Congress and headed toward ratification by three-fourth of your states."

I said, "This remains difficult to believe. And a balanced budget amendment would be a bad thing. Crazy policy."

"Mike," Tree replied calmly, "I'm simply reporting on the future. There is no point in arguing with me. It is what it is, except of course if it is not. And why does 'crazy' make you think that America's politicians will or will not do something?"

I certainly would not argue with his crazy point. "But let's get back to dogs," I requested.

"Expenditures by Americans with money on pets came to be a visible irritant to Americans without money. So, when the government needed to give a nod toward financial sanity, with wide-ranging luxury taxes, pet taxes were an important component. Many States added their own versions of luxury taxes on top of the federal taxes."

"How high are the taxes?" I asked.

"You do not need to bother yourself with the details, but that $400 bill you just paid would become $600 after the taxes."

Of course, I thought, this would be a significant hit to the financially "ok" citizenry but scarcely noticed by the ultra-rich… compared to a rise in progressive tax rates.

"Precisely," Tree observed. This was my consternation. There was enough that made sense to me in Tree's various narratives to be worrisome.

"Speaking for dog owners specifically," I intoned, "the costs are enough already. This would drive many owners out of the dog market: fixed income, struggling young families, a wide range of more-or-less middle-income people who would have otherwise owned dogs, even some hunters. Especially southern folks, from my experience, would not be amused."

"In fact," Tree offered, "there were pro-pet, anti-tax demonstrations across the nation. Concerned legislators in at least five southern and western states considered secession."

"So, what happened to all of the cats and dogs?" I asked haltingly.

"I really do not wish to burden you with that, Mike, but one consequence was the rapid rise in the market for Artificial Intelligence Pets -- AIP's. Japanese and American companies, particularly, had new incentives to pursue the technology of -- your example -- AI dogs."

"Tree," I said," it is difficult, from my experiences with dogs, to believe that an adult or child would accept an AI dog versus a real dog: soft, warm, great listening skills, and loving responses.

"I'm just telling you, Mike, that the luxury taxes were the last straw, so to speak, for the widespread ownership of dogs." After a pause, he added, "You are also underestimating what entrepreneurs, and technology, can accomplish when a market unfolds for them. The AI dogs and other pets were rapidly made more similar to real ones, in looks, feel, and response to human inputs. They would be able to learn from past interaction with particular humans and alter their future responses accordingly. If one wished, their 5-year-old's AI puppy would begin to teach basic arithmetic during tummy-ups. Even better, the puppy of the morning could become a monkey in the afternoon. Your adult's dog could teach you to speak French."

Frowning, I listened as Tree continued, "All of the annual dog costs go away, Mike, and they are exorbitant after the taxes. The one-time purchase price of an AI dog actually declines, especially given the improvement in features. You know how your back hurts after Teddi's weekly bath, and you grumble about tinkle-and-poop trips at inconvenient times. These also go away with AI dogs, unless you like to do these things and wish to purchase these options. Issues of boarding, giving medicines, and biting family friends are gone. Veterinarians, as a group, did not fare well in the new environment, except for the ones who diversified early into AI pet retailing."

"Tree, I probably don't want to know this answer, but would not the logical extension of this technology be AI mates… children… friends?"

"Indeed," said Tree, "you really do not wish to pursue that one."

"Then the next question is," I ventured, "would the Big not consider similar issues and tradeoffs regarding actual versus AI humans?"

"You really don't want to go there, Mike," Tree advised. He kept smiling, pleasantly, but did not laugh, as I pondered the discussion. The thought crossed my mind that he would certainly have the ability to be belly-laughing, somewhere beyond my cognition, at my inability to ascertain the truth about the future.

Tree concluded, "So, the luxury taxes on pets brought little revenues to the government after a few years, but they did largely eliminate real pets."

"And a great sadness covered the earth," I thought eloquently.

Tree pushed ahead in a different direction, "On the topic of government debt, Mike, some of your younger expert witness colleagues across the country will become involved in the children's class action lawsuit against adults, for starting them off in adult life with staggering government debt. The balanced budget amendment issue, along with reparations for slavery, started precocious children, and their lawyers, thinking. Why would children born as American citizens since the millennium assume the burden of prior generations, when government came to accept huge, budget deficits while making no efforts to pay down previous debt?"

"I'm not a lawyer Tree, but I would not bet on the success of that endeavor," I commented, while realizing my new role as a defendant.

He replied, "Of course, that is what various tobacco, asbestos, and pharmaceutical companies thought at first. And we are talking about a lot of money."

This story was not particularly farfetched, given my experience with trial lawyers. Even a small probability of realizing a large pot of money yielded the expectation of a still-mighty-large pot of money. My economist-self sought out numbers, and I mumbled, "Tree, federal government debt was five-plus trillion dollars in 2000. It is almost $20-trillion now…."

"And almost $27-trillion in 2020, after the tax cuts, the viral pandemic, and such," Tree added.

"So, the youngers' lawyers came after the twenty-or-so-trillion difference of added debt?" It bothered me that some of us now talked about trillions the way we once talked about nickels.

"More or less," Tree answered, "plus state and local government debt added a couple of trillion, and then money to ensure the solvency of the social security system. An interesting argument was also made to add some of the $14 trillion in household debt."

He had sucked me into this conversation before I realized it, and I asked, "Ok, Tree. How did the plaintiffs expect older generations to cough up that kind of money?"

"Mostly from wealth and estate taxes," he replied.

"How much of estates did the youngers propose to take?"

"All of it."

"Yipes, Tree. The effect on the incentive system in regard to economic activities would be disastrous."

"When a group of plaintiffs are looking at 25 trillion dollars or so, they don't worry much about the economic incentives of others," Tree advised.

I said again to Tree that lawyers pushing such a claim did not surprise me, but a significant jury award or settlement would be surprising. There were some practical limits to the amount of money available. Tree then suggested that one should never underestimate the ability of the central bank to create money nor of lawyers' attempts to take it. He was still smiling, but not laughing.

"What viral pandemic?" I asked, because his comment had not gone past me unnoticed.

"The one that killed more Americans than died in the world wars plus the Vietnam war combined," Tree answered.

"Like the Spanish flu in the World War I period a hundred years ago?"

"Yes, of comparable magnitude in cases and deaths in every part of the earth."

"How many Americans died from the Spanish flu?" I followed up, because I knew he would know the answer. I also recalled from somewhere that the Spanish flu did not originate in Spain.

"Almost 700,000."

The answer made me skeptical. "A new virus with those kind of death counts does not seem possible. Not in the U.S. and the so-called developed nations. Not with the advances in public health, medicine in general, vaccines, and treatments. If a new pandemic was that bad in the United States, what about the rest of the world?"

"Actually, your country fared worse than other countries," Tree said. He was neither smiling nor laughing, but he was clearly making this one up.

"Not that it matters, but where did this pandemic start?" I played along.

He replied, "It did matter. The answer is very complicated. And you don't want to hear the explanation." Then, he said, "It turned out that if humans had diligently worn facemasks, the really horrible outcomes would likely have been avoided."

"So, how long did it take for governments and the public to figure that out and shut down the virus?"

"You don't want to know, but mask wearing did not stop the virus."

The answer made no sense to me, but I countered, "With the CDC and all of the government and private capabilities for pharmaceutical research, surely it did not take long to develop a vaccine that could be used around the world."

"Several vaccines were developed, Mike, in record time."

"And that finally stopped it?" I asked offhandedly.

"No, the vaccine didn't stop it either."

"Why? If they worked, why would not the vaccines stop the spread?"

"You don't want to know."

"Did the pandemic at least make Americans closer, pulling together?"

"No, just the opposite." Tree seemed to grimace.

"And I suppose the economy and the stock market tanked?"

"High unemployment. Wide-ranging business failures. After a sharp dip, however, the stock market recovered nicely."

"Tree, sorry but I'm not being sucked into this one. It is not believable."

He laughed. It was an odd laugh, and rather than giving up the effort, he said, "I haven't even covered the effects of the pandemic on American sports. College basketball cancelled. No March Madness. Professional basketball and baseball closed down when the virus was bad, but then opened back up and held championships when it was still bad, or worse."

My interest in the tale perked up. Perhaps, he would slip up and reveal a future champion. "What about college football?"

Tree opined, "The various athletic conferences took charge and made their own decisions. On your west coast college football was cancelled but then reinstated late in the fall. The Big Ten conference – which by the way has 14 schools that apparently don't teach addition -- also began the season late with fewer games: plus, a championship, because you Americans don't play unless you can have a champion. But only a small percentage of ticket holders were allowed in stadiums, even for championships."

I had previously noted to myself that Tree became extremely agitated with conferences which did not get their numbers right. Fortunately, the Southeastern Conference had not limited itself to a number, or a region for that matter. It would be a hoot if Notre Dame ended up in the SEC. I lightly observed, "So I suppose the SEC actually added football games?"

"That is exactly what they did, Mike. They added two conference games and played a 10-game SEC schedule." He seemed pleased with the prescience of my question, and he was smiling again.

For the first time, the pandemic story began to bother me because the reaction of the various conferences is what I would have predicted if thinking about pandemics. Moreover, Tree had not mentioned Ivy League football. This also rang true because, well, no one cares about Ivy League football.

Nevertheless, I said, "The football part makes some sense, Tree, but otherwise I'm not biting on the virus story. If you are doing humor, you have lost the element of surprise in telling me a whopper."

"Suit yourself, Mike," he was still smiling and enjoying himself. "I had two more to tell you about, but we could end this discussion if you wish." He was a bit prickly, and I reminded myself not to give Tree anything resembling negative feedback. Yes, he heard that too. It is easier to be circumspect in one's talking than in one's thinking.

"By all means. Please keep going," I implored, genuinely, because there was no bound to the possibilities for what might come next.

"Two natural phenomena greatly affected your country – the Great Western fires and the southeastern hurricanes, attacking your coastal areas from the mid-Atlantic states to Texas."

"Both of these things are significant problems now, Tree."

"They got worse. Not every year, but a rapid worsening over a small number of years. Either one problem in a year, or both in the same year."

This was not good to hear, as Tree had returned to the domain of the plausible. I was more eager to hear answers than further elucidation of the severity of these problems. "Tree," I ventured, "It would be great if you would tell me that we stopped the fires before the entire western United States burned up. My daughter and granddaughter live in California."

"I'll skip some of the story, but your Congress finally provided the money for a massive series of irrigation-and-canal projects extending from the Pacific Ocean to the Rockies. It included the forests, but no attempt was made to irrigate most of the deserts. Your Congress isn't stupid."

I laughed out loud. "Tree, this story is unbelievable on so many levels." Yet, he was not laughing or smiling, and I felt badly for having sucked all of the joy out of the air.

I played the set-up for Tree, "So are you going to tell me how this massive system was constructed, how the country paid for it, how saltwater works on soil and vegetation."

"Mike," he interrupted, "you wanted the short version of the story, so I have given you the solution to the problem. It is up to you to conjure up the details. I will tell you an interesting side note, that the alternative to the national investment in an irrigation-and-canal system was simply abandoning the land west of the Rocky Mountains. This had some support in the northeastern states and the Congress, but mid-Atlantic and Gulf states had their own problem and were willing to compromise."

"You mean the hurricanes?" I asked.

"Yes. I was focusing on the hurricanes, versus the rising sea levels, pollution, and so on to save your time. The hurricanes became worse by any measure – number of storms, size, and intensity. Again, technology solved the problem."

I simply could not wait to hear this one and was smiling along with Tree. "How?"

"The country did have to abandon a few cities and jack up a few others, and the map of the coastline changed some, while the windmill system was under construction…."

"What windmill system?" I asked, beginning to smile.

"The sets of windmills were strategically located and roughly paralleled the coastline," Tree replied and waited.

The least I could do was ask the next question, "I am not an expert on windmill technology Tree, but how are ocean windmills supposed to stop a hurricane… versus being blown away by it?"

"Ah, the obvious question," he said without giving me any indication that he knew this tale was preposterous.

"Because the windmills were dual-use wind technology systems. They collect wind power to generate electricity in their traditional mode, but in hurricane season, when necessary, they are easily converted into wind suppression systems, which largely solved the hurricane problem."

"What does largely solved mean?"

"Your Department of Defense contributed some technology and tools which were part of the suppression system, but that is classified and above your pay grade."

"Great," I thought, "they bombed the clouds," but I said to Tree, "Are you going to tell me how the wind-suppression-mills worked?"

"No, Mike, once again I gave you the answer, whether or not you choose to believe it, but your job is to fill in the details. Another interesting note is that a few greedy windmill operators learned the hard way that power generation and wind suppression systems do not work at the same time. And everyone regretted the unintended consequences of this new system for Hispaniola and Cuba, especially."

For some reason, I commented, "Isn't there some future tension between the costs of these massive investments and a balanced budget amendment?"

"I should say so," Tree said emphatically, "and, Mike, let me offer two pieces of advice as you consider my comments."

"OK."

"First, you are continuing to underestimate the wonders of technology in solving future problems. And, as I suggested before, never underestimate the ability of your Congress to appropriate money."

I shrugged at this advice. He simply would not laugh as he spun these stories, except the once, even as his tales of the future became less believable. The realization struck me that my reaction to what he was saying wasn't particularly important to him. He was doing humor and having a terrific time, which is a genuine possibility with humor. However, discussions about the future were bringing me down. Tree was only foreseeing scary things, probably to teach me a lesson… again. I had to admire Tree: he had become quite adept at bullshitting.

A whistle sounded, and both Tree and I heard the band. Lynn, Chloe, and I occasionally heard the George Washington high school band in late summer and in the fall, but that sound would have come from precisely the opposite direction. This mysterious marching band sounded to be heading our direction from below the opposite side of the ridge, but only the distant hills were visible as the ridge dropped away beyond the small cemetery.

"Tree, what is happening?" I asked.

Tree seemed to smile broadly. "It is your parade coming here to entertain you. A gift."

"A parade for me?" Of course, this was a surprise. "Why a parade? Why for me? What did I do to deserve a parade?"

He replied instructionally, "Mike, please don't ruin your own parade by asking questions. Just enjoy yourself. This is likely your only parade."

In an instant, my eyes were attracted to the five cultivated bushes spaced equidistantly down the slope of our side yard bordering the small forest beyond. As I watched, the dark color of the bushes turned to a brilliant fall yellow. Indeed, all of the trees in the forest behind the bushes and up and down the ridge changed to the most vivid of fall colors, on leaves which had reappeared. As my eyes then surveyed down the ridge, each of the dark tree trunks and branches, beginning with Tree, were transformed into peak fall foliage, so that the houses and neighborhood visible in late January disappeared behind the brilliant colors. There were noticeably more orange colors in the mix, which was appropriate for my parade and appreciated. Even the temperature seemed to warm a bit toward a slight October briskness.

Tree said, "I decided to throw your parade in the Fall."

While struggling not to ask "Why?" my eyes were drawn back to the edge of the side yard, where the middle of the first bushes had been transformed to a different, taller bush, with long swaying branches. The bush was singing "She'll Be Coming Around the Mountain." Then, three men appeared simultaneously in front of the bush and asked it questions, as the singing bush changed songs to "For He's A Jolly Good Fellow."

"It is the Three Amigos movie," I thought, as the approaching band played the theme music from one of my favorite comedies. This was my most enjoyed scene from the movie. Steve Martin, Martin Short, and Chevy Chase, the Amigo heroes, looked over their left shoulders, as I thought this, and waived to me. I beamed with delight. Their silent-movie, fancy-western costumes were even more funny in person: black with white design, red scarf at the throat, wide-brimmed sombreros.

The amigos were halfway into the movie, having found the singing bush, where they could summon the invisible swordsman who could direct them to the hideout of the evil El Guapo, who had abducted the beautiful heroine, Carmen, and terrorized her small village, Santo Puco.

Tree whispered to me, "I thought it was appropriate to begin your parade with some of your favorite humor."

As I smiled at him, Steve and Martin offered their predetermined chants and shot once into the air, in order to bring forth the Invisible Swordsman. Chevy said his chant and shot to the side toward Ridge Road. This is both dangerous and illegal, and in fact, Chevy had shot and killed the Swordsman, who we all could hear fall to the ground from his invisible horse. While Steve and Martin began to yell at Chevy, the band topped the ridge.

My first thought was "Loud!" as the reality of what was happening struck me. What about my wife in the house, not to mention our neighbors, or the neighborhoods below the ridge? Has there ever been a secret parade, with only the honoree conscious of the event? Secret parade was an oxymoron, but by definition, the rest of us would not know that one was occurring. Frantically glancing inside the house, I saw that Lynn was preoccupied with whatever was in front of her on the counter. She might have missed the singing bush but not the band topping the ridge.

"This is your parade," Tree assured me, "so don't worry about others being disturbed."

My second thought was "Short" as I watched the first of the band appear and continue marching down the cemetery toward Ridge Road and then my side yard. This was The University of Tennessee "Pride of the Southland Band." It was my college band, of course, and my eldest daughter, Kristi, was also a Tennessee graduate. The band was led by a V-formation of flag bearers, then majorettes, then row after row of band members playing a familiar song from their pre-football-game marches. The traditional black uniforms, with orange and white headdress and vests, made me smile. Their size was amusing. The rows of 10-abreast band members would not have fit into the available path between clusters of grave markers, nor in the side yard. But the size of the band members began about one-third of a normal size, which decreased seamlessly among visible band members as necessary for the space available.

As the band filled the side yard, their size adjustments allowed the entire band, about 350 members as I recalled, to fill the available space, and they all turned toward me on the porch – the reviewing stand. Behind the band, the singing bush had resumed its normal form, and the three amigos had vanished. All five bushes, and all of the trees, were dancing with the music, in synchronized up-and-down, side-to-side movements. Occasionally, each tree would shake its top at the parade, brilliantly colored leaves would fly over the band, and at their apex the leaves would transform to a spray of the same colors settling upon the band. It was a ticker-tape parade, except better.

After many rows of band had crossed Ridge Road, I glimpsed a neighbor's car heading to town and approaching the parade. It proceeded through the band members and moved unmolested past my house. As the car would have smashed into two rows of marchers, those crossing the road simply disappeared, as if they had sunk below the road, and then popped back up as the car passed. Tree had gone to considerable trouble to orchestrate this event.

Moreover, as I watched, a pop-up crowd began to appear on both sides of the parade route. A circle of 2-4 persons, usually adults and children, would materialize – watching, cheering, having fun – and then after a few seconds disappear. Some of these persons looked familiar, but it was impossible to focus on specific images in their brief appearance, with all of the activity in the parade demanding attention.

Then, the band began to play "Rocky Top," the unofficial fight song of UT athletics. Of course that would be their featured song!

Tree whispered, "I know of your misgivings about this song, but the band will not perform without playing it." I nodded at him and smiled thoughtfully while enjoying the upbeat tune. It is dangerous to criticize this song in a group of Tennessee fans, but the words of the song were problematic to University administrators and faculty who actually read them. Many fans only know the words of the chorus, which celebrates life on a rocky hill in East Tennessee. There is nothing here which would seem to encourage University athletes toward sacrifice, effort, and victory. This could be overlooked, but for the other lyrics in the song. They describe the Tennessee fan, singing the song, as a male, with a mate who is half bear and half cat -- as if that was a good thing. This Tennessee Vols couple have tried jobs, and life, in the city, disliked both, and chosen to live on a rocky hill. Here they engage in the illegal manufacture of spirits. When necessary, they shoot, kill, and bury federal law enforcement officials on their celebrated hill.

"That is why the song is not the <u>official</u> fight song," I whispered to Tree. "It might discourage potential employers of University graduates, particularly those in the cities and towns."

But the band continued through an inspiring rendition of the song. I applauded and cheered, having assumed Tree was also causing my reaction to the parade to be obscured from family and neighbors. The band finished, brilliantly performed their iconic circle drill in the small space available and returned to their marching formation. Each row somehow squeezed through the ten yards between Tree and the corner of the house. After marching several more yards down the ridge, now much steeper, each successive row simply vanished into the autumn day.

A float labeled "Grand Marshall" was traversing Ridge Road, our gravel driveway below, and entering the side yard. The three tiers of a woodland scene offered the same fall colors which surrounded the parade route. Seated upon a top tier throne was the human-like Tree from the Charlotte airport. The large nose was hard to miss, but Tree sported groomed, orange hair which flowed backward in the breeze. He was laughing with pop-up crowd members on both sides of the parade route, and he was throwing candy bars and ripe persimmons from his colorful, branch-like arms. Crowd members appeared to catch these objects before anything hit the ground, which was satisfying to the obsessive-compulsive self remaining within me. He looked up and waved.

Tree beside me was also waving to the Grand Marshall tree. "Yes, Mike, that is one of my traveling selves. This is your parade, but since I put it together and will narrate for you, it seemed appropriate for me to serve as Grand Marshall. That's a first for me, and as you see, I'm having a great time." The float reduced its size to fit between me and real Tree and then disappeared a few yards further down the slope. Looking back up to the cemetery, I saw a pack of dogs more-or-less prancing down the parade route, occasionally playing with each other or running over to be stroked by a pop-up child. There were six dogs, each wearing a vest made of the thematic-colored autumn leaves and a collar of matching flowers. The dogs were young and full of energy, and I was smiling at the happy procession.

"Do you recognize any of them?" Tree asked.

"Brownie," I exclaimed in wonder… my first dog Brownie, it's Brownie!" No small boy could have been more excited at the sight of his dog, and I said to Tree, "My parents let me name her. She was brown; I was a kid and not very creative. My daddy explained to a friend that her mother was a rat terrier and her father was from somewhere on the other side of Drake Avenue."

Brownie now saw me, yelped with delight, and began jumping in the air as she led the others, now single file, down the yard. "Thank you, Tree," I said gratefully. It had been over fifty years since Brownie ran away just before Christmas. "Can I see her later?"

Then I realized that these were all of my lifetime dogs and they were in chronological order: Brownie, Blackie, Taffy, Johnson, Wilson, and Teddi Rose. I glanced around the porch and Teddi Rose had disappeared. A many-years younger version of Teddi had somehow joined the parade, as all of the dogs were at prime health and friskiness. They danced in delight as they saw me waving and calling their names. Each remained focused on me, as dogs will do, while jumping and barking below the porch. After a brief time of joyous reunion, they trotted past Tree and vanished. Teddi barked once behind me to announce her return to the porch as her correctly-aged self.

The float coming next over the road was large, although scaled down in size like everything else, with a circular surface. The border around the sides was primarily of red, white, and blue colors, and the circular surface held a Broadway set. The scene in progress was Annie and her compatriot ragamuffins in the orphanage singing "It's A Hard Knock Life."

The float stopped in front of me as the scene was ending. The stage then began to move through various scenes in the musical drama, some with quick bursts of song. Annie, now dressed in her red satin dress, stood to the side of the stage through this fast-forward. There were glimpses of Daddy Warbucks and Grace, Miss Hannigan, and Rooster. I unsuccessfully searched for Franklin Roosevelt in the quick sampling of scenes, since having a president in my parade would have been terrific. Thinking of my love for Broadway musicals in general reminded me that there was at least one niche of musical appreciation in my middle.

Both Tree and I knew why this was my favorite Broadway musical and why it belonged in the parade. We smiled at each other. This was the first Broadway musical which Chloe saw as a child, with Lynn and me -- part of her memorable first trip with us to New York City. She became obsessed with the Annie character. So often did she wear the red satin dress which Lynn made for her that a replacement Annie dress became necessary.

This was such a pleasant recollection that it seemed the parade stood still for a time, until the float restarted, moved along, and disappeared. Any doubt about a Macy's parade connection was removed by the trailing urchin holding a colorful tether to a large hot air balloon – large in relation to the Annie characters. The balloon was Goofy, and he sported a belt that was labelled "Goofy Dog" at the buckle. The balloon floated by me just above the porch level, and Goofy did a Goofy chuckle, said "Thanks, Mike," and evaporated into the air.

Next came two groups of (small) humans, walking along the route. Some were talking animatedly to each other, and they all waved and appeared to speak with the pop-up spectators.

"This is the march of family and friends,' Tree told me, and I began to look closely at the first group of scores of (little) humans, who were in no particular formation as they walked down the side yard.

It took a few moments reviewing the first few persons to realize that the walking humans were at the age I knew them when our relationship was at its most importance. My grandparents were first… my Mammaw, who lived in our household from my mid-schooling through high school. My parents, Pooky and Leo, at middle age, aunts, uncles, cousins. Then children and grandchildren, all female. Many of these persons were deceased, of course, but now they were all very much alive and celebratory as they stopped in front of me on the porch.

A rush of indescribably happy emotions embraced me, with a flood of good memories impossible to adequately sort out. It felt as a tidal wave of comfort and good cheer. My emotional processing systems were overwhelmed, so much love and gratitude was needed to share among these persons. "Thank you Tree," I said, "this is incredibly joyful." I thought that no human could ever expect such a wonderful family reunion. Religion aside.

My family members turned away at the same instant and moved down the ridge, which brought a second of anguish, but a solitary marcher came into view. It was Lynn, apparently at her age when we married, waving at me. A quick glance at the kitchen confirmed that current-age Lynn had absconded from the house and joined the parade.

"Smart move," I said quietly to Tree, "assigning my wife a place apart from all others."

"Yes," he replied, "it seemed appropriate and prudent. She is very special to you, and she is also co-owner of the parade route."

Lynn was saying something to me but with the pop-up crowd noise, it was difficult to discern her exact words. My best guess was that she was thanking me for all I had done for her in our time together and complimenting me on how enriching it is to live with me... and how she was looking forward to giving me care and comfort as I aged and grew infirm.

She turned and walked away. Teddi barked once, and I noticed that Lynn had returned to the kitchen and was walking upstairs.

Looking back, the yard in front of me contained a group of friends. Upon quick perusal, I saw that these were friends of all ages and circumstances of my life. They were happily waving to me in greeting, as I was doing back to them. Some were deceased, some current friends, who did, or would do, something to help me -- something hard to do -- while expecting nothing in return. And me to them.

I whispered to Tree, "The couple on the right side... I can't recall them."

"Yes, they represent friends you have had who you did not know that you had."

After another moment, I mumbled, "Not to complain Tree, but this seems to be a relatively small group of friends over my lifetime."

"Can you think of anyone else who could be added?" he retorted gently.

A few seconds later, I answered, "No."

"That's the reason. I can't just make this stuff up, Mike." And the friends departed.

Another float was crossing the road. It was a second float with red, white, and blue coloring, had many flower arrangements around the sides, and featured a circular surface. The front of the float was attractively labeled "Presidential Float" and the line below said "George H. W. Bush 41st President." The surface was dominated by the Presidential Seal and the colors in the flowerful symbol were gorgeous: the gold outer rings, the brown of the bald eagle, the green of the olive branch. Seated just outside the seal, at the back of the float, was a sixtyish President Bush, who was chatting with a young man seated next to him, while both waved to the pop-up crowd.

"I thought that the first George Bush might be appropriate for the President in your parade, Tree said to me, and I nodded my head in appreciation. This was the only president to have shaken hands with me in my lifetime. It was his time as the U.S. ambassador to the United Nations in 1972, and I was the cadet commander of the largest ROTC brigade in the nation. This somehow merited me an invitation for a 50-person briefing at the U.N. headquarters by Ambassador Bush. He shook hands with each attendee after his impressive briefing on world affairs, although no photographer was present to record the event.

Thereafter, I closely followed his career and was certain that he would become president. While our politics sometimes differed, I was proud of his successes. The Berlin Wall fell in his presidency and the cold war ended, a valued gift to adults who had learned duck-and-cover drills as youngsters in 1962.

It was me on the float with President Bush, a 1972 me. The President waved up to Porch Mike and I yelled thanks. The 1972 me ignored me, as this younger me was disturbingly wrapped up in himself, and the float moved past and disappeared.

Now about to cross the road was a lone female, who was walking carefully and waving to the crowd. She claimed the same space as a float, which was a curiosity. As she came closer, I could see that she was a high-school-age brunette, dressed in a jumpsuit-like garb of my high school days. She was prettier and prettier as she walked closer, looked up at me and blew a kiss.

"Tree," I said excitedly, "that girl is….."

Tree interrupted, "Don't say her name out loud, Mike. It is both good manners and wise to refrain from shouting out a female name during a parade." This seemed to be a strange parade principle, I thought, but Tree continued, "She was your great crush in high school -- your age, your grade, often sitting next to you in class."

"The problem, Tree, is that she was so beautiful, smart, and popular that she dated seniors when we were in 10th grade and a college guy in the 11th grade. We were good friends, but I never had the courage to ask her out, not even our senior year when she was largely unattached. She was above my pay grade for romantic purposes. I chose to avoid the risk of asking her out, being shot down and emotionally scarred, and facing humiliation as male classmates simulated an airplane with one hand, a machine gun with the other, and the devastating crash of the airplane on a nearby desk or table."

She had stopped and was looking up at me, flirtatiously, as Tree continued. "She is in your parade, Mike, so that you can know that she <u>really</u> liked you. During your senior year, especially, she wanted you to ask her out. That is why she so often sat next to you in class. In fact, she had a mutual friend suggest to you that you should ask her out."

"But I did not believe that message," I answered. "It did not seem possible to me. She was a 10 of 10, and I was a… well, no one ever bothered to give me a number; it was certainly below 10."

"You were wrong about that one. The longer you didn't ask her out, the more she wanted you to do so. This is good news from your past suggesting that others valued you more highly than you valued yourself."

It occurred to me that Tree might have little experience or knowledge about romantic relationships. "I'm not sure that this is a happy revelation. Do you have any idea what my senior year would have been like with her?"

"I do know, and you need to leave well enough alone. You got in enough trouble as it was, and besides, you had a terrific girl friend at the end of high school."

"True," I thought, "but I also had several, unrequited crushes in college...."

"Don't say the names, Mike," he again interrupted, "it is not appropriate during your parade."

I persisted, "Why weren't the others in the parade?" After a pause, and while waving back at my almost girlfriend, I asked, "Is it because she was the only one?"

"Are you asking if any of the others actually wished for you to ask them out?"

"Yes."

"Mike you are thinking too much. Try not to glum up your own parade."

I dropped the topic, as my high school friend disappeared, but it was noted that Tree did not answer my question.

A food float was about to come across the road. I knew this because a male and a female chef, white frocked with tall white chef hats marched ahead carrying a "Food Float" banner. This was unnecessary because the delicious aroma had already reached me on the porch. Individual smells came one at a time, as Tree apparently could manipulate olfactory matters along with everything else. Each distinct aroma remained a few seconds and then rotated away.

The rectangular float was inching along because three chefs walking on each side were serving samples of food to the pop-up crowd along the route. These pop-ups increased in number and lingered longer as adults and children accepted their offerings, began eating, and disappeared. Happier crowd noises could not have been heard. New dishes appeared instantaneously on the serving trays to replace what was being gratefully received.

I could see that the flat surface of the float was covered with what appeared to be a chocolate sauce but then saw that a mixture of sauces were somehow bubbling up from the surface – raspberry, perhaps, either caramel or peanut butter, strawberry, cherry, and a darker chocolate. The lava-like mixture continuously spilled over the sides, flowed to the bottom and was presumably recirculated. It was a self-propelled fountain of decadence. From the surface rose six towers of different heights, each ending in a table's surface containing a changing array of foods. There were three rows of two such food stands.

"These represent the six food groups which can be identified from your lifetime of eating: meats and potatoes, international exceptions, breads and baked goodies, breakfast foods, ice cream, and miscellaneous. Your unusual groupings of favorite foods make recipe classification difficult. For example, peanut butter and jelly sandwiches appear on the breads tower."

I was too mesmerized by the float to reply. Meat and potato combinations appeared and vanished across one top in the first row -- steaks, ribs, chops, roasts, fried chicken, hamburgers, hot dogs; baked potatoes, mashed potatoes, french fries. Tree and I knew that if my father asked what was for dinner as I grew up, it was understood that the appropriate answer was what meat was for dinner, and often the potato dish accompanying it. My mother would never answer with the name of a miscellaneous green or yellow vegetable, for example. First things first. Some meats were conspicuously absent from the rotating selection, I noted approvingly, such as liver and possum. Seafood dishes also appeared on this table -- beloved fried shrimp, salmon, lobster, crab claws -- although rarely encountered before my adult years.

Likewise, the dishes appearing on the international foods tower, exceptions to all-American meat and potato dishes, were rare before adulthood. I do recall Chef Boyardee pizza and occasional spaghetti, but I did not know that noodles meant pasta until college. Now before me were adult-life favorites from France to Italy to Asia. I smiled at the sushi, because Alabamians during the 1960's did not do sushi. It was pleasing to see that no dishes from England were included.

A new set of smells turned my attention to the next row and the bread tower, where my Mom's iconic cornbread was an initial dish. Every scrumptious bread from my recollection appeared, then pies, cakes, and cookies. There was visual and olfactory intoxication. This float was already overwhelming.

Also in the middle, and on the tallest tower, was the ice cream food group. Nutrition aside, I could live a reasonable gastronomic life on this group alone. Bowls of alternating flavors, cones, shakes, and sundaes.

It was then that I noticed Teddi Rose standing next to me, with her front paws on the screen. She was too excited to bark, apparently, but her stubby tail was moving faster than hummingbird wings. Realizing that she had no means to approach the float, she looked up at me in agony. "Your ice cream," said the chef who appeared behind us, placed the dog's bowl of ice cream on the floor and handed another to me. My bowl began with a homemade vanilla and peanut butter mixture, my favorite, and replenished continuously with new flavors. I turned back to the float and the chef disappeared.

While swilling the ice cream, I realized something about the pop-ups, which remained visible longer as food was served. In the crowd were ex-students. Also, I noticed favorite teachers, neighbors, colleagues, clients. Surrounding them in a pop-up might have been their own family members, who I may not have known or known well. All of the pop-up characters whom I saw brought good feelings and happy memories.

A breakfast food tower was on the final row, because if daily calories were not an issue, every day would begin with a breakfast buffet of impressive variety and quality. Such was before me: eggs of all varieties, bacon and sausages, pancakes, waffles. Reluctantly, I admitted to myself that these foods even surpassed ice cream for morning eating. Breakfast for dinner would have been great occasionally, except that the ladies did not share my breakfast food exuberance.

The last tower and shortest was Miscellaneous foods, which were primarily fruits and vegetables other than potatoes. Several items that I liked in both categories were appearing: pears, cantaloupe, raspberries, pineapple upside down cake, savory salads and dressings, squash casserole, fried okra. The truth is that if shipwrecked on a remote island, I would work on bringing forth steaks, hot dogs, and ice cream long before thinking about beans, broccoli, or bananas.

Towed at the back of the float was an actual-sized 105-mm howitzer, the foundation piece of my field artillery training. It was made of chocolate, with a huge cherry at the end of the barrel.

"This represents your brief period of military service. Your service wasn't long enough to merit a marching, military formation, or a tank, and I had to attach the howitzer somewhere."

That was a nice touch, I thought, as the food float disappeared. If all weapons were made of chocolate, the world would be a better place. Perhaps this was my destiny, to be the first advocate of chocolate weapons. We could eat ourselves to disarmament and if we did not they would melt away. The chocolate weapon disappeared.

The next float was already in the side yard and moving. This one was anticipated somewhere in my parade. It was a rectangular float, somehow self-propelled like all the others. Rising vertically from the back was a large, brown-decorated football, with "1998 Tostitos Fiesta Bowl" colorfully emblazoned. This was the first NCAA national championship game, and my team won. A green football field then extended to the front of the float, and printed at midfield in bold letters "Tennessee 23 Florida State 16." Reduced-sized players mingled on the field: Tennessee orange and Florida State with red and gold. I recognized #17 Tee Martin, the quarterback who led them all the way in the season after Peyton Manning departed. Ironic. The coaches, Phil Fullmer and Bobby Bowden, were shaking hands. Coach Fullmer and the Vols' players waved at me as they passed.

Tree sensed, I suppose, that he did not need to narrate this one. What a good feeling. It occurred to me that eight such floats would have been required to celebrate national championships in Lady Vols' basketball, but I would be required to think about Pat Head Summit, our legendary coach. The previous summer, she had died at age 64. The early onset of Alzheimer's had ended her storied career. So, these floats would have made me happy and very sad, and sad was not allowed in my parade.

I had heard the next float before it topped the ridge. It was Petula Clark singing "Don't Sleep in the Subway." I had forgotten that she had other hits in the 1960's besides "Downtown." The float was another beautifully decorated rectangle, but this time the long side was leading over the road and down the yard. The entire surface was a green football field. Colorfully imprinted on the left side of the field was: "Super Bowl #41 Colts 28 – Bears 17," right side: "Super Bowl #50 Broncos 24- Panthers 10." Rising up in the middle of the field was an outsized stage, presumably a half-time show. By this point, a 30ish Petula Clark was identifiable, in a sequined silver gown, standing before a microphone. She was now belting out "A Sign of the Times." Of course, this would be in my parade: Peyton Manning's two Super Bowl wins, with the greatest of all singers performing at the halftime. The float and Petula's stage stopped just short of the porch and facing toward both Tree and me.

Petula shouted to me, "This one's for you, Mike," and the hidden orchestra changed to the tune of "Downtown," her iconic song about the search for human connection in an urban setting. As the music began, a man dressed in a tuxedo rose from the stage to stand next to Petula before the microphone.

"Tree," I said excitedly, "That's Peyton. It's Peyton Manning and Petula Clark." Of course, Tree already knew that. And Petula began to sing…

When you're alone

And life's making you lonely

You can always go…

Peyton, who towered over Petula, leaned down into the microphone and sang/said "Downtown." He then leaned back out of the way. And so it went, with Petula singing and Peyton interjecting the title word as required. Peyton actually seemed a bit embarrassed and, while it is unfair to judge singing ability based upon the singing of one word, he had good reason to feel uncomfortable.

I was ecstatic. Petula and Peyton live from my side yard, singing the greatest pop song ever. The song ended, and the float moved between Tree and me. As they passed, Petula blew me a kiss, and Peyton said, "Go Vols." I said the same back to him, so that we would be like blood brothers from that time forward.

"Thank you, Tree," I said again, happily, and the Super Bowl float disappeared.

The band which could be heard approaching had topped the hill and was approaching Ridge Road. A banner leading the parade proclaimed "The Marching Virginians," which was followed by a flag corps, major-ettes, and the Virginia Tech band members. Each wore a white top with a maroon and orange sash. They were playing what I assumed was their fight song. It was an upbeat, energizing tune, and the trees and bushes again were gyrating to the rhythm, with the colorful ticker-tape mist adding to the celebration.

Tree's selection of this particular band was assumed to be that Virginia Tech was Lynn's alma mater. I glanced back into the kitchen, and Lynn was still preoccupied. Her own fight song had failed to expose my parade. The band members were, once again, small and became smaller as necessary to navigate the choke points along the route. Piccolos, clarinets, trombones, snare drums, and other instruments also changed size to fit the musicians. An SUV returning from downtown drove through a couple of rows of the band, which reappeared as the car passed.

This band did not stop, pivot, and play a special song for me on the porch. Rather, the band marched past me down the ridge, and row after row disappeared. Tree was not offering a narration, so I guessed this might be a deliberate snub. The Tennessee football team had come from behind to defeat the Hokies in the first game of the season that had just ended. The Vols then accomplished their best season in many years. These thoughts made me happy, which was perhaps the point.

My next thought was that I might be projecting my own sore los-ership upon the innocent Virginians. Perhaps this was a purist marching band that only played music when marching. Or, maybe they only knew how to play this one song. Hearing me, Tree shook his head in disappoint-ment, but he was smiling. "We now turn to the Wishes section of your parade," Tree said.

An unusually-shaped float was florally labeled "World Series 7th Game" around its front. As it tipped down and across the road, the shape was a major league baseball field, from the screen behind home plate to the outfield fences. Diamond, mound, outfield, a team on the field, but all scaled down, of course. The dugout tops on the two sides of the float had the New York Yankees logo and the Cincinnati Reds logo, my lifetime favorites. The scoreboard along the left field fence line indicated that this was the deciding 7th game of the series, with a 1-0 lead by the Yankees, top of the 9th inning, two outs, bases loaded, 3-2 count on the batter.

As the float came to a stop in front of me, I could see individual Yankee players, which meant the venue was the Yankee stadium of my youth, the house that Ruth built. The players were not time consistent, however, as #2 Derek Jeter was at short stop but #6 Cletis Boyer was at third base and #7 Mickey Mantle -- the Mick – was in left field. The Yankees were one pitch away from either victory or disaster, as a change of pitchers was being made.

On the mound, Whitey Ford handed over the baseball to the diminutive new pitcher. Also at the mound were #8 Yogi Berra, the catcher, who may have been doubling as manager, and pitching coach #32 Sandy Koufax of the Dodgers, who had apparently been hired as a consultant by the Yankees for this game. My heart began to race as I realized the new pitcher was me, the left-handed little league hurler whose pitching idols were Whitey and Sandy. My uniform was the blue-and-white uniform of the Mallory Sparkplugs, the auto parts manufacturer that sponsored my team. Sandy placed his hand on my shoulder, gave me last-minute advice, and then all three left the mound. Yogi took his place behind the plate.

Warm-up pitches were apparently unnecessary for little league Mike, as the Reds batter #5 Johnny Bench stepped back up to the plate. Pop-up crowd noise was rising. I shook off Yogi's first sign and then nodded my agreement with his next choice, took a deep breath, and began my unnecessarily complicated little league wind-up.

It was the slowest pitch that I had ever seen and looked to be a knuckleball as it erratically moved forward. Odd, because little league Mike could only theoretically throw a knuckleball, but not surprising in the context of this parade. Porch Mike had stopped breathing several minutes previously. Johnny had time to hitch and re-hitch himself as he moved forward in the batter's box, gleeful for the pitch to arrive. His mighty swing was a model of power hitting perfection. But the ball zigged when Johnny expected a zag, and Johnny Bench struck out.

The pop-up crowd noise became deafening, as Mike was swarmed by his Yankee teammates and the pop-up fans who spread out over the field. I knew that little league Mike had relived such a scene many times in his mind, but this time it was real… or at least parade-real.

"Have you ever had a feeling as good as when Johnny struck out?" Tree asked with a big smile.

"Never, Tree, not from my own athletic exploits or even fanship. This was the World Series, Tree." I spontaneously added, "This is why we keep score." Tree let the comment pass, however, as Yankee stadium was absorbed into my back yard, and both Tree and I looked back up the ridge at another float.

Moving through the cemetery was a float with a color scheme around its decorative sides which was beautifully done but in somber, dark colors of black, gray and brown. It was a marked contrast to the brilliant fall colors of the parade route and other, happy colors of the various bands and floats. No bushes or trees were dancing, and crowd noise had disappeared.

As the float tilted downhill past the road, a courtroom scene was the entirety of the squarish surface. The elevated bench of the judge dominated the courtroom and, at the back of the float, faced forward. The witness box was attached to the left side of the judge's fortress, and a jury box lined the same side as the witness box. A table with a court reporter and clerk sat before the judge, and, facing the judge, were the two tables of opposing lawyers, a waist-high barrier, and several rows of spectator benches. Pop-up circles of persons had abandoned the parade route and quietly filled the spectator space at the front of the float.

It was the first quiet of the parade, but reduced-size persons were animating the courtroom. The witness had to be me, current-age me, because he was older, resembled me, and was wearing my testimony uniform: dark blue suit, white shirt, and red tie. It appeared that cross examination may have ended as a lawyer at one table sat down, the judge dismissed me, and witness Mike gathered his files and stood up to leave the witness stand.

As he did, a juror on the front row stood up and slowly began to applaud, then two others on the middle row rose and joined the applause, and quickly the entire jury erupted in an outpouring of respect and admiration. The judge, who should have been admonishing the jury for such outrageous conduct, also stood and began to clap loudly. The pop-up audience rose and began to applaud and cheer. Finally, my side's attorneys joined in and, reluctantly, the attorneys who had just cross-examined me and would now settle the case as fast as possible. As a crescendo was reached, individual "hurrahs" and "way-to-gos" were drowned out.

I had begun laughing several moments before, as the audacity of the courtroom scene consumed me. Tree was also chuckling, and he asked, "What is the chance that this would actually happen to you in an American courtroom?"

"Slightly less than the chance of me winning a Nobel prize in economics," I replied. There was a silence between us that grew awkward, the courtroom float passed, and with a long floral attachment, a new float had been tethered to the previous float; it had the same solemn colors. On the surface was a table, and a formally dressed man was seated beside the table in a dark wooden chair.

"Here you go, Mike, the Nobel prize in economics. Congratulations."

Smiling broadly, I inquired, "What is on the table?" as gold reflected in the sunshine.

"Your prizes, Mike -- the gold medal, the certificate, and money -- these are stacks of all of your prize money in cash."

I had never before seen stacks of money, except in the movies, and shamefully realized that my mind was quickly allocating these new funds for various purposes, after payment of all federal and state taxes, of course.

"Ok, Tree, who is the guy with the Santa Claus beard and wire-rimmed glasses?"

"He is a stereotypical older Swedish economist who represents the awards committee," Tree answered seriously. "You could have had the complete awards scenario for a float but then you would need to make a speech revealing breathtaking insights into economic theory and, well...."

"Good enough Tree. The table and the old guy are good enough." I then struggled with myself before saying, "I cannot bear not to ask this, Tree… are you able to tell me the piece of my research which brought the prize?"

Tree seemed delighted with the question, but he answered without expression, "Brookshire's Law of Infinity." He stopped.

We certainly could not stop now, so I gave him what he wanted, "And can you remind me, perhaps in a sentence or two, exactly what that law is?"

"Surely, I can. Your law says that any whole number of dollars, from $1 to $9, when multiplied by infinity, results in an infinitely large number of dollars."

This made me begin to laugh again, "I never said or wrote that, Tree."

"Yes, you proposed this to your fellow students before a class in mathematical economics… to break the fear and tension. But a Swedish student wrote it down, and the rest is history as they say."

"What about ten, Tree?"

"What do you mean?"

"If the law is about 1-9, what about 10, for example? What happens at 10?"

Tree seemed to pause and think, "Economists are continuing to work through the implications of one through nine Mike. It will take them a while to start on ten." He added solemnly, "Your original thought evolved into the new field of infinity economics, which was adopted by governments around the world as a cornerstone of their economic policy." Tree was really enjoying himself as Grand Marshall.

The old Swedish dude was disappearing as another float moved toward Ridge Road, and another band could be heard coming from over the ridge. This new float had a rectangular surface ending in a seashell-like back wall. The color scheme involved various shades of blue. It was the stage for the long-running television show "Jeopardy," and a hidden orchestra played the Jeopardy theme song. The trees moved again with the music, but the music and the pop-up crowd quieted.

It was exciting to watch the Jeopardy float headed my way. I could see that Alex Trebek was standing in front of this wall and behind his lectern, apparently introducing double jeopardy. Alex's show had been a pleasant fixture in my life for the last third of a century. In my side yard, he was now talking to three contestants, who were facing Alex but would be facing away from me. It was unnecessary to see their names. Grand Master, all-time champion Ken Jennings occupied the returning championship module closest to Alex. A reduced-sized Mike, current aged, occupied the middle, and the incomparable Oprah Winfrey was in the third module. "Of course Oprah Winfree is standing next to Jeopardy Mike," I thought, "Anything is possible in my parade."

Facing the contestants, and me on the porch, was a flowery game board, with the five rows of money values in double jeopardy. The six category columns across the top held the same caption, "Meaning of Life." Was Tree about to reveal to me the meaning of life? This would be a terrific addition to almost anyone's parade, I thought. Or did the thirty entries on the board mean that life had thirty different meanings? The float was moving slowly, but there would be time for only one or two turns on the board.

When the float was almost directly beneath me, the action began. All 30 screens on the scoreboard grid flipped over simultaneously to reveal the same answer. Unfortunately, the answer was written in Greek. I was at least familiar with Latin, but this had to be Greek. "Aw c'mon, Tree," I started to say as he began to chuckle.

Quickly, Oprah rang in with a guess at the correct question, but she apparently missed. Ken tried but also missed. "Jeopardy Mike," I said out loud, "the question is not difficult. It must be 'What is the meaning life?'" Mike rang in and said something I could not understand but that must have been correct. The board blinked and bells sounded to signify victory.

He must have won the entire $30,000 on the board, give or take the two Daily Double options. Little Mike inappropriately jumped around in circles pumping his arms, and Oprah hugged him in congratulations.

"This is paradoxical, Tree," I said to him as he struggled not to laugh, "Little Mike there won Jeopardy, but all I know is that the meaning of life is written in Greek."

The Jeopardy float disappeared as Tree replied, "All you needed to do was take out your cell phone, click a picture, and have it translated later." He was right, I thought, momentarily deflated by my lost opportunity. No more than 10 to 12 pictures had been taken and stored on my phone, so that this and other functions of the technology were never at the front of my mind.

Can you back it up for me, Tree? Please?"

"Sorry, Mike," he replied, "even I can't reverse a parade. But you did learn one other thing."

"What is that?"

"The problem here is not in finding the answer, but rather in asking the question."

Before this comment could be pondered, the band music overwhelmed me. A banner introduced the "Auburn University Marching Band." Hundreds of members marched along, as with the previous university bands. White pants, blue tops, orange trim, and the distinctive, stacked AU logo was prominent. Also, the band members played the War Eagle fight song as they marched quickly down the parade route.

"Why the Auburn band?" I thought. Auburn was an SEC sports opponent of my beloved Vols. Tennessee was only slightly behind in the 50-or-so-game football series. It was true that I actually liked Auburn, as enemies go, because of growing up in Alabama and my admiration for their exceptional school spirit. Also, in my senior year of high school, my football team played Pat Sullivan's Birmingham football team. Pat

Sullivan would become Auburn's first Heisman Trophy winner, which did not surprise anyone who had watched his high school game films. These did not seem sufficient reasons for a gig in my parade, but the band was too loud to ask Tree. The porch was vibrating, and Teddi Rose, who disliked war eagles anyway, was frightened.

As with the Virginia Tech band, the Auburn marchers did not stop at the porch, re-form, and play a separate song, but quickly disappeared below Tree. I thought that perhaps marching bands held grudges. My team beat Pat Sullivan's team 62-21, and the Auburn people had tracked me down. That thought made me smile.

Tree finally spoke again, "And last, Mike, possibilities for your future," and another float crested the ridge.

As the float angled downhill, I observed the shape of a pottery vase with a smaller base flaring wider at the end. There was a raised stage at the back and auditorium seating with rows narrowing to the front of the float. This float was also decorated, but in darker, richer colors as befitting an important lecture, because the flowered sign at the front of the float said, "Annual Brookshire Lecture, Thank You Officers of the USA."

The seats were packed with attendees either in police uniforms or business dress. By now, it had become very easy to recognize the same-age, but smaller, parade Mike. He was apparently completing his address and had returned to the title slide on the screen to his side, "Thank You Strategies and Enforcement Speed Limits." Lecturer Mike's comments could not be understood beyond "blah… blah… blah."

"I attempted to prepare a speech for Lecturer Mike to be giving on this topic, but logic escaped me. If you wish to stop the parade and speak to this assembly and the pop-up crowd, however, we could do that."

I quickly demurred, because Tree would see me as egregiously narcissistic, and it would also have required several hours of preparation. Then, I laughed, "Tree, you know that nothing like this will happen in my future. At the same time, the audience erupted in applause, and the lecture float moved beneath. I also recalled that one member of the Charleston City Council had proposed reassigning the entire Thank You unit to regular patrol and redistributing thank you responsibilities over the entire police force. Just so thank you is in there somewhere, I thought, and admired my flexibility on the topic.

"Such a speech is indeed possible for your future, Mike. You are far ahead of your time on this subject. The future is all about possibilities, Mike, which can be an attractive feature of the future. You would need to leave this for the future, rather than dwelling upon it now, which is something with which you still struggle. And Lecturer Mike is much smaller. Don't miss that part of it."

The next float was almost at the road. It was the most visually attractive float yet, and perhaps the largest, in reduced size. The broad side of the rectangle traveled first, and the scene, left to right, was a mountain, a valley with a large creek or small river cutting the land approximately in half, and another mountain. Lest I miss the point, a little sun was rising over the first mountain, and an equal-sized sun was painting a sunset over the other. Moreover, a flowered sign introduced this beautiful picture as "Day Float."

I smiled as the characters came into view. To the left of the creek was Ron's farm; the county road was the front of the float. Ron could be seen behind his farmhouse seated on the hood of his jaguar, Bessie, while talking to his cow, Bessie. His corn extending to the fall-colored mountain was ready for harvest, ears dark green with brown silks. The other side of the waterway was more pastureland but bereft of animals. Seated on a small rise in the bank, a bit closer to the front of the road than Ron, was an apparently meditating, my-age Mike.

Little Mike was not immediately identified because he sported a full beard, but the orange sash on his simple brown robe gave him away. Mike was meditating. Meditating, little Mike. The look on his face was serene. He looked to be so very peaceful and safe, and joyful. The parade route had gone motionless, silent, reverent. Teddi Rose was on the floor snoring softly.

"Am I really likely to wear a robe like that, Tree?" I asked, breaking the silence.

"Time will tell, Mike. Time will tell. But it is possible."

My next thought was that, while this day-scene was appealing, the same scene day after day might be a bit stifling. It would have been good to know that alternative daily scenes would allow me to spend sufficient time on the food float, for example, but I hesitated to ask Tree.

He replied anyway, "Yes, of course the scene changes within a day. All sorts of fast-or-slow-changing scenes are in every day. Your challenge is to keep the scenes between the mountains. It always has been."

We were both distracted by the large, circular float now traversing down the parade route. The side colors were shades of blue and dark green. As it tilted downward, the flat surface was of the same colors. It was the height of this float that was striking, however, because this was a circus performance of a high-flying trapeze act, and this feature made porch Mike automatically edgy. Trapeze ropes were attached to circular disks high above the circus ring on the floor, but the disks were not attached to anything. I was moving past allowing such details to bother me. Rope ladders faced each other across the circus ring and extended to two platforms on one side, and one on the other. Here, the "catcher" had already started, swinging by his knees and gaining momentum. Standing on the high platform on the other side was a young female flyer, in a sparkling red leotard, who jumped off holding her trapeze bar and using the high starting point to accelerate her swing. She released the bar with perfect timing, accomplished a 1½ backward somersault, was easily caught and re-deposited on the lower platform, and bowed and waved to the cheering, pop-up crowd. The act was even more impressive because of the complexities of moving downhill, but the laws of physics had not proved limiting to my parade.

All eyes turned upward, to the higher platform, where now stood two burly men, dressed as gladiators, bookending a slight man, dressed in a sky-blue silk top and white tights. It was Flying Mike, which was stitched across his blue top in orange. He was the same age as me, on-the-porch Mike, and it immediately felt as if part of me was physically merged down on the float with him. The pop-up crowd was wildly cheering for Flying Mike. But he did not look well: very pale, with anguish on his face, and I felt fear with him.

Flying Mike either jumped, or was pushed, off his platform. In his acceleration downward, he managed to hang onto his bar, but his body was inert. The crowd had become silent, except for the occasional gasp. When Mike reached the point to depart for the catcher, he simply swung on by him and upward. After a heart-stopping moment at the top of his arc, he began the reverse arc backward and still held on as he paused in mid-air before another arc would begin, probably his last chance to be caught and saved.

The scene was directly beneath me now, although not far beneath. It had appeared that Flying Mike briefly attempted to climb back up the ropes above his bar, but then he turned, looked downward, and began his second descent. Rising from the crowd were shouts of "Let go, Flying Mike… let go, Mike… you can do it." He did let go, but he clearly would not connect up with the catcher. The catcher was scarcely into the necessary arc, as any chance of appropriate timing had vanished.

Flying Mike seemed to suspend in mid-air for a moment, and then dropped like a lead weight. Strangely, for the first time I noticed there was no net, which had probably not escaped Little Mike. Teddi Rose dropped to the floor and covered her eyes. As fast as this was happening, it continued to feel as if all or part of me was there with him, falling to the circus floor.

Except it wasn't a floor. It was water. Mike descended below after a tremendous, reduced-size splash, re-emerged, and held up his hands above the water in exultation. Water did not flow downhill in my parade. The pop-up crowd exploded in happiness and relief, as the last of the little Mikes disappeared.

I was shaken, and said to Tree, "I saw Little Mike's face in the pause, and then in the moment before he fell. And I felt it too. He knew that he was surely about to die, but the moment he knew that his face turned to peaceful, maybe joyous. Better than Meditating Mike because it was better than acceptance. It was anticipation, not resignation, in his face. Perhaps it was eagerness, to get on with it. He was smiling, Tree. There was no fear.

"That would seem to be a very good place for a person to be, at the end," I continued. "Whatever one would be doing, however he would be living, to have a face like that, at a time like that. It would be great to have a Flying Mike in my future." I thought some time would be needed to process this one further.

Perhaps Tree saw no need to comment, but we were both attracted to movement across Ridge Road, to the right of the parade route in the direction of downtown. It was the neighbor lady rising from a flat rock formation along the road and beginning to walk toward the parade route. She waved at me, and she smiled a special smile. Then she walked down the road. Had she witnessed the entire parade? What could I possibly say to her? Before Tree intervened with a comment, however, I reasoned that if he could have pulled off the parade, he could easily resolve my need for an explanation to the neighbor lady. This was important because I had no explanation for the neighbor lady.

As she walked beyond sight, a ten-member jazz band marched snappily over the ridge playing "When the Saints Go Marching In." The procession which followed was a New-Orleans-style funeral parade. Charleston had crafted its own version as a featured part of one of our annual festivals. The marchers wore black clothes, primarily, out of respect for the occasion, but there were flashes of purple and gold as the marchers gaily dispensed dark beads and other souvenirs.

Surrounded by the marchers was an elongated procession of three horse-drawn carriages, each towing a casket on a dark, wheeled flatbed. The horses were black, chestnut, and black. Crowd pop-ups turned silent as this procession moved by, and then disappeared as the procession moved under the porch and was gone.

"Why three caskets, Tree?" I asked, but a blaze of color diverted my attention to the horizon beyond the ridge. It was a cloud-like swirl of colors, which constantly folded into itself in a wondrous mixture as new colors appeared to accelerate its movement toward the parade route. As it became tightly compact and focused in my direction, the various colors became noticeably softer – just as beautiful but more soothing. Before anything could be said to Tree, the Swirl travelled down the side yard and surrounded me on the porch.

A first sensation was a pleasant warmth, but my feeling was also that I was part of this Swirl around me, somewhere blended with it rather than separately existing. The good emotions, sights, sounds were beyond my experience. But this immersion only lasted a moment, as Teddi Rose began barking.

I slowly focused on Teddi Rose, barking from her bed on my side of our upstairs bedroom. The Swirl was gone. Seeing me propped on an elbow waking up to her, Teddi feathered down her barking and padded over for some morning love.

Still blinking myself out of the dream, I sat up on the edge of the bed and processed my changed environment. Lynn, having also been awakened by the barking, said, "What in the world were you dreaming about all night? You woke me up all during the night talking."

"Do you mean like I was having a recurring nightmare?" I asked.

"Not a nightmare. You were excited, happy, chattering away. So happy that if you had said a woman's name, besides mine, you would have been in big trouble. What were you dreaming about?"

"I don't have a clue," I lied. "You know I can rarely remember my dreams." Tree had saved my butt on a female-name crisis. Comprehension that the conversation with Tree and then the entire parade had been a dream soaked through me. "So, I take it that you didn't sleep well?"

"Actually, I went back to sleep easily every time your oohs, aahs, and giggles woke me up, but then I started having dreams in between waking up to whatever party you were having."

"A parade," I began to say but caught myself and said, "What were you dreaming about?" Unlike me, you remember your dreams."

"It was bizarre," she laughed, "you would never believe it."

"Try me."

She briefly paused and replied. "I was somewhere near the Macy's Parade, but I couldn't see anything, just hear it a block away. Annie sang "The Sun Will Come Up Tomorrow." And I remember your Petula Clark singing "Downtown." There were marching bands, very loud sounds from the crowd. What did we eat last night?"

We adored Teddi and processed her downstairs and outside, and I seamlessly moved through my coffee, newspapers, and TV news routine. A late January snow of a few inches had fallen overnight. Tree stood cold and silent.

It proved impossible to keep my mind off the parade while moving through the day. Everything about this dream was unusual compared to what had been read on the subject and to my previous experiences. It had been an all-night dream, through REM and non-REM sleep, that I remembered in incredible detail, and that apparently spilled over into my wife.

The next day was very cold, and I was settled in my downstairs office for an afternoon of work. "That was some dream that you had, Mike," Tree began. He seemed to be speaking from the corner of the wall behind my computer screen. I was facing in that direction working, and

Tree stood outside, ten feet beyond the corner. It had been the narrowest point on the parade route.

I smiled a grateful expression at Tree, as we briefly reviewed my distinguished parade guests and the food float. "It was all terrific, Tree, all good memories or fantasies or improvements in me."

Then, some sad crept into me, "I must admit, though, that I thought you were showing me a miracle, beyond human capabilities to create, but as it turns out, the parade was simply a dream." I thought to myself for a moment and meandered through a query, "But how did my unconscious mind organize and implement a dream parade that thoughtful, in such specific detail, with information from my past that presumably only you know, but I did not? How were deceased people so seemingly alive and well? How do I possibly remember every detail?"

"Perhaps because the dream was a miracle -- the sign that you wanted in the beginning. Yet, miracles have their own timing. It is the nature of miracles. Moreover, it was time for you to see the parade, with me as Grand Marshall, and I have never had so much fun." He chuckled lightly.

"I can accept that. Dream or miracle. I choose to believe it was a miracle, and I thank you for it. Turning again to a question, however, "Why now, Tree? I no longer needed a sign that you were real or that you were bigger than me."

"Because it was my gift to you, and gifts do not require occasions or reasons. Nevertheless, it was time to move your middle from future worry or regrets from the past, so that you can settle where you belong, in today. No matter what."

"Tree, as joyful as this parade and this miracle have been, I am troubled. It was so very good and positive and hopeful, but it is not accurate. There is a bad parade, of failure and regret and sadness, of which you are surely aware. What do I do with the bad parade?"

Tree answered, "That parade no longer holds a purpose, for you or the Big or the All. You need not dwell there anymore."

"What will keep me from moving back there again, as I always have before, and dragging myself down?"

"It is that I forgive you, Mike, for the bad parade," he said simply. "This is the real miracle. The parade that is forgiven."

Not often in my adult life had I been so quiet, stilled by words to me. These words were entirely unanticipated, and the words were bigger than me. "Why would you forgive me, Tree? It is not what I deserve."

"Because I love you, Mike. That is why. What you deserve is not the issue, and what you deserve has never been your decision to make. Let go of that notion. You are now free to forgive yourself. You can do that, Mike. You can do that."

I almost asked him again about the three caskets but perceived somehow that an answer would not be forthcoming. Instead, I said, "The Swirl of colors at the end... anything that you can tell me about that?"

"You diminished your autumn worrying about the end of your parade. And how did the end look to you?"

"It was wondrous, incredibly beautiful."

"And how did it feel?"

"Warm and secure and comforting. Like a place that I belonged."

"Then, there you go, Mike, and, meanwhile, do the next right thing today."

CHAPTER TWELVE –
THE ECLIPSE

Tree and I did not speak with each other through the bleak and cold wintry days which extended through February and March of 2017. The high of the parade and follow-up conversation with Tree motivated me back to my path prior to the distractions of olding and death. Much of the return simply required mindfulness and persistence in what had been working for me.

Start and stop-of-the-day, bookend conversations with myself were reinstated, and this alone seemed to reduce daily time either in the past or in the future. When out of the day, I was once again likely to notice my transgressions and admonish myself to move back to the day where my mind belonged.

The improvements in my way of living were interconnected and reinforcing. Returning my focus to the day meant seeing myself smaller and that, in turn, was a reminder of the narrow scope of my control. My mental sorting machine for dividing the small set of what I might control from everything else began to crank back up. Then, the feeling of expectations relaxing for myself and others was almost palpable.

Driving strategies re-emerged, and several basketball games were Giffered during February. The look on Lynn's face was priceless when I began discussing how a stereo system could be wrapped around my man cave to enhance my ability to relax with music.

Surprisingly, less time than typical was devoted to news reading and viewing. A presidential transition was underway, and early signs had appeared that breaking news might begin to break faster and less predictably than had heretofore been true. Yet, none of that could be controlled by me, and there were more positive uses of time.

One such use was help to a friend who had been in a serious accident a few months before. Providing, and arranging for, his transportation to various doctor's appointments, meetings, etc. was a weekly activity. It was one of three periods during 2017 when the attempt at more and deeper friendships allowed the opportunity to focus on someone else. During a year of sometimes frenetic work activity, the periods in which help was needed coincided with days and weeks when in-town time was available. Coincidence or not, this use of my time proved far more valuable to me than to them.

March 3 was a Friday, with a prediction of clearing skies and warming into the fifties for the afternoon. My day began early with a downtown breakfast meeting of friends from my discussion group. Chloe had first been dropped off at her nearby high school. For the remainder of the morning, I had been in my downstairs office preparing for upcoming depositions. At 11:15 the phone rang, and the caller was seen to be my first wife and mother of my two daughters. It was 8:15 in California. A call from her this time of day was very unusual, and I recall thinking, "This is not good."

"Mike," she said when I answered, "the thing that we have worried about so long has happened. Nikki is dead." My recollection is that these three words saturated through me. I may or may not have said anything, and she explained that a short while earlier, she had been moving through my granddaughter's routine of breakfast and preparing for school when she glanced out her window. Three policemen were standing in her front yard. She walked out to them and said, "She is dead, isn't she? You are here to tell me that Nikki is dead." They asked if she would go inside with them where they confirmed Nikki had been found dead earlier that morning in the room she rented. Her room was not disturbed, and no drugs or paraphernalia had been found. A drug overdose appeared to be the cause of death, consistent with her appearance and history, and a toxicology report would be forthcoming.

We made plans to talk later in the day, as she needed to be with her granddaughter, and she agreed to call Nikki's older sister Kristi. Lynn was already at a luncheon honoring a good friend in town who was an accomplished circuit judge, but I texted her and she returned home. After speaking briefly to my two first cousins in Alabama, who knew Nikki and whose mother had been Pooky's twin sister, Lynn and I waited for the 3:15 dismissal of high school. One of us typically picked Chloe up but not both of us, so she was alarmed when both of us sat in the front seat waiting. As Lynn drove away, I looked at Chloe in the back seat and told her the tragic news. It was a long ride home, but Chloe's story is hers to share if she wishes, not mine.

Later in the day there were calls with my daughter Kristi and with two of my closest friends in Charleston. They asked about Chloe, but that is all that can be recalled. If anyone asked how I was doing, an accurate answer would have been impossible. My conscious self was functioning adequately, albeit by rote. The only feeling that can be remembered from that day is the emptiness of grappling with the knowledge that a child of forty years had been taken away.

Within a day or so, it had been decided that we would not fly to California immediately, but rather wait for a memorial service to be organized in April. Since Nikki had never lived in Charleston, few persons were aware of our loss, and I was not inclined to talk about it. My schedule and activities did not change, so that my days were busy. The loneliness of the last hour or so of each evening in my office/cave left me very sad at the end of the day. Yet, this is recalled as if part of a bad dream.

Tree came to me on Sunday evening in my private place, where the ladies rarely visited, after our dinner and common time together in the living room above me. I can recall that in this and other visits over the next month, he did not promote conversation but ensured I knew he was there for me. These visits are also hazy in my memory, but on the Sunday, I observed that we had never discussed Nikki in all of our time together, and he said, "We can discuss that anytime you wish, but now you are numb." It was the first such observation to me, but at that time, I was neither ready nor anxious to talk with Tree. In the times when my mind was devoted to this loss, the review of Nikki's history scrolled around and around, without regard to the feelings which might typically be aroused. Some of this may have been discussed with Tree, even though he already knew the story, but I am uncertain.

Nikki was born in the Fort Sanders Hospital, located on a hill overlooking some of the University of Tennessee, Knoxville campus. My favorite picture of her is at the age of three, with her sister age nine. In that year, 1980, the family moved with me to a new job at the University of Cincinnati. Three years later, I moved back to a faculty position in Charleston, my wife and I divorced, and my life with children became that of a non-resident father. Time spent with Nikki increasingly involved soccer. She was the leading scorer of Select soccer teams in a great city for youth soccer. Her championship Age 13 team played in a pre-game soccer match on New Years Day before the Orange Bowl. A trip that the two of us took to a tournament in Toronto is also a highlight of those days.

Then, when Nikki was 15 and her sister in college, Nikki's mom and her husband relocated to jobs in San Clemente, California, and Nikki moved with them to the other side of the country. Her new high school in

Orange County did not have soccer teams available, nor was she able to find another team. The drug use that had likely begun in Cincinnati only worsened, and addiction to heroin and other drugs quickly came to dominate her story.

The cycle of drug use; treatment, half-way houses, or other attempts at recovery; and relapse repeated. Nikki ultimately graduated from a private high school that catered to young adults with such problems. She became very close to my wife Darrance, before and during her five-year illness. Nikki's longest period of being missing and on drugs correlated with Darrance's lengthy stays in the hospital, and then with her death.

Having heard, or read, the accounts of other parents in this situation, the basics of struggle and sorrow were the same, except that this was my daughter and our situation. The lack of her progress toward a sustainable life was a disturbance which one could choose to feel anytime. Financial impacts and uncertainties were always around or just below the surface of reality. Soul-shredding decisions regarding the continuum between enabling and letting go often appeared quickly and without warning. Not knowing about a child's safety was an awful weight.

Jeff came along in 1999. They met in a treatment program, visited Lynn and I once in Charleston, and married. It is a memorable experience to give a daughter away at the Elvis Presley Chapel of Love in Las Vegas. Chloe was born on October 1, 2000, and we would see the family of three once or twice a year.

A few years later, the family moved to my ex-wife's new location in California, where they depended on her but (mostly) did not live with her. They struggled with drugs and financially. Being the parent of an adult addict who is raising one's grandchild was difficult enough by long distance, but my ex-wife faced the turmoil up close and personal, as the saying goes. One positive action that Lynn and I took was to ensure Chloe's preschool years in an excellent Montessori school, which also served a hot lunch.

Jeff and Nikki were on and off recovery efforts, and the use of methadone, by 2004, when they were part of a my-side-of-the-family Thanksgiving vacation at a beach house near Pensacola. Lynn and I were becoming very close to Chloe. In August of 2006, Chloe lived with us when her mother was in a hospital and then nursing home with carditis. In December 2006, the family moved to southern California, living with Jeff's mother. Jeff worked in an old friend's music store – Jeff was a talented guitarist – while Chloe attended California kindergarten.

Pooky and I were talking in our kitchen on April 3, 2007, when my ex-wife called to tell us that Jeff was in the hospital with an infection that the doctors could not control. He died of sepsis two hours later. Lynn and I flew to California the next day. Chloe, who by this time adored her Lynnie, stayed in the hotel room with us. The next day we met with Jeff's family, and we agreed that Lynn and I would raise Chloe. Nikki was indisposed for these discussions, and she was also less than three months from delivering her second child. The baby was born on May 25, and Chloe finished kindergarten with her familiar Montessori class. On June 5, Chloe came to live with Lynn, Pooky, and me in Charleston. She was six years old, which was Nikki's age when our time living together ended. It was a thought-provoking irony. Since Lynn did not have children of her own, we were grandparents facing parenthood for the first time, plus Pooky. Lynn had welcomed a mother-in-law and a granddaughter into our household within a couple of months.

We spent another year or so dealing with Child Protective Services and fending off the possibility that Nikki might reacquire custody of Chloe, but drug test results ultimately eased our attaining permanent custody and then adoptive parenthood. Meanwhile, Chloe's little sister was adopted and raised by my first wife.

Nikki lost her husband when she was thirty years old and pregnant. Then, she lost both of her children, and, at times, was legally denied any access to them. She had no job skills or work experience. Her addiction was progressive. I often had no mail or email address or telephone means of communication with her. Nikki began to receive SSI benefits after awhile, which helped her survive, but prospects for breaking her addiction were not good. Then, she died.

The weeks after March 3 were busy with normal work, school, and home activities, except for Chloe's spring break vacation to London and Amsterdam. I remember that the London cabbies were furious about the recent appearance of bicycle lanes on the streets, which they claimed were responsible for the gridlock of surface transportation. I recall the canals and the flower farm. Tree sat next to me once on a park bench facing a fine Amsterdam restaurant, but there is no recollection of the content of conversations with him or anyone else.

After only a few days back at home, we flew to the late April memorial service in California. I remember the lovely place where her cremation vase would be interred and the girlfriends who spoke at the ceremony about Nikki's kindness to them. Time was spent with my ex-wife's sister, brothers, and their spouses. There is recall of my attempts to be available for Chloe and her younger sister but little reason to believe that I could have been much help to either. My world had lost both depth and detail.

In the period from May through the summer, my paralysis of normal feelings may not have been known to me, except that Tree apparently thought it important for me to know. Tree brought up Bell's Palsy to help me understand, and only Tree had the history to know this analogy might be useful. This medical condition, sometimes called facial palsy, causes a temporary weakness or paralysis of the muscles on one side of the face. The drooping of the affected side is most noticeable with the drooping side of the mouth. The condition is associated with inflammation of the nerve that controls the muscles on the affected side of the face, but the cause of the inflammation is debated. It is very rare, and a person having the condition does not have a greater likelihood of having it again, so that a recurrence would be freaky.

When Tree brought it up, Bell's Palsy had visited with me on three separate occasions – two left and one right face – and the longest occurrence had lasted six weeks. Lecturing to a class and testifying in court were challenging with half a mouth functioning, but the condition resolved itself each time without lingering effects.

Thus, I knew the feeling of paralysis. It feels like nothing. There is no feeling to it. That is the defining characteristic of complete numbness. The physician who diagnosed me the first time asked me which side of my face was paralyzed, and I guessed the incorrect side. He said that mistake was common as people typically have no experience in the feeling of nothing, and it confuses them.

Tree observed that it is very difficult to know if one is numb with grief, because he is feeling nothing, and nothing is very difficult to feel. It is even more difficult for others to sense one's feelings, because another's feelings of nothing are even more difficult to feel than one's own.

The analogy reminded me of how strong and sometimes uncomfortable it felt in the period during which the face paralysis was departing, and the feeling was coming back. It reminded me of the strangeness of living with every part of oneself functioning normally, except one-half of the face, which was not functioning at all. Others could see the facial paralysis, but not this current numbness, which was all over and nowhere at the same time.

At some point, I asked Tree, in one way or another, how long this numbness would last, and he replied, "As long as necessary and as strong as necessary." He may have advised me not to make any big decisions for a while. It felt uncomfortable to talk for very long with Tree, but it was useful to have the numbness presented to me.

Meanwhile, work and family life seemed to proceed as normal. The steady flow of cases from Baltimore, added to the traditional business, occupied plenty of time, but thankfully cases involving out-of-town testimonies or other travel resolved themselves somehow. It would have been great to help Chloe or her younger sister in dealing with the death of their mother, but one cannot give what he does not have. There is no recollection of a conversation with family or friends about how I was doing or feeling, but nothing in me at the time invited such a discussion. The only response which could have been given about feelings was "numb," and even that observation came from a tree.

A close physician friend of mine, who knew me and my history very well, observed that it was ok for me to have feelings of relief. While the comment seemed odd at the time, it would be very helpful to me. Like numbness, it was information about how I did or would feel, and such information was not being self-generated. In these months, an attorney, who had become a close personal friend, spent many weeks in the hospital and then a rehab facility. We visited daily and had the time to discuss a wide range of topics that we would have been unlikely to find the time to converse about with our mutually busy schedules. Little detail of these conversations can be remembered, or it is remembered but cannot be made public, but I am certain that these daily talks helped me move forward.

Late one evening in my office, a first stream of thought peeked out from the numbness. What kind of situation is worse in dealing with the death of a child? Would it be worse if the death was sudden and unexpected, as with an accident? Or is it worse if the death culminates a long illness? Does the cause of death make a difference: suicide or overdose versus accident, cancer, or line-of-duty service? What of the child's age – unborn, infant, toddler, adolescent, young adult, adult? What if it were two children versus one?

At some point, I realized this line of thinking was insane, but for the possible excuse of numbness. Why would one wish to rate the degree of bad in relation to the death of a child? Why would one do that? It is bad. It is really, really bad to lose a child. If there were an "Unfair" list of life circumstances, the death of a child would be high on the list. A club to which one would never wish membership is parent of a deceased child. The jolt to the middle does not seem to go away. The feelings are bad enough that further analysis is unnecessary.

Yet, experiences are certainly different, and my mind wandered to Nikki's and my own story. The fact that the experience stretched from her age 15 to her age 40, and my age 42 to my age 66, had effects on me that I recognized and probably some that I did not. Grief at the disease and its consequences had been felt in each of these years, sometimes intensely. Fear and anxiety had visited. Feelings of guilt about what was happening would be overwhelming whether or not they were rational. Thus, even as difficult feelings might begin to emerge from the paralysis, I had felt these feelings many times before, often with a connection to the possibility of her death. If this had been the unexpected death of a child, much would have been avoided over time, but a tidal wave of heartbreaking feelings would befall a parent, it seemed to me.

This was perhaps the trigger for a related thought, which may have pulled me down further. In those 25 years, I remembered uncertainties, experiences, situations, and decisions that felt as painful as her death. That is a hard thing to think. It is because the progression of her disease had such dreadful consequences along the way, not that the death was less impactful. The jolting feelings at and after her death were not removed by this long history, and there is no way to know if they were attenuated by previous, wrenching experience.

Then, I was thinking about the cause of Nikki's death and whether that really mattered to me. Others have more difficulty knowing what to say, so that few people say much of anything. The feelings of others about her cause of death were not an issue or trouble for me. The addiction had been affecting Nikki's family for a quarter of a century, but few around me knew the story. As would become important, however, plenty of parents in Charleston had their own similar stories.

Another thought was that the 25-year period had provided me with exposure to the disease concept of alcoholism and drug addiction. I knew it was a chronic disease that can be arrested by abstinence, and it is a progressive disease leading to death or insanity. The disease is neither a sin nor a personal failing per se but destroys good judgment and sometimes results in bad behavior, often to support the habit. I came to believe this concept, and it was a way of thinking that provided at least a slice of comfort.

A thought emerged from the middle of me that when my 40-year-old daughter Nikki died, my three-year-old daughter Nikki died too. The one whose innocent, loving eyes looked up at the father who adored her and held the knowledge that he would take care of her and keep her safe, had died. And the six-year-old died. The soccer player died. The young adult and the adult who had good times with me and who sometimes gave more love to me than may have been deserved died.

Hope died too. Hope that the possibility of recovery from the chronic progression would somehow win over the possibility that she would reach a tragic end-of-life died. It is a circumstance when certainty is no prize. Even in past attempts to consciously let go of her, some part of my subconscious held hope that my conscious self was mistaken. The thoughts of all of this death were crushing to the middle of me.

Tree came to my office a short time later, and we talked about the losses of the 25 years and the losses of the death. Details elude me but we agreed it was a gruesome trade. This mental escape from the numbness brought me down, which is likely the reason for numbness.

Tree checked on me through the summer, with brief visits to my downstairs office and to the porch as I slowly reclaimed porch time for reading time alone. I recall two specific conversations.

"It is surprising as I focus upon it, Tree, that in six years together, we never talked about Nikki. I certainly knew you knew her story and the story unfolded over our time together."

"You were not ready to talk on this topic, and it was yours to raise whenever you wished," Tree replied.

"It was not customary for me to introduce the topic of Nikki, even to family and close friends. My relationship with her was a part of me, no question about that, but compartmentalized."

"Mike, all of the changes that you were attempting were helping in this part of your life, too. You actually realized that a couple of times. And we can talk about Nikki any time you wish."

The next conversation, later in the summer, was one that I had been dreading but could not stop myself from initiating. This was despite my knowledge of the grief literature and denial, anger, bargaining, and related topics. One may not be hindered by what he knows, so downstairs late one night I said to Tree, "You could have intervened Tree. You could have prevented Nikki's death. I am your friend. Why did you let it happen?" For the only time, I was angry with Tree, and the feeling had surprised me.

Tree, of course, knew that this had been in me for a while and clearly had been waiting for my anguish to find expression. "There is an answer to your question, Mike, but the simplicity of it is complex and out of bounds for us. Your anger denies the possibility that Nikki is on a path of joy and any intervention would have been a grievous mistake. Part of the anger is because of what you can't know and can't control, but we can talk about how you feel as you move along.

"You know how sorrowful I feel alongside of you because of this great loss. One truth which might be said now is that Nikki is the one who died, not you. Her death was about her, not you. It was not yours to cause or prevent."

"But, Tree, you know that I would have traded, me for her, if you had given me the chance," I argued.

"The answer is that this is not a trade you can make or a gift that you can give. Her path is now and always has been bigger than you. All of this is so very hard for you to accept, but you need not believe that the path where your daughter walks is hard for her."

In retrospect, the two of us might have taken the conversation much further, but I believe that Tree knew to keep my tentative forays from numbness as small and simple as possible. My next memory is of August 15, when I privately celebrated the 50th anniversary of ending two-a-day football practice in Alabama. It was really a few minutes of thought and perhaps a smile, because anything more would have approached joy and the numbness held joy out of reach.

On Monday, August 21, 2017, a total solar eclipse could be viewed in the entirety of the continental United States. This had last been true in 1918. Labelled "The Great American Eclipse" by the press, the event stirred significant public interest, school trips and other special travel for viewings, and repeated safety warnings about how to view, or not, an event that required not looking directly at the sun without protection.

Lynn was worried that I would look directly into the sun. Over the weekend, I had unexpectedly learned of a testimony on Tuesday. It was only a short drive away, but Monday would be consumed with unantici- pated preparation for a complicated commercial damages case. My wife knew that when the partial or total eclipse began, I would forget the warn- ings and look directly at the sun to discern what was happening. She was correct to have this concern. So, we pounded into me that I could look out my window at the unfolding event, but not up. Also, Lynn agreed to call me at strategic times during the afternoon and remind me not to look up. This was somewhat demeaning, but worth the assurance that my eyeballs would not be incinerated.

When the partial eclipse began, seconds after Lynn's preparatory phone call, I remembered to look out but not up, but it was difficult to concentrate when the sunny afternoon turned violet. The forest beyond the side yard was viewed through the eerie, purple haze -- a visual which was new to my memory. Chatter from the birds and insects in the forest seemed to slightly increase during the violet period, as the typical volume was usually unnoticed. Only when the cicadas emerged every 17 years would one experience the cicada volume down the length of the road, such that it was almost intolerable to walkers. It made sense to me that the forest dwellers might have been discussing their anxiety at the new color of the air. Yet, the increased volume would not be remarkable except for what happened later.

The total eclipse began a few seconds after Lynn's next phone call. It is difficult to admit that I almost looked up when darkness covered the earth. What will always be remembered, however, is the sound. The second that the total eclipse began, all chatter from the forest ceased. No chirps or insect sounds, or any other sounds, existed at my little place on earth. This two-minute-or-so silence during the afternoon darkness was an awesome experience as I sat at my desk looking out my office window. There had been no expectation on my part that such a phenomenon of silence could or would happen. No quietness in my experience before or since was quite like this silence. Then, the first sunlight reappeared, and the forest chatter instantly returned at normal volume. This was equally amazing.

Soon the normal afternoon returned to Ridge Road, the forest, and me. A lingering, powerful feeling from the eclipse event stayed with me, but I could not identify the feeling. My thinking also slowed my necessary preparation for the next day. By late evening, the work was almost completed.

Small. That was the feeling that I felt when the violet turned to darkness and the earth became silent. I had felt very, very small compared to what was happening around me and above me. It was a feeling that had been felt before, and a priority in recent years, but this time it was dramatic, powerful.

Tree was in the room with me. I sensed his presence, even though he was not speaking. So, I said to Tree, who was bigger than me, "Tree, I don't know what to do or to think. Will you help me?" My anger had apparently given way to smallness.

Tree smiled his warmest smile at me as he answered. "Let's talk about your loss and your grief as you feel ready to do that. We could start with your anger over a timeframe for moving on from your loss."

"You know that I have quickly come to detest references by others to 'getting past' or 'leaving behind' the death of my child, even when a good-hearted friend tells me there is no time deadline for my moving on. The notion of 'moving beyond' my daughter feels to me as another way of saying 'leaving her behind' and I cannot accept that she should be left behind by me. It is not something that I can do or am willing to try to do."

Tree, as always, was prepared for this discussion, and he said to me in a most comforting tone, "Let me lift this trouble off you, Mike. Your discomfort is well taken, and you will learn that others dealing with the loss of a child feel similarly. It is not now, nor will it ever be, your objective or chore to move past Nikki's death or her story. It is an impossibility for you to do so, and it is a false map for your future direction."

It was very encouraging for Tree to agree with me on this one. "So, what do I do? What is my direction?"

"You carry her with you, Mike, and you work on how to make the carry better, easier for both of you, a comfort not a sorrow. Your daughter is not left behind."

Then, Tree gave the conversation a twist. "Mike, you are at a jumping off place."

"What do you mean?"

"It is a place in your grief where you can choose to remain in numbness, or you can jump to a path that requires little effort, may reduce your pain somewhat, but eliminates your growth. Or you can jump back to the path you were on, the best path which you have known, while you deal with your new carry moving along with you."

"Why now Tree, why is this a jumping off time?"

"Because the eclipse moved the middle of you back to small, which is the very best time for such a leap. You asked me for help, Mike. The old, bigger you never asked for help. And I and others around you will be pleased to give it."

"I'm not sure that I can succeed in a jump back to that path," I said.

"Success is not your worry. All you need to do is try. There will be no scoring, and I will be around when you need me."

It made me smile that only Tree could say "when" I needed him, because he knew when I needed him even if I did not. A human friend would more likely say "if." I thought about it. He waited.

"Ok, I'll try."

"One other thought for you," Tree said, "If you are to carry your daughter forward with you, carry her along a path of joy, not of despair. Do not deny either of you that, nor your family or friends."

In the next week or so, first steps that might be taken in a try were considered, but a series of separate and unplanned encounters made this beginning much easier than it would have otherwise been. I had four conversations with persons, or couples, who had lost a child. Three of these four deaths had been drug overdoses. West Virginia often led the nation in drug overdoses per capita. Two of the four did result from a minimal try on my part to attend a meeting of my discussion group, where several persons close to me had shared their experiences. Another was a professional friend, and another a friend from racquetball playing days. The extent that Tree played a role in orchestrating these conversations is unknown, and I did not ask him. These original conversations led to more contact persons and either one-time or continuing conversations through the fall and beyond.

The comfort and restorative power resulting from such conversations was learned, or perhaps re-learned. Only persons who know similar tragedy or pain or fear can help in the way that such humans can help. It is one of the most fulfilling human contacts that a person might have in this world. Both the listening and then some talking helped me.

It seemed to me that everyone was attempting, in one way or another, to carry forward with their lost child. While persons may have used very different words in their sharing, no one seemed to hold the notion that their aim was to leave the child or their death behind. We were all over the scale in our carrying progress, and the same person could be in a different place in one week than in the next. Great tolerance was seen in the treatment of others in this regard. There was sharing of experience but not judgment about whether, or when, one should jump off, for example.

It took a while to realize that most humans who lose a child feel guilt, and there may be added or special guilt over a child who dies of a drug overdose. In one case, the parenting skills and activities of a parent were admirable, and yet she struggled with guilt over her addicted child's life and death. Perhaps if a surviving parent can find no logical reason to feel guilt, they create one or several reasons anyway. We are drawn to it, like a nail to a magnet, but talking to the others began to reduce this particular burden.

Out of numbness, one of my first feelings which can be recalled from these persons and our interactions was gratitude at their kindness. They are kind to each other. Grief of a lost child brings a special brand of loneliness. The others could reduce this loneliness, and that is what kindness means. It causes one to strive for this kindness to new travelers likewise burdened, which is also a kindness to oneself.

Tree and I talked every other week through the fall of 2017, and he more often visited me in my office at night than on the porch in the daylight. As important as was my human support, discussion with something bigger than me had special significance given what was on my mind. These conversations were brief, primarily because my own mood was not chatty, and my natural curiosity remained numb. A part of one conversation is remembered, after a day of self-induced, bubble-up guilt and remorse from the middle of me.

"Guilt is an oppressive, burdensome feeling, Tree," I said, "that will apparently never leave me. It is complicated because it is mainly about what I did not do, not what I did, and because it is often not clear what has truth versus what my mind has made up."

"It is human to feel the way you feel, and your contacts with others will help you, as you may help others. Remember that whatever ball of guilt remains in your middle, you only must deal with a day's worth of it today. And, Mike, we both know, and Nikki knew, that things you wish that you would have done, you could not have done under the circumstances of her disease at the time, or you would have done them. Because she was your daughter, and you were her father."

This was a difficult conversation to have, even with Tree, but I continued, "And it seems impossible, Tree, to get past the feeling that I do not deserve to be happy if my child is dead, or to attempt to make myself more joyful."

"You know, and we have talked about this before, that what you deserve is not your judgment to make. It is above your pay grade."

"And you know that what I know does not stand in the way of how I feel," I replied.

"Yes, I know," he said sadly. "These human feelings stick around, and yet all of the guilt and despair helps no one. Not you, not her, not your family." His response was consistent with what he had said before, but it was good to hear again.

"For lack of a better word, Tree, it feels disloyal to move toward happiness or fulfillment when your child cannot move at all."

"If you are carrying her with you, Mike, then it would be disloyal to move in any other direction, or to stand still. Carrying makes no sense in a life which does not move,"

Finally, I can remember saying, "Sorrow. The feeling of sorrow surrounds me much of the time. It is over the hard life that she lived in her 25 years of addiction. I am sorry that she felt sorry that she let me and others down. Thinking about what might have been is also sad."

"Of course you feel sad, Mike. It is another feeling which you grapple with as you adapt to what you carry, so that some day the carry feels more natural and more comfortable. Again, Mike, don't allow yourself to take on more than a day's worth of it in a day, and Mike, take heart that she has neither pain nor sorrow now."

Perhaps a month later, also downstairs in the evening, another conversation brought relief to me, which only Tree could provide. One of us made reference to our previous talks about olding, death, and after, and this led Tree to ask, "Let me ask you, Mike, do you trouble over issues of judgment and punishment for your daughter?"

My answer surprised me, "I do not remember thinking about that topic in regard to Nikki, ever, until you just brought it up. Maybe it is because of my belief that she had a disease and, but for the disease, was an innocent, who deserved better than she got. But I can't remember scoring her or worrying about her score."

Tree asked, "Do you forgive her, Mike?" It was another unexpected question.

After a pause, I answered, "To the extent that forgiveness is an issue, of course I do. She was, she is my daughter. Since you bring this up, it is like the judgment question. I do not recall any thinking about forgiving her. My thinking was about whether she could forgive me … for letting her down, for attempting to let her go."

Tree said softly, "What you have felt about forgiving her, she is quite capable of feeling back at you. Her attributes are as lovely as the granddaughters who are a gift to you."

"What it comes down to, Tree, is that I so much want to know that she is somewhere in the universe and that she is doing well."

Several minutes seemed to elapse as we sat together in silence. Tree said, "You know that we cannot go there in our talks."

Another pause, and then, "I will tell you, Mike, that you need not trouble over the welfare of your daughter Nikki."

These were the exact words which he had said about my mother. Again, a first thought that these words were so ambiguous as to be meaningless did not stick in my middle. Tree's tone and his non-verbals convinced me to accept these words in the most positive manner, as he had tiptoed on his own boundary to give me such a promise. There was something else this time. When he made the promise to me, the air embraced me with the feeling of the Swirl, if only for a few moments. Nothing was said to Tree in reply. It was unnecessary.

The Fall of 2017 held enough difficult days, when making the effort to move forward was not attractive. It did not feel as if such effort was in me. In freezing to death, the easier thing to do is fall asleep and die versus struggle to stay awake and live. By simply being around, Tree kept me from freezing. We talked more about the difference in the 25-year carry and the carry after her death. As had often occurred before, the talking through of a topic with Tree was a positive for me, even if a result of the talk could not be identified. The same was true for sharing with other parents, but Tree was, well, bigger than both me and them.

It must be noted that the sport of football was also played in Fall 2017. It would be nice to say that The University of Tennessee produced a season which provided some degree of comfort. Not so. 0-8 in the SEC. By the laws of nature and chance, plus home field advantage, even a poor team will win one or two games. Zero wins requires bad luck and referees at a level which is unimaginable. Yet, it happened in 2017. The coach was fired (again), and the Vols started over (again).

Worse, the Vanderbilt Commodores defeated the Vols for the second, consecutive year -- by a lot. Vanderbilt is a small, private school west of Knoxville, which features eggheads in various fields of academic endeavors and somehow puts forward an SEC football team. Losing twice in a row to them is as if David required two stones to fell Goliath, and Goliath made no apparent attempt to swat away the second stone or simply squash David while reloading. As bad as it was with only one stone, the Goliath boosters would be egregiously humiliated by the second stone.

Thanks to Giffer, I watched none of these sorrowful games. Notably, the football outcomes did not evoke significant anger or increase my level of sorrow. More important things had gone down and were going on. There is nothing like real life to remind a person that football is a game.

With encouragement from Tree, I slipped back toward the routines of thought and actions, which were being practiced before the old age diversion and then Nikki's death. I came to see myself as a mule, whose daily task is to pull the plow down as straight a line as possible and then to turn around and do it again. Muling is not mentally taxing. The primary skill involved is showing up, someone else determines the direction, and perfection is not an issue. The mule worked on his new carry, when able. He also reflected on how Tree's prescribed path had helped with the old carry in the past several years: living smaller, aware of lack of control, with fewer and lowered expectations. The trudging and plowing efforts were not poisoned by oppressive thoughts of a scorekeeper God.

Thus, time advanced to January 26, 2018, when my daughter Nikki would have had a 41st birthday. Tree visited in my home office that evening. Toward the end of our conversation, he complimented me on my try thus far and added, "You have found help from others and are helping in return. This is the way you humans are at your very best. It is a pleasure to observe."

His last words that evening were, "Your path did not change with your loss, Mike. You will walk, different, and you will walk differently, because of what happened and what is carried along. In the worst of times, your path does not change, but you may need to trudge it harder than before for whatever time that takes."

After he departed, I thought that little of whatever progress had been made could have occurred without Tree's aid. What did others do in such a sorrowful situation without a personal Tree, bigger than them, giving solace and advice? I thought that any comfort coming my way depended on my belief that Tree, and his words, were real. Either Tree was everything, or he was nothing. I either believed him, or not. There was no halfway on this one. A last thought ended my evening. There was a difference in Tree's tone of voice. Something was changing, and it made me afraid.

CHAPTER THIRTEEN –
THE END

A week later, now in February, I was driving out of Huntington and returning to Charleston around 9:00 in the morning. Earlier, a client attorney and I had met in her office to prepare her for cross examining another economist at trial later in the day. Interstate 64 connected these two largest West Virginia municipalities - - both slightly below 50,000 in population - - along a straight corridor of around fifty miles, which is unusual in the mountain state.

Cold rain earlier in the morning had stopped, traffic had lightened on this busy interstate after commuting hours, and I relaxed. Many were concerned about the seemingly high rate of accidents on such a straight, multi-lane interstate, but West Virginians are not accustomed to straight roads. Undoubtedly, Great Plains drivers have trouble driving in the mountains and are probably terrified in bad weather. West Virginians on a straight road are instantaneously aware that curves, and the voids beyond, do not threaten them. The problem is complacency, and once complacency takes hold, it spreads, so that one veers off the road occasionally just to see if the rumble strips are there. Then, one begins to push the enforcement speed limit a bit too much, perhaps follows the truck somewhat too closely. It is a recipe for disaster.

My high-performance vehicle had settled at 72 mph, less than 1 ½ percent above the posted speed limit. There is a limit beyond which even my wild side does not wish to go, because I am also afraid of excessive speed. Thus, I was enjoying the overcast morning and not thinking about anything in particular.

"Hi, Mike," Tree said, which caused me to jump in my seat and otherwise be startled. He appeared to me as traveling Tree, appropriately sized into the passenger seat. We had not spoken with each other since the evening a week before.

"Hi Tree," I responded. "Is there something that you would like to talk about as we drive home?"

"Not particularly. I thought we might have some fun together," he said lightly. This was a different reason for a visit, although we had certainly had fun together. But it made me feel anxious.

Tree did not wait for my reply but asked, "Why don't you allow me to drive your car for a while? I have never actually operated an automobile. While my means of moving around are much faster, as you would suspect, so many humans spend so much time doing this activity that it is useful for us to do it together. Or, rather that I do it and you watch."

"Tree, you can't simply drive for the first time on an interstate. And, with my luck, after we change places, we would pass a state trooper who would see no one driving and me in the passenger seat."

"That is not a problem. It is just as easy for me to drive from the passenger side. All you have to do is sit back...."

"No, no, no Tree, we really don't want to do that. There are rules. There are skills.

It is not rocket science, but you might make a mistake and kill some-body. Like me.

"Not to mention," I added hastily, "you don't have a driver's license, and I would be allowing an unlicensed person to drive my car." Worse, I realized it was not a person but a tree, a compact little tree that would probably remain unseen and unheard.

The conversation was already feeling to be the role reversal which it was. "I have been watching you and am sure that I can do this. But I have also cleared the road a half mile ahead of us, so that you would not revert to worry. So, lighten up, Mike. Take your feet off the gas and hands off the wheel and I'll take over." As he said this, however, the automobile locked me out of any control, and it was clear that Tree was taking over.

"Besides, he reasoned, "if the law pulls us over, my lack of a driv-er's license will be the least of our problems."

Grimly, I at least agreed with that, but Tree was driving the vehicle, and after the pause for transition, it began to accelerate in a jerky sort of way… 60, 65, 70, 75. "Tree that is fast enough," I said with alarm, "and you are driving in the passing lane with no one to pass."

Tree immediately moved to the right-hand lane while still accelerat-ing. "You have to signal before changing lanes," I said, and Tree responded by moving back into the passing lane where he started.

"Your speed indicator goes up to 120 miles per hour, Mike. Let's crank her up."

"No, Tree," I exclaimed, "you need to change to the other lane and slow down." He did not seem to be happy to comply, but it felt as if he had taken his foot off the accelerator. He also steered into the right lane and then, remembering, turned on his right turn signal.

"Thank you, Tree." I exhaled a breath of relief. Then, the flashing lights and burst of siren from the state trooper closing behind me captured my attention. The control of my vehicle returned to me, and I slowed further into the shoulder lane of the interstate.

Having the presence of mind not to turn my head toward the passenger seat, I whispered urgently, "You apparently did not clear the interstate of state troopers, Tree. Now what are we going to do?" He had disappeared. "Tree… Tree… Where are you?" He was not talking either. I could not believe that he had abandoned me.

Meanwhile the trooper had been communicating with Trooper Central, I supposed, and he departed his vehicle to walk toward me. Looking into the side mirror, I said to myself, "I cannot believe it." Walking up was the same Charleston policeman who had given me a ticket several years earlier. He had filled out his frame a bit, moved with more confidence, and obviously had become a state trooper. Without saying anything, he took the driver's license I offered, looked at me, and smiled.

"Mr. Brookshire. We meet again," he observed.

"You actually remember me?" I asked, surprised.

"It was my first day patrolling on my own, and you were my first citation. So, I remember."

Since he knew my name, it was natural for me to look for his name. There was a tag on his uniform shirt that said HOWDY and that threw me off for a second. It was perhaps my involvement in the Thank You Officers movement which made me think HOWDY might be the moniker for a friendliness initiative by the state police. Maybe it was an acronym.

Then, I foolishly asked. "Howdy. Are you Officer Howdy?" And I smiled, which was not a wise thing to do but simply could not be suppressed.

"Yes, Officer Howdy," he said curtly, and he seemed to glare at me in warning that further comments about his name would not be prudent. While my immediate problems burdened me, a few thoughts were shed for the dumb joke experiences over his name which had likely befallen him.

"Mr. Brookshire, do you know why I pulled you over today?" Officer Howdy asked. It was exactly the same trick question that he had asked years earlier. Not often, but sometimes, my mind will expand a moment in time into a bubble of thought, which is somehow fast forwarded through the time available. This was one of those moments, when Officer Howdy asked me his trick question.

Do police across the country ask this question at the beginning of every traffic stop as a means of apprehending serial killers and other serious offenders? Out of every ten serial killers, stopped for a traffic violation, would one blurt out, "Because you obviously must have found all the bodies buried under my concrete back yard." Whether the admission is triggered by surprise, stupidity, or arrogance, one of ten would certainly yield a productive outcome justifying the mass asking of this trick question.

Then, in this moment, I thought about Truth. Veritas. Always tell the truth. George Washington told the truth. The truth will set you free. What got you in trouble was not telling the truth. Find a policeman and tell him the truth. The truth, the whole truth, and nothing but the truth.

The truthful answer to Trooper Howdy's question was known to me and could be given in a straightforward and concise manner. I knew that we were here talking at the side of the highway because an invisible, sometimes talking tree had, arguably, taken away from me any control of my vehicle and had begun driving erratically. It was through my efforts that the car had slowed and stopped, and the tree had meanwhile disappeared. That was the truth.

Apparently, Officer Howdy had grown impatient with my expansion of the moment, and he volunteered the reason why he pulled over my high-performance vehicle. "When your car blew by me," he started, "it took me a while to catch up. Then, I clocked you at 43 miles per hour and fiddling with your turn signal.

"So, Mr. Brookshire, you were doing, in the least, fast-and-slow driving, not a common violation but potentially serious." He added, "The textbook case of fast-and-slow driving from the police academy, Mr. Brookshire, is the guy who was transporting large quantities of amphetamines and downers in his trunk and sampling both as he drove."

Officer Howdy paused, and I had no idea what to say.

"Mr. Brookshire, you don't have any amphetamines, other drugs, or anything else that is illegal in your trunk, do you?"

"No sir," I answered quickly and politely, because that was the truth, and he had thankfully chosen to ask one of the few questions where truth was not problematic.

"And," he continued, staring hard into my eyes, "you are not in any way impaired in your driving this morning, Mr. Brookshire, are you?" The thought occurred to me that this would be a really bad time for my Graves disease, which could randomly move the muscles around my eyes, to suddenly bug out one of my eyes at Officer Howdy.

This did not happen, however, I again said, "No sir," and after a few seconds Trooper Howdy said "Ok. I believe that. So, Mr. Brookshire, do you always drive the way that you were just driving or is there some particular reason for your fast-and-slow episode?"

It was back to the telling-the-truth issue. Not a chance. If there was an iconic book of exceptions to life rules, my current situation with the tell-the-truth rule would certainly be in the book. On the practical side, even Trooper Howdy would not wish me to tell him the truth if he had any idea beforehand what I would say. He couldn't simply let me drive away after I blamed it on a tree. The paperwork and aggravation which would befall Trooper Howdy would be substantial. And to no avail. Even if I was tortured into telling the truth, I would still be blaming the incident on a talking tree.

Thus, I came to lie to a trooper named Howdy. "Officer," I said, "sometimes driving early in the morning like this, especially with absolutely no traffic..." I stopped because Officer Howdy had jerked his head up and first noticed the ghostlike inactivity on both sides of the interstate.

Tree's half-mile-ahead zone was apparently still in force. A puzzled look crossed his face as I continued, "… my mind wanders to something that I need to do, or is ahead of me in the day, and I just have a lapse … Usually a second later, I'm back but my foot might freeze up on the pedal, just for a second. I need to stay focused. I'm sorry, Officer Howdy." The look given to Officer Howdy attempted to highlight every ounce of old age, infirmity, pitifulness, and helplessness that was within me.

Officer Howdy looked at me again, intensely, sighed a long sigh, glanced around at the lack of traffic, and said, "Mr. Brookshire, if I let you go with a warning, do you think that you can make it home driving the posted speed limit and paying attention?"

"Yes sir. Thank you." I said eagerly.

"I'm not sure, Mr. Brookshire, that I would have done this except for the paperwork headaches that a fast-and-slow driving charge would bring down upon me. So, this is your lucky day."

"Thank you again, Trooper Howdy," I replied and drove carefully down the highway. Traffic was instantly normal. A thought of sadness intruded. Ten miles or so down the interstate, Tree reappeared in the passenger seat. "So, you are back," I said, with a certain sternness, "Where did you go when I needed you?"

Tree replied calmly, "First, Mike, my hanging around would not have done you any good with Trooper Howdy. Second, who do you think influenced Trooper Howdy to let you go with a warning?"

"Where were you?"

"In the trunk. Hiding in the trunk. Then, when you and Howdy began talking about the trunk, I almost panicked."

"But Tree,' I interrupted, "if he had opened the trunk, he would not have seen you."

"I know that now, Mike, with the pressure off, but it is amazing how unnerving it is to be pulled over. Even if you have done nothing wrong."

"You <u>had</u> done something wrong, Tree," I emphasized. "He probably could have charged me with reckless driving, which would have been a case of mistaken identity that no one could ever sort out."

"Of course, you should not have allowed me to drive your vehicle without some at least minimal instructions, but it all worked out. You and Officer Howdy had a chance to see each other again."

I held my tongue, but then said, "Tree, please don't ask to drive my car anymore."

He did not seem to be displeased and changed the subject, 'Let's have breakfast together. Why don't you drive us to the restaurant where you and Chloe have breakfast?" He was referring to the downtown Charleston restaurant where Chloe and I had our every-Saturday-morning breakfast. Just the two of us, it was a great tradition since her coming to Charleston. I was starving as we drove into downtown, so such an outing made at least that much practical sense.

As we drove into the adjacent parking garage, I looked ahead but said to Tree, "How are you actually planning to eat, Tree? You don't eat. Or at least it has never come up. Not to mention, you realize that people will see me walking in alone and eating two meals while staring at an invisible companion. Is this something that we really want to do?"

"Absolutely. Maybe ask for an out-of-the-way table. It will be fine."

Tree walked in the front door ahead of me, and I feared that an idling teenager had noticed the door being opened for me. The three people at the counter knew me, we chatted, and the reduction in customers by mid-morning allowed me to obtain the corner table in the far room. A friend will join me for breakfast soon, I told the three. Truth issues again. It was a problem of the day.

As our entourage, visible and otherwise, navigated around tables, I spoke to an ex-mayor, a tailor whom I like, and an attorney client. This knowing people pleasantness was a real benefit of living in a city of this size. I was seated in the corner table of the far room, against the plate glass window at the front of the restaurant and facing the low wall which divided the restaurant into two large rooms. Tree, and/or an empty space, had his back to the divide and faced me. The swinging kitchen doors were over my right shoulder on the back wall of this service area.

The waiter had worked there for many years. He left for coffee and juice after I told him that I would also order breakfast for my friend who should be just behind me. Tree indicated to me that watching humans talk while they ate breakfast was fascinating, and I noticed his keen interest in the lengthy menu of choices. He listened to me order my favorite egg dish with avocados and then dictated his order to me in spurts of excitement, which I repeated to my waiter friend.

"My friend would like two scrambled eggs and two poached eggs, bacon, link sausage, hash browns... And a loaded oatmeal... And three chocolate chip pancakes... Coffee when he arrives... And a large grape-fruit juice.

The waiter, who had been writing furiously, looked up at me with a furrowed brow and said, "Mike, you know how big our pancakes are. Nobody eats three of them."

"Just trust me here. This guy wants three." The waiter placed a neighboring table next to Tree, as extra surface space would be needed. He said quizzically, "Who are you bringing in here? Paul Bunyan?"

I smiled but thought, "If you only knew who was in here, Paul Bunyan would not be so unbelievable." He walked away muttering to himself. Meanwhile Tree and I used our out-of-the-way view to choose customers and wonder who they were and where they would be headed after breakfast. The Russian spy, who was here to assess the hundreds of underground missile silos secretly located in abandoned coal mines, was by far the most interesting of these customers. He had been speaking something that sounded like Russian to his waitress, although he could have simply been from Boston.

The apparently empty space and I were soon served the enormous breakfast by our waiter and another staffer. The waiter filled both coffee cups, said nothing further about my ravenous friend who had still not appeared, and returned to the kitchen. My eating commenced immediately, our conversation stopped, and it took me a few minutes to realize what was happening on the other side of the table. Tree's substantial inventory of breakfast foodstuffs were being consumed, or at least disappearing, at a uniform rate. First the egg dishes, I assumed because eggs get cold, disappeared at 10 percent gone, 20 percent gone, through 100 percent of clean plate, from the far part of each plate toward Tree. Then, all of the other foods and the drinks disappeared at the same rates. I thought I heard him in a mouth pucker from the grapefruit juice. Our waiter refilled our coffee once, stared at Tree's space and, literally, his 50 percent eaten food, gave me a really strange look, and walked away. Tree recommenced moving his eat lines from 50 to 100 percent.

"You know that I have to live here with these people after you finish your one-time breakfast," I silently muttered to Tree.

"Yes," he replied, "but they will forget the details, so relax and enjoy yourself. By the way, Mike, what is this bacon and sausage food I just ate?"

I told him, and he said, "So that is what they are doing back in the kitchen. That's disgusting. If I was human, it might cause me to pass out."

"But bacon smells better than almost anything, Tree."

He shook his head, "You are right about that… and it tastes great as human food goes… if it would simply be possible to eat it without thinking about it."

Our waiter cleared the table, saying nothing to me. I also said nothing because what could be said? It was necessary to tell him I would wait a few more minutes to see if my friend might still arrive, and my eyes conveyed to him promise of a really big gratuity.

Tree was, meanwhile, surveying the other customers at their tables, and I sensed mischief. "Mike," he said, "do you see that couple across the room sitting next to the kitchen?"

Glancing over my right shoulder, I saw a couple in their twenties. The man was tall and well built but looked rough, as with either a hangover or the end of a double shift. His companion was a petite and pretty brunette, who did not appear to be especially happy with him. They had finished breakfast.

Then Tree said, "Watch the guy for a minute." It was an easy surveillance from my position, as I appeared to be casually glancing toward the kitchen. The lady was looking behind her, perhaps talking to a friend at a neighboring table. The man took a last bite of something, and his coffee cup rose vertically from its saucer and laterally to hover next to his hand, which likely was about to reach for the cup. The man's mouth dropped open, his right hand froze in the air, and the coffee cup returned itself to the saucer. My eyes immediately shifted back to Tree across the table, and I heard him. Of the various types of Tree "sounds" which I had experienced, this was a new one. My immediate guess was a giggle, a giggle which one was attempting to suppress before it grew larger. The giggle quickly became a chuckle, which I had heard before. The thought of the expression on the man's face when the cup traversed back to the saucer made me begin to, in the least, chuckle. Neither one of us could stop laughing, even though we both attempted to hide our merriment.

"Uh oh," Tree whispered across the table. I looked across the room, and the big guy was standing up and looking at me. His wife, who was conversing rapidly with him, also looked across the room at me, and they began to walk in my direction.

"This is bad, Tree," I blurted and looked back across the table. Tree had vanished. Again. "Tree … Tree." Great. He was probably back in the parking garage hiding in my trunk. It was at this instant that it struck me only I had been laughing insofar as anyone else would see it. Then, they were standing next to my table looking down at me, who was suddenly as serious and yet innocent looking as a human with direct knowledge of what had happened could possibly be.

The big guy started to say something, and I also had a vague sense that he was planning to hit me either before or after he said it. His wife put her hand on his chest, however, and said to me, "Did you do something to my husband's coffee?"

My mouth was open but silent. This might have been taken as genuine surprise at such a strange question. Actually, in expert-witness mode, I was buying time to think through the question-and-answer scenario which might lie ahead. My first answer was truthfully easy if she would leave it there. "No." I did nothing to the coffee cup.

But what if she watched Perry Mason or Law and Order reruns and then said, "So, you have no knowledge of what happened to my husband's coffee?" or, "And you weren't laughing at my husband?" Many questions might prompt a Tree-necessitated obfuscation of the truth, which in turn could trigger a subconscious, probably non-verbal, signaling of my prevarication. The combination of Graves disease and extreme stress could cause an eye to wobble around a bit, and the big guy would surely hit me if that happened.

Perhaps the length of my open-mouthed pause combined with the lady's own doubts about whether coffee-cup-diddling had actually occurred and, further, if the old guy across the room dressed in a business suit had been the diddler. She patted her mate in the chest and instructed, "Just go pay the check." He looked at me with mean cow eyes but did what he was told. A few minutes later, I escaped the scene, under the watchful eye of my waiter. Tree was not in the car or at home, but we needed to talk about his behavior.

That evening, dinner and family activities occupied me until 9:00 or so, when the ladies moved upstairs to bedrooms and I to my downstairs office and hangout room. On this occasion, Teddi Rose came downstairs with me, because she loved to idle on the couch while I either worked or watched the TV screen above her head. She had to be carried down and back up the stairs because of old age and arthritis. "What a princess," I thought. It was my hope that Tree might show up, and, indeed, his presence was felt soon after Teddi was settled on the couch.

"Hi, Mike. Before you start with me, everything is fixed between the big guy and his wife, and neither the waiter nor others will bring up your spontaneous burst of laughter from the corner table, nor your large consumption of food." His voice was in the corner of the room and above my computer screen, with the actual Tree ten yards outside. I sat in the recliner in the middle of the room, facing this corner voice.

"Tree," I was unmoved, "have you noticed that when you let your hair down, so to speak, you have a tendency to push the boundaries of we humans which, in turn, increases the chance that someone, like me for example, could find themselves in serious trouble?"

"Yes, Mike, you are absolutely correct," Tree replied.

"I am?" His response surprised me, as this conversation was, once again, a role reversal of our time together.

"You are. It is apparently as dangerous for a Big to become too small as it is for a Small to become too big. Sure is fun though."

"Perhaps fun was given to humans as recompense for heartbreak and hemorrhoids," I volunteered, but realized that Tree had turned serious.

"Which leads me to what I am here to talk with you about, Mike. It is time for me to leave our active relationship -- it might be called – of the past six years. We will not talk again or be together as we have been. Before you ask, we cannot discuss Why, except that it has already been six years of your life for this unmatched relationship between the two of us.

This was apparently my day to be stunned. My mouth was opened. My heart did not beat. It had not occurred to me that Tree and I would stop talking. Me, the whatiffer, and this possibility had not heretofore entered my mind. Now that the announcement had been suddenly made, I felt panic, and the sorrow which followed me stepped up. "When?" I asked urgently.

"Tonight," he replied. "This is our last conversation, Mike."

"Why so fast, Tree?" I asked in despair. "I need more time with you … and to think of questions that have not yet been asked. This is such a huge change for me. It is a loss of something that could never have been expected but nevertheless has been there."

Tree paused a moment and then observed, "In truth, the out-of-bounds topics have been defined for us, and we cannot go further. With everything else, you need nothing further from conversation with me. It is yours to seek, not mine to give." Then, he added, "but ask questions now if you wish."

My mind was not well functioning, burdened as it was with a dispirited middle of me, so I hesitated while Tree waited patiently. He was correct. There was no obvious new ground to cover. I knew, or thought I knew, how he would answer questions that were arriving in my mind.

Finally, in order to say something, "Thinking back to the Why Me? questions that I first asked. These are not very important to me anymore. It doesn't really matter why. This experience happened, it has been a very good thing for me, and I can accept the mystery of why."

"That is a sign of your smaller self and is to your credit and benefit."

"Then let me try again about you, Tree," I said without much confidence, "you have told me that you are not the Big, and I will not ask that question again. But in the hierarchy from human to Big, where do you fit? We have been together for six years, Tree, so can you shed some light on that for me?"

The likelihood of an answer felt low, but Tree answered without hesitation, "Admiral-of-the-oceans would be a rough equivalent for earthly understanding of where I fit. Fairly high up there in power and influence. Three-fourths of the surface." He stopped abruptly.

I gave Tree a long look through the corner wall and then smiled and observed, "So you are not answering that question, right?"

"Right," Tree agreed, "you knew that I would not answer such a question when you asked it. On the topic of the Big, however, it might be a universal problem of sorts if the Big ever came to be intrigued with humor, particularly of the type with which you have helped me become proficient. None of the admirals, prophets, and others would know for sure what was truth versus what was the Big doing humor."

This struck me as an odd, spur-of-the-moment comment as I offered my own, "Is it possible, Tree, that the Big has always known humor, and you are the only one in the Bigger crowd, if there is such a crowd, who had heretofore been outside the humor loop?"

Tree fell silent, as if he was giving this possibility some serious thought. I felt surprise from him. Perhaps the quality of my questions was improving.

"The quality of your questions is improving, Mike," Tree acknowledged.

Emboldened, but still of low morale, I asked another one. "Tree, how did our time together go for you? Did you accomplish what you came to do ... whatever that is? Did I help?"

Tree paused a few moments and answered, "You would like to know your score in an activity that you have no possibility of understanding?"

"I was not thinking of a score ... well, maybe indirectly ... but did this experience matter, for anyone or anything beyond me?"

"Mike you did not hear this from me, but you have performed so well in your assignment that the human race is being extended another one hundred years beyond the previously determined expiration. And, as a special reward for your good efforts, University of Tennessee football players will have a third leg on game days to help with running the ball, block-ing, tackling punt returners, and so forth. This courtesy will be extended through your remaining life expectancy. Of course, the third legs will need to be invisible, or the Vanderbilt fans especially would be sure to notice."

"Because of their exceptionally high IQs, I suppose."

"Precisely," Tree answered.

Then, I said, "So you are not answering this question either, right?"

"That is correct."

While my mind was blanking on further questions, Tree added, "The rules about our conversations, I should say, no longer apply because this is our last conversation, but all the rules are off. Even number 4. If you should be so bold as to tell other humans about the two of us, don't expect anyone to believe you."

"So, I am being left without another soul who knows this has hap-pened, Tree? It is a new kind of lonely."

"Good point," he said, "let me see what I can do about that."

Teddi Rose, who had been temporarily forgotten on the couch, jumped to the floor and slowly walked over to Tree's voice in the corner. She sat down on her haunches with her back to me and seemed to look up through the corner of the ceiling at Tree's head outside. It was entirely quiet. Then Teddi Rose did a Sit Pretty and held it awhile. She finished and turned to me with sadness in her large, brown eyes. Before this could choke me up, her look turned to determination. Dog determination. She walked the couple of steps to me and sat down on my feet. She had never before sat on my feet, but it felt good to have her there.

"I'm currently unable to think of other questions which you might actually answer, Tree, but I don't want to say goodbye to you. You have given me so many gifts, and we have become so close, it is difficult to imagine a future without our talks. I love you, Tree."

"You need not imagine your future at all, Mike, but have joy in your days. There is much ahead for you to learn and say and feel … in your statistical life expectancy, of course. Only our conversations and encounters are ending, not our relationship. I am still here for you. Around you. This is my space. You often talk to me now with no expectation that I will talk back. You can do this. You are ready."

He felt sad to me, perhaps because that was a feeling which I wanted him to share. "Thank you for humor, Mike. It is quite a gift and will require great care. Goodbye to you, Mike, my human friend. I love you, too."

A very specific and memorable feeling overcame me at that moment, which held me together. I felt Tree's presence leave the room but at the same time his presence was also with me. However much presence was left behind, it has been just enough.

And he has been since. Around.

* * *

It is not the ending that I would have chosen for my two-way relationship with Tree, and certainly not with the abruptness of our ending conversation. It was unlikely that I would ever have chosen to end our interaction, however. This was on my mind the next morning as the reality of this new change in my existence took hold. Perhaps Tree had little experience in saying goodbye. Perhaps it is as difficult for a Big to leave a Small as for a Small to leave a Big.

The day was a busy work day, with two long calls to attorney clients about current cases. Teddi and I were strolling at the early dusk of winter when the neighbor lady walked toward us. She sometimes walked despite the cold weather, unless the death curve iced over.

This evening, she stopped in front of Teddi and me and looked at me with concern. "Are you alright, Mike?" she asked. Before thinking about the question, I answered, "Better than I might have expected, so far anyway." Then it struck me that this exchange made no sense unless she knew about Tree and his departure. How did she know? How much did she know? Who else knew? How did she know my first name was Mike? Tree would not have allowed such a mistake, if it was a mistake.

She touched her hand to her heart, smiled her kind smile, and said, "That is good. I shall be thinking about you and Teddi Rose. Please tell Lynn and Chloe hello for me."

I promised to do so and called her by her first name. How did I know her first name? The neighbor lady gave Teddi a pat and continued down the street.

My next time alone with Teddi Rose was later that evening, after Chloe and Lynn had gone upstairs. I had watched a news special in the living room because I did not wish to be in my downstairs office and reminded of the departure. I walked out on the porch, with Teddi trailing, and closed the door to keep outside the 20-degree temperature. Standing in the middle of the porch, silent, I looked up through the porch roof at the head of the persimmon tree.

Lynn opened the door, to my surprise, walked onto the porch past me, and to the screen. She looked up at the tree and said, loudly enough for me to hear, "Thank you Tree … for your help to my husband. We will miss you."

I was once again stunned and staring at her with my mouth opened. The telepathy of long-marriage communication eliminated the need for me to ask, "How did you know about Tree?"

She took a step and poked me in the chest, saying, "Because you talk in your sleep." Her eyes sparkled with glee, mischief, and intellectual superiority.

"You never told me that before," I exclaimed.

"Why in the world would I give up a source of information like that? Except to say goodbye to Tree?"

I asked, "What does Chloe know?"

"That something has been happening out here on the porch, but I doubt she would ever bring it up with you. She has said to me that you are much more chill than you used to be… high praise for a teenager."

I smiled and Lynn opened the door to return inside. She turned again to me and said, "I think Tree wanted to leave with some others around you who knew something of your experiences. Me. The neighbor lady. The dog, and to some extent, Chloe. So that you do not feel alone with this." She closed the door, and I watched her walk upstairs.

Lingering in the cold, I walked to the screen, looked up at the proboscis, and was silent. Of all the feelings about Tree being processed, this was a new one, which was felt strongly in the middle of me. Everything was going to be ok. It was not clear to me what "everything" meant, nor how "ok" was defined. Yet, the feeling was not diminished because of this lack of precision, but rather even more valued. I felt very grateful, which is the perfect wrapping for such a wonderful gift of feeling.